A SLIGHT CHANGE OF PLAN

Other Books by Dee Ernst

A Different Kind of Forever
Better Off Without Him

A SLIGHT CHANGE OF PLAN

Dee Ernst

Montlake
Romance

Text copyright © 2013 Dee Ernst

Printed in the United States of America.

Published by Montlake Romance, Seattle

www.apub.com

ISBN-13: 9781477848227
ISBN-10: 1477848223
Library of Congress Control Number: 2013909205

This one is for Toni, Marsha, and Jane, who were with me from that first flush of true love to the final, bitter, Sara Lee days.

CHAPTER ONE

Look out, New Jersey! After living alone for the past few years, I'm ready to take a new chance on love. I already have everything I need—a successful career, a beautiful home, great friends, and three fine adult children. Now, I'm going after what I want—a smart, fun-loving, and adventurous man to share it all with. At 55, I don't need young and handsome, but I insist on kind, honest, and thoughtful.

I sound old and desperate."

"No, you don't. You're overreacting. You sound fine."

"I need to take out the part about living alone for a while. And about having three children."

"Kate, first of all, it's not like you have toddlers. Three adult children is a good thing. It sends a signal that they are out of the house, you are alone and independent, and if you run away for a romantic weekend, you'll have a built-in pet-sitter."

She was right there. My youngest son, Sam, was graduating from college in two months with a degree in something to do with computers that I didn't understand at all, but he assured me it would guarantee him a very good-paying job. My middle child and lovely daughter, Regan, at twenty-five, was getting married sometime in the not-too-distant future, and had already moved in with her intended. My oldest, my son Jeff—a year and a half older than Regan—was living with his soul mate, Gabe, in a West Village apartment which was the only place I could ever see him living. So yes, I was alone.

Independent? Well, sure. I had to be. I'd been a widow for the past eight years. I'd learned to kill spiders, empty mousetraps, change flat tires, and hook up a cable modem to my computer. If that wasn't real independence, I didn't know what was.

"Then maybe I'll take out the part about being fifty-five."

"Then you wouldn't have anything."

"Exactly."

My sister, Laura, smacked the side of my head with her open palm. "Kate, I'm telling you, this sounds amazing. You'll have men snapping you up like a bright new penny."

"Why am I Kate Freemont Everett? I was married way longer than I was single. I'd almost forgotten my maiden name."

"In case anyone from your past stumbles over your profile, you need for them to be able to recognize you. I mean, you look pretty good for your age, but I can't say you haven't changed."

"My past? You make it sound like I left a trail of broken hearts behind me."

The truth was, I hadn't been the breaker of any hearts. If anything, I was the breakee, having been seriously dumped in college by the guy I thought I was going to live happily ever after with.

"I can't imagine anyone from high school being remotely interested in me now. And I can't imagine my being interested in any of them. Not after thirty-seven years. Maybe we should just forget this whole thing," I suggested.

Laura is my little sister. After my father died, our mother had to work, often pulling the three-to-eleven shift, leaving me in charge of Laura during the long evenings of her childhood. It was then that she formed a rather distorted view of my life: She thinks I'm perfect. Possibly because I let her stay up as late as she wanted when she was a little kid, or maybe because she grew up on a diet of Coke and Hostess Twinkies, which I think would affect any person's rational thinking.

Laura was trying hard. "Honey, fifty is the new thirty."

"I bet the thirty-year-olds don't say that."

She sighed. "You need to put in your age, Kate. It's for everyone's protection. Do you want men answering you who say they're sixty when they're really seventy-two?"

Trying an online dating service was all Laura's idea. Let me get that out there right away. My husband, Adam, had died of a sudden heart attack. I was over the pain of his loss and had been quite content in my singlehood. But lately I really wanted somebody who was happy to see me when I got home who didn't have a separate water bowl. I did not enjoy the solitude as much as I used to. I really didn't like going out alone anymore—restaurants, movies, places like that. And I was tired of spending long weekends in interesting places when I had no one to share the experience with. I had kind of been hoping a perfect gentleman would somehow fall into my lap, but Laura pointed out that if I wanted somebody, I'd have to go out and find him, and online dating was the quickest and most sensible way to go about that.

I was moving on to what was generally called "the next phase," and was looking for things to shake up my life. I was seriously thinking about selling the five-bedroom home I had raised my family in, even though the real estate market was still deader than a doornail. I had my eye on a very chichi townhome in a gorgeous complex that had its own pool, jogging trail, and health club, as well as basketball and tennis courts. And a golf course.

Maybe, in the "next phase" of my life, I could become a professional athlete.

Two weeks earlier I had given notice at my law firm that I was planning to cut my hours there in half, starting on May first, which was two months away. As I expected, they immediately offered me a very nice little package to just leave, which is what I had wanted in the first place. I had been sniffing around the possibility of teaching. Because I had an MBA on top of the law degree, I got a sweet offer from a small private college to teach Intro to Tax Law and Business Law 101. It was going to be perfect, and they wanted me to start in the fall.

Which would leave me plenty of time to work on the professional-athlete thing.

But for right now, I was unemployed. Which was why I was sitting home in sweatpants and a flannel shirt on a Wednesday afternoon, arguing with my sister.

"Laura, I'm not comfortable with this. I haven't been on a date in thirty-two years. Besides, I'm starting to get hot flashes. I have to pee every ten minutes. I'm very short-tempered. I have a very uneven libido. I'm pretty sure that menopausal women are not ideal dating material."

"You don't have to put that in your profile, silly. Besides, most of these men have been married before and have probably been through that once already."

"So why on earth would they want to go through it again? Laura, men my age don't want me; they want twentysome-things."

Laura sighed. We looked very much alike, my sister and I. We both had our mother's dark eyes and wavy hair, our father's lean build and square jaw, and the curse of the Freemonts, big, flat feet. Being five years younger, Laura hadn't started dyeing her hair yet, so hers was a dark, rich brown. Mine was slightly lighter, with hints of auburn that came from trying to cover all that gray with Medium Golden Brown.

We were both tall and thin and flat chested, another family trait, one that drove my daughter, Regan, to tears of despair as a teen. Not the tall-and-thin part, but being flat chested was something of a trial for her. Poor thing. She swore that she wanted implants for her eighteenth birthday, but that was the year her father had died, and she finally realized what was important to have and not have, and big boobs ended up at the bottom of the list.

"Listen," she said. "I have to pick up Wade in twenty minutes. Just go through the site, Kate. Read what the other women have to say. Then read some of the men's profiles. You don't have to go live right away, but you're all set to go when you feel the time is right, okay?"

She leaned down to kiss my cheek, then scurried away to pick up her son. Laura had two boys in high school, both involved in sports. She was also a fairly successful Realtor, and had mastered the art of sandwiching clients in between ferrying her sons from one ball field to another.

My two boys had never been involved in sports. Jeff started drawing in crayon at thirteen months and never stopped. He was now a very successful cartoonist, with his strip syndicated in more than fifty daily newspapers. You may have read it—*Bennie's World*. It's the one about the cute little boy who wants to be a ballet dancer, while the world around him thinks he should be a baseball player. And as for Sam, well, Sam was a geek in preschool and never outgrew his love of fantasy action figures, old sci-fi television shows, and math. It was kind of sad, because when he talked about what he loved, my eyes glazed over after thirty seconds and then my hands started to twitch. I couldn't even tell you what his major was in college. He'd tried to explain it to me several times. He was very patient and always used small words. He was doing something with computers. That's all I got.

But not even Sam could explain the attraction so many people have to online dating. I had actually asked him, since he was my only unattached child, and therefore the one most likely to be trying it himself. But he'd just grunted, leaving me to ponder: Is this how people really meet now? Whatever happened to hanging out in bars?

I did not read anyone else's profile. I turned off the computer, made a cup of tea, curled up on my couch, and watched the birds in my backyard fight over sunflower seeds.

I also napped a little, waking up with two cats on my lap and a dog on my feet. Maybe I wasn't having hot flashes after all. Maybe it was just additional body heat that was causing me to break into a sweat at random times. My cats were rescue cats, both gray. They were named Seven and Eight. Without the kids around to name them, I'd just counted thirty years of family cats on my fingers and came up with the perfect names.

Seven, by the way, was much friendlier. She would always find my lap. Eight was more typical, seeking only food and a soft, sunny spot, rather than company.

I also had a dog. Adam had never wanted a dog, but after his death, I went to the local shelter and found Boone. She was a mix, part spaniel, part terrier. She also loved the cats. In fact, I was pretty sure she thought she was a cat, because she was a big fan of soft, sunny spots. She never complained about what I fed her, was always happy to see me, and never argued with me. She was a perfect companion. But whenever the phone rang, she raced over and barked, looking up with eager anticipation. Was she expecting a call?

I read for a while, napped a little more, and ate some leftover lasagna for dinner. I watched eight episodes in a row of *The West Wing*. Then I went to bed. Alone. Except for two cats and the dog.

Maybe Laura was right. Maybe I should start getting out more. So I spent the next morning in my yoga class, where I visualized myself in my new home, hosting a party of attractive and eligible men from my new complex, all of whom were disgustingly physically fit. There was wine flowing and gentle laughter, and I had to make several calls to my adult children explaining that I was going to Cabo, and could one of them take the dog for a weekend?

There's an old saying—man plans, God laughs.

And let me tell you, he has an interesting sense of humor.

When the holidays come around, my children and I don't gather around a long, scrubbed pine table, laughing and sipping wine from fragile crystal while fondly remembering the past. I blame Adam for all that. Not that it was his fault that he died—I'm fairly certain that was unintentional—but he was an ob-gyn, devoted to his patients, always on call, and had managed, in the course of our twenty-two-year marriage, to miss every birthday party ever given for his children . . . and his wife. He also was never around for Halloween, most Thanksgivings, and every other Christmas. I know—women can't help when they have babies, but I often thought that Adam took on new patients only if he thought they could go into labor at the exact moment he should have been helping his five-year-old daughter blow out her birthday candles.

The upside to his absence was the fact that he—I mean, we—were rolling in money. Adam earned the money, and I spent it. When I decided to go back to work, it had been on a part-time basis at first. The kids were all little—Sam had just started first grade. I told everyone it was just an excuse to get out of the house and use that fancy law degree I'd spent so much money to get, which was partially true. It was also because I was desperate to have an adult conversation, where PTA meetings, playdates, and the value of organized T-ball were never, ever discussed.

I had gone into law in the first place because I wanted to be a champion of the oppressed and downtrodden. But when I looked at my three kids, and realized that being a champion was very time-consuming, I got my master's in accounting and went into tax law. Still big bucks, but no night court to deal with.

But a few years later I decided that Adam was probably having an affair, and I was thinking about divorcing him. I wanted to make sure I could support myself and the kids if he turned into a major jerk over money when papers were served. That's when I went full-time. So in addition to Adam never being around, my kids were kind of on their own during the two years prior to his death. It's not like they were latchkey kids—by then, Sam was in middle school, Regan was a high school sophomore, and Jeff was sending out college applications.

Sam and I had talked about it a little. He insisted his childhood was a happy one. Of course, Sam spent most of the aforementioned childhood in an imaginary world anyway, where bad things happened to you only if you ran into an orc or evil wizard.

Regan had always refused to discuss her father. She worshiped him, hated his being away all the time, probably blamed me for it, and still got teary when she talked about him. So I'm just guessing she does not look back fondly on her teenage years.

Anyway—the point is, I had no qualms about selling the great big house I had raised my kids in. It was not dripping in rich, fond memories. They didn't even have any stuff left there. Their rooms were not shrines to their youth—no posters or pillows, no snapshots tucked around the mirrors.

I had three perfectly good guest rooms, in addition to the original guest room, and, frankly, that's about three bedrooms too many. I wanted to sell.

So that weekend, when I called Laura, I mentioned my idea. She immediately drove over, clipboard in hand.

"How long have you had carpenter bees?" was the first thing she said.

I stared at her. "You've been here hundreds of times. You never noticed before?"

She shrugged. "I don't wear my Realtor's hat when I visit family. But you know they're a problem, right?"

Yes, I did know. That's why I had an exterminator come every month. Which is also why I wanted to sell the house. Five bedrooms, three and a half baths, a three-car garage, pool, and finished basement sounds like heaven on paper, but it requires several people to take care of it, and those several people are all highly trained professionals who want to get paid lots of money.

"Anything else?" I asked.

"No. The outside looks great. But these floors—you should get them all redone. Hardwood's a plus, but not if it looks shabby. And that red wall in the kitchen—got to go." She was making notes as she spoke. "You know I love your house, Kate, but in this market, you'll need to do a lot of work. I was even thinking about a stager."

"I don't want to do a lot of work. I'd be happy to sell it for less than market value."

She frowned. "Less? What the hell is wrong with you? And why are you selling in the first place? You love it here."

"I know. But now I want to move to Castle Crossings."

She narrowed her eyes. "Wait a minute. You quit your job. You didn't fight the dating idea nearly as hard as I thought you would. And now, you're selling the house. Are you having some sort of midlife thing?"

I shrugged. "Maybe. But I went to an open house at Castle Crossings last weekend, and I loved it. I remember when it was first being built, like twenty-whatever years ago. I fell in love with it then. The condos are still fabulous, there's a pool and walking trails for Boone, and I'd never have to worry about carpenter bees again."

She grinned. "I just listed a three-bedroom over there. Completely redone last year and it would be great for you. And if money is not an issue, I can get this place sold in a month. Are you sure? What do the kids think?"

"I don't know what the kids think. Does it matter? They don't live here anymore; you know that. And I don't know if I want three bedrooms."

"Of course you do. Better for resale. And besides, the two small bedrooms are upstairs. You never have to go in them if you don't want. And it's a corner unit, right next to the woods, with a finished walk-out basement."

"Why would I need a basement?"

"To store all your stuff in, Kate. You're a friggin' pack rat and you know it. It's perfect. Gorgeous. Let's go."

She was right. It was gorgeous. I'd have to get rid of half my furniture—or stash it in the basement—but that broad expanse of copper-colored granite whispered to me, the fireplace actually sang, and the walk-in shower in the master bath winked knowingly. I had never been so seduced in my life.

So I signed papers for the rest of the day: the contract for buying the new place, the contract for selling the old place, and the membership forms for the on-site health club.

Then I went home. I pulled up my online profile and hit the button. I was now officially Out in the World.

Cheryl Drake became my best friend when we were seven years old. When she moved into the house next door, she immediately found the tree fort that the previous neighbors had built for their three sons and called to me as I ate an apple on my back porch steps. I grabbed another apple from the kitchen, climbed the ladder to the top of the tree fort, and sat with her and watched as the movers hauled things from the truck to her new house. In that brief span of time, she told me that she was an only child (like me) and that her mother was a great cook (also like mine), and now that she was living in a house instead of an apartment, she was going to have six dogs, three cats, and a pony. I was instantly jealous, but quickly got over it when she assured me that I could have full access to all the members of her menagerie.

She then announced that the tree fort was going to be a penthouse apartment from now on, and would I care to be her roommate? I said yes, although I wasn't sure what a roommate was. This was 1965, remember, and all I knew of life was married couples and their children. I didn't know that two single girls could live together. Cheryl assigned us each a job. I was a teacher. She would be a nurse. I could set up a schoolroom on my back porch. She could have her hospital on her patio. We could meet for lunch, and visit each other at work. After work, we'd make dinner together, then take care of all the dogs and cats, and ride the pony.

In one short afternoon, my entire world changed. Because of Cheryl, when Mary Tyler Moore became a sensation on television for being a single woman with a job and her own apartment, it was all old hat to me.

Cheryl never got six dogs, three cats, or a pony. She did get a puppy for Christmas that year, as well as a baby brother, whom her parents would not trade for a pony no matter how much she begged. When I got my own baby sister, I thought that maybe we could trade them both in, but no luck.

When my father died, during my freshman year of high school, I had to come home every day after school and watch my baby sister, because my mother had to go to work. So I missed out on lots of things that I should have been enjoying in high school—football games after school, getting drunk in the parking lot of the old movie theater, and smoking pot in the park on sunny afternoons. Luckily, Cheryl sat with me out in the penthouse, and we got drunk and got high, and since I never really cared about football, it wasn't nearly as awful as it could have been.

We went in two different directions after high school. Her parents divorced, and she moved to New Mexico with her mother, so when I came home from college during a break, she was no longer right next door. We wrote to each other for a while, and she flew out to spend a week one summer when we were both twenty-one. But after that, life happened. I went to law school, got married, and moved to Rhode Island. She also married and was rumored to be in California somewhere.

But fate is strange, and at our tenth high school reunion, there she was. She'd divorced her second husband

and moved back to New Jersey. Adam had just been offered a job at Morristown Memorial Hospital, so we were also looking to move back. Ta-da! Instant best friends again.

The best thing about Cheryl is that we don't live in each other's back pockets. I see her for lunch about every other week, usually for lunch, occasionally for a long afternoon of shopping. We tell each other pretty much everything. She was the first to hear me say out loud that I thought Adam was having an affair. I was the first to know she was remarrying—a much older gentleman, pretty much for his money and vast Far Hills acreage. I'm also one of the few people who knew how genuinely sad she was when he died.

We met for lunch that Monday. Cheryl was the exact opposite of me—blond, very curvy, and dressed for complete success. I had not put on a suit in almost a month, since I left my job, and had taken to wearing dressy sweatpants and J. Jill tunics. She was shiny and sleek, where I was fighting back frumpy with lots of silver jewelry and a variety of new haircuts. She was plucked, powdered, and polished. I'd started biting my nails again out of sheer boredom. But we both liked cold white wine for lunch, which was the important thing.

Cheryl fluttered. Her hands were always in motion, her head was always nodding, and she often tapped her foot for no apparent reason. Time spent with her I considered exercise, because I always came home exhausted from just watching her.

"And, what's new?" she began, while reading the menu, sipping her drink, and keeping one eye firmly fixed on her cell phone.

"I put the house on the market," I told her. "And I joined a dating site."

Her mouth dropped open, and she actually paused for a fraction of a second in surprise. "Really? Which one?"

"Match Made in Heaven."

I could feel the tip of her foot against the table leg. "I'm on Catch a Star. I'm having so much fun."

I stared at her. "Really? That's great, Cheryl. How long has this been going on?"

She shrugged. "About two months now."

"And you never thought to mention it before now?"

She made a face. "I wasn't exactly sure if I was doing the right thing. It felt a bit strange at first. But I'm pretty happy with how it's worked out."

"And have you met anybody?"

She shot me a look. One of those "Are you kidding?" looks. "I've met three anybodies."

"Oh, that's great," I said, and I meant it. Robby had been gone for almost two years, and Cheryl had always been one of those women who needed a man in her life. "Do you think you'll start to date any of them?"

"Oh, honey," she said, waving over the waiter, "I'm dating all of them."

I managed to keep my astonishment to myself until after we ordered. Then I zeroed in. "Are you really dating three men at once? Isn't that a little much, even for you?"

"Well . . ." She waggled her head back and forth. "It's not like I'm full-out dating."

"Then what's it like?"

"There's not a lot of face-to-face. We meet for lunch, or drinks, about once a week. Mostly, we tweet and text."

I took a gulp of my wine. "Tweet? And text? Is that all?"

"Well, we're all very busy. Paul lives in Brooklyn, he's in real estate, and so he's always on the go. Marco is a professional musician, and right now he's performing with a small opera company and in his free time he gives private lessons. Brad lives down the shore. So I just keep them all in my phone, like those little Tamagotchi pets the kids had back in the nineties. I smile and wave, and talk to them, and they talk back. Very sweet."

"What about, well, you know. Sex?"

She made a face. "I'm never having sex again. Seriously. Robby and I had sex once a month for the first few years of our marriage, and when we stopped altogether, I was perfectly happy. Sex was never one of my big things, you know that. Frankly, at this point of my life I've pretty much forgotten all about it. That's what's so good about this online thing. We never really have to touch."

I was trying to absorb this. "Cheryl, what if one of them wants to touch?"

She looked at me with shaking head and clucking tongue. "That's why I'm keeping them on the phone instead of in person. Besides, they're all pretty old. They probably can't get it up."

"But—" I stopped. I knew by now to never judge the rest of the world by anything Cheryl had to say. She'd been living on her own private planet for years, and liked it that way. If I wanted to find out about online dating, I'd have to look elsewhere.

To change the subject, I mentioned her grandson. She had one. I did not. I tried not to hold it against her, but it was hard. I had three healthy children, all well into their childbearing years, and none of them had thought to pro-create. Jeff is gay, but that was not an obstacle anymore, and I know he had mentioned adoption sometime last year. I had been trying very hard not to pump him for informa-tion. Regan was getting married any day, but she had this whole "I need to start my career" thing going on. True, she had spent many years and many dollars going to veterinary school, but you can heal sick puppies at any age, and you're only fertile for so long. As for Sam, well, I wasn't sure Sam had even had sex.

"How's Tyler?" I asked.

She beamed. "I spent all morning with him yesterday. I taught him how to say 'chair' and 'taupe.'"

"Interesting choice of words. Are you training him to be an interior designer?"

"Very funny. So, I guess since you're selling the house and thinking about dating, you're going through a midlife thing?"

I sighed. "Why do people say that? Midlife? Seriously, I'm fifty-five. How many one-hundred-and-ten-year-old peo-ple do you know?"

"Honey, if everyone had a midlife crisis at thirty-five, the world would implode. So, are you going to be having sex?"

I sighed again. "This menopause thing is killing me. Just when I think my libido has taken a permanent vacation, it comes roaring back, and suddenly I miss sex. God, an orgasm is one of life's few pleasures that isn't harmful or illegal."

Cheryl arched an eyebrow. "Don't need a man for one of those," she said.

"I know. But I'm tired of naming my vibrators so I have someone to thank."

After lunch, she wanted to drive out to Castle Crossings to see my new place, but I had to explain to her—several times—that the old owner was still living there and we couldn't just walk in and poke around.

She sighed. "Just as well, I suppose. I have a bra fitting at two thirty."

I stared. First at her face, then at her rather amazing boobs. "Bra fitting?"

"Yes, Kate. I've been having bras made for years."

"Made? As in, custom built?" Adam had often joked that Cheryl's bras needed not so much to be sewn as engineered.

"Yes." She sounded impatient. "I know that you don't need to wear one. I can't tell you how much I envy you that. But when you're built like me, well, let's just say that with great breasts comes great responsibility."

And on that note, she left.

I talked to my daughter, Regan, on the phone three times a week. Her idea, not mine. And we usually lunched together at least one day during the week. I went over to her apartment for dinner on the occasional Sunday, and once a month I tried to have a big Saturday-night spaghetti thing, with Regan and her fiancé, Phil; Jeff and Gabe; and whatever friends and/or relations I could gather together. So I knew for a fact that everyone was aware that I had put the house on the market. I mean, didn't they see the big yellow sign in the front yard? And I talked to Sam about it, because he specifically told me not to get rid of the shoe box that was on the top shelf of his closet, behind his old chemistry textbooks. Of course, after he asked me this, I quickly ran upstairs to see what was so damn important, but the thing was taped with enough duct tape to seal up a submarine, so I let it go.

And when a very nice day trader and his wife made an offer, and I took it (even though it was a bit less than the asking price), I believe I put the whole thing on Facebook. In fact, I may have even posted a picture of me waving the check in the air and grinning like an idiot. I know that I told everybody when I got a closing date for the new place, because I sent everyone an e-mail asking if they could help me move.

But, somehow, my children remained oblivious.

I didn't know that, of course. I thought the lines of communication were open and flowing. After all, they had plenty to say about me dating again.

Dating in the digital age was very different from dating in the seventies. For one thing, most of the flirtation was done in front of my computer in my jammies and slippers. I considered that a plus, by the way. I had always hated getting all dressed up, ironing my hair straight, and worrying about falling off my platform shoes just to meet some jerk I would never, ever see again.

The picture face on the screen had no expectations. He didn't buy you a drink or two, for instance, then get upset because you wouldn't blow him in the unisex bathroom. He wouldn't take you out to dinner because he needed a date for his cousin's wedding, and he thought you'd look hot in a red minidress and could show up his brother with the pregnant wife. No one asked if I was holding. No one mentioned his waterbed. And no one would ever expect you to wait a few weeks to see whether he was getting back with his old girlfriend or not. No, the face on the screen was very low-maintenance.

At first, I got a lot of "waves." That's online dating–speak for a show of interest. Two gentlemen waved all the way from Florida. Like a long-distance relationship at my age was a good idea. I didn't wave back. I exchanged two or three messages with a very sophisticated New Yorker, until he mentioned that he still had a wife, and how did I feel about open marriage? He was a little *too* sophisticated for me.

Then there was the week of Daves. DaveOne was a banker who had been out of a job since 2009 but still got dressed every day and commuted to New York City, where he'd sneak into museums or stake out his old office building. Why is it that people online tell a stranger things they should seriously never mention to anyone? Ever.

DaveTwo seemed sweet and funny. We actually got as far as suggesting to meet in person for coffee. Then he asked if he could bring his mother, because she'd gotten used to him living back home and got lonely if he went out without her.

Oh my.

DaveThree seemed rich with promise. A lawyer. Widowed. Three kids. I was thinking we had so much in common. But he started sending things to my e-mail address, you know, those rants about politics and such, and although I'm not all *that* liberal, when he confessed that he rewatched Ronald Reagan's old State of the Union addresses I had to draw a line.

My children found this all very entertaining. Sam actually laughed, and he's not big on spontaneous expressions of delight. Jeff suggested I start a blog, and went ahead and bought the domain name ohbabybaby.com. He promised to give it to me for Mother's Day. Ha-ha, sweetie.

Regan got very analytical. She brought a file to lunch filled with articles about dating after "a certain age" and all the pitfalls involved. I read part of her offering with a mixture of amusement and horror, then promised her I would never give a stranger any of my bank account numbers. She seemed unconvinced.

I was kind of glad the dating thing remained low-key, because I had so much other stuff to do. Although I'm not actually a pack rat, as Laura suggested, I do have a hard time letting go of certain things. But I got very hard-core. I went through four closets of old clothes and gave away anything I hadn't worn in two years. Or anything that still had shoulder pads. Or was tie-dyed. I did keep my business suits. All of them. They represented not only my career, but a serious financial investment, so I decided they would stay.

I had to get rid of records. I had LPs dating back to the sixties—did you know that Sally Field released an album as the Flying Nun? Some of these were harder to get rid of than others, but, as Jeff pointed out, I had already downloaded everything of importance into my little MP3 player. Since I could now listen to every Dan Fogelberg song ever recorded without having to get up and flip anything over, out went the vinyl. Books were also a bit of a problem. So I just got rid of all of Adam's and kept mine.

I fretted over furniture until I decided to just buy new. I don't care what kind of shape the living room couch is in—every twenty years, whether you need to or not, you should buy a new one. I sent an e-mail to my kids asking them if there was anything they wanted me to save. Nobody got back to me, which I thought was a little strange. Were they ignoring my e-mails? Or were they just in denial about my moving?

I had to drive up to Boston for Sam's graduation a week before the closing was scheduled, and planned on major shopping on Cape Cod. I would have liked someone to come with me, but both Jeff and Regan were vague. I should have realized something was up, but I was too busy, so I resigned myself to going solo.

At the end of April, three weeks before Sam's graduation, I spent a few hours online making a list of all the places on Cape Cod I wanted to visit. Virtual shopping isn't as emotionally satisfying as real shopping, but it is cheaper. I also found a few painters and a guy to redo the floors of the condo. All without putting on real shoes. God, I love the Internet. Then, because I hadn't been there in a few weeks, I opened up my profile on the dating site. Three more waves. A retired teacher. A career military guy. And Jake Windom.

Boy, was God laughing now.

CHAPTER TWO

R emember your first true love?
Not the high school first love, because, really, that was all about angst. Where is he? Will he call? Why was he talking to Jenny? When should I let him take off my bra? Does he really love me? Should we have sex? When? Where? How can I go away on vacation with my family for two weeks and leave him alone when that bitch Cathy just broke up with her boyfriend and has her eye on him?

And I don't mean your first sex boyfriend, either. For some smart people, high school boyfriend and first sex boyfriend were one and the same. But for a few late bloomers—like me—first sex boyfriend was in college, and (let's get real) sex was pretty much the only thing holding you together. Ever remember having a conversation with that guy that lasted longer than five minutes? And that wasn't about where you were going to be taking your clothes off next?

No, I mean your first Real True Love. The one you talked to for hours. The one you knitted a sweater for. The one you dreamed of going to Colorado with, where the two of you would build a cabin together and live off the land.

Maybe those of you who did not have that first love in the seventies had different dreams. I must admit, the building-a-cabin thing is pretty lame these days. But you know the guy I'm talking about.

He was the one.

You never, ever loved another man the way you loved him.

And when it was over, he broke your heart like it would never be broken again.

For me, that was Jake Windom.

He was tall, dark, and handsome. Hey, some men really are. I met him the first week of my sophomore year in college, when he hit me in the head with a football. Not on purpose—it was fate. I was walking across an intermural field with my roommate, barely paying attention to the guys tossing around a football on the other end of the field, when I heard someone yell, "Watch out!" As I looked to see who was yelling, a football hit me right on the top of my head. It hurt. Not a lot, but enough to bring tears to my eyes, mostly from surprise, but I didn't tell that to the incredibly gorgeous guy who ran up and apologized, and then insisted he walk me to the student center for a drink of something. That was Jake. We had coffee, then went to the pub for a beer, and then we had another beer or six, and then we sat on the steps in front of my dorm until dawn, and when I finally stumbled back into my room, I was in love. So was he.

I never got used to the idea that someone as handsome as Jake could want somebody as normal-looking as me. He was a year older than me, a business major. We were inseparable from then on. We both lied to our parents about staying on for the summer sessions, got a studio apartment together, and worked crummy jobs for money to pay the rent. My mother thought I had gotten the apartment with

MaryJo, the girl who'd been my roommate at the dorm. Luckily for me, Bloomfield College was far enough away from home that Mom would never just drop by.

When Jake got accepted to a master's program at Penn State, I told him I'd follow him up there and finish my degree later. He said no. I wanted to graduate and go on to law school. If I dropped out to follow him, he said, I might not get back on track. Besides, he said, we loved each other enough that a little distance couldn't hurt us. I knew that other women would go after him. He was so handsome—how could they not? But, stupid me, I believed him. He graduated in May. He went away in August. I was lonely and miserable and could not afford to take the bus to see him, and by November he'd started seeing somebody else. A teaching assistant, a few years older than he, who understood all the pressure he was under. It was nothing I had done, he told me. It just happened.

I spent three days crying and eating nothing but frozen Sara Lee pound cake. MaryJo almost called my mother to come and take me home, but I rallied, because I decided the best revenge was to get into a great law school, find a terrific job, and make the cover of both *Time* and *People* magazines as the wealthiest, most beautiful woman in the world that he didn't have anymore.

And now, thirty-odd years later, there he was. Waving at me.

I stared at the computer screen. I was afraid to move. If I clicked on his picture, would he know that I did it? Would he know I was interested enough to check him out? Would he immediately get a message, like the Bat-Signal, telling him that yes, I saw your wave. Did it matter?

Wait—maybe it was another Jake Windom. It was not all
that unusual a name. I bet there were hundreds of Jake Win-
doms out there, all looking for a feisty and attractive widow
like me. Why did it have to be *my* Jake Windom?

So I clicked on the link, and up came his picture.

Yep, it was him, all right.

He looked almost exactly the same. Going gray, but
only at the temples. Why is that? Why don't men have the
dreaded white stripe down the center of their heads the way
women do? His face was rounder, the sharp jaw and cheek-
bones softer, but, God, he was still so good-looking that he
took my breath away.

He didn't look fat, either. Or bald. Or like he had really
bad breath and farted in his sleep.

Damn him anyway. How was it possible, after all these
years, for him to piss me off so easily?

I needed to talk to somebody. Immediately. Before I did
something stupid—like wave back.

So I called the one person who had been with me
through the entire Jake Windom experience, from that first
flush of true love to the final, bitter, Sara Lee days.

I called MaryJo Rooney.

MaryJo had been my roommate at college before, during, and after Jake. We'd met our freshman year. We roomed
together sophomore year. As far as my mother knew, we
were also roommates my junior year, the year Jake and I
were camped out in a one-window studio only slightly bigger
than a bread box. And after Jake left, I moved back in with
her and rode out my senior year. She not only saved my life;
she made me get out of bed to go to classes, badgered me
into completing my applications, and made sure I looked

presentable at all my interviews. She was the reason I got into law school.

She had been happily married for a long time, with kids grown up and out of the house, like mine. She was a guidance counselor at a suburban high school outside of Chicago. I checked the time; she was still a big church person, unlike me, but even with the time difference, and a really long service, she should have been home.

Thank God, she was.

"Kate! Hi! I was just thinking about you. Oh, this is so funny. You must be psychic. Wait, let me sit and get comfortable. So, how are you? And the kids?"

"Jake Windom just waved at me," I blurted.

There was a moment's silence. "From where, honey?"

"I signed up for an online dating service," I explained.

"Well, that's fine. You've been alone for a long time. But I still don't understand. Were you driving in a car and he passed you? Did you see him at a restaurant? How did this happen?"

"He's on the same dating site. He must have seen my profile. So he expressed an interest. It's called waving."

She was quiet again. The best thing about MaryJo was her patience. She was originally from Atlanta, and always had that slow, Southern way about her. She could never be rushed. And she always thought very carefully before she spoke.

"Kate, you know I love you. And I want you to be happy. That man broke your heart. If there had been any justice in the world, he would have been struck down dead for all the pain he caused you. He is not worthy of your time or energy, not now, not ten years from now. Do not even think about waving back."

There it was, the worst thing about MaryJo: She really held on to a grudge. "MaryJo, that was thirty years ago."

"So?"

See what I mean?

"Well, we're both older and have moved on with our lives. It might be fun to just, you know, catch up."

"Didn't you once tell me that you still dreamed about that man?"

Ah, yes. The other worst thing about MaryJo: She never forgot a word anyone said. Which tied in perfectly with the whole grudge thing.

And she was right: I did still dream about Jake. I'd never stopped. Even when Adam and I were first married, and I thought that Jake was just a piece of my history, he would haunt me. Not often, but every once in a while, I'd wake up with my heart in my throat, thinking he had just left the room. Adam and I had been married for twenty-two years, and I had never, since his death, dreamed about him. But I still had dreams about Jake.

"He looks exactly the same," I told her.

"Well, shit. Not even bald?"

"No. He lives in White Plains," I said, reading his profile. "Divorced, no children, loves theater and football. Go, Giants."

"The Giants can kiss my ass. And so can Jake Windom. No kids?"

"Nope."

"Don't suppose there's any info on the ex-wife? I'd love to know if he ever married that stupid Penn State bimbo he left you for."

I laughed. "See, if I waved back, I could ask him."

MaryJo did not laugh. "Honey, I am so afraid that if you see him, all that old stuff will come rushing back. And you're right: You've both moved on with your lives. Do you really want to do that to yourself?"

The final worst thing about MaryJo: She was one smart, savvy woman.

"I'm curious."

"And?"

I sighed. "I sold the house. I'm moving into a condo next month. Regan is getting married any day now, and my baby, Sam, is graduating from college. I'm lonely. I want someone in my life again."

"How can you trust a man who took the best thing he ever had in his life, you, and threw it away?" I could hear her take a deep breath. "I know that you called me because you wanted somebody who would talk you out of this. But I don't think I'm doing a very good job."

"You're right. I did want somebody to tell me what a bad idea this was. And you're doing a great job."

"But you're going to wave back, aren't you?"

"I don't know."

"Baby, be careful. Do not let him stomp all over you again. Okay?"

"I'll try."

I hung up the phone. I stared at the screen. His dark eyes were smiling at me, the same way they did back in 1978.

I took my hand away from the mouse and turned off the computer.

Even after thirty years, it still hurt.

CHAPTER THREE

The best thing about living alone are little rituals that you can count on. When I realized I would never need the little dinette tucked into my kitchen alcove, because my kids were never going to do homework there again, I got rid of it and replaced it with a soft, squishy chair and ottoman and a low wicker table. Now, every Sunday morning, I could curl up with my coffee and the Sunday *Times* and spread it out all over the place without having to worry about running out of space.

While I was trolling through the Arts & Leisure section, looking at ads for shows I'd never see, I called my kids. Sam was first on my list. He was always awake on Sunday morning because he was never out drinking or sleeping around the night before. And I began every Sunday-morning conversation with Sam with the same question. It's not like I was being a pushy mother. But I knew Sam: He was not particularly good at social interaction, and I just felt the need to remind him that there was a world out there where women lived, and that sometimes he should visit it. For three and a half years, we'd had pretty much the same conversation on the subject.

"Morning, sweetheart. Did you meet anybody?" Since I already knew the answer, I leaned away from the phone to put cream in my coffee.

"Yes. Her name is Alisa, and we're thinking about living together after graduation."

Whoa. I stopped pouring, put the creamer down very gently, and pushed the cat from my lap.

"What did you say?"

"Here's the thing, Mom. She's going for her PhD at Columbia. So, I applied as well, and I've been accepted. It will probably be another two years, but it will be so worth it. The problem is housing. I mean, apartments around there are really expensive. So I was wondering if we could just live with you and, you know, take the train to the city every morning."

I pressed the palm of one hand down against the tabletop and readjusted my grip on the phone.

"What did you say?"

"I know it's a lot to ask, but there's plenty of room at the house, and you're going to be hanging out at that new job of yours all day, I know how you are. You can meet her when you come up for graduation. We were going to drive down to Manhattan, check things out for a few days, you know, being tourists. Then we'll go back to Boston, rent a truck, and move down for good. How does that sound?"

"Sam," I said at last, "when we talk on Sundays, do you ever actually listen to what I'm saying?"

There was a long pause on the line. "Of course, Mom. Why would you ask such a thing?"

"Didn't I tell you that I put the house up for sale?"

"Well, yes, but everyone knows it's a terrible market. You probably won't be able to sell it for a couple of years."

"I signed a contract last month. I'm closing in four weeks. I'm buying a town house in Madison."

Now it was his turn to be struck dumb. I was still trying to process how he could have met this Alisa person, gotten to know her, fallen in love, and planned this elaborate scenario without ever mentioning anything to me.

"And anyway, how long have you known this girl?"

"You sold the house?"

"When did you meet her?"

"There won't be much room in a town house."

"I thought you were getting a job with that German company."

"I guess finding an apartment shouldn't be too hard."

"Sam!" I yelled. "Stop and tell me about this girl. And going to grad school. We talk once a week. Couldn't you have maybe mentioned this to me a little earlier?"

He sighed. "I know how you are, Mom. If I told you about Alisa, you'd get all starry-eyed and goofy, and we weren't sure what we were going to do after graduation, so I figured the less you knew, the better."

"I do not," I said coldly, "get starry-eyed. Or goofy."

"How long ago did you write up the guest list for Regan's wedding?"

I cleared my throat. "Four years ago."

"Exactly. And how long has she been engaged?"

"Six months. But that's different."

"No, Mom, it's not." He was quiet. "I met Alisa last summer. She's doing work in neurobiology and she's super-smart and three days older than I am and I really love her.

She gets me and I never have to explain myself to her. She knows me. And she loves me anyway."

Aw, Sam. "Of course she loves you. What smart girl wouldn't love you? You're the best kid in the world. You're also a royal pain in my butt. And what's this grad school thing? Were you afraid I was going to get starry-eyed over paying for you to go to school for another two years?" Which was not entirely true. MIT had offered Sam a full scholarship. That's how smart he was. But I still had to pay for room and board, living expenses, and the occasional round-trip ticket home.

"The tuition part is all covered. Seriously. Not to worry. We'll be fine. I still have Dad's money, so we'll be able to afford a place near school, I'm sure. We can spend our vacation looking for a place. It'll be fun."

That's my Sam. He and his brother and sister had each inherited a substantial amount when their father died. Jeff used his share as a down payment on an apartment in Manhattan. Regan used it to go to Cornell School of Veterinary Medicine. Sam invested very conservatively and had actually made money over the past eight years. I knew, because I did his taxes every year. Not only could he and his girlfriend live fairly well, but if they could find something reasonable, they could also have a nice chunk of change left over.

"Sam, I'm happy for you, really. So happy that you've found someone. And I can't wait to meet her."

"Thanks, Mom. She can't wait to meet you, either. She's all alone. I mean, her parents died when she was little; she has no siblings, and was raised by her grandmother, who went into a nursing home two years ago. She can't wait to be part of a real family."

Tears came to my eyes. "Oh, Sam, we'll love her like crazy, I just know it. I have to go. This is way too much for me right now. I need some deep breathing. Maybe I'll call during the week, okay?"

"Okay, Mom. Love you."

I put the phone down and stared at it. Then I stared at Seven. She had jumped up onto the chair next to me, her tail twitching with disapproval. She arched her back and purred.

Well, that was one way to start the morning. I closed my eyes and took several cleansing breaths until my heart rate was back to normal and the tears were gone from my eyes. I picked the phone back up and called Regan.

"Mom. Hi. I was just about to call you. We have a date picked out. We just decided, isn't that great?"

Her news knocked me back for the second time. "Really? Oh, honey, that is great. And thank you for telling me. Did you know that your brother not only has a girlfriend, but that they're moving in together? And they wanted to move in here?"

"Oh, he told you? I'm so glad. I hate keeping things from you, but he made me promise."

"What? You knew about Alisa? And you didn't tell me?" What was wrong with my children?

Regan made clucking noises. "Mom. We all love you and try to keep you from worrying about things. If you knew about Sam and Alisa, you'd go into your mother bear mode, and we didn't want that. Phil and I have decided on the last Saturday in October. What do you think?"

"What do you mean, mother bear mode?"

"Mom. Seriously. Does that sound good?"

I got up and found my five-year planner. I had a five-year planner because, as a lawyer, I had sometimes needed to plan things way in advance. I flipped pages.

"Lucky for you, it seems like any Saturday next year looks good."

"Not next year, Mom. We mean to get married this year. Six months from now."

"That's not a lot of time to plan a wedding."

"We want a small wedding, you know that. In fact, we were thinking about maybe just having it in the backyard. By the gazebo? The weather will be gorgeous in October. We could have a little afternoon thing, about sixty people. What do you think?"

What did I think? The wedding list I had made up, even though it was four years old, was still an accurate representation of whom I wanted at my daughter's wedding, and it had one hundred and sixteen names on it. That was not even her list. Or her fiancé's list.

"Regan. You're killing me here. You and your brother both. I sold the house. Doesn't anyone ever listen to me?"

"Really?" She sounded surprised, but also genuinely pleased. "That's great, Mom. Honest. So we'll get a hall or room or something. Not to worry."

"Honey, places are booked a year or two ahead of time. You might have trouble."

"I don't think so. After all, we just need a small room."

How could I put this delicately? "Are you sure about sixty people?"

"Mom." Her voice got a little tense. "Yes. Sixty people. Maybe seventy. I know about your list, but you're going to have to readjust your thinking. I refuse to be part of a circus. Would Jeff walk me down the aisle?"

"Oh, I'm sure he'd be thrilled. What a lovely idea. But, seriously, sixty?"

"Stop it. Sixty. How about the rehearsal dinner? Do you think wherever you're moving to will be big enough to have the rehearsal dinner?"

"Absolutely. But I'll be happy to help out. Money-wise, that is. You know that."

She sighed. "Yes, I know. And thank you. But Phil's mother is giving us a seriously hard time, so we've turned down all help from her, and Phil told her we were doing it ourselves, and if you give us money, then there will be an issue. A big one. You know what she's like."

I wandered over and poured myself more coffee as I spoke. "Yes. I know exactly what Elaine is like. She's a complete and total bitch. Are you sure she's Phil's mother?"

Regan laughed. "Yes. Sadly, I'm sure. But his dad is coming from England, so you'll finally meet him, and then you'll understand why Phil is as great as he is."

Philip Pendergast was indeed great. He was handsome, charming, smart, and well employed as the director of pharmaceutical sales for a fairly large and stable company, and he loved Regan with every fiber of his being. She was lucky. So was he, of course, but Elaine was the kind of mother-in-law they made bad movies about. Nothing in life is perfect. And along with the son-in-law from heaven, I was about to become attached to Elaine, who was such a cliché she made my head hurt.

I hung up the phone a second time. Should I call Jeff? Was there any other news out there, lurking just below the smooth surface of my life, waiting to reach up and catch me by surprise?

"Jeff? Happy Sunday. Do you have a secret someone in your life that you're not telling me about? Somebody you're planning to move in with?"

He chuckled. "Sam finally told you? He was really worried. I met her, by the way, when I went up last fall. She's lovely. A little shy, but sweet and maybe even smarter than our Boy Wonder."

"Jeff, that's all great. Really. But I sold the house. The contract is signed. If you all had trusted me enough to let me know what was going on, I would have held on to the house, not to mention my job. Now it's too late. I'm closing on the condo. I may even learn to play golf."

He made a noise. "Mom, please. Golf? So you're going to move to Madison?"

Thank God, someone was listening. "Yes. Sam wanted them to live with me here at the house. I wouldn't have minded, not really. Even for two more years. Does grad school really take that long?"

"I don't know, Mom, but think of it this way: Once he's done, he'll be making so much money, we'll be able to put you in the best nursing home in the state."

"What a comforting thought. You always know the right thing to say, honey. Your sister wants you to walk her down the aisle. What are you doing the last Saturday in October? Of this year?"

So we chatted a bit longer, and when we hung up I spent a long time staring out the back window. The yard looked like it always did at the end of April—tulips and daffodils pushing through the dark, damp earth, a green haze on the trees. When I was up in Boston watching Sam graduate, the lilacs would be in bloom. A perennial bed that I had planned as the world's best cutting garden surrounded the pool. I hoped the day trader's wife would take care of it for me.

My new condo had a deck, and overlooked a stretch of county park that ensured privacy and quiet. Instead of spending the summer on my knees, weeding, I could sit in the shade and sip white wine between golf and tennis dates.

While slashing the guest list for my daughter's wedding.

I'm sure there are many misconceptions about the young people who attend the Massachusetts Institute of Technology. Let's get a few of them out of the way.

Yes, they're all really, really smart.

Yes, most of them have no problem with doing whatever they want after graduation. They can get jobs, go to graduate school, pretty much whatever they'd like because—see above. They're really, really smart.

And MIT looks great on a résumé.

They are not, however, all geeks. Or at least, they don't all look like geeks. Sam is a very tall, well-built, and good-looking guy. It's not just a mother's pride saying this. I know cute when I see it, and Sam had always been cute. Unlike Jeff, who, thank God, has a wonderful sense of humor and a great heart to make up for his close-set eyes and lack of chin.

I don't know where Sam's physique came from—I can only thank genetics. Adam was a baseball player up until medical school, and Sam inherited his broad shoulders and muscle tone. He sure didn't get it huddled over a table, shaking dice, saying, "You are about to enter an enchanted forest."

But I have to admit to being a bit surprised when he introduced me to Alisa and she was not a pale, bespectacled waif with hunched shoulders and an overbite. She was beautiful. Tall, graceful, and full-figured, she was very deserving of my almost-gorgeous son. And on top of all that, she was obviously really, really smart.

Jeff was with me at the graduation. Regan could not make it. She had just started at a new veterinary clinic, and it was her weekend on call. I wasn't sure why Gabe, Jeff's other half, was not there. Jeff muttered something about the shop. Gabe, ten years older than Jeff, owned a very successful wine-and-cheese shop blocks from their place in the West Village. I always missed Gabe when he wasn't around. Aside from being charming and very funny, he always had a bottle of amazing wine, that no one had heard of, to share.

We were a happy, lively group. We made it through graduation. I was very proud of myself. Only one hot flash, and it did not require me to loosen any clothing or even fan myself frantically. I remembered people's names and did not suffer any vocabulary gaffes. I had been known, at times, to use the word "elephant" when I meant "car."

We then had a great dinner together at someplace Sam found right on the water, and I lasted until midnight on the post-dinner Revolutionary War pub crawl along the Freedom Trail. When they started doing shots, I caved.

I finally got a chance to get to know Alisa a little better the next morning. The guys were so hungover at breakfast that they winced at the sunlight and huddled silently in their clothes. She and I were clear-eyed and unsympathetic. She was very sweet, but also very ambitious and determined. She had just about every minute of their New York City trip planned out, and showed me all the apartment listings they were going to look at, right there on her tablet. They all looked small, dark, and incredibly overpriced, but she didn't seem to mind. In fact, I got the impression that she was relieved they would be getting their own place, rather than bunking with me. When I mentioned that, she blushed just a little.

"Mrs. Everett, I have to admit I was a little worried. You are obviously a very nice person, but you could have been a raving bitch, you know?"

My mouth dropped open. "You're right. I'm so glad you're this honest. As a family, we're not big on being polite to each other. We kind of let it all hang out, you know? So, since I'm not a bitch, and I'm not going to be your landlady, please call me Kate."

"Thanks." She glanced over at Sam and lowered her voice. "He thinks you're terrific, you know. And it's not that I don't trust him completely, but he thinks the Three Stooges are funny. Let's face it. Sam has crappy taste in lots of things."

I was liking this girl more and more. I beamed at Sam. "You picked a great one, Sam. Really. Maybe she'll finally convince you to get rid of your G.I. Joe collection."

Sam turned pale. "Never. She'd never ask me to do that. Would you, Alisa?"

She just smiled. See? Really, really smart.

Over the second cup of coffee, I looked over at Jeff.

"Honey," I told him, "Alisa and Sam have got the next few years tied up, and Regan is just now getting started on her career. You know that I want to be the cool grandmother, not the old grandmother, so if it's going to happen anytime soon, it'll be up to you."

He shuddered—had I spoken too loudly? "As soon as I grow a uterus, Mom, I'll get right on that."

I sat up a little straighter. "Wait. What happened to that adoption agency you and Gabe were talking to? I thought things were moving along there."

He closed his mouth quickly. Sam ducked his head.

"What's going on?" I asked slowly.

Jeff shrugged. "Gabe and I are having a few issues. That's all."

I pushed back my coffee cup. "Issues? About adopting?"

He shrugged again. "No. Well, yes. We're having issues about everything."

I glanced at Sam, who seemed intent on tracing a circle into the tablecloth with a spilled drop of orange juice. "Sam, did you know about this? Is this another secret you've all been keeping from me?"

Sam shook his head. "No, Mom. Honest. Jeff just talked about it last night, after you left us."

I glared at Jeff. "You had to wait until I left to talk about this?"

Jeff shook his head. "No, Mom. I had to wait until the fifth shot of tequila to talk about it. It's all very new. In the past few weeks he's been acting strange, and he's out of the house a lot. . . ." Tears welled in his eyes. "I think there's someone else."

My heart dropped. Not my baby! I reached over and squeezed his hand. "Oh, honey, really? Are you sure? I can't believe it of Gabe. He's so devoted."

He sniffed. "I hope I'm wrong, I really do, but . . ." He trailed off, shaking his head sadly. "Come on, Mom, you should know better than that. Look how devoted everyone thought Dad was."

My heart dropped even farther.

"What do you mean, honey?" I asked, keeping my voice even. I didn't dare look at Sam.

Jeff squinted, fumbled with his toast, and cleared his throat. He drank some coffee, squinted again, opened his mouth, and closed it.

"Jeff?" I asked. "What do you mean? About your father?"

He made a noise. "I always thought Dad was cheating on you," he blurted. "It was just a feeling, mostly. And, well, I overheard him. Once. On the phone. And I thought you thought the same thing." He finished up in a hurry, then drank more coffee.

The world got very quiet. I looked down at the tablecloth and took a deep breath. "Yes, I thought he was having an affair, too. That's why I went back to work. I was going to divorce him. I'm sorry you, well, suspected. It had nothing to do with you. Or Sam or Regan. Things between us just got sloppy. We stopped paying attention to things. Marriage is hard. Any relationship is hard. And if you don't work at it all the time, and try to keep it going, it falls apart."

Sam snorted. "That's no excuse, Mom. Dad was a real prick."

I looked at him in surprise. "Sam, that's a terrible thing to say. Your father loved you."

He shrugged. "Yeah, I know. He just had a shitty way of showing it." Sam reached over and grabbed Alisa's hand. "I promise you," he said solemnly, "that I will never, ever cheat on you."

She smiled sweetly. "I know, Sam. I'm not worried. Because if you ever do, I know exactly how to kill you so no one will ever suspect a thing."

Sam smiled back. I stared at her. Then I stared at Jeff. He raised his coffee cup in salute.

"Welcome to the family, Alisa. Mom's right, as usual. You're going to fit right in."

My original plan had been to drive to Chatham, on Cape Cod, check into a quaint bed-and-breakfast, then walk out to the beach and have a long talk on my cell phone with Laura about the weekend. Sadly, I hit traffic outside Boston (big surprise), the B and B lost my reservation, so I ended up in a very conventional motel, and by the time I walked to the beach, it was almost eleven o'clock at night, way past my sister's bedtime. Besides, it was cold, the wind kept throwing sand in my face, and I couldn't get a cell phone signal.

On to plan B.

I moved the next morning to the B and B, and called Laura from a quiet park nearby with a lovely windmill and an empty bocce ball court. I'd been texting her all weekend, and had even made Jeff send her pictures, but I needed to talk to her.

"How's the girl?" was her first question.

"Alisa is great," I told her. "Did you get the pictures? She's as sweet as she is beautiful. She also has a big 'no bullshit' clause in her life, which I appreciate. She was very happy to not be moving in with me, even though I was not the complete bitch that I could have been. Sam is completely smitten, and she knows it, but I think they'll be great. Jeff and Gabe are having problems."

"No. Really? But Gabe seems like, I don't know, perfect?"

"Yeah. I thought so, too. Then Jeff pointed out—at the breakfast table, in fact—that Adam seemed perfect and he was cheating on me. Seems like Jeff actually overheard something."

"Whoa." I could hear Laura moving around. She probably decided to settle someplace a little more comfortable for the duration. "He said that?"

"Yep."

"And Sam heard?"

"Yep. And then Sam said his father was a prick."

"At the breakfast table?"

"Yep. I feel awful. I never wanted any of them to know. And they never said anything to me. I know that Adam was not the best father in the world, but he did love those kids."

"Well, Katie, let's face it: You've got three smart kids there, and they were all living through it with you. It makes sense that they would have figured stuff out."

"I know. But still. Anyway, I'm going to shop for fab accessories and antiques while I'm here."

"Good. Remember, strike up conversations with any attractive, age-appropriate men. Unless you've met somebody online and you haven't told me because you hate to admit when I'm right."

I chewed my lip. The first Christmas that Jake and I were together, he drove up from his home outside Philadelphia and spent a couple of days with me and my family. Laura was quite taken. In fact, when I told her we had broken up, she was so upset, you would have thought it was *her* heart that was broken.

"Jake Windom waved at me," I told her.

I could hear her on the line. She actually gasped. "Jake? My Jake?"

"I always kind of thought of him as my Jake," I said.

"When?"

"A few weeks ago."

"Are you going to meet him?"

"I didn't wave back."

Dead silence on the phone. Finally: "What?"

"I didn't wave back, Laura. What would have been the point?"

"Kate," she said slowly, "there are so many dating sites out there. You and Jake happen to sign up for the same one? It's like a sign from God."

"Ah, Laura, I don't think God cares about my old boyfriends."

"No, but he cares about your happiness. This is kismet. You can both start all over."

"Have you been reading Danielle Steel again?"

"I'm serious, Kate. The two of you were perfect together. Can you really go through the rest of your life wondering?"

Well, she was right there. Jake had been gnawing at the back of my brain ever since I'd seen his picture. "I don't know. Listen, I'm going shopping now. Maybe I'll run into a handsome millionaire trolling for old candlesticks."

"Well, if you do, remember Jake. He was always the one you were meant to be with."

I made a noise. "Laura, then why aren't we together right now?"

"Because you didn't wave back at him, idiot. Think about it."

I clicked off the phone. Three old men had started playing bocce ball. I watched them for over an hour, sitting there in the sun. They didn't say much, just grunted, pointed, and laughed together. I didn't understand the game at all, but it was a joy to watch them. When the game was over, one of them came over and kissed my hand.

When they were gone, I sat there some more. Remembering.

I sometimes surprised myself when I realized that Jake and I were together for only two years. It had seemed, at the time, that we had always been a couple, that our souls had somehow formed this perfect unit ages ago, and when our bodies finally came together, it was a great . . . "at last."

It wasn't just the sex part, either, although that was pretty spectacular. We had both been somewhat experienced when we met, but together we became adventurous. We often ended up in the middle of the floor, because no bed was big enough for our energy and exploration.

We were best friends. We saw the world through the same mind's eye, wanted the same things, had fought the same battles. We were both ambitious. I wanted the law, he wanted the business world, and we were not willing to take any prisoners along the way. And while we would lie together some nights, talking about going up to the mountains somewhere and creating our own little paradise, we both knew that our real lives were about doing and going and being someone who mattered.

From that first meeting, we were together almost every day. When we were apart, for those few vacations and breaks when we went to our respective homes, there was no sense of "missing," because our connection was so real and powerful. He would be waiting for me. I never doubted that he would always be waiting for me.

Our friends at college had marveled at us, our closeness, our commitment to each other. In an age of casual sex and fluid relationships, Jake and I were the original power couple. Our apartment became the place for everyone else to gather, for beer and pizza and talk, long into the night.

When we broke up, people treated me as though he had died, like I was a grieving widow rather than a callously dumped girlfriend. It took me a long time to get over him. In fact, there had been no one between Jake and Adam. And when I did meet Adam, I was so lonely and still so sad that I made myself accept his attention, because I realized if I didn't, I could end up alone for the rest of my life. When Adam proposed, I was so grateful that I wept.

But I always thought of Jake as the man who had been meant for me. It was his name that had been written in the stars, right next to mine. Sitting in the sunlight on a May afternoon on Cape Cod, I wondered if our names were still there, somewhere, together.

I spent a lot of money on Cape Cod. I bought a great old wing chair that barely fit in the back of the minivan, even though I'd taken all the seats out. I bought paintings and quilts, a faded Oriental rug, and lots of what my mother would have called tchotchkes. My main problem was that I didn't know what I wanted my new home to look like. I only knew what I didn't want it to look like—like the widow of a doctor lived there. So while I had spent hours of my life looking through glossy magazines and watching HGTV, I still didn't have a vision. But I figured I had lots of time.

I closed on the condo as soon as I got back, before I closed on the house. Which meant I needed something called a bridge mortgage. It seems the bank didn't quite trust me to pay off the condo after I sold the house, even though I had all sorts of signed contracts. I know that I went through the mortgage process the first time with Adam, but I don't remember it being such a pain in the butt. I wanted to scream and throw things and just wait until I had the check from the sale of the house in my hot little hand, but, even more, I wanted all the condo walls painted a soothing taupe and the hardwood floors refinished dark coffee before I moved in. So when I signed away my old house and followed the movers to my new place, it looked just the way I wanted it to look—except I had almost no furniture. I had saved all the outdoor stuff, so my deck looked great, but inside was pretty empty. I did have the wing chair, covered in ivory silk, and a rug from Cape Cod, and lots and lots of boxes, as well as a queen-size sleigh bed and brand-new mattress. I had kept a very few sentimental pieces, like some of the kids' things, but that was all stashed in the basement. My home was going to be all new, a fresh start. I popped open champagne, sat alone in my one chair, and looked at my life. Thirty-some years of my home and family, reduced to mountains of brown cardboard and a row of pictures lined up against my new fireplace. The cats had gone into hiding, Boone whined and would not settle down, and I couldn't figure out which wires went where on the television, so I went to bed early. By morning, all the animals had found their way to the new bed, so I figured we'd all be fine.

My new condo was three levels. The garage and basement were on the street. From the driveway, you'd go up a half flight of steps to a beautiful brick courtyard where I had already planned for a few tall, colorful planters with lots of flowers, a really cool water feature, and a low stone bench. Then up another half flight to the front door. I really liked the courtyard, and could imagine sitting out there in the evenings with my wine, watching the comings and goings of the neighborhood.

Jeff and Gabe showed up early, brought bagels, and helped me unpack. I kept looking for a sign that something was wrong between them, but they seemed to be their usual selves. Gabe left just before lunch to go to the grocery store, and came back with enough food to fill the fridge and then some. Afterward, we left the boxes and shopped for furniture. Jeff and Gabe brought their van, a long, battered thing Gabe used to haul stuff to the shop. I followed in the minivan. We were going to do some serious shopping.

Maybe I wasn't sure what I wanted the condo to look like, but Jeff and Gabe had a vision. We power-shopped six stores, including every HomeGoods we could find. We bought pieces off the showroom floor and packed as much as we could in both vehicles, then unpacked and had everything arranged by dinner.

Finally, I said, "This is how you see me living?"

Jeff was smiling happily. "Mom, the place looks great."

I looked around. Shabby velvet club chairs, faded leather love seat, and chunky black tables. And, because they were on sale, four fake palm trees. "It looks like the Abercrombie and Fitch store at the mall."

Gabe clucked. "No, Kate, it doesn't."

"That's because there's too much light in here," I said. "Imagine the place in near-darkness."

Jeff shook his head. "You're crazy."

"Okay. Hollister then."

Gabe's face fell. "Well, maybe a little."

"All I need is a surfboard on the wall," I said. "And a rack of skinny jeans."

Jeff was hanging tough. "You're both crazy. This is shabby-chic-slash-eclectic."

I shook my head. "This is 'Do you have this in size triple zero?'" I flopped onto one of the chairs. Granted, it was very comfortable. "I'm going to have to start subscribing to all those weird music magazines. And play the Beach Boys in a continuous loop."

Jeff dove into another box. "We just need to add a few accessories."

"My God, Jeff, can you possibly say something a little less gay?" Regan came into the room. She had knocked, I'm sure, but had not bothered to wait for anyone to open the door for her. My fault, I knew—I never locked my doors, because all the people I knew were so used to letting themselves in. *Mi casa es su casa,* no matter what *casa* it was. Phil was right behind her, struggling with another palm tree, which I assumed was my housewarming present. I waved tiredly from my chair.

"Hi, baby girl. How do you like the new digs?"

Regan had hugged Gabe and was looking around critically. She was a very pretty girl. She looked more like Laura than me, thank God, because my face is all strong angles, with a jaw that could be Jay Leno's second cousin. Regan's face was soft and gently curved. So was her body, but you could hardly ever tell, because her standard uniform was something big, baggy, and drooping. For a woman with a great shape, she never showed it off. She told me that since she was flat chested, nobody was going to look at her anyway, but would it hurt to flaunt great legs and a nice butt?

"Why does this place look familiar?" she asked.

I stood up to kiss Phil. "Think forty-dollar tank tops."

"Wow," she said. "You're right. Except it's way too bright. And there are no black shutters. Where's the checkout?"

Jeff had artfully arranged a wooden bowl, a stack of books, and three oversize chess pieces on the coffee table. "See, this looks better," he said.

Regan shook her head. "No, not really. And I can't believe we bought you a palm tree. It already looks like a rain forest in here."

I waved it aside. "Yours is real, honey, and it's beautiful. Thank you. We can put it out on the deck. In fact, why don't we sit out there for a while?"

So we sat in the twilight on old, familiar patio furniture, cast-iron tables, and creaking Adirondack chairs. Gabe went into the kitchen and came back with fruit and cheese, crackers and wine, and we ate and talked, looking out over the woods that were my brand-new backyard. We talked about Sam and his new life. He and Alisa had found a place, and were moving in in a few weeks. We talked about Regan's wedding, and where she was looking for her dress. Phil complained about his mother, who was already being a royal pain in the ass. No one mentioned our old house. No one mentioned Adam. No one seemed sad to see me in such a new and different place.

But I was sad. Just a little.

The best thing about my future son-in-law, aside from the fact that he was crazy about Regan and would make a noticeable contribution to the good looks of my grandchildren, was that he could do things. Jeff could arrange furniture and find the perfect shoe to go with any outfit. Gabe cooked like a chef and was pretty good at money advice. Sam could hack into any government database and arrange for a long-range nuclear missile to hit any target I desired. But Phil was good at practical things, like finding the cable box in my new den, and making sure the washing machine was hooked up properly. He laughed at me because I also had a telephone line installed, but I'm still old-fashioned enough to believe that if you have a home, you should have a home phone.

In a week I had pretty much unpacked the important stuff, waved at a few neighbors, and walked to the health club. I hadn't gone into the health club, but Boone and I passed it at least once a day. I nodded to the golf pro in passing. I even looked at the pool.

Cheryl came by to take me to lunch and check out the place. She stood in the middle of the living room, looked around carefully, then glared at me.

"Why did you let Jeff decorate your house? Have you learned nothing?"

I shrugged. "He seemed so excited. He and Gabe both. And they brought the van, and Gabe always has great wine. . . . Is it that bad?"

"Kate, it's gorgeous. Two gay men from the Village? How can it not be? But let's face it, this room looks nothing like you."

I looked around sadly. My animals had all adjusted nicely. Boone had claimed a corner of the love seat. Seven perched on top of one of the velvet chairs in a patch of sun. Eight hung out under one of the fake palms, looking for all the world like a gray tiger stalking a gazelle. But try as I might, I did not feel comfortable.

"The den is better," I told her, leading the way. The den was an alcove right before the master bedroom, with my desk and computer, a wall of empty bookcases waiting to be filled with all my books, a wall-mounted television, and the squishy chair and ottoman that had been in my old kitchen.

"You can't live in here," Cheryl said. "You've got those beautiful windows overlooking all that green space, and you spend your time in this cubbyhole? Grow a backbone, Kate. Send the stuff back and go to Ethan Allen."

"I know. I'm going to have to do something. I can put the stuff downstairs, or some of it on the upstairs landing. The good thing about all these extra rooms is that I can buy all sorts of furniture and keep moving it around. Let's eat."

Cheryl drove, always an interesting experience. Once, she rolled down her window so she could scream at the guy idling next to us at a red light to stop talking on his cell phone. We got to the restaurant without inciting a riot, and ordered. We chatted for a few more minutes before she nailed me.

"So what's bothering you?"

I played with the stem of my wineglass. "Do you believe God is interested in our happiness?"

My Italian mother belonged to one of the more complicated religious affiliations—Lapsed Catholicism. She made
sure that both my sister and I received our first Holy Com-
munion, but after taking care of that first brush with sin,
she ignored any further religious education. My father was
a Methodist, the most laid-back and undemanding of organized religions, so I spent most of my young life believing in
God but not taking him too seriously.

Cheryl frowned. As well as I knew her, I had never discussed religious beliefs with her. I knew that she'd been
raised Catholic, but beyond that, I had no idea what her
spiritual outlook was.

"Do you mean in a general sense, like God loves us and
tries to keep us on the right path?" she asked.

"No, not exactly. Do you think God personally cares if I,
Kate Everett, die alone in a rest home somewhere instead of
holding the hand of a man I love?"

Cheryl looked at me through narrowed eyes. "How hy-
pothetical is this question?"

"Well, an old boyfriend is on the same dating site as I
am, and Laura thinks it's divine intervention and that we're
meant to be together."

"What kept you from being together before?"

"He cheated on me and broke my heart."

"Ah. That old boyfriend."

I looked at her. "I don't remember ever telling you about
Jake."

She shrugged. "Is that his name? We've all got one, Kate.
The guy that should have been. Mine was Will Marcetta.
Bass player in a folk-rock band. I would have lived in the
back of his van and traveled all across the county with him,

if he'd let me. But I don't think he was willing to give up the freedom of the road, you know? The one-night stands? I never thought I'd love again. But I did. Just like you did." She stopped and let the waiter slide a Cobb salad in front of her. She picked up her fork and played with her food for a minute.

I leaned forward, listening. Cheryl could be a real space cadet at times, but she had a rock-solid core of good sense.

"I'm not sure going back is a good thing," she went on. "We can never be the same people we were. Do you want to risk finding out that the great love of your life has turned into a boring old fart? Or do you want to keep remembering him the way he was?" She shrugged. "I don't think God has set you up. There's a difference between God and fate. And fate is not always kind. Neither is God, for that matter, but he always has better intentions."

"I know. You're right. I'm actually meeting a retired science teacher for coffee next week. He seems very smart and friendly, and no bizarre personality traits have emerged so far, so I'm giving it a shot."

"Meeting someone? You're stepping out beyond the world of virtual relationships and going to try someone in real life?"

I made a face at her. "Yes, a real someone. Not a real Jake. I still haven't decided what to do about him. Maybe meeting somebody else will prove to me that going forward is better than looking back."

"Good for you, Kate. I'm proud of you. You are a shining example of the New Single Woman: facing the world alone and unafraid of change, putting everything on the line, willing to take chances with the unknown. Some magazine needs to do an article about you."

I stared at my lunch. Lettuce and grilled chicken swam in and out. I felt suddenly nauseous. I didn't want to face the world alone. I didn't want to put everything on the line. I was only taking chances because I didn't have that many choices. Any magazine article about me would be titled "Caution: Midlife Crisis Coming Through."

"Would you be disappointed in me if I told you that I hope the retired teacher and I hit it off, get married, and live Happily Ever After so I never have to take another vacation alone?"

She reached over and patted my hand. "I'd never be disappointed in you, Kate. You're one of the best people I know. But you really need to do something with that living room. Ever since I walked out of there, I've had this weird urge to go shopping at the mall."

I had invited Sam and Alisa to have dinner with me. Twice. They declined, saying they were trying to get their own place set up. But then they invited me to see their apartment. I was quite excited about the whole thing.

I must admit that my feelings about New York City were first and always colored by the movies I had seen as a kid. Remember Audrey Hepburn's apartment in *Breakfast at Tiffany's*? Even though she had no furniture, it was cute and chic, in a great neighborhood with fascinating neighbors. *Barefoot in the Park*, anyone? What Jane Fonda did with that little place was amazing, and again with the great neighborhood, etc. Even during the late sixties, when Times Square had hookers and junkies instead of Disney, I still thought that living in Manhattan would be as close to perfect as anyone could imagine. So even though Sam's new place was in Harlem, and I had never been to Harlem, my expectations were high.

I took the train, then the subway, and was in the general neighborhood in a little over an hour. Then I had to walk twelve blocks. Luckily, it was not raining. Or too hot. And I had comfortable shoes. The block they lived on had no quaint cafes or gleaming outdoor markets. Faintly ethnic music did not waft through open windows. It was a block totally devoid of charm or grace, but loud with the sound of traffic.

The building was prewar, but not in a good way. It did not have a doorman, but they buzzed me in and the little lobby had only one broken light. They lived on the sixth floor, and I had to wait a long time for the elevator, which was small but did not smell of pee. I got off the elevator and they were standing in the hallway, waiting for me. They looked beautiful together, so I ignored the blaring of horns, cracked ceiling, and worn linoleum. But once inside, I caved.

"Your window overlooks the alley," I said.

Alisa pulled out one of the two bentwood chairs that were crowded around a tiny table. "Yes, but we get some light in the bedroom," she said.

I sat. I looked around.

The kitchen was along a wall about six feet long, with a tiny sink and the smallest gas stove I'd ever seen. The living/dining room held the table we were sitting at. There was also a huge desk covered with two laptops and three printers. The other huge desk had a desktop and a fax machine. There wasn't room for anything else. The walls were pretty, a pale yellow that tried to, but did not quite, brighten the place up. There were curtains framing the window and the view of a solid brick wall, and over one of the desks was a gorgeous reproduction of a J.M.W. Turner painting, all stormy skies and a brilliant ray of sunlight shining through. The only ray of sunlight in the whole room.

The floor was the same worn linoleum as the common hallway. The ceiling had the same cracks. I could still hear the blare of traffic. I sniffed discreetly. No funny smells. Thank God.

"I love the wall color," I said.

Alisa grinned. "Me too. Sam wanted white, but I thought we needed some fake sunshine. Can I get you something? We'll be going out to eat. I hope you don't mind, but I'm not a very good cook, and every time I turn the stove on, I smell gas."

Sam made a noise. "She thinks she smells gas. I keep telling her it's all in her head."

Alisa reached over and kissed him lightly. "I have a highly developed sense of smell." She looked so pretty in a short denim skirt and a bright polo shirt. Her dark hair was long and shiny, her blue eyes bright and hopeful. All I could imagine was her in six months' time, all the life crushed out of her from coming home every day to this crowded, dingy space.

"Bathroom?"

I had to walk through the bedroom. Yes, it did have a window, set so high in the wall you couldn't look out, but it was noticeably lighter in there. There was room for the bed, barely, and there was a closet with no door. I realized the door had been removed because otherwise, there would have not been enough room to open it.

The bathroom was the size of my walk-in shower. The tile on the floor was stained, but everything was scrubbed clean. When I sat, my knees hit the pipe under the sink.

I could not believe that apartments like this still existed. The whole thing could have fit into my new living room. This was worse than anything Neil Simon could have thought of when he was writing *Barefoot in the Park*.

I went back to the living room. "Storage must be a real challenge," I said brightly.

Sam shrugged. "Well, we've got stuff in boxes under the bed. And I'm thinking about renting a space for my books and old paperwork. Right now, Jeff has a bunch of stuff in the back of Gabe's shop. Alisa still has her skis and some of her old furniture in a pod up in Boston."

"Oh? Jeff has been up here?"

Alisa made a face. "He and Sam got into a bit of a tiff. I don't think Jeff liked our place very much."

Sam sighed. He still had big puppy-dog eyes that made me want to hug him and protect him from the big, bad world. "Jeff called it a frat boy's wet dream. I know this place is kind of a dump, but it's only forty minutes from Alisa's lab, and four subway stops from my campus. It's fairly cheap, and the neighborhood is not too bad. We've got a month-to-month lease, so we'll keep our eyes open for something bigger. And we can try for student housing next year."

I took a deep breath. These were grown-up people here. Their combined IQ was probably greater than the combined IQs of both the offensive and defensive lines of any major professional football team. If this was where they wanted to live, I had better keep my mouth shut.

But . . .

There was no way in hell any kid of mine was going to live here.

"So, I have no idea how a doctorate program works. When do you both start doing whatever it is you're supposed to do?" I asked, sitting back down on my little chair. I felt a hot flash coming on. I resisted the impulse to grab a manila folder off one of the desks to fan myself with. I just hoped they wouldn't notice the beads of sweat at my temples.

Sam, leaning against the wall, was off on the topic. After five minutes, Alisa must have noticed that my eyes were no longer in focus, because she leaned forward and gently asked if I'd like a glass of wine. I smiled gratefully.

"That would be perfect," I said.

She nodded in sympathy. "There's a pretty little place just a few blocks from here where we could sit outside and see the sky. Are you up for a walk?"

Of course I was. My God, anything for a breath of fresh air. I wasn't quite prepared to walk down the stairs, rather than wait for the elevator, but going down five flights isn't really that bad, and there was a nice breeze in the stairwell from a few broken windows. Once we were outside, I felt fine. The sun was shining, the traffic was humming, and only four short blocks away was a tiny bistro where the wine was cold and we sat outside. Sam continued his monologue, something about starting to teach in the fall, and research all summer. I waited for him to take a breath before turning to Alisa.

"And how about you? When do you start teaching?"

She shrugged. "My arrangement is different. I'm not obligated to work in the classroom. I'll be assisting one of the faculty members in his lab. This summer I'll be free to just do my own work. Starting in October, I'll be working three days a week for Dr. Manheesh, and taking classes on the other two days."

"So, you'll be spending the summer in some library somewhere?" I said.

She shook her head. "No, I can do most of it from the apartment. I'll probably only have to come to campus once every couple of weeks."

Work from the apartment? From that miserable shoe box? "Ah, well, let's hope the air-conditioning doesn't break down," I joked.

Sam had finished his wine and was looking around for the waiter. "We're still trying to figure out how to put one in," he said.

"Put one what in?" I asked.

"An air conditioner."

I stared at him, then at Alisa. "The apartment doesn't even have air-conditioning?"

Sam shrugged. "That's why it's only seventeen hundred a month," he said.

Alisa was looking down into her wineglass. I could have sworn I saw her lip tremble. "I need to pee again," I said. "Alisa, can you come with me?"

She followed me inside and down the stairs to the restroom. As soon as I was certain Sam was way out of earshot, I stopped short and grabbed her by the shoulders.

"Do you really want to spend the summer in that place?" I asked her.

Her blue eyes filled with tears. "No. It's awful. I feel claustrophobic. Two nights in a row I woke up and couldn't breathe. I'm afraid to go out by myself. But Sam found it, and he was so proud, and I don't know, I think it's really the best of what we can afford. I don't want Sam to spend all his money; we'll need it when we want a house and family. All I'll be bringing in is my stipend, which will barely cover my lab fees and some groceries. I just don't know what else we can do. We'll qualify for student housing next year, and I know that will be so much better. For now, I'll just tough it out." She sniffed long and hard. "Please don't tell Sam. He'd be so upset if he knew how I felt."

"Listen, honey, first of all, you and Sam deserve better. Second of all, why doesn't he already know how you feel? I was so happy you were the kind of person who didn't hold back anything. I know, with Sam, you just want to keep him safe and happy, but this is your life. Don't start hiding things now. It's a hard habit to break. Tell him how unhappy you are."

She wiped her face with her hands and shrugged. "What would be the point? It's not like he can do anything about it."

"Yes, he can. You guys can still live with me."

She sniffed again. "What?"

I heard the words as they tumbled out of my mouth, and I knew I couldn't stop them, but it felt okay. "You two can still live with me. At least for this year. My second floor has two bedrooms and a loft area, and is three times the size of what you've got now. It's bright and sunny, and there's a bathroom you can actually turn around in. It won't take you that much longer to commute, and if you insist, you can keep this place for late nights or whatever. But you'll have room to spread out. You'll be able to have real furniture, more than two desks and a bunch of computers in your living room. I'll be working and playing lots of golf, so you won't see a lot of me. Really. I'm extending the invitation. What do you think?"

She swallowed. "I think it would save my life. But Sam . . ."

"Sam wanted to move in with me in the first place. If he had bothered to let me know last winter, this would never have been an issue. Let's face it, plan B sucks so far. You with me?"

She nodded. Then she smiled. Then she frowned.

"We gave away most of our furniture so we could afford a smaller storage space in Boston."

I chewed my lip, thinking. I was staring at the emblem on her polo shirt. "Where did you buy that shirt?"

She looked startled. "Hollister, probably. I'm always there."

"Then don't worry about furniture. I've got the perfect solution."

I went into the restroom, because I'd learned to take advantage of every bathroom opportunity that came along; then we went back upstairs. Sam was sitting with more wine, blissfully unaware. We sat down. Alisa took his hand and smiled sweetly.

"Sam, I love you with all my heart. I hate where we're living. I feel like I'm in prison. Your mother has just offered to let us move in with her for the year, and I think it could work. So I'm moving in with your mom. If you want to keep the apartment, fine. I'll stop by between classes so we can have sex. But I think you should come there with me."

Sam grinned. The product of eight thousand, six hundred, and fifty-three dollars and four years' worth of orthodontia gleamed. "Thank God," he said.

Smart boy. Really, really smart.

CHAPTER FOUR

My kids all liked one another. There were times, when they were younger, that I was sure they were going to kill one another, but by and large they grew into their siblings' foibles and were friends. Watching the three of them together was like watching an old, well-rehearsed vaudeville act—they completed one another's punch lines, passed off one-liners, and traded inside jokes like the seasoned pros that they were. They were yin and yang and yin-yang. I was proud of them.

So I was a little surprised at Regan's reaction when I told her that Sam and Alisa were moving in with me.

I had stopped by her apartment to ask if she'd like to go furniture shopping with me. She was all smiles until I mentioned Sam.

She stared. "He's moving into your condo?" she asked. "With Alisa? You're going to let them live there together? Are you crazy?"

"No, not at all. Have you seen that place they're living in? It's horrific. I couldn't not ask them. They'll have to drive to the train, but the commute is a small price to pay for fresh air and a bathroom where they can turn around."

"This is your adult son, Mom," she said slowly. "Wasn't the whole point of selling the house a statement about going forward with your life without your kids?"

I looked at her. "Regan, there is no way I will ever go on with my life without my kids. It's impossible. When you're a mother, you'll understand. Yes, I wanted to move in a different direction, but it was never about leaving you guys behind. Is that what you really thought?"

"Why else would you sell the house?"

"Because I was tired of living in five thousand square feet all by myself, that's why. I didn't want to worry about taking care of it, cleaning it, and hearing my footsteps echo through vast, empty rooms. And I wanted to buy floral chintz sofas and lots of foofy pillows."

She rolled her eyes. "Is that why you let Jeff decorate for you? Honestly, Mom, for a woman who always knows what she wants out of life, sometimes you amaze me with your willingness to let your kids roll over you."

I settled back into her couch. "Really? Wait until *you* have kids." I tilted my head at her. "Did my selling the house bother you? You never said anything. I never had the idea that you were emotionally attached. It's not like you didn't take every single thing that was yours with you when you left."

She shrugged. "It's just weird to think that Sam is going to be living with you again. He was always such a baby about leaving home in the first place, and now he's managed to find a way to get back."

I looked at her quizzically. "Is that jealousy I hear?"

She shrugged, then laughed. "Maybe. Pretty stupid, right? I mean, Phil and I will probably buy our own place by next year. We've kind of been looking, but this wedding stuff is just so ridiculous. We found a place for the wedding, by the way. It's called Clareview House. It's a beautiful old mansion, but we need to bring in our own catering. I was going to ask you about that."

I beamed. My daughter was very independent. Being the middle kid and only girl, with an absent father and a strong mother, had left a mark. That she was asking me for help was a real breakthrough for her.

"I know a few people who would do a great job," I said, speaking slowly. Didn't want to scare her away. "I'll make a few phone calls and let you know some names. How's the guest list?"

She shot me a look. "Don't push it, Mom."

I held up my hands, palms out, in defeat. "No problem, honey. Now, will you help me find a soft, squishy sofa in a shiny chintz print?"

She grinned. "Sure. I've got clinic tomorrow and Thursday. How about Friday morning?"

Perfect. The good thing about being between jobs was a completely open schedule.

I went home and walked Boone past the health club again. Someday soon, I swore to myself, I'd actually go in. I was starting to recognize a few people in the development. There was the very attractive couple who jogged together in color-coordinated outfits, identical headphones, and very big watches. A sweet older lady—I think she said her name was Marie—lived across the cul-de-sac and petted Boone whenever she saw us. There was also a very attractive gentleman, maybe in his sixties, who drove a Lexus and had no visible roommate or partner. He did not smile or wave, but when I saw him unload golf clubs, I gave trying golf at least seven minutes of serious thought.

When I sat down at my computer, I found a brief e-mail from the dean of business at Centenary College, the woman who was supposed to be my new boss, telling me that, due to funding cuts and slipping enrollment, I would not be getting the contract we discussed. In fact, I would not be getting anything.

I stared at the screen. I had quit a very high-paying job so that I could relax and take it easy in the world of academia. Sure, they weren't going to be paying me a lot of money, but then, I had agreed to teach only two classes. It was going to be perfect. I would make just enough to cover the taxes and fees on the condo, as well as basic living expenses, and in return, I would give about twenty hours of my time and expertise to a hundred or so students.

I was not hurting for money. My biggest expense had always been the house. Now that I was living mortgage-free, my nest egg could last a very long time. But I was counting on a job. I was counting on *that* job.

I could not go back to my old firm. I knew for a fact that they were glad I had left, because business had slowed considerably, even in the tax department. I suppose I could look for another job as a lawyer—after all, I was qualified and experienced. But that would not work in my favor, not in this economy. I did not want to run through my savings, or have to go into the 401(k).

I called Cheryl. "I got fired," I told her.

"From what?"

"My job. At the college."

"But you hadn't started working there yet. How could they fire you?"

I sighed. "You're right. I didn't get fired. I just didn't get hired."

"Kate, that sucks. I'll be right over. I have just the thing to make everything all better."

She arrived forty minutes later, a bottle of wine in hand. "Happy new unemployment. Where's a corkscrew?"

I handed it to her; she poured wine into two glasses, then wandered through the condo. She came back into the kitchen frowning.

"Kate, this furniture is still giving me a very funny vibe. Is this really the kind of place you want to live in?"

I shrugged. "It isn't. Regan and I are getting new furniture and moving all of this upstairs for Sam and Alisa." I took a long drink of wine.

"Why would Sam and Alisa need furniture upstairs?" She was searching in her purse for something.

"Because when I saw the hellish shoe box they were living in, I invited them to move in with me."

She pulled a baggie out of her purse, looking triumphant for a moment before turning to me with a frown. "Your son and his girlfriend are going to be living with you?"

"Yes. Is that pot?"

"Why would you want that, Kate? You've been living alone for a while now. Won't that be a huge disruption? And yes, I thought we'd smoke a joint in honor of your losing your nonexistent job."

She emptied the contents of the bag on my granite countertop. She gazed down at the twisted buds and sighed.

"This has to be cleaned. I need an album cover," she said.

"Cheryl, where the hell did you get that? You haven't smoked pot in years."

"I know, but wine adds on pounds, and I'm tired of eating salad twice a day. I got it from the nice young man who works at the gas station on the corner of my street. I didn't know where else to go—all my contacts went to prison or died years ago—so I figured a high school boy would be the best chance at a source, and he was happy to get it for me. He graduates next week. I may have to find another supplier."

"Are you crazy? You just asked a strange high school kid?"

She gave me another one of her "Are you kidding?" looks. "Of course not. I get my gas there all the time. I've known Kyle for a couple of months now." She had pulled a packet of rolling papers out of her purse as well. "Now, again—album cover?"

"Cheryl. I don't have any albums anymore. I have CDs and an iPod. Nobody has albums anymore."

Her face fell. "Then how the hell do people clean their pot?"

"I have no idea. You're serious? You want to roll a joint?"

She pushed everything across the counter. "I just had new tips put on; I can't do a thing with these damn nails. You roll one."

"Cheryl, I'm a lawyer."

She wrinkled her nose. "Not anymore. Listen, you and I used to smoke every afternoon, all through high school, sitting up in that old tree house. Remember? We could use a little bit of the naughty. Go ahead and roll. It's like riding a bike. You never forget how."

Well, she was right about that. I found my wok and used it to separate the seeds, and rolled three very respectable-looking joints. The only lighter I had in the house was one of those long, skinny things I used to light the grill, so we lit a candle and used that. Cheryl took a long, deep drag, then spewed out a lungful of smoke and coughed for a whole minute. I stared at her until she stopped. Her eyes were watering; her face was red. And she was grinning from ear to ear.

"Oh, Kate, why did we stop doing this?"

"Because it's illegal. I'm an officer of the court, Cheryl, and this is against the law."

"Well, it shouldn't be." She took another hit, a tiny puff, and grinned again. "I can't figure out why this wasn't made legal years ago. You can't tell me all those senators and congressmen have never smoked. So many of them are our age and older, and they never inhaled? That's a crock. And they could tax it, make a bundle, and lower everybody else's taxes. The whole recession would be over! I need to write to the President about this."

I took the joint from her and tried a small, tentative hit. Just enough to feel it in the back of my throat. I exhaled gently.

I closed my eyes and took another hit.

Wow.

"Cheryl, this is the best idea you've had in a long time. I'll help you with that letter."

We carried the wine bottle, our glasses, and the joint out to the deck and sat in quiet contentment for a few more minutes. I didn't have an ashtray, but I used the saucer from one of my small clay pots to stub out the roach. The birds were singing, the sun was filtering through the trees, and I felt totally at one with the glory of Mother Nature.

"You know," Cheryl said, "you could throw a few seeds into one of these clay pots out here and grow yourself a nice little crop."

"That's a brilliant idea. It will blend right into the tomato plants, and no one will ever know."

"I've got a few seedlings in my rose garden. I'm just hoping that Tyler doesn't pull them up and ask his mommy what the funny plant is."

Cheryl's daughter, Heather, was twenty-six. "Would Heather disapprove, do you think?"

Cheryl sighed and took a long drink of her wine. "She joined one of those antidrug things in high school and never stopped believing. She doesn't even like my drinking wine in front of her. Insufferable prude, that girl." She shook her head sadly. "I love her, but she is a real pill. Remember Rutt's?"

I frowned. "Rutt's? Rutt's Hut? Home of the world's best deep-fried hot dog?" I was getting confused. "What does that have to do with Heather?"

"Nothing. I'm not talking about her anymore." She sighed. "Those hot dogs were the best things I'd ever eaten. Remember how we'd make a whole road trip out of going down there? I bet one of those babies would taste great right now."

Cheryl got the munchies faster than anyone I had ever smoked with, and since I was in college during the seventies, believe me, that was a lot of people.

"Well, I'm not driving down there today," I told her.

She sipped her wine contentedly. "No, I suppose not. Besides, I can't eat like that anymore. Remember Dairy Queen? And maple walnut sundaes?"

"We're not going there, either. Do you really have pot plants growing in your rose garden?" Cheryl lived in a very exclusive gated community, in a detached three-bedroom with a small, enclosed backyard where she had at least two dozen rosebushes that she tended with religious fervor. Sitting out on her patio on a hot summer night, the smell was intoxicating.

"Yes. I have about twenty. I'll wait till they're at least a foot and a half high before I pull them up and dry them out. I don't want them to get too tall. Somebody might notice and complain to the HOA board."

Or the police. "Cheryl, what are you going to do with twenty plants' worth of marijuana?"

"Smoke it, of course. I've noticed that I'm drinking way too much wine. It might help me relax; plus wine has a lot more calories than you'd think, so I'm going back to my roots." She giggled. "Roots? Pot plants? Get it?"

Good lord.

That was the funniest thing I'd ever heard.

When I finally stopped laughing, Cheryl and I went back into my kitchen and made brownies. As they baked, we scattered seeds in all the clay pots on my deck—the tomatoes and peppers, the hibiscus and Regan's palm tree. We passed on the impatiens—the seedlings would be noticeable way too soon. We had some more wine as we pulled the brownies from the oven, and, while they were still warm, spread peanut butter on top of them. Then we added a scoop of vanilla ice cream. And some chocolate syrup. And nuts.

Best. Dinner. Ever.

Tom Smith, according to his profile, retired from teaching three years ago and was using his experience as a science teacher/guidance counselor/wrestling coach to privately tutor high school students in college admissions testing and assist them in the application process. So I figured he was smart, compassionate, and well built. He was also charming in his e-mails, and our one phone conversation had lasted forty-five minutes and ended with us agreeing to meet for coffee.

He was short. I'm five eight, and although I know that's considered kind of tall for a woman, I didn't consider myself a tall person. But when I stood next to Tom, that was how I felt.

He cracked a smile. "You should have mentioned your years spent on the women's basketball team."

I grinned down at him. His eyes were about three inches below mine. "And how long were you in the touring company of *The Wiz* as Munchkin number four?"

We laughed. We had spent the entire time on the phone laughing at each other's jokes. When we sat down, we were exactly at eye level, and I thought he was pretty cute in person: gray-white hair, lots of it; dark eyes; and olive skin, with big teeth that flashed a great smile. His profile said he was fifty-eight, but he looked younger.

"So, I have to ask," I said. "Is there a Napoleon complex I'm going to have to deal with later on?"

He shook his head. "Nope. What I lack in stature, I make up for in towering intellect and superior sexual prowess. My self-image and my height are entirely unrelated."

DEE ERNST

"Thank God," I said. "It took me an hour to figure out what to wear to my first date in over thirty years. If you had turned out to be a dud, I'd probably wait another thirty."

And we were off.

It's interesting how adult relationships work. I'd had men friends in college, purely platonic men friends with whom I had long conversations about deep, important things, like "Is there a God, and what does he want from us?" and "In the future, will we really be able to beam up?" Once I was married, my men friends morphed into the husbands of my women friends, or business acquaintances. As "wife," that was all that was allowed. And I had been happy with Adam most of the time, so I never went looking for anything else.

It was great to sit down with a man and know that maybe, just maybe, this so-far-interesting dynamic could become something more. Something better. I missed having a man to talk to. My own sons drove me crazy, and conversations with them usually ended with me thanking God I didn't have to live with a man anymore. But this was different. Sitting and talking to Tom was nice. It was more than nice. He was a little rough around the edges, looked at things from a slightly different angle, and had a deep, gruff laugh.

We went from coffee to dinner. We both loved Thai. We went from dinner to a drink. We almost went from the bar back to his place, but I shook my head, and he said fine, and then he said he'd call, and when I got home, I was almost regretting saying no. Why shouldn't I go home with someone if I wanted to? I was a grown-up woman with no emotional entanglements, and if I wanted to sleep with someone, well, I should be able to. And that lost libido of mine had sat up and looked around sometime after the second white wine. But sex was something I hadn't had in a while, and I wanted to go slow.

Besides, I hadn't shaved my legs.

But on the next date, I might.

The monthly spaghetti Saturday had been a tradition at my house for years. It was my one big concession to the whole "family dinner" idea. My kids were always invited, and my sister, Laura, and her family, but there were always other people, like Cheryl, and sometimes neighbors or coworkers to add to the mix. It's not that I didn't love my family and want to have dinner with them, but I had other people in my life who I also wanted to have dinner with, too, and why should I have exclusively family versus nonfamily dinners? So I'd make a huge pot of gravy (which is what my Italian mother called her spaghetti sauce), cook a few boxes of pasta, toss a salad, and toast some garlic bread. Then I'd top off the evening with cannoli and other pastries from the Italian bakery in Morristown that was always worth the trip, even if finding parking was the absolute pits.

Laura always got there a little early so we could talk about Mom.

Our mother, Rose Gianelli Freemont, had lived in a seniors' development outside of Cape May, at the southern tip of New Jersey, for almost twenty years. She had never remarried after Daddy died, and seeing what kind of woman she had turned into was part of the reason I didn't fight the whole dating thing as hard as I could have.

The two of us had had a falling-out right after Adam had died. She had really loved Adam, and when I had told her about the cheating, and how I had been thinking about leaving him anyway, she had become very angry. Angry, grieving people should be careful what they say to each other, and she and I had not been careful. We ended up screaming, terrible things leaving our mouths that nothing could ever make right again.

A month after the fight, I called her and apologized. She hung up on me. I drove with Laura to see her. She closed the door in my face. After the third time that happened, I stopped going down. I sent her flowers for her birthday every year, and a basket of fruit for Christmas. She never acknowledged the gifts. I'm pretty sure she got my cards and letters, but she never wrote back. Every month I called, said, "Hi, Mom," and she hung up on me. It had been going on for so long it didn't even hurt anymore, because I knew that even though she hung up on me, she had caller ID, which meant she deliberately answered the phone so that she *could* hang up on me, and that meant something. Once my mother found something that worked, she was very reluctant to change.

Laura traveled down every three or four months, and talked to Mom several times a week. My kids had gone with Laura in the past to see their grandmother, and she still sent them birthday and Christmas gifts. Regan, I knew, called her every month or so, and Jeff sent her postcards all the time. Sam wasn't too good at keeping in touch, but managed a birthday card and a thank-you note at Christmas. I just kept calling and hoping for a miracle.

"Mom's getting worse," Laura said, slipping onto a stool by the breakfast bar and reaching for the wine.

I glanced at her. I was chopping stuff for salad. "Worse how?"

Laura sighed. "Her piles are getting bigger. She can't walk across the room without getting winded. And she's starting to forget things."

This was not good news.

My mother was always someone who felt that every single item that came through the U.S. mail was very important. So important that throwing it away was, if not a federal offense, at least a misdemeanor punishable by a large fine and possible prison time. Consequently, there were always piles of opened, read mail all over her house. It was stacked, rubber-banded or paper-clipped, and covered all horizontal surfaces. The last time I had visited her, a few months before Adam's death, I had been alarmed by the small mountains of paper that had sprung up all over her house.

"How bad is the paper?" I asked.

Laura sighed. "Well, she's started getting a lot of magazines."

Okay. Very bad. Magazines had always been, to Mom, sources of profoundly important information that could not be found anywhere else. At one point, Laura and I had to sneak six years' worth of old *TV Guide*s out of Mom's house while she was in the shower.

My mother had also spent fifty years of her life smoking. Granted, smoking, for her generation, had been cool and acceptable before it became rude and fatal, but Mom smoked until she was diagnosed with emphysema twelve years ago, and the damage had been too far gone. Her ability to engage in any physical activity had been dwindling for years.

"What about the walker?" I asked.

My sister rolled her eyes and drank some wine. "What do you think?"

Ah, yes. Good old Mom. Denial was her middle name.

"What kind of stuff is she forgetting?"

"Where the garbage can is. Her doctor's last name. What a can opener is for."

Well, shit.

At that moment, Laura's two sons, Devon and Wade, came bounding in from the deck.

"Hey, guys," I said. "How's school?"

"Okay," Wade said. "I like your new house."

"Thanks. Me too."

"How's the driving going?" I asked. Devon was turning seventeen, and had been driving on his permit.

He shrugged. "Okay. I'm a really good driver, but Wade is afraid to drive with me."

Wade, two years younger, made a face. "I'm not afraid," he said hotly. "It just makes me nervous because you go so fast."

"I don't go too fast," Devon began, and I immediately jumped in.

"I guess you two want to play Xbox?"

They nodded, disaster averted, and I showed them into the den. I had gotten an Xbox for them a few years ago, because while I enjoyed their company in short spurts, they quickly became bored with plain television and then grew tiresome. Video games allowed them to engage in open warfare without ever leaving the couch. Much better than playing soccer in the living room.

Laura's husband, Bobby, also came in from the deck. Poor Bobby. He was a quiet, mild-mannered geek, happiest when designing some Internet website, and his two physically overactive sons wore him out.

"I really like your new place," he said, reaching for the wine. "As the boys pointed out, you could put a basketball hoop at one end of your deck and have enough room for a one-on-one game."

I smiled. "Yeah, well, I'll keep that in mind. Did you see Mom, too?"

He looked grave. "Kate, it wasn't good. But the thing is, she didn't realize it wasn't good. She wasn't at all bothered by the fact that she needed to hold on to something just to walk across the room. It was like an obstacle course; chairs and tables everywhere, so there was always something for her to lean on. And when I offered to take some of her magazines to the recycling center, she said she hadn't finished reading them, even though they were three years old. All she would let me do was take out all the cardboard. There was a pile by the doorway almost three feet tall. But she's perfectly happy."

I sighed. "Mom is always perfectly happy as long as things are going exactly the way she wants them to and there's nobody telling her what she doesn't want to hear. She'll be perfectly happy until the roof falls in, and as soon as she figures out how to live in the open air, she'll be perfectly happy again."

"We need to do something," Laura said.

I shook my head. "You need to do something. I'll be happy to help you help her, but you know how things are, and they're not likely to change."

She shrugged and snatched a stub of carrot from the cutting board. "Whatever. I have a feeling that she's inches away from disaster, and she knows it. So, anyway, what about Sam?"

"He and Alisa should be moving in next week. I think as soon as I find a job, things will be fine. Until then, we'll just stay out of one another's way."

Jeff had come up the stairs and into the kitchen, Regan and Phil right behind him. "What about finding a job?" he asked, placing three bottles of wine on the counter and giving me a kiss.

"My planned excursion into academia has been canceled. So now I have to find something else to do with my life."

Regan was carrying flowers and more wine. "What happened to the college thing?" she asked.

"Budget cuts," I said. "This is a lot of wine, even for us."

Phil was also carrying two bottles. "Stockpile, Kate. Just don't drink it alone while you're sitting around all day not working."

I shook my head. "Not working is not an option. I've got to find something, and by the fall. Unfortunately, I'm not qualified for anything but tax law, and that's what I don't want to do." I shook my head again. "On top of the latest Rose report, maybe I do need all that wine."

"What's with Grandma?" Regan asked.

I glanced at Laura, who took a deep breath.

"Your grandmother is starting to unravel," she explained. "She's forgetting things. I don't think she can live by herself too much longer."

Jeff uncorked the first of the bottles he'd brought. "And where else could she live?"

Good question. Once upon a time, about ten years ago, my mother and I had made a major tour of several assisted living places, a few of them so nice that I seriously thought about signing myself up. But nothing was quite good enough for Mom, so she went back to Cape May.

Laura shrugged and looked at Bobby, who carefully avoided looking back. Jeff, watching them both, passed around the glasses and started pouring.

"Well," he said, raising his glass, "here's to Mom's first spaghetti Saturday in her brand-new place. May she have many more."

We all clinked glasses and drank up. After that, conversation turned away from unpleasant things like dementia and unemployment, and we started talking about Regan's wedding. We were all getting along just great when Cheryl came in, carrying more wine.

"Thanks, I think," I said, giving her a hug. "Why are suddenly all the people in my life showering me with wine? Do I need it? Or do you think I have a problem and you're all turning into enablers?"

Cheryl gave me a knowing look. "What else for the woman who has everything?"

I rolled my eyes and handed Regan some plates and forks. Cheryl immediately started folding napkins.

"The place looks great. Love the new furniture," she said.

My new furniture had been floor samples, all on sale, so I grabbed them right off the sales floor and had them delivered the day before. I had two love seats, one in a rosy floral with green vines, the other a green-and-white stripe. I also had two matching slipper chairs in rose with green trim. Everything went with my ivory wing chair and the faded Oriental rug. The effect was feminine but not too sweet. I had tipped the delivery guys an extra fifty bucks each to cart the other furniture upstairs, where I was sure my son and Alisa would appreciate it. I spent the morning buying pillows and throws and cool shabby-chic lamps and candleholders, and was pretty happy with the new arrangement.

Jeff twisted his head around toward the living room. "Oh, right. Very nice, Mom. A little twee for my taste, but . . ." He shrugged expressively as I punched him hard in the arm.

Cheryl handed the napkins to Regan and turned to me with a bit of a glint in her eye. "What did you decide to do about the love of your life?" she asked.

Regan made an immediate about-face and came right back into the kitchen.

"Love of whose life?" she asked.

Oh, dear.

I cleared my throat. "An old boyfriend of mine happens to be on the same dating site as I am, and he waved." I tried to sound nonchalant, but Regan eyed me sharply.

"Wasn't Daddy the love of your life?"

Oh, damn.

"Regan, honey, I met Jake way before your father. He was my first great love. You always have a soft spot in your heart for your first great love."

"But what about Daddy?" she said, her voice cracking a little.

I scooped the last of the grape tomatoes into the salad bowl. "This isn't some kind of contest. Jake broke my heart.

Your father married me, and we were together most of my adult life. What else do you want me to say?"

She whipped around and marched back into the dining room. Her righteous indignation would probably have played out better if she had a door to slam behind her. Just marching through an open archway was not nearly as effective.

Cheryl caught my eye and mouthed, *I'm sorry.* I shrugged and put the pasta on.

Laura came over and stood very close to me in front of the stove.

"So, what are you going to do about Jake?" she whispered.

Jeff had sneaked up behind us both. "Is that his name?" He was whispering as well. "Jake?"

I stirred the steaming pasta. If you're standing over a pot of boiling water and you have a hot flash, does it even count?

"Stop it," I hissed. "I'm not doing anything."

Cheryl was nudging me on the other side. "Laura," she whispered loudly, "did you know this guy?"

Laura nodded and sighed. "Most beautiful man I'd ever seen."

Bobby's voice rose up from behind us. "You all having some sort of conference over there?"

Laura leaned over to Cheryl, forcing me to take a step back. "He totally broke her heart," she hissed.

"Trying to cook here," I said loudly.

Jeff leaned in. "When was all this?"

I wiped sweat off my forehead. "College. Can I get in here? Please?"

Cheryl gently pushed my head forward, directly over the boiling water, so she could lean behind me toward Laura. "Those are the ones you never forget," she murmured.

Jeff sniffed. "I had one of those. Jason. He was a Swede. A Nordic god."

"Mom?" Regan called. "Do you really need that much help to stir the pasta?"

"She needs to see him again," Laura said.

"No, she doesn't," Cheryl shot back.

"See who again?" Regan asked.

I turned around. Laura, Cheryl, and both of my children were huddled around the stove, and there, at the far end of the kitchen, Bobby stood, frowning.

"People," I said loudly, "I'm in the middle of a hot flash and you all need to step back *now!*"

They all backed away, and cool air hit me like a wave. I closed my eyes and took a couple of deep breaths. When that didn't help, I grabbed the lid to the soup pot from off the counter and used it as a fan. In a few seconds I felt much better. I looked at all the waiting faces.

"I am not going to see Jake Windom," I said loudly. "In case any of you were interested. And dinner will be ready in four minutes. So can we all finish setting the table?"

Regan swept the salad bowl off the counter and headed into the dining room. Jeff grabbed wine bottles and his glass and followed her. Laura turned and started slicing up the bread. Cheryl tilted her head at me and smiled.

"Good," she said.

"Thanks."

"Do you mean it?"

"Absolutely," I said.

But then I thought, *Well, probably.*

There are some people who are born to move furniture. My son was born to invent a robot to move the furniture for him. So when he told me that he and Alisa would be moving their own stuff in, I was skeptical. But they showed up bright and early with his battered Corolla and a U-Haul, along with three other young men I would have never mistaken for professional movers. All three of them were short, wore glasses, and had a vaguely nerdish air about them. They tumbled out of the Corolla like clowns out of a VW Bug, and then stood around for ten minutes while Sam and Alisa argued about where they would be living.

I had invited them to use my second floor. It had two empty bedrooms, a bathroom, and a large, open loft area that overlooked the living room. It even had its own tiny balcony. When I described it to them, they seemed happy. But when Sam walked into the house and saw the basement, he wondered aloud why they should cart all their stuff up two flights of stairs when it would be so much easier to slide everything through the garage into the basement.

Now, granted, my basement looked pretty good. It was a long, L-shaped room with double sliding glass doors that opened onto a small cement patio, and it looked directly into the woods. The bathroom downstairs was pretty big, with double sinks and a walk-in shower. The carpet was new and the paint was fresh and clean.

"But it's one room," Alisa pointed out.

"Yeah, but we could put the bed into this little alcove, the desks by the stairs, and have a little seating area right there by the sliders. It would be cool."

"Our bedroom in the little alcove would mean that your mother would have to pass our bed every time she walked to the laundry room to do clothes."

"She wouldn't mind. Besides, look at all the sunshine coming in."

"There's plenty of sunshine coming in upstairs, Sam. We could put the desks in the smaller bedroom, and use the loft like a living room. So when you're working, you could shut the door for privacy, and I could sit and read without bothering you."

"Alisa, you never bother me."

"Okay, then how about this? I can sit and read without hearing you yell at the computer and mutter about the idiots you have to work with."

"I don't mutter."

"Yes, you do."

"Alisa . . ."

"Or what if I want to surprise you by buying sexy underwear, and be stretched out in the bed when you come home from work? Your mother might mind doing laundry then."

I had been standing next to an Asian American young man in skinny jeans and what looked like an old bowling shirt. When Alisa said that, he made a loud, rather rude noise. Sam glanced around.

"We'll be right back out, guys," he announced, then led Alisa into the house.

"Too bad," I said. "I was about to bring out the lawn chairs and a cooler of beer."

He grinned and stuck out his hand. "I'm Tim. Yeah, they can really put on a show."

I shook his hand. "Kate. How did my son rope you into this?"

Tim shrugged. "We've known each other a long time. We started out as partners in the computer lab. I introduced him to Alisa, so I feel a certain obligation to the relationship."

"Well, you do good work. But I didn't think they were the arguing type."

"Alisa usually isn't, but Sam can get a real bug up his ass sometimes, and I think she fights back just to put him in his place. She can be pretty tough."

"I see that. Any woman who uses sexy underwear in an argument is a force to be reckoned with. But Sam's right. It would be easier to just put everything in the basement."

Tim shook his head. "The stairs are the challenge. Hai built this planking system that he thinks will get everything up there with only one person exerting force, and Sam says it's a crock."

I looked over, and another Asian American man, a very tiny one, waved at me.

"Only one person? Really? But those desks looked pretty big."

"Exactly," Hai said excitedly. He started to explain how it would all work. His English was not very good, and I think he was talking about thrust versus resistance, or maybe he was reciting the Pledge of Allegiance in Korean or Vietnamese, but then Sam and Alisa came out of the house and Sam called out that they were all going up to the second floor.

I never did find out the name of the third young man. I don't think he actually spoke a word all morning. He helped Hai take out a series of slender planks made of a stiff black material, and Sam asked me very politely to stay out of their way for a while. So I called for Boone and took a long, leisurely walk around the complex. I stopped and chatted with the golf pro, and set up an appointment for a lesson the next week. I also found out that the pool would be open in less than two weeks, and that there was a block-long garage sale planned for the first week in July. I had so much to look forward to.

When I returned home, all the furniture was up on the second floor. Hai was looking smug. I helped walk up a few boxes, but they really didn't have too much: the bed and dresser in one room, the desks and their computers and printers in the smaller room. The furniture Jeff had loved so much looked very nice in the loft. The fake palm trees screened the area, and Alisa was filling a bookcase with books when I came upstairs.

"Everything looks great," I said.

She smiled. "Yes. And thank you again, Kate. This is so much nicer than our apartment, and I promise we won't be in the way."

I waved it off. "No worries. You guys can hang out up here, I'll be downstairs, we'll meet at mealtimes, and everything will be fine."

"Yes. I think so, too." She glanced at Sam, who was coming out of the bedroom. "Right, honey?"

Sam frowned. "Right what? What did I do now?"

"Nothing, sweetie," I said. "We were just saying how we should all get along fine."

"Sure."

"And we need to talk to your mom about rent."

Sam looked at her. I looked at her. We both said, at the same time, "Rent?"

Alisa nodded. "Of course. We're two adults, Sam, and we need to be paying our way."

"But she's my mom."

"Yes. But she is also a person in her own right who should not be taken advantage of."

"But," Sam argued, "this place is paid for. It's not like she needs to pay a mortgage or anything."

"That's not a reason, Sam. There are still expenses. If nothing else, I know how much you eat, and that's worth several hundred dollars a month alone," Alisa said.

I hadn't thought about charging them rent, because I am a total pushover when it comes to my kids, but the girl was making a lot of sense.

"I don't know, Sam," I broke in. "Alisa is right. You were willing to pay almost two thousand dollars a month for a shoe box. And feeding you has always been a very expensive proposition. I'm not working right now, so I don't see why I shouldn't charge you a little something."

Sam looked stricken. "Mom?"

"What? It's not unreasonable. In fact, I read somewhere that it's a good idea to charge rent when children return home. If you are my tenant instead of just my son, then I'm less likely to treat you like a fifteen-year-old with a bunch of rules and restrictions. Like when you need to turn the computer off, or how loud you can play your music."

Sam's eyes narrowed. Those had been two of the many running battles of his high school years. "That makes sense," he said slowly.

"Of course it does," said Alisa. "I think two thousand a month is good."

"What!" Sam yelped.

She stared at him, and he visibly wilted. "Sam, I've been online and I know what it would cost to rent an apartment down the street. We essentially have a two-bedroom with a garage and private balcony with easy access to the train station. Two grand is about right."

Even I thought that was excessive, but I was not about to get in the middle of this.

"Alisa, this is my mother. Can't we at least get the friends-and-family discount?"

They both looked at me. I straightened my shoulders. "Okay, you two. I agree about the rent. But you are my son, Sam. So, one thousand a month. Payable the first of every month. We're adults here, so I'm sure loud noise and other inconsiderate behavior will not be an issue. I'll be happy to do the shopping, so any food in the fridge belongs to all of us. If you have any requests, write them on a list."

Sam looked a bit sulky, but Alisa seemed relieved. "Good," she said. "I'm glad this is settled. I've always had to pay my own way. I'm much more comfortable now." She gave Sam a hug and a kiss on the mouth. "Now, that wasn't too bad, was it?"

He kissed her back. "Alisa, whatever you say. Listen, I need some more cable, and then I have to run the guys back to the city and return the van. I'll bring Tim back to help set up the office. Can you pick me up at the train station?"

She nodded, and he bounced down the stairs. We heard him yelling to his friends, the door slammed, and we were alone.

"Well," she said.

"Yes. Well. Why don't you do what you have to do up here, then come on down and have some tea. And I made a coconut cream pie. It's Sam's favorite, but I don't think we need to wait for him."

She nodded, and I went back downstairs. I put some water on to boil and took the pie out of the refrigerator.

Alisa came down a few minutes later. I poured tea in silence, and cut two slices of pie. She took a bite, then closed her eyes.

"This is heaven," she said when she finally stopped chewing.

I smiled. "Yes. Best recipe I ever found. You're not a vegetarian or anything?"

She frowned and shook her head. "No. And I'm a lousy cook. Sam usually cooks, and I'll eat anything he wants to make."

I was surprised. "Sam cooks? Since when? The boy never made so much as a peanut butter sandwich when he lived at home."

She swallowed and sipped tea. "Yes, he told me. But he taught himself last year, when we started dating, and he realized that unless he wanted to eat every meal out, he'd better learn, 'cause I sure wasn't any kind of meal ticket." She glanced at me. "He says you're a great cook."

I looked modest. "I have moments of greatness."

"He also says you're brilliant, funny, beautiful, the perfect mother, and all-around best person ever."

I was a little surprised. Sam had never been one to gush about anything involving human beings. "Well, I am his mother."

"True. But he usually only gets excited about theoretical things."

"He obviously got excited over you," I said.

She blushed. "Well, only after I chased him all over campus and threw myself at him repeatedly. For a brainiac, he's very dense about things."

"I know." I finished my pie and leaned back, then sat up again. I could feel a hot flash coming like a slow-moving train.

"I finally got his attention when I dressed as an elf at a *Lord of the Rings* mixer the CompSci department threw. If it weren't for Galadriel, I'd be dating a law student right now."

I was trying to look interested, but was too busy fighting the urge to pull off my shirt and fan myself with a pizza pan. "Really?"

She had finished her pie and was watching me closely. "Are you all right?"

She probably noticed the beads of sweat on my temples. "Hot flash," I said shortly.

She nodded. "My grandma used to get those all the time," she said.

Oh, why, thanks so much!

"Are you really dating again?"

I looked at my tea, thinking I'd rather die than put anything hot anywhere near my body. "I'm trying. I'm not exactly sure how it will all turn out."

"I think it's great," she said. "I mean, Sam is the love of my life, but if anything ever happened between us, I'd want to try again, you know, to find another person to share my life with. There are all kinds of ways to love a person. You should never give up on finding love."

I looked at her in surprise. "That's a very wise thing to say." I decided to take a chance. "And a really funny thing has happened. The man who was the love of my life—back in college, I mean—is on the same dating site I am. And he wants to get together."

Her jaw dropped. "Oh, Kate, how romantic. Did you answer him? Have you seen him?"

"I haven't decided what to do yet. He broke up with me. I was pretty crushed."

She leaned forward. "Kate, aren't you dying to know what he wants to say to you?"

I shrugged. "Yes, I guess, but he can't say anything to me until I wave back at him."

"So, do you know what he's been doing all these years?"

I shook my head. "Just what's on his dating profile."

Alisa jumped up. "Let's Google him," she said, and ran off.

I stared after her. Google him? Why hadn't I thought of that?

She was back in the kitchen, laptop open.

"Okay. Spell his name?"

I did, and went around to look over her shoulder. My mouth felt dry. My heart was starting to beat a little faster.

What would the Google gods reveal?

It appeared that Jake Windom was a fairly important guy. He was, for one thing, the CEO of a very successful company, Nesco, with corporate headquarters down on Wall Street. There was mention of his divorce. One bio said that he met his ex-wife at Penn State. It looked like he'd married the woman he left me for. Was I grateful that, at least, he had broken my heart for something akin to true love, instead of some casual fling? No, I don't think I felt grateful at all. After all, he had divorced her in the end.

He also had a charity that he was involved with, was on the board of directors of a handful of nonprofit organizations, and had recently bid thirty-five thousand dollars on a Dalí sketch at Sotheby's.

Alisa sighed. "You have to talk to him, Kate. He's reached out to you, even though he must know how much he hurt you. Maybe he's regretted it every single day of his life. Maybe he tried to find you again, right after it happened, to beg you to take him back, but couldn't. How do you know that he hasn't been searching for you all these years, just to beg your forgiveness?"

I stared at her. "I know because I don't live in a Nora Roberts trilogy," I said. I couldn't believe I'd found another believer in fairy tales. I was surrounded by happily-ever-after groupies. I needed to change the subject, and fast. "Have any idea what you'll be doing all summer?"

She closed the laptop and shrugged. "I'd like to get a job somewhere. I know it's a little late to be applying anywhere. And other than neuroscience, I have very limited job skills."

I gave up on the tea, got up, and cleared the table. Anything to create a cool breeze. "I'll be looking for a job as well. Maybe we can tag-team. We're both pretty much only qualified to do only one thing, so that narrows our options quite a bit, but still."

"Maybe we should go into business together. We could sell your pies."

I laughed. "Good idea. Maybe have one of those cupcake shops that are opening up everywhere."

"Kate's Cakes," she offered. "But we'd put a K in 'Kakes.' So it would look really cute."

I wanted to gag a little but didn't. "I hate to break it to you, Alisa, but the middle-aged widow and the wildly popular cupcake shop only works in cozy romance novels. In real life, it's a hard, long battle for success that usually ends in failure, and if I fail, I'll have to start charging you and Sam more rent." I smiled at her. "Besides, aren't you going to be doing something brilliant in the next few months?"

She smiled shyly. "I hope it's brilliant. That's the only way I'll get to France."

"France?" I asked. "What's with France?"

She stood up and stretched, like a cat. "That's where I'm going when I finish school. There's a lab right outside Paris doing amazing stuff, and I've already been in touch with the director. I hope to fly over there next year and meet him in person. I can't wait. I'm going to love living in France."

I stared at her. "You want to live in France?"

She nodded, beaming.

"And will Sam be going with you? To France?"

She nodded again. The sweat on my body began to dry and I felt suddenly cold.

"You're going to take my son to France and raise all my grandchildren there?"

Being an MIT graduate, she immediately noticed the sudden change in my tone. She may have also seen my jaw tighten and my eyes narrow. As I watched her, I could see her backpedaling.

"Well, Kate, nothing has been decided. I mean, it's just an idea I had, that's all."

"What would Sam do in France?" I wasn't letting her off the hook.

She made a face, thinking fast. "Whatever he wanted. There are tons of technology companies over there. With the kind of work he's doing, he could write his own ticket. But like I said, it's all in the planning stages right now. Nothing has been decided. We have the next two or even three years to figure it out."

"Of course," I said. We stared at each other for a few moments; then she cleared her throat, thanked me for the pie, and mumbled something about unpacking. She practically ran out of the kitchen, laptop clutched to her chest.

I'd spent a lot of time lately planning changes to my life: changing my job, starting to date, buying a new house. It had looked pretty good on paper. But now I was finding out how planning your life really works.

It doesn't.

The new house was feeling crowded. Not that I minded Sam and Alisa living with me. I welcomed the idea of getting to know my son again, and his girlfriend seemed like someone who would fit nicely into both of our lives. Even though it looked like she was planning to take my baby and shuffle him off to live in France, where I'd only see my future grandchildren once a year unless I wanted to move there myself and live in an attic on the Left Bank.

Until then, there were some things I'd gotten used to that would have to change. Like leaving the bathroom door open, and playing seventies disco music really loud in the middle of the night when I couldn't sleep. But those things I could adjust.

I was unemployed. Not at all where I expected to be at my age, which was way past the desirable employment age. Where was an ex–tax lawyer going to find a job that could cover all her living expenses so that she'd be able to leave her 401(k) and other investments intact? Just in case she had to drop everything and move to Paris?

And I was dating again. Why did I live in a society that insisted you find your own mate, when there were so many other places in the world where a name was pulled out of a hat and, bingo, instant marriage? Those who pooh-poohed such arrangements were sadists or extreme optimists, and I couldn't decide which was more annoying. Tom Smith was a very nice person, but we had a long road ahead that would be fraught with potential disaster. I didn't want to do all that work and then end up with nothing.

What I wanted was to find Jake and have a beer with him, just like back in college. I wanted to be with somebody who knew my thoughts, finished my sentences, and would rub the exact spot on my left foot, right below the middle toe, that still cramped up at the end of the day. Adam had come close, when things between us were good and full and happy, but Adam never made me feel the way Jake did.

I wandered into the den. All my books were there, in no particular order, but grouped together by author. I scanned the shelves. Sure enough, there was a cupcake romance. I made a face, grabbed one of those Nora Roberts trilogy things, and went out on the deck and read the rest of the afternoon.

CHAPTER FIVE

It took me about a week to realize that Alisa Patterson was the sweetest girl in the world. She was completely without demands, always asked if she could help around the kitchen, and stayed out of my way. My son, however, my brilliant baby, was a royal pain in the ass.

Part of it was my fault, and I knew that right away. Sam had always been the needy one, and I had been more than happy to play along with him when he was a kid. These days, I'd be called an enabler. Back then, I was a good mommy.

But as an adult, he was really hard to get along with. He went out every morning to go to Columbia, and didn't return until late afternoon. He and Alisa spent time together before they both came back down around dinnertime, and then the two would go upstairs for the evening. You would think that since I only had real contact with Sam for a few hours a day, there would be no issues.

You would be wrong.

First of all, he left a trail of personal belongings through my house. It began at the front door—a sweater, jacket, or baseball cap. He always managed to drop something on the kitchen counter. It was usually a crumpled bag of half-eaten sandwich or stale bagel. I could understand the connection. Food belonged in the kitchen. But used food belonged in the garbage, and for some reason he never made it those extra few steps.

Then there would be his backpack. On the stairs. In my mind, the dividing line between their living space, which they were paying for, and mine began on the first step going to the second floor, so technically, the backpack was on his turf, not mine, but I could see it from my turf, and it bothered me. He was going upstairs anyway. Couldn't he at least bring it to the top of the stairs before dropping it to the floor?

Alisa did not leave anything around. She also did not pick up any of Sam's stuff. On this, I was torn. Yes, as a modern, independent woman, she should not be picking up after her slob of a boyfriend. But didn't it bother her? Couldn't she tell it was bothering me?

I spent the first few days asking him politely to put away his things. He was always apologetic and did it immediately when asked. But if unasked, as I discovered when I decided to stop asking just to see what would happen, he did nothing. By Friday, there were two different baseball caps by the door, two days' worth of *New York Post*s on the table by the living room, and four pairs of sneakers on the steps going upstairs. I was starting to feel a little frayed.

"Regan," I asked her Friday at lunch, "was your brother always a complete slob?"

She laughed at me. She was on break from her clinic and dressed in scrubs. I often thought she chose veterinary medicine because it would be a good excuse for her to wear oversize clothes.

"Well, yeah, Mom. It made me crazy. You never even made him make his bed, which both Jeff and I had to do as soon as we were tall enough to smooth the sheets. I could never understand why he was so special."

I sighed. "I don't understand it, either. I had trained you and Jeff so well. I guess I was too tired with Sam. But what should I do now? I mean, I can't ground him for making a mess like I did when he was eight and tried to re-create Vesuvius erupting in the laundry room."

She laughed. "That was pretty funny. You were so pissed off at him. There were soapsuds everywhere."

"Yes, there were. Even your father was ticked off at that one, and he forgave Sam everything."

"Look, Mom, I know it must be weird for you. I mean, Sam is a grown-up and all that. But it's still your house. You can set rules, you know."

"Setting rules is not the issue. Getting Sam to follow them is. How do I get a grown man to do what he doesn't think is important?"

"Find something that is important to him."

"Like what?"

She grinned. "Food."

I'd never thought of that. The way to Sam's anything was through his stomach.

When I got home, there was a flannel shirt draped over the bannister and an empty Starbucks cup by the sink. I smiled. Then proceeded to make chili with cornbread. Not really early summer food, but one of Sam's favorites. Around six they came down. I was sitting, eating calmly. Sam reached for a bowl.

"Sam, I'm sorry, but there's no food for you," I said.

Alisa, sensing something, grabbed a bowl, filled it with chili, and sat beside me. Sam was standing there, frowning.

"Mom, what are you talking about? There's plenty of chili."

"I know," I said. "But you can't have any."

"Why not?" He was sounding annoyed. Good.

"Sam," I said, pushing my bowl away and turning to look at him, "this is my house. I invited you to live here, and I have no problem with that. I don't charge you much rent, and I don't mind cooking for you and Alisa. But it's my house, and my rules. I've asked you half a dozen times to not leave your crap all over the place, but you don't seem to get the message. So, here's a new rule. If you come into the house and leave any sign of your presence, like that empty paper cup sitting two feet away from the garbage can over there, you cannot eat any of my food. Got it?"

His mouth dropped open. He stared at me, then at Alisa. She shrugged and bit off another piece of cornbread.

"But, Mom . . ."

I looked at him and raised an eyebrow. "What?"

He turned and threw the paper cup in the garbage. Then he went into the hall, and I could hear him going up the steps. There was a flurry of activity.

Alisa smiled at me. "Great call, Kate."

I smiled back knowingly. "Thanks. It was actually Regan's idea. All my kids are pretty smart."

She got up and ladled out some more chili.

Sam came downstairs, looking sheepish, and grabbed the bowl again.

"Wait a minute, Sam."

He turned.

"This will be the one and only time you get a break," I told him. "Next time, you will not be able to clean up after the fact and get a do-over. Next time, you'll have to go and get takeout. Okay?"

He made a face, nodded, then filled his bowl. He sat down beside Alisa.

"Sorry, Mom," he mumbled.

I waved my spoon around graciously. "No problem, honey. I know it's partly my fault you're such a spoiled brat, which is why I'm taking it upon myself to try to change your ways. It may very well kill us both, but I figure it will be worth it in the end."

He glowered. Alisa giggled. I got more chili.

Tom Smith and I had another date. We went to an antique car show out near Lambertville, then had dinner in a converted mill right on the Delaware. It was late when we got home, and I almost invited him in, but then I realized Alisa and Sam were probably still up, watching TV in the loft, and we'd have to introduce everybody, then wait for them to go to bed, and then there was the whole breakfast thing. Here I was, a grown-up woman, thinking about having sex with another grown-up, and I had to worry about what my kid would say. There was something wrong with that picture.

Tom seemed to get it, though. He smiled as I stepped out of the car, and suggested, quite casually, that maybe he could cook me dinner on Saturday night.

I smiled at him through the window. "Sounds good. Can I bring anything?"

He frowned, thinking. Then he brightened. "A toothbrush?"

I laughed out loud. "Yes. I have one of those. Anything else?"

He said no. I went inside and had a great night's sleep. The next day I called my favorite spa and made an appointment to get my hair done. I was thinking about getting a full-body hot mud treatment. I also thought about a Brazilian wax and a boob job, but, let's face it, at my age the expectations can only be so high.

Laura, of course, had something to say on the subject. "You're going to have sex with a man you hardly know?"

We were sitting on my deck Friday afternoon. She was in between baseball games. I was thinking about whether to buy sexy underwear or stick with good old-fashioned nakedness.

I sighed. "Laura, I was in college during the seventies. I spent years having sex with men I hardly knew. Besides, Tom and I aren't kids. We're not losing our virginity to each other in a grand gesture of undying love. We're two adults who are attracted to each other and want to act on that attraction. We've talked about it, but there's no need to get deep and philosophical about it. We're both lonely and a little horny. That's pretty much it."

She looked sorrowful. "But what about Jake?"

I made a noise that may have been a snort. "What about Jake?"

"Did you ever get in touch with him?"

"No."

"Well, I think you should. At least have coffee with him or something. Aren't you curious?"

Yes, I was very curious. I had not clicked on his page since I first saw his wave. But now that I knew some of the hard, cold facts of his life, it was as though the ice had broken a bit. It felt easier to go back there, just to have another look. "Well, maybe I could wave back, just to see if he wants to, you know, meet and talk about old times."

She jumped up and squealed, then raced off to the den.

I was right behind her, but she had already turned on the laptop and was going through my desktop apps.

"Where is it?" she muttered.

I wrestled the laptop away from her and found the site, clicked on my page, and sat for a moment looking.

Jake's wave was still there. I had not been on for a few days, and I had gotten another wave, this time from a very nice-looking podiatrist I had waved at a few weeks ago, so technically he was a wave-back. I thought for a minute about Cheryl, with three suitors dancing around her in virtual courtship. I didn't think I'd have the energy. But I did click on Jake's wave.

We both sat there and watched as the cursor blinked. I'm not sure what we were waiting for, exactly. I did not really think I'd get an immediate response. After all, his wave was weeks old. If he had been waiting breathlessly for my response, I don't imagine he would have been waiting this long.

"Now what?" Laura asked at last.

I shrugged. "Well, now he'll have my e-mail address, so he can get in touch with me. I guess I just wait." I tossed the words off lightly, but my heart was racing. Wait? How long was I going to be waiting? Would he be angry because I had taken so long to wave back at him, and not get back to me at all? What if he had abandoned the dating site entirely because I had ignored him?

Alisa had wandered in. "Wait for what?" she asked.

"I waved back at my old boyfriend," I told her. "You know, the one I told you about."

She leaned over my shoulder. "The one we Googled?"

Laura shot me a look. "Googled?"

I shrugged. "Alisa was curious, that's all."

Laura snorted. "Whatever. Is there a picture of him? He was so good-looking when he was young."

"Sure," I said as I clicked my way to his page.

Laura sighed. "He's still handsome," she said.

"Wow," Alisa said. "He really is. Are there any more pictures?"

I sat, staring.

"What?" asked Laura.

"His status," I said slowly. "It's changed. He's dating someone."

"He's dating someone?" Laura gasped. "Oh, Kate, how could he?"

I made a noise. "He could because he's a single man on a dating site. That is kind of the whole point."

Alisa reached over. "Do you think people post pictures of who they're dating on these sites?"

I shrugged. "Probably not." I had a very small but distinct pain in my gut.

"Well, he had a Facebook page," Alisa muttered. Her fingers flew over the keyboard. "We found it last time—you didn't bookmark it?" She was muttering some more. "Oh, God. Look at his status. In a relationship. Just scroll down," she said, doing the actual scrolling herself. "Who's that?"

Good question. There, at the bottom of his page, was a picture of a stunning woman, maybe thirty, with carefully tousled blond hair, a wide white smile, and an amazing set of boobs.

"'A picture of Sandra the beautiful,'" I read slowly.

Laura made a very impolite noise. "Are you sure that's his girlfriend? She's young enough to be his daughter. Is he kidding?"

"Apparently not," I said, reading on. "She works at a mall."

Laura was getting huffy. "Of course she does. Sephora, probably. Where else?"

"Now, Laura," Alisa said soothingly, "don't make assumptions. She might be a very accomplished person." Alisa, being a scientist, was occasionally annoying in her insistence on fact before rampant speculation.

"Well," I said, "he doesn't describe her as Sandra the brain surgeon, or Sandra the financial analyst, or even Sandra who feeds starving orphans. Looks like 'beautiful' is her best asset."

"Maybe," Alisa suggested, "she works in the Apple Store, you know, at the Genius Bar."

"I bet she couldn't get hired at RadioShack." Laura was on a roll. "In fact, she probably wanders around holding perfume for you to sniff, because they don't trust her with a cash register."

"Well, if he answers me back, I'll ask him what she does," I told them.

Laura started to say something, probably something nasty, then caught herself. "Wow. I'm sorry, Kate. This must be a real bummer for you."

It was. It's not that I expected Jake to refuse to settle for anyone else after he found out that I was possibly available to him again. Well, maybe that was a momentary fantasy, but I didn't think he'd want no one else but me. I had hoped that he'd want someone else *like* me. But instead, when given the choice of all the women on the dating site he could have chosen, he chose someone like Sandra.

I shook my head. "Hey, at least her name isn't 'Autumn' or 'Fawn.' I'm glad he's seeing someone. Now, if he does happen to get back to me, there won't be any question about why. We'll just be two old friends checking in."

I shut the laptop and looked at Alisa. "And by the way, if I don't come home tomorrow night, don't call the police, okay?"

She smiled. "Okay."

In the end, I bought the underwear, because although I was pretty slim and relatively toned, the same genetics that kept the weight off made me completely flat chested, and I felt the need for a little pizzazz. Tom was very appreciative, but they didn't stay on all that long. We ran into a few technical difficulties.

"Do you need help?" he asked. I was trying to unhook my bra. The wine I'd just had certainly relaxed me, but my powers of concentration were slipping. Besides, I still had my wineglass clenched in my fist. I wasn't used to reaching around behind me and unsnapping the thing with one hand, all the while maintaining a come-hither expression on my face.

I spun around. "Please."

He moved his hands down my back. The bra dropped to the ground. I hadn't been naked in front of anyone since Adam. That had been a long time ago, and I found myself feeling just a little insecure. Which is why, when the bra fell to the floor, I didn't turn around.

He came around to face me. "You're nervous," he said, taking the glass from my hand and putting it on the nightstand.

I nodded.

"But you want to keep going?"

"Yes."

"Good. But here's the deal. You're taller than I am."

I had to giggle. "Yes."

"Yeah. About that. Can we lie down and continue this?"

"Can we turn the light off?"

He smiled. "But I really want to see you."

I smiled back. "Okay."

Once lying down face-to-face, I didn't feel quite as exposed. He didn't seem quite as short, and once skin started moving against skin, the remaining wisps of clothing came off very easily.

I didn't mind the light on at all.

I had decided to spend the whole night, because I wasn't as sharp at driving in the dark as I used to be. I had only two hot flashes during the night, which I cleverly disguised as trips to the bathroom. On my way back from the second trip, I put my sexy underwear back on, so neither of us would have to face my naked body in the harsh light of day. But he was up and out of bed before me, so I got to make an entrance with the benefit of full wardrobe and makeup. He was one of those chipper morning people, which normally would have irritated the hell out of me, but I was in a pretty good mood as well, so after hot coffee and bagels with cream cheese and terrific lox, I got into the car and headed home.

I had turned off my phone at the beginning of the previous night's activities, but once I was on my way home, I turned it back on. There were six messages. All from Cheryl. All left between nine and midnight the previous night.

I pulled over. Yes, I know I could have just used that Bluetooth thing, but I never really figured out how to work it. She answered right away.

"Where were you last night?"

"At Tom's. What happened?"

"Really? Already?" she said.

"Cheryl? You called me, remember? Like, a million times? What happened?"

"Can you come over? I had a little sexual adventure myself last night, and I may never recover."

I turned around and headed toward Cheryl's. She had left my name at the gate, so the little man let me through. She must have been watching from the window, because she had the front door open before I turned off the car engine.

She was silent as she closed the door behind me. Her face was tight. We stood for a moment in her hallway. I wasn't sure what to do or say, so I just looked sympathetic. Then she threw her arms around me and started sobbing.

I hugged her, my mind racing. Had she been hit? Raped? I patted her back and made mother-hen noises until she pulled away from me, wiping her face with both hands.

"What, honey?" I asked gently.

She grabbed my hand and pulled me out to her patio, where we sat in the morning sunlight. She took a deep breath.

"I finally decided to sleep with Marco," she said at last.

"Marco? Okay, Cheryl. That's good. What made you choose him?"

She shrugged. "He's a musician, and very romantic. I mean, he has a deep, loving soul. And I love all artists, you know that. He hadn't been pressuring me, I mean, not really, but I could tell it would mean a lot to him, so last night I invited him over." She sat still, staring off into space.

"And?" I finally prompted, when it looked like she could be meditating on that particular thought for quite a while.

"Well, I cooked for him, of course. My cassoulet. And I had some great wine, and a rustic apple tart." She tilted her head, as though remembering a fond but far-off memory.

"And," I prompted again, hoping she would not start describing what each of them was wearing.

"And he was very happy with everything, especially the part where I told him we could finish our wine in the bedroom." She took a deep breath. "I was quite looking forward to, well, everything. He was a very good kisser. It looked as though he was going to be very good at everything else."

She stopped again, but there was no wistful look in her eye. "I farted on him," she blurted.

I think my mouth dropped open, but I recovered quickly and snapped it shut. "You what?"

"I farted on him!" she yelled.

I jumped back a bit. What in the world was I supposed to say? "Ah . . ."

"He was down there, you know, trying really hard, and the damn beans from the cassoulet, well, you know what can happen. I tried to move his head out of the way, but he was very intent, and I just couldn't stop myself." Her eyes filled with tears. "He was so nice about it, but it was ruined for me.

I was too embarrassed, so I put my clothes back on and sent him home. And now he'll probably never call me again, and I liked him best of all."

"Oh, Cheryl," I said, getting up and hugging her again. "I'm so sorry, sweetie. I really am. But stuff happens all the time. I bet if you asked him, he'd love another chance."

"How can I even talk to him again? It's not like we were an old married couple, where all those body noises are just, well, nothing much. I wanted everything to be really special for him. I had candles. I even wore my custom-made black bustier. And it was all ruined."

She was crying now, blubbering on my shoulder as I hunched over her, trying to pat her on the back without losing my balance. I finally stepped away, ducked back into the house, grabbed a handful of tissues from her bathroom, and ran back outside. She grabbed the tissues and blew her nose, wiping her eyes, and snuffling just a little. She finally took a deep breath and exhaled loudly.

"See what happens when I decide to have a real relationship with somebody? I fart in his face." She glared at me. "But I bet you and Tom had a cosmic experience, worthy of a letter to *Penthouse* magazine."

I laughed out loud. The two of us had often sat up in the tree house on warm afternoons, reading from her father's copy of *Penthouse,* marveling at all the inventive ways people could have sex, and wondering if either of us would ever be so adventurous and lucky.

I shook my head. "Sorry, Cheryl. It was fine. I mean, I hadn't been naked in front of another person for the purpose of pleasure in years, so I wasn't expecting instant ecstasy. The earth didn't move, although he was very generous. No revelations, no new positions, no celestial choir singing out praises. For two fiftysomething people having sex for the first time, we did okay."

She sniffed. "Really?"

"Yes, really. I needed wine; he needed Viagra. We took a while to get going, and things moved a little slower than I remembered, but it was lovely. What exactly were you expecting?"

She shrugged. "I don't know. But at least you didn't fart on him."

I started to laugh. I couldn't help it. There she was, sitting in the sunshine, dressed impeccably in white slacks and a gorgeous lime-green top that clung to her breasts and wrapped around her waist, with her hair perfectly done and her makeup, although slightly streaked, just right. She looked as poised and sophisticated as ever, the visual so completely out of sync with what she was saying.

She started to laugh, too, thank God, and we sat there for quite a while, unable to look each other in the eye without erupting into another round of giggles. Finally, she waved her crumpled tissues in the air like a ragged white flag of surrender.

"Marco has a great sense of humor," she said. "I'll call him up right now and see if I can coax a laugh out of him." She pointed a finger at me. "Don't move. If this goes badly, I'll need you again."

She got up and went inside. I took a brief tour of her garden, admiring the roses and noticing the little sprouts of marijuana peeking up beneath the thorny bushes. She was going to have quite a crop here soon. I wondered whatever happened to the seeds we had scattered at my house. I'd have to remember to look for them. I'd hate for my adult son or, worse, his girlfriend to discover I had an illegal harvest on my deck.

She came back out a few minutes later, beaming. "He thought I was adorable and funny. We laughed together, and he's coming back over tonight, and I'm having grilled chicken and something else totally lacking in fiber."

"Good," I said. "Can I go home now?"

We said good-bye and I drove home. Sam and Alisa were gone, so I took a long bubble bath, something usually reserved for snowy Friday nights, then took Boone for a walk.

I was both pleased with myself and a little disappointed that I felt no urge to wait by the phone for Tom to call.

CHAPTER SIX

I did not like Elaine Pendergast, the woman who would soon be tied to me indefinitely through the marriage of our respective children. Mainly I didn't like her because she did not think Regan was good enough for her son, Philip Evans Pendergast. My feeling was that she wouldn't think that Pippa Middleton would be good enough, but that did not soften my opinion of her. I think my kids are pretty special, too, but I try not to get too nasty and superior about it.

Elaine had divorced Phil's father twenty years ago, and never chose to remarry. Perhaps if she had, she would have had something else to occupy her time, and she would not have been such a continual pain in her son's behind.

She did not like me, either, because we once had a minor pissing contest—that she started—and I topped her "Philip's great-grandfather was an executive with the Union Pacific Railroad" with "Regan's great-grandfather was on the Board of Trustees at the Metropolitan Museum of Art." She is exactly one year and one day older than I am, a fact I remind myself of whenever I doubt the existence of God.

She has probably called me fewer than a dozen times in the three years we have known each other, but she obviously thinks I should recognize her voice, because she has never identified herself to me. I have caller ID, but I refuse to play along.

She called the Sunday after I'd spent the night with Tom. "Kate, have you spoken to anyone about a shower?" she asked.

I sounded annoyed, mostly because I was. "Who is this?"

"Elaine. Is there a bridesmaid or someone doing anything about this?"

"Hello, Elaine. So nice to hear from you. How's the weather out there in Denver?"

"The weather? Really? How droll, Kate. Is there going to be a shower, or should I fly out there and try to organize something?"

"Everything is under control, Elaine. The shower is going to be the Wednesday before the wedding, and the bachelor party on Thursday. Rehearsal dinner Friday night. This is so that people who are flying in can just come out for the shower and stay, rather than make the trip more than once."

"How odd. Who else is coming from a long distance?"

I settled into the couch. It was a faded floral, peonies and cabbage roses, with a great fringe around the bottom in moss green. "Well, Regan's best friend from high school, Kim, is the maid of honor. She's in Dallas, but her family still lives in Morristown. She's in charge of the shower. Phil has a couple of friends from Pitt coming out. My old college roommate is going to be staying with me—she's from Chicago—and, oh, yes, your ex-husband is flying in from London. I can't wait to meet him."

The silence on the phone was deafening. "He's coming there?" she said at last.

I was really enjoying myself. "Is who coming here?"

"Dammit, you know. Edward. He's going to be at the wedding?" She sniffed. "Philip didn't mention it."

"Did he have to? I mean, this is his father. Of course he'd be at the wedding."

"He is a philistine," Elaine huffed. "I only hope he stays sober and doesn't try to pick up one of the bridesmaids."

Well, that was interesting. Regan had met him and never mentioned that he showed any undesirable character traits, but I wasn't giving her an inch. "That would be tough. Kim is married with twin two-year-olds, and the other bridesmaid is a lesbian."

Elaine snorted. "You'd be surprised. They refused any help from me, you know."

I sighed. "Yes. They refused me as well, so don't take it personally. They are two very independent kids, and they know exactly what they want."

"Is the food going to be good, at least? Regan isn't a vegetarian or anything, is she?"

I bit back a nasty crack. "Why, no, she's not. Just because she's a vet doesn't automatically make her a vegetarian. And I helped her pick out the caterer. It's a very good group; they used to cater the functions at my old law firm all the time."

"Old law firm?" Her voice took on a little life. "Did you quit law?"

Damn! Why had I let that slip? "Yes, a few months ago. I wanted to free up my time. I have a new place now, you know, and I was thinking about taking up golf for the summer before looking for something else to do. It's not about the money, of course," I lied, but only a little. "But at my age,

I can't imagine just sitting around the house all day." Which was exactly what Elaine did.

But she was a smooth operator. "Well, I'm sure you'll find something, dear, provided you don't hurt yourself while learning your new, uh, sport. Well, I feel a little better about this. What color is your dress?"

"What? Why?"

"Really, you can't have two mothers of the bride and/ or groom wearing the same color. I was thinking something metallic, but not too showy, of course. Not silver. Maybe a nice bronze. Or gold. Those are very hot colors this season. I'll let you know as soon as I pick the dress. Don't want to look like bookends, now, do we?"

God forbid. "No, Elaine, we don't. Listen, I have to go. Thanks for calling. If something comes up, or if I find a dress first, I'll let you know."

I hung up and immediately called Cheryl. We had planned on having lunch that afternoon, but I asked if instead we could go mother-of-the-bride dress shopping first. She was agreeable, so we met at the mall instead of the restaurant.

Short Hills is the kind of mall where you need to get dressed up to shop there. All the major designers are represented in beautifully decorated shops, each with a person whose only job is to bid you welcome. There is no food court. There are palm trees, piped-in classical music, and valet parking. Cheryl spotted me gazing up at one of the fountains, and sneaked up behind me, hissing in my ear, "I bet this is all about Elaine."

Ah, what a good thing it is to have a friend who knows you so well. "She wants metallic, preferably bronze. The good news is that because of the time difference, I have a jump on her. I've got to find something before ten o'clock, Colorado time."

Cheryl laughed and followed me into Bloomingdale's, where a very helpful young woman grabbed every appropriate metallic dress in my size the store had to offer. But I'm pretty tough on myself, and after nine try-ons, I wasn't happy.

"This one is too short," I griped.

Cheryl shook her head. "No, it's not. You've got great legs, and it's mid-knee. It's perfect. And the draping around the neck almost makes it look like you have boobs."

I straightened my shoulders. "I like the third one better, with the drop waist?"

"No. The sleeves made you look like you were wearing Batgirl's cape."

I looked around. The helpful salesgirl was nowhere to be found. I didn't blame her, really. After she heard my first three critiques, she realized what she was dealing with and got the hell outta Dodge.

"How about the one with the jacket?" I asked, shuffling through the rack. "See? It's not as short."

She fixed me with a look. "Maybe you're having low-blood-sugar issues. Why don't we eat something, and you can tell me what is really wrong, because all those dresses look perfectly fine, and you are in a real mood."

"I am not in a mood."

"Yes, you are. Buy that one. If, after a nice lunch and a good night's sleep, you still think it's too short, you can return it."

I snarled, but just a little, paid for the dress, and made for Joe's American Bar & Grill. I completely ignored every healthy thing on the menu, and when the waiter came I ordered fried chicken with a double order of mashed potatoes. When the waiter left, Cheryl smirked.

"See, I knew there was something wrong. What's up?" she asked.

"Elaine is a bitch. I waved back to Jake a week ago, and he hasn't gotten in touch with me. I mean, he's dating somebody now, but I figured he'd at least want to say hello. I had sex with Tom again, and it's still more work than I remembered. I need a job. Oh, and yeah, I have my first golf lesson tomorrow, and I don't want to play golf."

She stared, then took a deep breath. "Okay. Well, what should we fix first?"

I grinned sheepishly. "Yeah, I know. I don't know what's wrong with me. I had this great life plan, you know, and now . . ."

"Now what? You're not happy with how it's going?"

I shrugged. "It's not that, exactly. I mean, everything is going pretty much on course, but, it's not . . ." I shrugged again. "Not what I expected."

Cheryl made a face. "Kate, really? You're just finding this out now?"

"I don't want to play golf," I muttered.

"Well, thank God you started with that one, because at least we can fix that. Cancel. Where is it written you've got to play golf?"

"What the hell else am I going to do with my time?"

"That we'll save for your second piece of chicken. Get over Elaine. I know that she doesn't think Regan is the most wonderful woman in the world, and that hurts your feelings. It doesn't bother Regan, so why should it bother you?"

The waiter came with our food, so I couldn't make my icky face.

"And get over Jake," she went on. "He's not part of your life anymore."

I smashed four pats of butter into my potatoes, and ripped open three packets of salt. "I know. It just freaked me out to see his face after all these years, and I thought he might actually want to see me again. I even imagined he wanted to maybe begin a relationship with me. Then I find out he's in a relationship with a woman young enough to be his daughter who's all boobs and not much else. It's like a slap in the face."

"I thought you weren't even going to wave back. What changed your mind?"

"Desperation? Nostalgia? Whatever it was, it was too late. Or just a ridiculous idea to begin with." I took a bite of chicken and glared at her. "What else? Go on, get it over with."

"You and Tom had sex and it wasn't great? So what? You're not in love, you're not eighteen, what the hell were you expecting? Give both of you a break and some time to get used to each other. And I'm telling you, it may never be great. At our age, sometimes things work, and sometimes they don't, and all the technique in the world isn't going to change that."

I picked the last bit of meat off the bone. "Really?"

She nodded. "Yes. Really. It's not about the sex. It's about the closeness. It's about intimacy. It's about trusting someone enough that you can be vulnerable and real. Did you at least enjoy being in the same bed with him?"

I nodded.

"Good. That's a start. I've discovered that knowing that there's someone there to hold me in the middle of the night if I have a nightmare is worth more than anything the Kama Sutra has to offer."

I stared at my empty plate.

Adam and I had a marriage that had made me feel lonely and angry in the last few years before his death. Sex became the only real connection we had, even though I knew he was sleeping with other women. I wanted to feel safe, like I belonged, and I still mattered to him. And that feeling had come only when we were alone in the dark.

"You're right. Thank you. Now, can you find me a job?"

Cheryl laughed. "What do you want to do?"

I thought. "Maybe I could write. I've always wanted to do that. Remember that woman a couple of years ago, who wrote about going to Italy and eating, then going to India and joining an ashram, then going someplace else? I could do that. I mean, I'm great at eating, I love Italy, and I've taken a yoga class before. I'm already halfway there."

Cheryl laughed again. "You do know that she was a writer before, right? And that her editor paid for her trip? It's not like she was a random person who just happened to write a best-selling book. Have you ever written anything?"

"You mean besides letters to the IRS? No. What about travel books? I'm a very good traveler."

She pushed away her plate. She had eaten a very nice chopped salad and a piece of grilled chicken, and was looking smug and healthy. "I think you need to be more than a tourist to write travel books. My God, Kate, you have a law degree. Shouldn't you at least try to make some use of it?"

"If I wanted to do that, I never would have quit my job. I'm tired of the law. I'm tired of rich people trying to get out of paying what they legitimately owe the government. Maybe I could write about that. Do you think a riveting account of tax evasion has a chance of making it to the *Times Book Review?*"

Cheryl was gathering up her things—purse, sunglasses, and her Bloomie's bag. "Kate, you know I love you, but if you're having problems, have you thought about a therapist? Maybe if you talked to somebody, you'd feel better."

I stood up, gave her a kiss, and waved her away. I sat for a long time, looking at my drying potatoes and picked-over bones. I actually had thought about calling somebody, but I kept thinking I'd just wake up one morning and something would change that would make me feel so much better. So far that hadn't happened.

But when I got home, I clicked on the computer, and there it was—an e-mail from Jake Windom. Saying that he'd love to see me again, and would I consider coming into Manhattan for a drink?

I spent a long time looking at the e-mail. Then I clicked my way over to his Facebook page, which I had bookmarked as per Alisa's instructions, and looked long and hard at Sandra the Beautiful. How could I possibly compete with that?

But did I want to compete with that? Or did I just need to see him so that I could finally feel like it was over, thirty years after the fact?

So I e-mailed him back, asking him to name the time and place. I'd be there.

* * *

Alisa found a job. Being a brilliant girl, with a degree in neuroscience from one of the country's leading universities, and being a doctoral candidate with another one of the country's leading universities, she got a job completely in keeping with her education and intelligence—in a coffeehouse as a barista.

She was very excited. It was right in town, she could work four mornings a week, and they were starting her at ten dollars an hour.

Normally, something like that would have caused me to roll my eyes and mutter, "Are you kidding?" but since I couldn't even manage to get an interview at a coffeehouse, I kept my mouth shut.

When I told her I was going into New York on Thursday, to see the new exhibit at the Met that I'd been planning on seeing for weeks, and, oh, yes, afterward have a drink with Jake, she jumped up and down and dragged me into my bedroom.

"You need to wear something fab," she said, heading for my closet.

"I don't have anything fab," I told her. "I was a lawyer. I have seventeen different black suits. That is not fab."

She was staring into my closet. I kept waiting for her to say, "No, Kate, we'll find something," but she didn't. She finally turned around to look at me.

"How many black suits?"

I cleared my throat. "Seventeen."

"You kept seventeen black suits? That makes no sense. Unless you were thinking about finding a job at a funeral parlor."

"No, I was not, but I didn't want to get rid of thousands of dollars' worth of designer clothing simply because of color. It seemed wrong."

She nodded. "Okay, I can understand that. But where are all the rest of your clothes? I mean, you haven't worn one black suit since we moved in, and I know that you've been out with Tom a few times, so I'm assuming there's an alternative wardrobe somewhere."

I walked into the closet and pushed all the suits aside. There, stuffed into the corner, was a flash of color.

Alisa looked at me sternly. "Kate, get rid of the suits. Donate them to Dress for Success or something. At least half of them." She grabbed a five-foot length of black suit, lifted it up, and handed the whole thing to me. I staggered out of the closet and threw the suits on the bed, then went back in.

Now that there was a little more room in the closet, and the overwhelming sense of doom was lightened, she started looking through my clothes. She finally grabbed a few things and threw them at me. "Try those on," she ordered.

She was right. I had gone out with Tom, but for our first date I had worn my semi-chic standby—a loose pantsuit in sapphire blue that I usually wore to informal dinners with my former law-firm buddies. I'd worn it because I wanted to look confident and successful. What did I want to look like for Jake?

Alisa had found two very colorful sundresses that I had completely forgotten about. She also pulled out a few pairs of linen crop pants and some great sleeveless silky tops from Chico's. Perfectly acceptable to wear for casual drinks. We tried everything on.

"You have a great body for someone your age," she said.

I tried to not cringe at the age thing. "I've always been built like a piece of decking—long and narrow. I'd kill for boobs, or even a little butt."

"Yes, but you look so great in clothes."

I sighed. True. But out of clothes, I looked like a pale, slightly wrinkled two-by-four.

We finally settled on one of the sundresses, because the ruffles around the neckline gave the illusion of breasts. I didn't know why I was bothering—Jake had seen me naked—often—and he had never minded my flat chest. In fact, he told me more than once he was not a boob man. And he would joke—"Why bother with a bra? I like easy access."

Apparently, judging from Sandra the Breast-iful, things had changed.

Now all I had to do was stop feeling guilty about seeing him. Tom and I had spent another night together, with a bit more success in the ecstasy department, and he had been calling every day. Just to check in, he said, but I was not at all girlishly delighted by his attention. I didn't need anyone checking in on me. Not yet, anyway.

I did not feel like I was cheating on Tom, for several reasons. First, I didn't feel committed to him in any way. Second, I was just having a drink. With an old friend. Who was currently dating a woman who could easily slip into the Miss Universe bathing suit competition and feel right at home.

So there was nothing for me to feel guilty about.

"So then why," I asked Cheryl the next day, "do I feel guilty?" I had picked her up just a few minutes earlier, and we were on our way to New Hope for a day of shopping and lunch.

She looked thoughtful. "Maybe you feel guilty about all your fantasies about him," she said at last. "Because you dreamed of finding him again and jumping his bones and having him fall madly in love with you, and then you could live with him in his fabulous estate in White Plains and live the life of a pampered CEO's wife." She sighed. "So the two of you could vacation in Paris and Tahiti, and go to the kind of charity functions that get your picture in *Town and Country* magazine."

I glanced over at her. "Cheryl, have you been smoking again?"

"Oh, yes, but I still think I have a valid argument. You're not feeling guilty about what you've done as much as what you'd like to do."

"I don't think," I said slowly, "that I want to be a CEO's wife."

"Course you do. You were a great doctor's wife, so it's only natural. Yes, I know, you were a lawyer with a master's and blah, blah, blah, but really, wouldn't you love to be rich?"

"Cheryl, you can't do this anymore."

She glared at me. "What? Tell you the cold, unvarnished truth?"

"No. Get high without me. When you're stoned, my only defense is to be just as stoned."

She reached into her massive Coach purse and pulled out a joint. "Here. I found one of those great do-it-yourself rolling machines online. Do you want me to get it started for you?"

I instinctively looked in the rearview mirror, expecting flashing blue lights and a siren. "Please put that away. Not when I'm driving—are you crazy?"

She sighed. "Remember the good old days, when I would give you a shotgun at forty miles an hour?"

"Cheryl, don't you think you're smoking a little too much of that stuff? I mean, I get an occasional Friday night, but seriously? At ten in the morning?"

"Well, it's better than drinking at ten in the morning, which would have been my choice three months ago. I started smoking pot so I wouldn't drink too much."

"Maybe you need to figure out why you were drinking too much."

"I know why. I was lonely and bored. What the hell else does a fifty-five-year-old single woman do who doesn't work and has lots of time on her hands?"

Since that described me to a tee, I felt a little nudge of concern. "You're not lonely anymore," I said, grasping for any straw in the wind. "Aren't you dating three men?"

"No, just one now. Marco."

I glanced over. She looked fairly inscrutable. "Really? So, he came over . . . ?" I asked.

She continued the Sphinx look. "Yes."

"And?"

"Well, the good news is that I didn't embarrass myself. And I came so hard I practically threw myself off the bed. But he has a very tiny penis."

I concentrated very hard on keeping the car on the road. "Oh?"

"Yes. You know all the stuff about how it's not the size of the ship but the motion of the ocean? Well, that's crap.

Luckily, he's aware of his own, ah, shortcomings, and has found creative ways to compensate. And he's a lovely man, truly. But he's very busy. Sure, I've got great Monday nights to look forward to, but what about the other six nights? And seven days? That's a long time to be alone, rearranging closets and avoiding the treadmill."

I had absolutely no words to say, so I kept my mouth shut.

"So," she said after a few minutes, "how are you and Tom getting along?"

I shrugged and kept my eyes on the road. "Fine. Things are a little more interesting in the bedroom, and we're having a lot more fun doing a few things together. But it's weird—I had invited him to come with me today, but he said he was busy. Then I told him you were coming as well, and he was suddenly not busy and asked if I wanted to drive down the shore for the day instead. I mean, really? And now it seems like he's checking in with me. A lot."

"You don't want one of those insecure, possessive types. They're killers. Really. They choke the life right out of you." She suddenly sat up. "Look, a McDonald's. Could you pull in? I'm starving."

Of course she was. I parked and she ran inside, emerging a few minutes later with two bags and a large drink.

"Jeez, Cheryl, got enough food?" I said as she strapped herself in.

She put the drink in the cup holder and opened one of the bags. The scent of french fries filled the car, and I immediately wanted at least sixteen of them.

"I wasn't sure what I felt like, so I got one of everything. And extra-large fries. Wanna share?"

Of course I did, so we pulled back on the road, and I snacked on fries while she took four bites out of everything in the bag. When we arrived, I was bloated and slightly nauseous from the smell of fried food.

New Hope, Pennsylvania, for those who don't know it, is an odd combination of hippie, New Age, and biker. Lots of what used to be called head shops and turquoise jewelry, psychics, stores selling Wiccan supplies and leather, and biker bars. There are also lots of vintage clothing and jewelry shops, some great art places, and at least three pet-themed shops. If you cross the bridge to Lambertville, it's a bit more upscale—less Harley-Davidson and more twee.

Cheryl got out and began feeding quarters into the meter. "Is four hours enough, or should we count on staying a bit longer in case we have lunch?"

"Cheryl, honey, how can you possibly think about food?"

She conscientiously threw away both bags full of leftovers. She took a deep breath, flung open her arms, and pushed forward her chest, causing a man walking his dog up the sidewalk to bump into a tree.

"It's a beautiful day," she declared. "Walking around in this glorious sunshine will stir the juices, I promise. Let's shop."

It was a Wednesday, and during the week there were fewer motorcycles and more dog walkers on the streets of New Hope. The trees had all leafed out, the sidewalks were fairly empty and shaded, and all the shop doors were open to the warm breezes coming off the Delaware River. There was a hint of incense in the air, mixing with the smell of grilled burgers and roasting garlic.

We were trolling a vintage clothing store when Cheryl grabbed my arm and pulled me into a corner.

"This shop is for sale," she hissed.

I looked at her.

"What? For sale? How could you possibly know that?"

"Because I was eavesdropping, that's how. The owner over there was on the phone with a broker. The whole building, inventory and all, is up for grabs. Buy it with me."

I stared at her. "Cheryl, why would we want to buy this place?"

She looked around lovingly. "Didn't you read that great book about the woman who had the vintage clothing store, and how every piece of Chanel had a story, and there was an old lady, and kind of a romance? It was charming."

"That is not reason enough to buy something like this."

"Well, you need something to do with your life, and so do I. We could be partners."

"We know nothing about retail. Or vintage clothing. And it's an hour commute each way. And if I know you, you'd spend all your time wearing the inventory." I shook my head. "First Alisa and her cupcake shop idea, and now this. Why would I want to start my own business in this economy?"

"Because," Cheryl said, "you have nothing to lose. You're smart, hardworking, and if you don't find something to occupy your time, you'll end up like me. Stoned and miserable."

I looked at her. "Oh, Cheryl, I wish I could find something like in your book, really. I'd love to be your partner in something really great. But I don't think this is it."

She shrugged, and proceeded to buy six different outfits, including an amazing swing coat straight from Carnaby
Street. She paid for it with her Platinum American Express
card; then we walked over to the old rail station for a very
light lunch before heading back.

I went home, took a long shower, and set out my sun-
dress.

Tomorrow I was having a drink with Jake Windom.

I'm not saying that the world was against me, but as I was
getting dressed the next morning, Regan called and asked
if I wanted to help her pick out her wedding dress.

"I found three that I like," she said, "but I'm really torn
about which one looks the best. Can you help me? Or do
you have something else to do today?"

Well . . . I mean, really. Should I tell her that I was planning on meeting that old flame of mine she had been railing
against a few weeks ago? Should I send Jake a quick e-mail
and tell him that for the first time in *weeks* my daughter had
actually asked me for help, and could we reschedule? Or
should I blow off the Monet exhibit that I'd been looking
forward to and just meet Jake?

When in doubt, tell the truth, then lie. "Well, honey, I
was on my way into the city to see that Monet thing at the
Metropolitan Museum, but I'm sure I can catch it some other day. But I was meeting some people afterward. Do you
think we'll have this wrapped up by, say, three o'clock?"

Regan made a noise. "Mom. It's not even nine in the
morning. The dress place is twenty minutes away. And I'm
only trying on three dresses."

There is something to be said for a low-maintenance daughter.

So she picked me up and we drove down to Wayne, and she disappeared into the dressing room while I wandered around, looking at mounds of white, billowing silk, satin, and taffeta until I heard her calling for me. I scurried back to find her staring at herself in the mirror, frowning.

"What do you think? This is my favorite, but it's not very traditional."

I couldn't speak, because my throat was suddenly blocked and I felt tears in my eyes.

She looked stunning. The dress was a simple sheath, cut on the bias, a pale iridescent fabric over white satin. Her shoulders were bare. Her body, which so often looked flat and shapeless, seemed fluid and graceful as she turned to face me.

"Mom? You're crying? Oh, God, really?"

I sniffed. "Regan, you look beautiful. That gown makes you look like you have a real woman's body, instead of a Freemont woman's body." I used both hands to brush away the tears. "Really, honey, I don't know what your other options are, but I think that one is perfect."

The saleswoman was nodding. "I told her that. Only about ten women in the world can get away with wearing a dress like this, and she's one of them," she said.

"But it doesn't look, I don't know, bride-ish," Regan said.

"Yes, it does," I told her. "If I were you, I'd forget a traditional bouquet and carry long-stemmed white roses. Get some white baby's breath to put in your hair. You'll look amazing."

She made a face in the mirror and shrugged. "Okay. I'll take it."

And she did. She walked out of the store with it, because it was a discontinued sample. Then we went to the mall and had lunch, she dropped me off, and I drove to the bus stop, got on the express to Port Authority, and walked up Fifth Avenue to the Pierre Hotel.

We had agreed on the Pierre because I thought I was going to be right up the street at the museum all day. Of course, the Pierre was also wonderful and very romantic. As I crossed the lobby, I glanced around, half expecting Fred Astaire and Ginger Rogers to come gliding across the polished floor. The bar was practically empty at that hour. I walked in, admiring the deep leather chairs, hoping I'd look younger and more beautiful with all that expensive lighting, and trying to pretend that this was just any old place to grab a quick drink. Then, my throat closed up for the second time that day, and I had to turn around immediately and find the ladies' room.

I had spotted him right away, seated at a small table, staring down at his wine. He looked exactly like his picture—graying, older, still handsome. But what his picture hadn't shown was his body—he was no longer a lean and muscular twenty-two-year-old. He had grown not so much fat as soft, and slightly round.

But that was not what had brought me to tears. Just seeing him in the flesh—God, what was wrong with me? Why was I still so emotionally tied to someone I had not seen in over thirty years?

I looked at myself in the mirror and took several long, deep breaths. Then, of course, I peed. Because I could. I ran cold water, wet a paper towel and held it against the back of my neck until my heart rate returned to normal. Then I went back into the bar and walked right up to him.

"Hey, Jake," I said.

He looked up at me and broke into a smile. He stood up and put his arms around me, and I slipped right into that familiar place against his left shoulder, where I had been a hundred times before, long ago, in a galaxy far away.

My arms had gone around him automatically, and I could feel the heat of his body soaking into mine as it had hundreds of times before, and his arms felt strong and protective around me, and all I wanted to do was stay as close as I could, breathing him in.

"You look great," he said when we finally stepped apart.

I grinned as I sat down. "Thanks. You too. I would have recognized you anywhere."

A waiter appeared and I ordered a martini. I'm usually a white wine person, but under the circumstances, I needed a real bracer.

"So," he said. "Three kids?"

Thank God for Jake, knowing how nervous I'd be, and giving me something comfortable to talk about right away.

"Yes. My oldest is a cartoonist. He does a daily strip, *Bennie's World.*"

Jake raised an eyebrow. He could do that—raise just one. And when he was younger, his brows were full and black and etched perfectly above his eyes. Now they were grayish and a bit shaggy.

"I know that one. I read it. Your son is Jeff Everett?"

"Wow. You remember his name and everything? Most people know the strip but can't tell you the artist."

He laughed. "Yeah, I still have a great memory for totally random information."

"Oh, God, that's right. You were always pulling odd facts out of the air and boring people at parties."

He looked indignant. "I thought I was being wildly entertaining."

I laughed. "I only told you that because I loved you."

He looked straight at me. "Yes. I know you did."

Very long pause.

"And then I have a daughter who's getting married in October," I said quickly. "And my youngest just moved back in with me, with his girlfriend, no less, so he can work on his PhD."

"Sounds like a great family."

"Yes. We are."

"And your husband? Or, I guess, ex-husband?"

"He was an ob-gyn. He died eight years ago."

"Sorry. Your profile on the site just said 'Single.' I thought you were divorced."

"Well, I probably would have been if he had lived. I was getting ready to leave him."

"How funny. He never came up at all when I Googled you."

"You Googled me?"

He looked sheepish. "About five years ago. But it mentioned your children, so I assumed you were still married back then."

He had Googled me? "He was having an affair."

"That must have sucked."

Yes. It sucked as badly as it did when you *left me.* "You were always the master of understatement, Jake. And you? No kids? Didn't you want, like, ten?"

He shrugged. "When I was young and foolish? Yes. But Jill and I spent a lot of years working our way up our respective corporate ladders. She was older than me, by five years, and when we finally stopped to think about it, she was at an age where getting pregnant was very tough. We could have gone a few different routes, I guess, but by then I was into working eighty-hour weeks. I would have been a very absent father."

I had finished my martini and was feeling a bit reckless. "I bet if you had kids, you would have found the time."

He looked at me. "Your husband was a doctor. Did he find the time?"

I signaled the waiter. Two points, Jake. That deserved another drink. "No, actually, he didn't. Although he couldn't control when his patients decided to have their babies. But that's water under the bridge, or something. What happened to your marriage?"

He fiddled with his fork, took a sip of his wine, and cleared his throat. "She just came to me one day and said she knew she was never my first choice, and that she was sick and tired of waiting for me to love her like she felt she deserved. So she left. That was six years ago. She just remarried, and she seems very happy. She was a financial analyst, but she spent a lot of time managing my career. In fact, she pretty much guided me in my job choices, all the way to the top. She always wanted me to be rich and successful, and she got what she wanted." He shrugged. "But she realized it was never going to be enough."

He had said that she was never his first choice. I wanted to reach across the table, grab him by the throat, and ask what the hell he meant by that. Instead, I gazed into the spanking new martini in front of me, and took a great big gulp. My head exploded.

"That's sad," I finally said. "So you're living in White Plains?"

"You mean, you didn't Google *me*?" His eyes were glinting with laughter, but I looked at him calmly and lied.

"No, not at all. So, tell me."

"Yes, I still have the house there, but I also have a place down in the West Village. The company I work for has its offices on Wall Street, of course, and it's just easier to catch a cab and crash, instead of driving all the way home."

"The West Village?"

"Right off Carmine Street."

I stared at him. "That's where Jeff lives. His partner owns West Wine and Cheese."

Jake threw back his head and laughed. People around us turned to look. His laugh was like that—huge, booming, and infectious. I had spent hours laughing with him, and now, all those years later, it still felt the same—like he knew a great joke and you just wanted to be in on it.

"I'm in there all the time. Gabe and I have a very intense relationship. He's always yelling at me to try something new, and I'm always telling him to shut up and bring me the usual."

I couldn't believe it. Jake lived literally around the corner from Jeff and Gabe. He knew Gabe. All the times I'd been down there, hanging out at the shop, even waiting on customers, Jake could have walked in at any time. I drank the rest of my martini in a single gulp.

The same thought must have occurred to Jake. He smiled gently. "It's a very small world, isn't it?"

Oh, yeah.

"Are you okay?" he asked.

I shook my head sharply. Of course not. He'd married a woman he couldn't love enough to keep. He'd been living a stone's throw from my son for years. Five years ago, he'd gone looking for me. And he'd found me. Damn Google for not linking Adam's obituary. "I should not have ordered that second drink. I'm in danger of falling into a stupor."

"God, we can't let that happen. I remember how you used to get."

I grinned. There had been many a night we'd sat on our front steps, my head against his shoulder, because I'd been so drunk I didn't want to sleep for fear I'd get sick all over him in the middle of the night.

"Let's get something to eat," he suggested. "Do you want to stay here? Or I know a great pub just a few blocks from here."

I needed to move, so we got up and headed south. We did not talk, but walked slowly as I let the fresh air clear my head. When we reached the pub, I still felt buzzed but much better.

"This place has great burgers," Jake was saying.

"I can see that the years have not cultivated your palate any. Is a burger still your first choice for any dining occasion?"

"I never saw the need to fiddle with perfection," he said. We were led to a booth, where I asked for a very tall ice water, Jake had the house red wine, and we looked at the menus.

"This place has fifteen different kinds of hamburgers," I pointed out.

"Yes, and I've tried them all. More than once. In fact, the chef is thinking of naming one after me."

"Are you a regular?"

That moment, on cue, a very pretty waitress stopped, grabbed Jake's hand to give it a squeeze, and told him how good it was to see him again.

Jake looked sheepish. "Well, I guess you could say that. I'm part owner. I wanted something to keep me busy after I retired."

"I'm impressed. But a little upset that when we walked in, everybody didn't yell, 'Jake.'"

He flashed a grin. "That's my place across town."

We ordered—two burgers—and I took a drink of water.

"So, what about you?" he asked. "I'm assuming you went to law school?"

"Yes, I did, but why would you assume that?"

He shrugged. "Because it's what you wanted to do. I could never imagine you wanting something as badly as you wanted that and not finding a way to get it."

I had wanted him more than I had ever wanted anything in my entire life and hadn't found a way to keep him, but I didn't mention that.

"Yes, I did go to law school. Then I got married, practiced law for a bit, had some babies, got a master's degree at night, then started part-time doing tax law. Then I went full-time, and I just quit this past spring."

"Retired already? Good for you."

"Not quite retired. I thought I was going to teach a few classes at a small college, but that fell through. I'm sort of unemployed right now."

140

He shook his head. "Now is not the best time to be un-employed. There's this economic crisis thing going on."

I nodded. "Yes, I noticed, but thanks so much for point-ing it out."

He waved my thanks aside. "Hey, no problem."

We were quiet, but it was a nice quiet. I felt relaxed and very content. Maybe it was the safe, comfortable booth that surrounded me and made me feel safe. Maybe it was the company of a man who knew everything there was to know about me, and had once chosen to love me anyway. Maybe it was the martinis.

Whatever.

"So, how long have you been doing the dating thing?" he asked.

"Just a few months. After Adam died, I really had no interest in being with anyone else, but, I don't know, I guess it's part of the whole changing-my-life thing. I started feel-ing lonely. And my sister felt, very strongly, that it was time. How about you?"

He shrugged, and waited until the waiter set down our food. The plates were overfilled with meat, bread, onion rings, fries, coleslaw, and a whole dill pickle. He looked sheepish again.

"I wish they wouldn't do this," he muttered. "I spend hours at the gym, and every time I lose a pound, I stop here and gain three."

I laughed. "Yeah, well, that's old age for you, Jake."

He made a noise. "No shit. I remember being able to eat four or five subs from Manny's in one sitting without ever having to think about it."

"Yes, your metabolism was legendary. Didn't you eat a turkey one Christmas?"

"Not a whole turkey. Just the leftover carcass. If my mother had wanted to save it, she should have said something at the time. How was I to know about turkey soup?"

I laughed again. "And then there was the Night of Many Tacos."

He looked surprised. Did he think I wouldn't remember? It had been thirty-odd years ago, but in my mind it was as clear as yesterday. "Fourteen. But that was a dare. You haven't gained an ounce," Jake said.

"I haven't. I've just gotten flatter everywhere. This is a very good investment, by the way. Great burger."

"I know. I ate in a lot of pubs before I hijacked this one."

"So, this retirement you're talking about, is it anytime soon?"

Jake grinned. "Two years, six months, and fifteen days."

"That's great. Then what are you going to do? Besides hang out here every day and listen to your arteries slowly clog."

He shrugged. "I still like the idea of moving to the mountains somewhere, remember? Like we used to talk about? Get a cabin somewhere, nice and peaceful. Fish and read. I'd still love that." He sounded almost wistful.

I pointed a very crispy and delicious french fry at him. "Our original plan was to cut all the logs ourselves, make the mud to chink up the holes, and live off the land."

He made a noise. "Yeah, well, I'm not twenty-two anymore. I'd just as soon have one of those premade numbers trucked in and watch the experts put it together. Preferably

DEE ERNST

from beneath the shade of a big, old tree sitting next to a cooler of beer."

"That, my friend, sounds like a brilliant plan. How does the girlfriend feel about it?"

For the first time, he looked uncomfortable. He reached for his wine and took a quick sip.

"Actually," he said at last, "Sandra is very much a city girl."

"Really? And is she beautiful?" My voice was nice and even. Friendly. Like it really didn't matter at all.

"Yes, she is." He drank the last of his wine and waved for the waiter. "But we don't have too much in common. She thinks the West Village is too sleepy. She prefers loud music to good food. And she's a very big shopper."

"Good lord. You hate shopping. At least you used to."

He shrugged. "I still do. But she thinks I'm very good at holding bags and paying for things." He spoke lightly and almost smiled as he said it. "I just started this online dating two years ago. Most of the women my age have all this baggage—they complain about their ex-husbands, moan about their kids, have money problems—it's hard to find somebody who just wants to have a good time. And when I do manage to find a smart, successful woman with minimal issues and a reasonable sense of humor, all they want to do is prove to me what a great catch they are. I get it—it's hard for 'women of a certain age' to find men who want to date them. And I'm one of those men; I really am. But they have this agenda, and they're never relaxed enough for me to really get to know them. It's been tough trying to find someone who just wants to spend time with me for the sake of, well, fun."

143

"Oh."

We were kind of quiet again after that. We'd sat down to eat just after six, and now, almost three hours later, we had reached a sort of plateau. I had to make the nine-thirty bus, so he walked me down Central Park West until it turned into Eighth Avenue, and we looked in the windows at all the jewelry and electronics, brushing by the tourists who stood gazing up at the night skyline. We made small talk and quick jokes until we reached the Port Authority building. He insisted on standing with me at the gate until the bus showed up, and then he gave me a cool kiss on the cheek and told me how great it was to see me again, and he walked off into the sunset. Figuratively, of course. There are no real sunsets inside the Port Authority building. Besides, it was too late in the evening.

He was just the same as he'd always been, in spite of the lines around the eyes and the thickening waist. His voice was deeper, coarser, and he had a much tougher shell around him. Being the CEO of a big corporation would do that to you, I imagined. His hands were the hardest part of the evening, because every time I looked down at them, I remembered their tenderness and strength, as well as their playful teasing. It seemed like I had spent the best few years of my life holding on to one of those hands.

So I got to spend forty-two minutes on the bus, looking out the window, wondering how I was ever going to be happy with someone like Tom Smith, or anyone else for that matter, when there was a Jake Windom in the world.

CHAPTER SEVEN

I had turned my phone off when I was with Regan, picking out her wedding dress, because I don't consider myself one of those people who need to be constantly available to the world at large. No one is going to call me to advise them on an international crisis, or to walk them through a particularly delicate bit of heart surgery, so why do I have to always be "on"? Nothing was more important than Regan's dress, and then I went off to see Jake, so I didn't look at my cell phone until the next morning, and there were six text messages—five from Tom, beginning with *Hi, how are you?* and ending with *I can't believe you'd treat me this way!*

Seriously?

The sixth was a text from Laura, saying she had broken her leg, and could I give her a call?

"Laura? What happened?"

She sighed. "I fell down the basement steps. Stupid cat ran between my feet, and bam, down I went. It's a clean break, right above the left ankle, but I'm out of commission for a while. They don't put you in a cast anymore. They just tell you to keep all weight off the thing for six weeks. Thank God the boys are gone."

Her two sons had been sent off to a month-long sports camp the previous weekend.

"Well, I guess the good news is that you won't have to worry about who's going to drive them all over creation for the next month," I told her. "What about your job?"

She laughed. "I always slow down during the summer, and in this market, no one will even miss me. And I now have a perfectly good excuse to sit in the sun and read for the next few weeks, instead of running around trying to cover everything on Bobby's 'to do' list. How was your day yesterday? Did you see Jake?"

"Yes. I also helped Regan pick out her wedding dress. It's perfect, fits her like a glove, and cost less than five hundred bucks. She's one lucky girl."

"I'm sure she is, Kate, but what about Jake?"

I tightened my grip on the phone. "Jake is just exactly the way he was thirty years ago—smart, charming, funny—and I felt so comfortable with him. It was a great evening. After which he went home and probably banged his barely legal girlfriend."

"Did you ask him about her?"

"Yes. He's with her because he's looking for some fun." I had wandered onto the deck and was staring out into the woods. "He married the woman he left me for. She pretty much made his career. Then she left him. Six years ago."

"Wow. So, are you going to see him again?"

"What would be the point? He's got this other woman. And I've got Tom, who's a fairly good man. I'd like things to work out between us."

"Okay, but if Jake should get in touch with you again, remain open. I mean, if you had a great time, he probably did, too, and that could be the start of something."

I put the palm of my hand on the top of my head and pressed down hard, as though trying to push out all my confused thoughts. "I'm not sure I should be thinking along those lines, Laura. Jake and I had our chance. I don't know how useful it is to keep thinking about what-ifs."

"The world would be a dull and miserable place without the what-ifs, Kate."

"Maybe. Do you need anything?"

"Nope." She laughed. "I'm going to make Bobby wait on me hand and foot for the next few weeks. I think I deserve it."

I laughed with her. "You do, baby sister. Take full advantage."

I hung up, then called Tom.

"Where were you yesterday?" he said.

I took a deep breath. "Yesterday I helped my daughter pick out her wedding dress."

He was silent. "Oh. Why didn't you answer my texts?"

"Because I did not want to be interrupted while I was picking out my daughter's wedding dress, and turned off the phone, then forgot to turn it back on." I was proud of myself that my voice was still nice and even.

"Oh. Well, I didn't know that."

"Really? So you just assumed I was checking my texts every five minutes but chose to ignore all *five* of your requests for attention? It didn't occur to you that maybe, just maybe, I was doing something important, and didn't have time to play the 'Hey, how you doin'?' game?"

He was silent. Good.

"Kate, it's just that I was worried."

"About what?"

"About what you were doing."

There it was. I took another deep breath. "Tom, seriously, it's none of your business what I'm doing."

He was quiet for so long, I almost cracked. But having played the control game with Sam, the brightest and most stubborn of my kids, I knew when to hold 'em.

"Kate, it's just that . . ."

"That what?" God, were we really having a conversation like this over the phone? I really hated technology. We should be nose-to-nose in a dark room, sweat trickling off our bodies from the summer heat, so in case it ended well we could have great makeup sex.

"What is this about, Kate? Why are you so angry?"

Well, poop. That was a very unfair question. I was angry because I had met Jake Windom, and that big fantasy I had in my brain about "closure" was just that—a big fantasy. I wasn't happy I'd seen him because I could continue with the rest of my life with no regrets. I was miserable I'd seen him because it reminded me of everything I had lost.

This was not Tom's fault, by the way. And I knew that. So I would have to be very careful to separate the reason I was mad at Tom from the reason I was mad at the world in general.

"Tom, the thing is, I've been alone for a long time. I'm not used to having to answer to anyone. I felt stalked. I mean, I think you and I may have a future, but we're not there yet."

"You're right. I'm sorry. I'm used to clingy women, and my behavior has been conditioned over the years for me to play a very, well, active role. I need to step back and allow you your space if we want to be successful going forward."

The words were right, but the delivery felt like a very patronizing sales pitch. But I took it.

"Good," I told him, even though that was not how I felt. "I'll call you."

"How about dinner tomorrow night?" he asked.

Hmmm. I had already designated Saturday as a spaghetti Saturday. Since I felt a little guilty about dumping all over him, I said, "Come here Saturday. I'm making pasta, and there'll be some people. It will be fun."

"Okay." His voice was considerably brighter, so it must have meant something. To him, anyway.

When we hung up, I felt something was not quite right. I called Cheryl.

"Can you and Marco come over for spaghetti on Saturday?"

"We'd already made plans, dinner and a movie."

"I invited Tom," I told her.

She was making little clicking noises with her teeth, which meant she was thinking. "Then we'll be there, because you do need a crowd. He might think this is some sort of step forward, being introduced to your family and close friends. Are you ready for a step forward?"

"I'm not sure. Will he really think that? Isn't that a little high school?"

"Of course. But let's face it, that's where men learn most of their dating behavior. Do you have a few C-listers? That way Tom will understand that his being invited was not really such a big deal."

"C-list? I don't think I have a C-list."

"Of course you do. New neighbors? The golf pro? Cleaning lady? I know for a fact you can drum up a few lawyers."

"The lady across the cul-de-sac. She thinks Boone is adorable."

"Excellent. And a few lawyers?"

"Cheryl, in all the years I worked at that office, I did not find one person I would consider inviting to my home. But seriously, maybe he doesn't even know the difference between the A-list and the C-list."

She made another, even more impolite noise. "That's another thing we learn about in high school, Kate: Life's journey is all about working your way up to the cool kids' table. Don't forget it. Ever. What should I bring?"

"Chicken nuggets and Boone's Farm apple wine?"

She laughed and hung up. Boone came up to me and laid her head on my lap, her butt wagging gently where her tail should have been. Time for a walk.

Since I had canceled my golf lesson, I had changed the route Boone and I took every day. Now we came out of the cul-de-sac and turned left toward the walking trails, instead of down past the pool. I had never been a great fan of Mother Nature. I mean, I loved looking out at things, but I never enjoyed being in the midst of, well, a forest or a desert, for example. My idea of the perfect wilderness setting involved carefully weeded flower beds and comfortable seating. Plus, I was a little phobic about ticks. But I braved the wilds of Madison rather than face the golf pro, and I was meeting a whole new set of neighbors, the hardy, outdoor set. There was one very friendly man who walked his Jack Russell terrier who seemed very open to conversation, but his dog kept trying to hump Boone, so our exchanges so far had been rather short.

Boone and I braved our way through the trees. It was summer already—it was mid-July, and although Memorial Day was the usual start of summer, I always considered the Fourth of July to be the official jumping-off place. I never put on a bathing suit before then.

On the way home, I stopped by and knocked on my neighbor's door. It took a few minutes for her to answer, but since her front door was open behind the screen, I figured she was home. When she appeared, she gave me a big smile, opened the screen door, and reached down to pet Boone.

"Kate, hello. And Boone, how's the girl?"

Boone wriggled with delight.

"Marie, I'm having some folks over tomorrow for spaghetti dinner. Do you think you could come over and join us?"

She broke into a delighted smile. "Of course. I'd love to. Dane was coming over, but he's here all the time. I don't get too many invites these days, so I certainly won't say no. Thank you so much."

"Dane?"

"My son. We usually see each other on the weekends, but he'll understand, I'm sure."

"Invite him along," I told her.

She tilted her head in surprise. "Really? You don't even know him."

I waved a hand. "Well, you and I are going to be neighbors for a long time, so I may as well get to know him, right?" *Besides,* I thought, *nothing says C-list like a neighbor's son.*

She beamed. "How thoughtful of you, dear. All right, then. What time?"

So I was set. Tom was going to meet my friends, some family, and also some of the most insignificant people in my life.

Now, there was a step. I'm not sure if it was forward or not, but at least it was something.

Saturday morning, Sam came down fully dressed at a fairly early hour, surprising me just a little. He gave me a quick kiss and opened the fridge.

"Alisa and I are going to have to miss your thing tonight. We're going into the city to hang out with some of my lab people; then we're seeing Tim's—remember Tim? He helped us move?—his brother is in a band and they're playing in Chelsea tonight. And then we're going to crash at Tim's place, so we don't have to worry about catching the bus. Sorry."

"No problem, honey. Have a great time."

He had pulled out some organic cranberry juice and poured himself a huge glass. Then he started taking all his pills. He took at least eight different supplements, from fish oil, which I could perfectly understand, to blue algae, which I didn't get at all.

"So, Mom, how's it going?"

I settled back with my coffee. "It's going fine, Sam. Thanks for asking. Still nothing on the job front, but I'm not worried yet."

He nodded. "Good. Good. Listen, Alisa and I aren't being too big a pain in the ass, are we?"

I smiled. "Alisa is a great girl, and she can stay here as long as she likes. You have always been a pain in the ass, but

I'm used to it by now. Are you really going to move to France and raise my grandbabies in a foreign country?"

He made a face. "Mom, you have no idea what kind of opportunity this is for Alisa. She's not even begun her doctorate, and this guy over there is crazy to get her. Alisa is really brilliant."

"I know. And apparently she can also make a mean latte. But France?"

He finished taking his pills and put the glass in the sink, caught my look, then put it in the dishwasher. Good boy.

"Who knows what's going to happen, Mom? I know how you are about planning way too far in advance for everything, so let's just wait, okay?"

Fair enough. I resented the "planning way too far in advance" remark, but knew it held a kernel of truth. As I finished my coffee, it occurred to me that with the kids out of the house, Tom could spend the night with me for a change. I sent him a quick text, making the invitation, then went into the den to check my e-mails.

And there it was, a message from Jake, telling me what a great time he'd had, and maybe we could meet again next week?

My ears were filled with the sound of all my blood rushing to my head. Really? He wanted to see me again? But what about the girlfriend? I had been that girl, the one who had put her blind faith in Jake because I thought he was such a wonderful guy, only to have my heart stomped on because he really wasn't. Did I want to be That Woman? The woman who knowingly went out with an attached man in hopes of luring him away? And how did I feel about the fact that Jake seemed perfectly comfortable cheating on this girlfriend, too?

On the other hand, Sandra the Beautiful didn't look like the type to have too many sophisticated emotions, and would probably be moving on to the next guy before the back door even got close to smacking her on the butt.

Damn, I wished I knew what I wanted. I wished that there was some clear plan out there for me, and that all I had to do was follow the dotted line. What I was not going to do was be an "other woman," although since the other woman was usually the young, sexy one, the whole situation appealed to my sense of irony. So I sent him a simple line back—*What about Sandra the Beautiful?*

Take that, Jake Windom.

The next night, as I was chopping salad, I heard Boone barking and knew somebody had come up the driveway. But after a few minutes of no one coming through the door, I went down to find Laura sitting on the bench, Bobby standing beside her, holding her crutches.

"Hey," I called, coming down into the courtyard.

Laura looked up and smiled. "Can we eat out here?" she asked.

I gave Bobby a kiss and a quick hug before sitting down next to Laura. "Sure. We'll bring down the dining room table and chairs, set out a bunch of candles; it'll be great."

She nodded. "Good. Stairs are really tough for me. You know how uncoordinated I am. In fact, I may have to spend the rest of the month here, because going down is harder than going up."

"She won't let me carry her," Bobby explained. "She's afraid I'll throw out my back."

I shook my head. "Laura, you probably don't weigh more than a hundred and twenty pounds."

"I know. But Bobby's back is tricky. Picking up a six-pack can be fraught with peril."

"Well, Tom is coming, and Jeff and Phil and my neighbor's son. Hopefully, between all of them, we can find someone who knows the fireman's carry."

She rolled her eyes. "I am not going to be slung over somebody's shoulder like a sack of flour, with my butt stuck out for all the world to see."

"Laura, honey, you have no butt, remember? Can I bring you out some wine?"

She nodded, and Bobby followed me into the house.

"She's in more pain than she admits," Bobby said. "Devon is homesick and keeps texting her every five minutes for her to come and get him."

"Wait a minute," I said. "Those boys have been going to the same soccer camp for ten years. This year he's homesick?"

"This year he has a girlfriend, which is the only reason she hasn't sent me up there to get him. And on top of everything else, your mom got her cable shut off because she forgot to pay the bill." He sighed. "Laura's stressed and doesn't handle it the same way you do."

I wasn't so great at stress, actually, but Laura tended to crumple quickly. I poured the wine.

"Mom had her cable cut off?"

Bobby nodded. "And her cable is tied to her phone. So at first she thought the phone was broken, so she drove to RadioShack and bought a new one. But then when the TV stayed blank, she called a neighbor to try to fix it. That's when they figured out that everything was turned off. It took her four days to get it turned back on."

"Wait. She drove? I thought Laura said her car was dead, and she was using the bus that ran through the complex to get around."

Bobby made a face. "A well-meaning neighbor jump-started it for her."

I felt like banging my head against the counter. This was a woman who, according to my sister, could not walk across her living room without stopping for breath and who was starting to forget things. The last time she drove, about three months ago, she got on the parkway going in the wrong direction and went past six exits before she figured it out. And somebody thought she should have her car back? Well-meaning neighbors should be shot.

I carried the wine back outside, and found a small crowd had gathered. Cheryl was there with a very tall, very attractive man I assumed was Marco. I had imagined him older, but he was probably in his mid-forties, with dark skin, flashing white teeth, and a magnificent head of black hair, thick and longish, that surrounded his strong face like a lion's mane. Tom was also there, hands in his pockets, watching everything with a half smile on his face. Regan was sitting next to Laura, holding her hand. Phil was crouched in front of Laura, looking very sympathetic.

"Wow," I said, coming down the steps and handing Laura her wine. "Were you all lurking around the corner, waiting until there were enough of you for a mass strike?"

Regan stood up and gave me a quick kiss. "I was just telling Aunt Laura that Phil can easily carry her inside. This is silly."

I looked at Laura. "See? Man up and let Phil carry you. I've decided I cannot feed all you people out here. There's not enough room for the chairs."

Laura made a face, but put out her arms. Phil scooped her up and they went into the house, Regan carrying the crutches. I smiled at Tom and gave him a nice, long kiss.

"Welcome," I said.

He nodded. "Thanks. Is your family always so high-maintenance?"

What did he say?

"Well, she did break her leg, and crutches are tough to get used to," I explained, still smiling.

He shrugged. "If you say so."

I was trying to decide what to say next when I heard my name being called. Marie was crossing the street with a very large, dark man at her side.

She smiled and waved. "Hello, Kate. This is my son, Dane."

Marie was tiny, just under five feet, with snow-white hair, olive skin, and a very Italian look. Dane had skin the color of coffee with a touch of cream, long dreadlocks, and a decidedly Jamaican lilt to his voice.

"Glad to meet you, Kate," he said, holding out his hand. I shook it, introduced Tom, and we all went inside.

Laura was comfortably settled on the couch, her wine-glass handy, laughing at something Regan had said. I made more introductions, got more wine, and sat back to watch.

Marie and Marco were fast becoming friends. He, I knew, was a professional musician. What I didn't know was that Marie had also been a professional—she had sung in the chorus of the Metropolitan Opera for thirty years. Cheryl, left to her own devices, zeroed in on Dane. He was probably just under forty and very good-looking. He was explaining that Marie had adopted him when he was twelve years old, bringing him to live with her in New York City. Dane was the director of some sort of program in Newark that worked with the homeless. Bobby and Tom were discussing sports. It seemed that a good time was being had by all.

Regan left Laura's side to sit next to me. She gave me a look.

"What did you do to Elaine?" she asked.

"Nothing. I just bought a gorgeous metallic dress, bronze, before she could buy a gorgeous metallic dress. I may have pissed her off."

"Ya think? Why do you do that to her?"

"Do what? It's not my fault I found the perfect dress for your wedding that just happens to be bronze. She called your future father-in-law a philistine, by the way, and warned me that he'd try to sleep with the bridesmaids."

Regan snorted. "Edward is a perfect gentleman. It's all sour grapes on her part. Tom seems nice."

Her voice was very even. Tom had come through a few minutes earlier and asked everyone if he could freshen their drink. A nice gesture, sure, but—this was *my* house.

I glanced up and Regan's face was completely set. "Yes, he is. We haven't known each other very long, but I think if we give each other a chance, we could be good together."

She took a quick sip of her wine. "What about that other guy? The college one?"

Now it was my turn to keep my voice even. "We had a drink. It was good to see him again."

Cheryl came over, her arm draped through Dane's. "Kate, you must talk to this man. He needs your help."

"Oh?" I looked at him "Really?"

Dane laughed. He sounded just like that guy in the old Uncola commercials. "I always need help. Cheryl says you're a tax attorney?"

I nodded. "Yes. Currently unemployed, but I can still call myself that."

Dane flashed a smile. "Would you be interested in doing a little volunteer work? I run an organization called the Shadow People, and I could use a person with your skill set. Believe it or not, the people I work with have incredibly complicated tax problems, and since they're homeless and without resources, they are in desperate need of advice."

I was surprised, but just for a moment. "I could actually use something in my life right now, and although I really didn't want to go back to law, I would love to be useful again. Sure, I'd be glad to help out."

Dane handed me his card. "Call me. This is a very lucky day for me. Not only am I spared my mother's cooking, I've found a recruit as well. Thank you."

I laughed and went in to put the pasta on. Tom suggested I replenish a few olives and chips, which I did, then I checked the garlic bread. Soon we were all happily eating.

After dinner, Laura and Bobby left, and a short time after that Dane walked his mother back across the street. But he came back and the bunch of us sat on the deck, drinking more wine, and laughing quite a bit. For such an odd, last-minute mix, we all got along just fine. Cheryl and Marco were the last to leave, just after eleven.

I started gathering the wineglasses. Tom came back from the bathroom and came up behind me, kissing me on the neck.

"You have great friends," he said. "And your daughter is a hoot. She's just like you. Do you and your mother get along as well as you and Regan do?"

I shrugged and carried the glasses into the kitchen. "Well, you're right: She is just like me. I look at my daughter and see a strong, independent woman who knows her own mind and isn't afraid to go after what she wants. My mother looked at me and saw a spoiled, willful brat who was disrespectful, rebellious, and unappreciative. All a matter of perspective, I guess."

"So I guess you and your mom had a pretty rough time together when you were younger."

"Very rough time."

"Are you close now?"

"No. I haven't seen her or had a conversation with her in eight years."

"Really? I call my mother twice a week."

"Good for you, Tom. Hypothetically speaking, if you told your mother that you thought your wife had been cheating on you, would she have believed you? Or would she have called you an ungrateful liar?"

"What are you talking about?" He stopped wiping down the counter and stared at me. "Of course she would have believed me."

I took the sponge from his hand and set it in the sink. "That's why you talk to your mother twice a week, and I don't. Can we change the subject? Discussing my parental relationship is really killing any romantic vibe that may have been hanging in the air."

He grabbed me around the waist and spun me twice around the kitchen. Then he pulled me close and sang the first few lines of "Smoke Gets in Your Eyes" in my ear.

I laughed and put my hands under his shirt. His skin was soft and smooth. For a guy who was almost sixty, he was pretty buff.

"Much better," I murmured.

"I could recite some poetry," he said.

"Could you?"

"No. Maybe. The only poem I remember is 'The Owl and the Pussycat.' But I could sing you another song."

I kissed him long and hard. "No, that's okay. I think the romance is back."

And then we went to bed. I had a tiny bottle of body oil, lightly scented of musk, and we took turns rubbing it all over. Everything was warm and lovely, and I fell asleep curled against his back.

I woke up the next morning to the smell of coffee. How lovely. Tom was already up and had figured out how to work the Keurig. I got up, threw on my cute/sexy robe, pale violets on white terry with lots of lace for the trim, and padded out to the kitchen. Should I offer to make breakfast? Should we go out? Maybe go back to bed?

"Morning, Mom."

Tom, Sam, and Alisa were all sitting at the breakfast bar, all drinking coffee, all looking incredibly uncomfortable.

"Sam? Weren't you and Alisa supposed to be sleeping at Tim's last night?" *Oh, God, how did this happen?*

"Well, when we got there, Alisa saw a roach and freaked out, so we took the late bus home."

Alisa made a face. "I'm so sorry, Kate, really. But it was a *huge* roach, and it was crawling up the dresser right next to the bed, and I screamed so loud that I think I woke up Tim's neighbors, and I made Sam bring me home. Coffee?"

"Sure. Well, how lucky for us all. You've met Tom?"

Sam looked at Tom as though he were looking at a particularly nasty bug. "Yeah, just now."

Tom was not smiling. "Good morning, Kate. I was going to suggest we go out for breakfast."

"Excellent idea. Just let me get some clothes on. I mean, get dressed." *Oh, God.* "I mean, get dressed in something else."

"Tom was just saying you had a great time here last night," Sam said.

"Yes," I said, inching backward, hoping for a clean exit, but Alisa pushed a steaming mug of coffee into my hands.

"I'm so sad that we missed it," she said brightly.

"Well, next time," I said.

Tom made a noise.

"Tom was also saying that you met online," Sam said darkly, as though "online" were some secret place right next door to an opium den.

"Yes."

"Five weeks ago," Sam continued.

I sighed. "Yes, just about. Back in June, right, Tom?" I smiled encouragingly, but Tom just looked at me, a few faint lines of irritation across his forehead.

"Yes," he said shortly. "June."

"That's not a very long time," Sam pointed out.

I looked at him squarely. "For what, Sam? For one consenting adult to decide she'd like to sleep with another consenting adult?"

Sam turned bright pink, and Tom muttered, shaking his head and looking down into his coffee mug.

"Honestly, Sam, I realize this is the awkward moment when you find out that your mother is a real person who has a sex life just like everyone else on the planet, but don't make it some traumatic event that you'll be talking about for the next ten years in therapy. Get over it."

Tom stood up, put his mug in the sink, and walked over to give me a light kiss on the cheek. "Why don't I call you?" he said, and before I could argue, he slipped out the door.

Alisa hit Sam in the arm with her fist. "You are such a jerk!" she yelled at him.

Sam looked hurt and amazed. "What? What did I do?"

Alisa was still yelling. "This is your mother's house, Sam. We are guests. You have no business making snarky remarks about her behavior in her own home."

"I'm not snarky!" he yelled back.

She put her hands on her hips and turned to me, eyebrows raised.

"Yeah, Sam," I told him, "you were kinda rude."

"Well, sorry." He must have noticed he was still yelling, because he cleared his throat and lowered his voice. "I don't know the proper protocol for meeting the man who just had sex with my mother."

"Instead of dwelling on the sex part," Alisa said, not yelling but still with force and conviction, "why don't you be happy that your mom has found a person to share her life with?"

Sam looked stricken. "Mom, are you going to marry this guy?"

"Of course not, Sam. I mean, I don't know. It's way too soon to think about that. Tom and I are just getting started. Give us a little time, okay?"

"Well, it wasn't too soon for you to start sleeping with him," Sam muttered.

Alisa hit him on the arm again. "It seems to me, Sam, that you wanted to have sex with me after four days. Cut your mother a little slack. She doesn't need her geeky-but-sex-crazed son passing judgment."

That was way too much information, so I carried my coffee back into my bedroom and shut the door.

Then I did what I always did on Sunday morning.

"Morning, Jeff. I missed you last night."

"Hi, Mom. Wait." There was a noise on the line that sounded like gargling. "Okay, I'm back. Yeah, sorry about that, but Gabe and I were seeing a surrogate."

"Surrogate what?"

"Gabe and I are having a baby."

Full stop. Luckily, I hadn't taken another sip of coffee, or I would have spewed it all over my bedroom.

"When were you going to teil me this?" I yelled. "Oh my God! Jeff, this is wonderful!"

He was laughing. "I know. Remember how I thought Gabe was having an affair because he was sneaking around and not telling me where he'd been? Well, he was trying to surprise me. He got everything all lined up. We met the woman yesterday, and on Tuesday we're going to the sperm bank. We're both donating, so we won't know who the biological father is, but it's all very scientific and aboveboard.

The woman is a single mom from Maine who has a free ride to law school but needs living expenses for the next four years. Gabe and I are going to forget about the vacation house and give all our savings to her instead."

A baby. Jeff and Gabe were going to have a baby. This was going to be the wildest baby shower ever.

"I'm going to be a grandmother. Oh, Jeff, this is the best news. You're not going to France, are you?"

"What? France? Why would I go to France?"

"Nothing. It's just that's what Sam and Alisa are planning to do. But it doesn't matter now, because you two are going to have a baby. Oh my."

"Just don't make any formal announcement yet, okay? Meryl, that's her name, she has to get pregnant first. Then we should wait at least ten weeks to make sure everything is okay. Gabe was smart. He found somebody a whole day's drive away. If she were here in New York, I'd be baking her cookies and visiting her womb twice a week, like on a bad TV sitcom."

"Fine. But we need to celebrate. When is good?"

"Come Thursday night. It's the four-year anniversary of opening the shop. We're having some business friends and neighbors, so I hope you don't mind if you're the only straight person there. Virgil's, of all places, because Gabe didn't want anything too formal. But no baby mention to anyone else, okay? It'll be our secret. Eight o'clock?"

"Of course. Can I tell Sam and Regan?"

"Hey, Mom? Maybe I want to tell Sam and Regan?"

"Oh. Right. Sam's a bit touchy right now, so be prepared."

"Sam? My fabulous baby brother? Touchy? Why, I can't imagine. Did his subscription to *Scientific American* run out?"

"No. He came down to breakfast this morning and found my boyfriend having coffee in the kitchen."

"Really? Go, Mom."

"That was not his reaction," I said drily.

"Yes, well, he always was an insufferable twit. Now that he's finally got his own sex life, you'd think he'd be a bit more understanding."

"You might want to mention that to him."

"I'll call him now. See you Thursday."

I hung up, stared out the window, then did the happy dance all over the bedroom. I was going to be a grandmother. At last. I just couldn't tell anybody.

How long would it take for Jeff to call his sister? I needed to talk to somebody about this, and Regan was the best choice. Would Jeff call her first, or Sam? Would he even call them today? Would he want to wait, because, even though they were his siblings, he could really only trust news this big with his mother? Hmmm.

I walked out, got the Sunday *Times* off the front steps, and made another cup of coffee as I sorted the paper. As I sat in my Sunday chair in the den, Boone came and curled up on my feet. I nudged her with my bare toe.

"You couldn't have barked when they came home last night?" I asked her. Boone cocked her head in interest, but chose not to respond. "Just a tiny 'woof' to give me a heads-up?" She put her head down and sighed. Some watchdog.

And then the phone rang. Oh, yeah—Regan! Jeff did call her. Thank God.

"Mom, are you really sleeping with that man?" she asked.

Okay, so maybe Jeff didn't call her.

"Jeff didn't call?" I asked.

"No, but Sam sent four separate texts. Seriously?"

"Why are my children—all of them, I might add, unmarried but living in sexual bliss—so interested in *my* sex life? It's nobody's business."

She was silent. But not for long. "I just don't want you jumping into something too quickly."

"Regan, your father has been gone for eight years. Just how much longer do you think I need to mourn?"

"But you don't know him."

"So I should, what, date him for a year or two? Is that what you and Phil did?"

Oh, good. More silence. "Mom, that was a little different."

"How?"

"Phil and I are getting married."

"And you knew that was going to happen when you two first jumped into bed together?"

"Okay, Mom, I'm going to hang up now."

"Wait. Did you like him?"

"Who?"

"Tom. You spent a whole evening with him. Did you form an opinion?"

"He was nice."

"And?"

"Really?"

"Yes."

"I didn't think he was good enough for you. You're smarter than he is. And his sense of humor is a little forced. And he seemed a little too involved, you know? Like even though it was your house and your party, he wanted to run everything."

Well, just that one time, when he ran around pouring more drinks for everybody. And then when he told me I needed more chips. And olives. Oh, and that little bit in the end when he kept telling me to light more candles while we were on the deck.

"Regan, honey, those are actually very good observations. But we're still a new couple. Give us some time to find a way to fit together, okay?"

She sighed. "Okay. Sorry, Mom, but I need to get used to you as a dating person, instead of just my mom, you know? I hope you find somebody to be happy with, I really do. I don't think Tom is that person, but maybe you're right, and you both just need time."

"Thank you, honey."

"But can I say something without you getting too crazy?"

I sighed. "Sure."

"Shouldn't you be out there looking for a man who's going to sweep you off your feet, instead of waiting around with somebody until they find a way to fit?"

"I'm fifty-five. I'm not sure I'm still sweepable."

"Well, you should be. Don't you want to be?"

All I could see was Jake Windom's face. "Good point, Regan."

"Are you mad at me?"

"Of course not, honey."

"Good, because I have a favor to ask."

"Go ahead. Ask away."

"Edward Pendergast is flying in on Tuesday. He's going to spend the next few months here, looking up old friends, that sort of stuff. I think he has some business to do in New York."

"How nice! I can't wait to meet him."

I could feel her smile through the phone. "He's really such a good man. But he's flying into Kennedy, and I hate going out there. Would you come with me?"

"As long as I don't have to drive, sure. I'll be happy to ride shotgun."

"Thanks."

We hung up, and I sat looking at the phone in my hand, while Boone snored gently at my feet.

CHAPTER EIGHT

I had called Dane St. Germaine and told him I'd be happy
to volunteer at his center and give whatever tax advice
I could to his homeless clientele. That was Monday afternoon. I called Tom up that evening, and asked if he wanted
to come over for some pizza and TV, but he said no, thanks.
Tuesday morning Dane called me back and asked when I
could start. I laughingly said tomorrow, and he said great,
he'd line up some appointments, gave me an address, and
left me staring at the phone.

Regan was afraid she would be caught in traffic, get lost,
or have to battle the zombie apocalypse, so we left my driveway three hours before Edward's plane was due to land.
Since we ran into just a little traffic and no crazed undead,
we spent two hours wandering around the airport, where we
had an incredibly overpriced and tasteless lunch. I would
have called it a touching bonding experience, but she spent
most of the time on her cell phone, while I read *Vogue* magazine, something I hadn't done in years, not since I realized
I would never again be twenty-two, or spend twelve hundred
dollars on a single pair of shoes. But it was the fattest magazine on the rack, so I grabbed it.

We were waiting by the luggage carousel. I was watching
suitcases go by, playing "Name That Designer" in my head,

when she jumped up and ran. I looked over at Edward Pendergast, and a very strange thing happened when I saw him.

I smiled.

It's not like he was really good-looking. His face was narrow, and his nose a bit long and pointy. His hair was fair and thinning on top. His smile was wide, and his front teeth were a bit crooked. As he hugged Regan, I realized he was not that much taller than her, which would make him exactly my height.

So why was I smiling?

I stood up and got introduced. His hand was warm, his shake was firm, and he had the kind of accent Cary Grant impersonators would kill for. We stood and chatted about his flight, the weather in London, the weather in New Jersey, and if he could rent a car at his hotel, where it would be infinitely cheaper than renting it in New York.

By the time we had collected his luggage (totally nondesigner) and paid the exorbitant parking fee (two hours of which was totally wasted time), I had agreed to have dinner at Edward's hotel with him, Regan, and Phil. Regan was driving Edward to the Hertz rental place in Morristown. And, since I was going to be in the car with them anyway, I said I'd just hang out with him until Regan returned with Phil. That way, Edward and I could sit at the bar, have a glass of wine, and get acquainted, since we were practically related. Afterward, he said, he'd be happy to take me home.

So, that's what we did, and gosh, what a great guy. Why the hell had he been living in England all that time? Why couldn't we have met sooner? Because, seriously, if I had known about Edward Pendergast, I never would have bothered with that stupid online dating thing. At all.

* * *

Newark is a big city, with lines of traffic snaking around concrete and steel. Thank God for my GPS, because I never would have found the small alley where Dane had his office. Not that it was an actual office—it was a former warehouse, tucked behind a parking garage, a cool, dark space that went on seemingly forever, but packed with people and things—boxes of clothes, dry goods, food, as well as rows of desks manned by earnest-looking students on laptops and phones. I tried not to think about my car parked out on the street, unprotected, but Dane had assured me that all "his people" and their cars were taken care of. The locals took turns keeping watch.

It took me a few minutes to find him. I had been walking around in the dim light of the warehouse when I heard a laugh that I recognized and headed off in that direction. I found him at a long table, sorting shoes.

He looked up from his work and flashed a smile that lit up the room. "You're here," he boomed. "And on time. Kate, I cannot begin to thank you enough. So many volunteers think they can wander in at will. I can tell you're going to be a real asset."

He spoke briefly to a few kids who had been at the table with him, and led me to a large, empty desk with a huge pile of files on it. I had my own laptop and calculator, as well as copies of all sorts of tax forms. He let me sit down and get comfortable.

"We cannot give any of the people you will speak to today any financial assistance," he explained. "You look at their situation and tell them what the best plan is for them. Because people are homeless doesn't mean they are without income. Many of them have P.O. boxes and collect Social Security and pensions. Some of them own stocks and get dividends. They have inherited money or sold their homes but never got around to purchasing another. We have never been able to offer this kind of advice to them before, so we all really appreciate your being here."

I kept looking around. The place was vast. "What do you do here, Dane?"

He shrugged. "Everything. Distribute food and clothing, offer a place to get out of the cold during the day, although we are not considered a shelter and cannot allow anyone to spend the night. We are open to anyone, but the people who come here are mostly regulars, street people who have been in this section of Newark for a very long time. The Shadow People Solution is privately funded, with a board of directors and eight full-time employees, including myself. Most of our volunteers are college kids and retirees." He grinned. "And unemployed, overqualified attorneys."

I smiled. "I'll do what I can."

"Good. Around one o'clock I'll come by and take you away for lunch."

"Dane, that's okay. I'm sure I can manage lunch on my own."

He nodded. "I'm sure you can, too, but I find that once you get started with these people, you forget about things like lunch. Or coffee breaks. Or even going home. I've told everyone they are allowed thirty minutes. Which means you have fourteen people who will want to talk to you today. At the end of their time, make them leave. They won't want to. If you have any trouble, just stand on your desk and yell for me, okay?"

"Okay."

By the time Dane tapped me on the shoulder and told me it was time for lunch, I felt I had traveled to another world. As Dane had said, I could have spent a lot more time with every person, but each of them understood when time was up and collected their forms and notes, thanked me profusely, and gave their seat to the next person. I saw seven people that morning, and found seven situations I had never faced before. These people wanted to make sure they paid what was needed, because they understood that if they got into trouble with the IRS, they would never be able to get out. My former clients wanted to avoid paying anything at all, because they knew all that money they saved could be used to bail them out if necessary.

I followed Dane out into the heat and sun, to a run-down food truck that had the most amazing smells coming from it. He introduced me to Mel, who ran the cart, bought me two delicious tacos and an iced tea, and we sat and ate on a long bench outside the warehouse, elbow-to-elbow with Dane's people.

He had been very quiet until after I had eaten. Then, as he gathered up our trash, he asked me casually, "So, do you think you'll want to come back?"

I wiped my hands on the last bit of napkin. "Sure. Next time I won't wear khakis, because it's a little bit grimy here, but I'll come back. Why? Do your volunteers usually run away screaming after the first day?"

He threw back his head and laughed. "The respectable white ladies usually do, yes."

"Really?"

He shrugged. "These are the great unwashed. Sometimes it's hard to see them as individuals, with lives and personalities beyond their problems."

"Well, maybe to some, but I gotta tell you, Dane, these individuals are unlike any I have ever seen. And their problems present a whole new learning curve. I will be back for sure. Plan on every Wednesday, at least until I get a real job somewhere."

The rest of the day flew by, and Dane finally came up and told me to go home at six thirty, as I was scrolling through the tax laws on my laptop.

"See?" He laughed. "I told you you'd forget about going home. See you next week."

My car was where I left it, so I drove home and collapsed into bed after a quick shower and no dinner. It was the best, most exhausting day I had spent in a long, long time.

I got up early the next morning and took the bus into the city and finally saw the Monet exhibit at the Met. It was stunning. I wish I had been with somebody, so we could have stared in awe together. Tom had invited himself when I told him where I was going, but I brushed him off. If it had only been the museum, it would have been fine. But I was also going to be having dinner with Jeff, Gabe, and their friends, and didn't feel like having Tom around. I wanted to relax and enjoy myself, and did not want to think about whether or not Tom was having a good time.

When I finally left the Met, it was after three in the afternoon, pretty hot and muggy, and my crisp linen crop pants started wilting as I walked down Fifth Avenue. Here was my dilemma: Virgil's was in Times Square. I could walk there easily and spend an hour or three drinking wine at the bar, but I really wanted to talk to Gabe and Jeff alone, which meant going all the way downtown, and then coming back uptown. See the problem? In the heat and humidity, I'd be a wrinkled, sweaty mess.

So, I popped into Saks, cooled off in the infants' department, managed to *not* buy every cute baby thing I saw, then hailed a cab and rode downtown in comfort.

There are blocks in downtown Manhattan that seem frozen in time—faded brick, swinging signs, and tiny tables crowding the sidewalk, where you can sit with wine or espresso and watch people for hours. Gabe's shop is on a block like that, with a cute bay window jutting onto the sidewalk, filled with baskets of boxed crackers and jugs of olive oil. You thought you were going to walk into a dark, narrow specialty shop, but when you pushed your way in, it opened into a huge, well-lit emporium. The wine side, in one-half of the space, had bins up to the twelve-foot ceiling, and there was one of those cool sliding ladders that libraries used for books, but Gabe used it to climb up and bring down precious bottles. The cheese was on the other side, as well as sausages hanging from brass hooks, barrels of cured olives, and loaves of fresh bread from a bakery in Brooklyn, although those were usually sold out by noon. It smelled great, if you loved cheese like I did. If you didn't, you should probably stick to the wine side.

Gabe was with a customer, of course, but he waved when he saw me and, after handing over a few wine bottles, came over and gave me a huge hug.

"How excited are you?" he asked, grinning.

"Gabe, I am over the moon. You two are going to be the best parents ever." I whipped out a onesie from my Saks bag. It was tiny, yellow, with ducks embroidered across the front. "Happy baby!"

"They're that small? Oh, no, stop the insemination!"

"And they poop."

"That I know."

"Is Jeff home?" Home was literally around the corner, the bottom two floors of a brownstone.

"No, he's meeting somebody about maybe doing an animated cartoon series for *Bennie's World*."

"Really? How cool is that? Okay, then I'll just wander around."

Gabe gave me a look. "You have a key. You could always go over and hang out."

"I know, but it just feels weird being in there without you two. Like being the only live person in a photo shoot for *Architectural Digest*."

He laughed and went off, and I wandered happily for the next twenty minutes or so. The place was busy, but then it always was. Gabe had the perfect location for his shop—those West Village people loved their wine. I was starting to feel a little bored when I heard a very familiar voice.

Jake?

Really?

I peeked around a display, and there he was, in a three-piece suit, laughing with Gabe.

When he had met me for a drink, he'd been in khakis and a polo shirt, and had looked just like any other guy. Now he looked like what he was—the CEO of a multinational company: powerful, rich, and a little intimidating.

I came up behind him.

"You were right," I said. "Very small world."

He turned around and his eyes widened in surprise; then he reached out and hugged me, lifting me off my feet in the process.

"I was just thinking about you," he said.

Gabe was watching carefully.

"Really?"

"Yes. Really. Gabe, Kate and I were college sweethearts. And in all the time I've been coming here, I never knew that Jeff was her son. Isn't that wild?"

Gabe was grinning. "My favorite mom-in-law and my favorite customer. That is pretty wild. Was he stubborn and argumentative in college, Kate, or is this pigheadedness an old-age thing?"

I laughed. "Well, he was always reluctant to try new things. He had his favorites and stuck to them."

"But when it comes to wine, there are hundreds of new tastes. Jake, I mean it, this Shiraz will change your life."

"Go on, Jake, be daring," I said.

Jake looked at me. "Only if you share it with me, Kate. I live only four blocks away, and it's not too early in the evening for a glass or two. How about it?"

What? But Sandra the Beautiful . . . what about her? He had never answered my e-mail about her, so I had to assume she was still in his life. But I didn't want to ask about her in front of Gabe, who I could see was bursting with curiosity already.

I glanced at my watch. "Gabe, when are you guys heading up?"

"You've got plenty of time," Gabe said, moving toward the register. "The reservation is for seven thirty. In fact, Jake, would you like to join us? Jeff and I are celebrating the shop opening four years ago today. I think you were one of our first customers. We'll be at Virgil's because we want to lick barbecue sauce off our fingers later on. I could change the reservation."

Jake looked at me. "Kate?" His eyes were smiling, like they used to when the two of us would be alone and he was about to suggest we take our clothes off. I actually started to blush.

"Sure, why not?" I said. There was a hot flash building. I could feel it, so I moved in front of the air-conditioning vent and prayed that Jake would take a long time paying for his wine.

No luck. It took him less than, like, three seconds to check out, and he took my arm and steered me outside, where, luckily, the outside temperature was barely ten degrees cooler than my inside temperature, so the sweat on my upper lip and down my back was perfectly under-standable.

"This heat is a killer," I said, just to cover my bases.

Jake nodded. "Yep. I'm close, though. We should be able to make it before your hair starts to frizz."

I had to laugh. I spent a great deal of my college career trying to find ways to keep my thick Italian hair from look-ing like a Brillo Pad when the weather turned warm and humid.

"That is not a problem anymore. I finally found the mag-ical combination. Funny you should remember that," I said.

"After all the time you spent bitching about it, how could I forget?"

"That's true. Hey, Jake? What about your girlfriend?"

He didn't slow his pace. "She's not my girlfriend anymore. We ended things, quite amicably, just two nights ago. I think she realized I was too old. And I realized she was too, uh—not high-maintenance. That sounds like she was a gold digger. She just liked nightlife, and dancing, and drinking in clubs."

"I thought that's why you went out with her in the first place, to have a good time."

He shrugged. "True. But we were never able to agree on the definition of a good time."

Can I tell you that my heart did a little backflip?

It only took us five minutes to get to his place, on a quiet, tree-lined street with very expensive cars lining the curb. He led me to a gorgeous four-story brownstone with twelve steps up to a red front door. He unlocked the door and held it open for me. I was a bit confused, thinking I'd have to follow him up to whatever floor was his, and then I realized I was not walking into a lobby of an apartment building—I was walking into the foyer of his home.

"You own the whole house?" I asked.

He shut the door and walked down a long, cool hallway. A Dalí, probably that print he had picked up at Sotheby's, hung just inside the doorway. I followed him into a huge kitchen that took up the entire back of the apartment. Sliding doors opened onto a deck that in turn overlooked a tree-lined courtyard, complete with fountain.

He was arranging the wine bottles on a granite-topped island roughly the size of my entire dining room. "I really need to change," he said. "Do you think you can find the wineglasses?"

"Sure. Which zip code are they in?"

"To the left," he said, and went back down the hallway.

I put my purse on one part of the island and looked around. It was a beautifully designed kitchen, with a six-burner gas stove, double ovens, three sinks, and at least fifty linear feet of granite. I wanted to be buried in that kitchen. I tiptoed back down the hall. There was a vast dining room right inside the front door, walls painted an elegant robin's egg blue, drapes puddled on the burnished wood floor, and a table so big that my entire family, including cousins, could have had Thanksgiving dinner there, with room for a touch football game in front of the sideboard. Next came a powder room, then a walk-in closet. Who has a walk-in closet off the hall?

Back in the kitchen, I found the wineglasses. They were in the wineglass wing, between one of the sinks and the built-in wine cooler. He had one of those refrigerators where you open the door and think there's going to be a freezer back there somewhere, but it's all fridge. The freezer was the next full-size stainless-steel door. And that refrigerator? Another three inches deep, it could have qualified as a walk-in. It held two shelves of bottled water, an entire door of condiments, and lots of take-out containers and orange juice.

Next assignment? God was with me—I found the corkscrew in the fifth drawer I opened.

Since the Shiraz needed to breathe, I uncorked the bottle, then opened the sliders and went out on the deck.

It was hot as hell out there, with no breeze whatsoever, but the sound of the water from the fountain was lovely, so

I leaned against the railing, trying to identify some of the plantings. The courtyard was brick, with ivy growing up the tall fence that ran across the back. There were lots of ferns and big-leafed hostas, their small white flowers hanging in the still air. Then I heard Jake's voice. I glanced up, and he was coming down the spiral staircase tucked in the corner of the deck. From his bedroom, I assumed. Or maybe just his dressing room.

He was barefoot, wearing Dockers and a linen shirt. He stood next to me, looking down at the courtyard. "Want a tour?"

"Sure."

We went back inside and he poured two glasses of wine, then showed me around.

The house was very narrow. We went down the stairs to the ground floor, which was all living room, with small windows facing the street, but a wall of glass opening to the courtyard. There were lots of neutrals, beiges and taupes, on long couches and deep chairs, and beautiful hunting prints on the walls. All very masculine and subtle, classy without screaming expensive. He grinned like a kid when he showed me the dumbwaiter.

"Is that the coolest thing ever?" he asked, and I had to agree. Next to the dumbwaiter there was a full wet bar, so you wouldn't have to spend too much time running up- and downstairs fixing drinks when entertaining the forty or so people who could easily fill the space.

The floor above the kitchen was the master suite: huge bedroom, equally huge bath, a book-lined office tucked in front, and a dressing room. Everything was, again, beautifully done, elegant without being showy. Finally, two guest suites on the top floor.

Now, I'd been in a lot of really great houses in the past thirty years. After all, I'd socialized with doctors and lawyers for most of my adult life. But this house was something else.

"Pretty amazing, Jake," I finally said when we were back in the kitchen. In the corner by the sliders was a polished round table with a leather wing chair and two wicker chairs. The perfect place for breakfast or dinner alone, but why would he need three chairs for breakfast? I didn't ask. But it was also the perfect place to sip wine and eat a little sharp cheddar.

"Yeah. I was very lucky to find it when I did. I'm putting the White Plains house up for sale. The taxes are killing me, and I'm never there anyway. This place is where I want to be right now. Jill was always about the Upper West Side. In fact, that's where she's living. But this is more me, don't you think?"

"If you say so. This super-CEO Jake is new to me, remember?"

He shook his head. "Not really. I'm still the quiet, humble guy I was back in the day."

I snorted. "Jake, you were never quiet and humble. You always had a pretty good opinion of yourself, and weren't afraid to tell other people about how great you were. I was the quiet and humble one."

He threw back his head and laughed. "God, Kate, you? Quiet? In what alternate universe were you ever quiet?"

I laughed, too. "Okay, well, maybe not quiet."

He poured us some more wine. "I can't get over your being Jeff Everett's mother. And then to find out he's the same Jeff who's Gabe's Jeff? Wow. What's the word? Serendipity?"

"Something like that. How do you like the wine?"

"It's good. Of course. Gabe has never steered me wrong. The man has excellent taste."

"Except in decorating for the mature crowd."

"What?"

"Never mind. Who decorated your place?"

"A woman I was seeing for a while. Right after Jill. She called herself the rebound woman, and warned me it wouldn't last. I didn't believe her, of course. I thought she was going to make me happy again, but after a year, I could see she was right. She was a great Band-Aid, though. After I bought this place, I ran into her at a fund-raiser, and she was just starting her decorating business. I gave her carte blanche, and this was her first big job. She had some trade magazine in here, doing a spread. She's pretty successful now. I was glad to help her out." He'd been staring out the window, and as I watched his face, I could see the sadness there, something I hadn't noticed before. He glanced over and caught me staring. We both smiled.

"How's the job hunt?"

I shrugged. "The main problem is, I don't know what I want to do. I just know I have to do something before I chew my foot off from boredom. I started volunteering at a center for homeless people down in Newark. Giving tax advice, believe it or not. Yesterday was my first day, and it was amazing. These were people who had nothing, but still wanted to make sure they had done everything possible to ensure the IRS wouldn't be mad at them. Complete opposite of what I had been doing. I had to really think about their problems, and the solutions, and had to be creative and flexible. It was great. Just the exercise I needed for my brain. If I could find a job like that, I'd be thrilled."

"Can you turn it into a paying position?"

I shook my head. "No. This guy is privately funded, and I'm sure he's on a shoestring. I'll find something." I glanced at my watch. If we were walking, we had to start now, and I wanted to walk. I wanted to wind my way slowly uptown with Jake, my arm casually in his, shoulders bumping. I wanted his head to lean down to mine as we spoke, to see the flash of his smile. "Are you ready to head out?"

He nodded and cleared the table while I went to the bathroom—of course—and when we hit the street, the air was cooler, so we walked, talking, and were only a few minutes late to Virgil's.

They were at a big corner table upstairs, and Jeff shook Jake's hand, then hugged me, whispering in my ear, "This is your college Jake? Who broke your heart?"

Oh, dear. That's right, he'd found out the whole Jake story. I nodded and gave him a very fake smile.

"Not a word, Jeff. No discussion of this situation whatsoever. Got it?"

He raised his eyebrows and threw up his hands, signaling defeat. I knew tomorrow he'd be calling me first thing, asking all sorts of questions and making several suggestions. But for tonight, I was going to enjoy the food and Jake and the knowledge that sometime in the next year, I'd be a grandmother.

We stayed a long time. Jake and I were the oldest people at the table, and the only straight people. We spent a lot of time laughing. We spent a lot of time drinking. He walked me to the Port Authority again, and when my bus pulled up he said, very casually, "So, next time, why don't I come over to Jersey?"

Next time?

I was so friggin' cool: "Sure."

I waved as I got on the bus, still cool.

Next time!

CHAPTER NINE

Friday morning, I had three texts in a row from Tom. *Missed you last night.*

Busy later?

How about a drink?

Can I tell you? Right then, I felt guilty. I had really wanted to make things work with Tom. I thought we had a future together. I'd thought that, given time, we'd be pretty good.

But Jake Windom wanted a next time. And I wanted a next time, too.

Alisa noticed me staring miserably at my cell phone, and sat beside me on the couch.

"What?"

"I'm starting to like Tom."

"Well, that's good."

"And even though he was pretty freaked out last weekend, I think he's starting to like me, too."

"I don't see why that's making you look so unhappy."

"Remember Jake?"

"Jake, the love of your life?"

I winced. "Yes. Well, we saw each other again last night. He's one of Gabe's best customers, and he was in the store yesterday, so I went to his place and had some wine, and then he came to dinner, and I had a great time."

"Your Jake knows Gabe? Oh, Kate, this is the world telling you something. Do not ignore this message."

I narrowed my eyes at her. "Excuse me, Miss Science Brain of America. But since when do you advise listening to the cosmos? I thought everything had to be backed up with at least a fragment of reality."

"Not when it comes to the heart, Kate. I mean it. Call Laura; she'll tell you the same thing."

"I know she will. The two of you are like dueling cupids buzzing around my head. What about Tom?"

She folded her hands on her lap and looked serious. "I don't think that Tom is quite right for you. I know I don't know him well, but observing you together, I sense a lack of spark."

"Oh, so when it comes to Tom, you're going to get all analytical on me?"

Sam shuffled into the living room, coffee mug in hand. "Are we talking about Tom? He's a real douche bag. Gotta get dressed. Later, Mom." And he shuffled out again.

Alisa looked at me, eyebrows raised. "Just remember how brilliant he is," she said, and followed him upstairs.

Jeff called and was completely annoying, telling me what a great guy Jake was, how funny and sophisticated, not to mention rich.

"You could forget about trying to find a job, Mom, and hang out all day in the Village with the rest of us."

"It's not that simple, Jeff."

"Sure it is. And if you moved into his place, you could see your grandbaby every single day."

That kid did not play fair.

I had lunch with Marie. She flagged me down when I was walking Boone, and insisted I come right on in. Her condo was one level, with a beautiful baby grand piano in the living room, and a tiny patio out back where we had BLTs on her homemade bread with her homegrown tomatoes that she started way back in March in her windowsill. She also had crisp white wine and fresh baked biscotti for dessert. What a great neighbor.

Tom and I had been texting back and forth, and had agreed to meet at six at the Dublin Pub. It was a little odd that he didn't offer to pick me up, but that was fine with me. We managed a table outside, on the side terrace, and ordered drinks. I was telling him about the Monet exhibit, because I really didn't want to talk too much about last night's dinner, but when our drinks came, he knocked back his scotch in one gulp and took my hand.

"Kate, can I talk for a minute?"

Oh, no. He looked so serious. What was I going to do if he said something about our relationship? What if he wanted to take it to "the next level"? I liked this man, and did not want to do anything to hurt his feelings, but what was I going to say?

I stared at my wine, wishing I'd ordered a martini. "Sure, Tom. Go ahead."

"I don't think this is working out very well."

"What?"

"You and I. I don't think it's going as well as I'd like."

What?

"Tom, we've known each other less than two months. What isn't going well for you?"

"You seem to have a lot of other, well, distractions in your life. You're always off somewhere, with your kids or friends. I don't feel that I'm getting as much, well, private time as I'd like."

"Private time?"

"Yes."

"Monday night, when I suggested pizza and TV, you were the one who was busy."

"Yes, well, that was work."

"Oh. So if I had a job, it would be different?"

He threw up his hands. "If you had a job, it would probably be impossible."

"Tom, I would think that, at our age, we would be more appreciative of each other's lives and commitments, and would not be so, well, high school about things like this."

He drew back. "This isn't 'high school' at all. If you're not willing to work on building our relationship, I don't see where we have much of a future."

Whoa. He was breaking up with me.

"You're a very lovely woman, Kate, but for some reason, we can't get on the same page when it comes to how much time we spend together. That's a real issue for me. So I think we should pull away now, before one of us gets too attached."

I stared at him. "Tom, why did we never have this conversation before?"

He frowned. "What do you mean?"

"I mean that maybe, if I had known this was a—what did you call it? Real issue? If I had known this was a real issue for you, we could have probably resolved it."

He shook his head sadly. "Honestly, Kate, if you don't know how to read the signs, I'm afraid this dating thing is not going to end well for you."

"Wow. How passive-aggressive of you." I drained my wineglass.

"Now, Kate, that's really not very fair, is it?"

"Fair? How old are you, and you still talk about fair? And now that I think about it, you made a habit of suggesting we get together when you knew I'd already had something going on. The nights I was sitting home with my thumb up my butt, you couldn't be bothered, but I tell you I've got plans, and suddenly you've got three different places we need to go. When I tell you I'm spending the night watching TV, you don't call, text, or anything. But if I'm out, there's this constant stream of vitally important information you've just got to share with me immediately.

"And another thing. Saturday night, I introduced you to my friends. My family. You've never once introduced me to any of your friends or family. In fact, you haven't even mentioned that you have any friends or family. What the hell is that all about?"

"Kate, I think I should go now."

"Tom, I think you should have gone four weeks ago."

He shook his head sadly and left.

Tom had just broken up with me.

I signaled for the waiter and ordered a martini, then I texted Laura.

Tom just dumped me. At Dublin Pub and can't drive home.

She immediately texted me back.

SO SORRY!! U must b so upset 2 not drive. B there ASAP.

Not upset. So angry I had a martini. Hurry.

I was almost done with my bacon cheeseburger when she arrived—medium, extra bacon, with fries and onion rings.

She sat across from me, where Tom had so recently sat as he gave me the heave-ho, and shook her head, her crutches leaning against the table.

"Where's Bobby?" I asked. "I'm sorry, I should have never texted you. I know you can't drive by yourself."

She waved her hand in the air. "The boys are with us. They're getting ice cream. Family night out." She shook her head. "The cheeseburger I get. But what is that? Vodka?"

"I know. This is the second time in as many weeks I've had to drink out of my comfort zone."

"What happened? Tell me quick, because I know that drink is going to make you completely stupid in the next five minutes."

I swallowed. "He had the nerve to tell me I wasn't spending enough 'private time' with him. What is that? 'Private time'? Were we supposed to be reading aloud to each other? Having more sex? Did he want me to sit at his feet and fondle his toes? What the hell is wrong with men?"

Laura listened patiently. "Kate, I'm very sorry that things didn't work out with Tom. I know you were hoping that the two of you could find your way to a bit of happiness, but obviously the man was a douche bag. You're lucky to be rid of him."

"That's what Sam said," I mumbled.

"What did Sam say?"

"That Tom was a douche bag."

"I didn't know they had met."

"Believe me, it wasn't planned. They met at the condo. Over morning coffee."

"Oh, God, and I missed it." She took my hand. "I am sorry."

I pushed away my plate. It was pretty well picked over. "Me too. He was a nice man, really. Just not for me."

"Excellent attitude. Maybe you won't get stupid after all."

"No, it's too late. Jake may be back in my life."

I told her the whole story—the drink at the Pierre, the pub, our meet-up last night. She didn't say anything, just sat as I babbled like a schoolgirl crushing on a football star.

"Well," she said at last.

"I know."

"It looks like I've been wrong all these years. It's not the drink that makes you stupid after all. It's just a recurring thing, like a virus."

"Why is Jake being back with me stupid? No, I mean it. I really need a good argument right now."

"Look, you know I want the two of you to live happily ever after. But I'm afraid if you pick up where you left off, he's the man who betrayed your trust, and you're the woman who spent years fantasizing about getting back with him."

"Not years," I muttered. "Well, maybe, but not a lot of years."

"So it seems like this has to become more about the present. And the future. Are you willing to try to build something from scratch?"

"If I thought we could end up in the same place, yes."

"The same place? You mean two sex-crazed college kids planning the next fifty years of their life? You're living in the past again." She grabbed both of my hands and shook them.

"Look at me," she ordered. I lifted my eyes from my empty plate.

"What do you want, Kate? From a relationship with Jake?"

I sat and thought for a moment. "I want to be with some-body who knows me, so I don't have to work so damn hard to live my life. Tom was a constant effort for me, and we still never got off the ground. Sure, I can try another man, and maybe after a few months things will work out. Or not, and I'll have to start again. I'm not sure I have the energy for all that. But Jake, he already knows me. Yes, I know, thirty years is a long time, and I know we've both changed, but the truth is, the spark is still there. And I'm not talking about sex. I'm talking about the connection we used to have, where we got each other's jokes and wanted the same things in life. Last night, I'd look over at him and know exactly what he was thinking. We were in our own secret, special club. I can't be wrong to want that again." I took a deep breath. "By the way, he broke up with the girlfriend."

"Then go for it."

"This is not just the vodka talking."

"I know. I can tell. If you think you've got a chance, Kate, you need to try, or you'll spend the next thirty years kicking yourself in the ass." She sighed. "I want you to try. And I'm really rooting for the two of you to make it work."

"So I'll go for it."

"You should. But maybe instead of picking up where you left off, you might try going back to square one. Maybe you could be two people who met on a website for the very first time and have to start from scratch."

"That might be a good idea."

"It is. I may be the little sister, but sometimes I get things right."

I didn't have a lot of time to think about Jake, because the next morning Laura called to tell me that our mother had fallen, was in the hospital, and had been there for the past five days.

"Five days? Why did it take so long for someone to call you?"

She had been crying. "Because when the ambulance picked her up, they took her to a smaller hospital, one she's never been to before, instead of the big county ER where they have all her records. She had hit her head and was so out of it, she couldn't give them my phone number. It's taken her this long to realize where she's been and what's happened to her."

My heart dropped into my bowels and I felt sick. "Out of it?"

"Yes. I haven't even spoken to her yet. I just got off the phone with the social worker. They will not let her go home. They don't think she's capable of living alone any longer."

"I'll be right over."

I drove the twenty minutes in a daze. If Mom couldn't live alone any longer, then we'd have to find her a nursing home up here. Her being half a day's drive away wasn't going to work anymore.

I ran through the front door. Laura was in her living room, her broken leg propped up on an ottoman, on the phone.

"Mom, yes, I know," she was saying.

I could barely hear my mother's voice on the other end of the line; I could just get a slight, rasping sound.

"Yes, Mom. But that's not what the doctor said, is it?"

Laura's eyes were welled up with tears, and she kept taking long, deep breaths.

"But, Mom, you can't do that anymore. They won't let you."

Laura shook her head at me, rolled her eyes, and made her "She's killing me" face, something she hadn't done since we were kids. I almost laughed.

"Mom, Kate is here now. Do you want to talk to her?"

Obviously, no.

"But, Mom, I told you. My leg is broken. I can't drive down."

Laura tightened her grip on the phone as she listened. "Mom, I have to hang up now. Kate and I have to figure this out. I'll call you tonight." And without hearing Mom's answer, she hung up.

"What the hell are we going to do?" she asked.

"We need to find her a place up here."

"True, but she has no money left, so that may be a little hard."

I was shocked. "What do you mean, no money left?" Back when I knew what was going on in my mother's life, there had been my father's insurance money and a veteran's benefit that had been put together into a very tidy nest egg for Mom. "Where did it go?"

"Down the toilet with the rest of the economy. She had it all in stocks and things. She lost it all in '08 along with everybody else."

"Is her house worth anything?"

Laura wiped her nose with the hem of her T-shirt. "Maybe. If we could sell it. Her little development down there just opened a new section, and the new units are going for over two hundred thousand, but her place is almost twenty years old and, let me tell you, all original décor. Who'd buy it?"

I got up, went to the bathroom, brought back a box of tissues, and watched silently as Laura blew her nose and cleared her throat a few times.

"Where's Bobby?"

"Golfing. He doesn't want her here. We don't have the room."

"Of course you don't. And you can't very well take care of her; you're on crutches. I'll go down and get her. She'll stay with me till we figure something else out."

Laura made a noise. "With you?"

I took a deep breath. "My basement is perfect. She won't have any steps. There's a big bathroom, and it's a warm, sunny space. I'll get a double bed down there, and a dresser, maybe set up a small fridge and microwave. Sam and Alisa can help me, I'm sure. She'll have a whole floor to herself. I'll send down food on Boone's back. We'll never have to see each other. It will be perfect."

"You're serious?"

"Laura, what else are we going to do? We've avoided thinking about this for years, but we can't pretend anymore. Mom has to be up here, and the most logical place is with me. So. I'll do a little shopping today, get my son to move some boxes, and get this ball rolling. When are they releasing her?"

"Monday. But they want her to spend at least three or four days in rehab, so she can get her strength back. There was no concussion, nothing physically wrong with her, except that she's old and needs somebody to look after her." Laura sighed. "This is going to be very interesting."

"Oh, yeah." I got up, went over, and gave her a kiss. "It'll be fine, really."

Oh my goodness. What had I gotten myself into now?

Alisa and I spent Sunday shopping, while Sam cleared out the rest of the boxes in the basement. Some of it was my stuff, some of it was his, but it was all put away in floor-to-ceiling shelves we had put up in the garage. I had two extra dressers from the old house that had belonged to Regan, along with some stray tables that had been scattered around that I had pushed into a corner and surrounded by boxes, so it was nice to discover them once Sam had cleared things out.

Monday a double bed was delivered, along with a love seat and recliner. I put together a kitchen cabinet thing, stocked it with a microwave and toaster oven, and put it next to the minifridge Regan found on sale at Home Depot.

It was a very good thing I didn't have to worry about scheduling any "private time" with a pesky boyfriend. I never would have gotten it all done. Besides, the lingering anger gave me a boost of adrenaline that really helped.

That afternoon Regan came over and helped me hang drapes to cover the sliding glass doors in Mom's new space. The patio off the basement was partially covered by the deck above, but plenty of sunlight managed to get through. Regan is very good at using the electric drill, and doesn't mind that I hate to use the level and always eyeball things, usually resulting in having to reposition the same piece of hardware four times.

She was all business until lunch. Then . . .

"How's Tom?"

She was being social, trying on the "We're adults and can be just friends" hat, instead of the "I'm your daughter and I can't believe you're dating" hat.

"We broke up. Well, not we. He broke it off. I pretty much just sat there in disbelief."

"What a creep. You deserve so much better. Sorry."

"Me too."

"Are you going back on that dating site, or are you going to take a breather?"

"I think I'm going to go out to dinner with my old friend Jake."

We were out on the deck, eating chicken salad sandwiches on pita bread. She swallowed before speaking.

"And how, exactly, did that come about?"

"I met him for a drink, and then I ran into him at Gabe's last week when I was there. Jake and Gabe have known each other since the shop opened. Quite a coincidence."

She looked at me, looked down, and then stared off at my potted palm. "This was the guy who was the love of your life?"

"My much younger life, yes."

"Oh. Because Edward asked about you."

I felt a little tingle of excitement. "Asked about me how?"

"If you were seeing anyone. I didn't think to mention Tom. Maybe I'm psychic. What should I tell him?"

"The truth. That I'm going out to dinner with an old friend."

A pause. "Um, Mom, why is there a pot plant growing around your palm tree?"

I followed her gaze. Sure enough, there it was, about eight inches high. "Oh, that's Cheryl's. She planted them right when I moved in."

"But that is a pot plant, right?"

I cleared my throat. "Yes, it is. I should probably harvest it before it gets any taller. Don't want the DEA copter to spot it on a flyby."

"Harvest? You're going to harvest it?"

"Regan, look at me. Are you shocked? You smoke. Or you used to. All three of you used to. I know because I could smell it on you. And I recognized the smell because I went to college in the seventies, when we all smoked. And I inhaled. All the time."

She shook her head. "Is that what you are going to do with it? Smoke it? That's just so high school."

"Lately, it seems like everything in my life is high school. But I don't think I'll be doing any smoking, really. I'm just so proud of myself for being able to grow it. Usually I have a black thumb."

"Well, the tomatoes look good."

"They're cherry tomatoes. And look, green peppers."

"And more pot. Honestly, Mom, you're not going to turn into one of those hippie-dippy types, are you?"

"No, honey, that ship has sailed. I can't even remember the words to 'Truckin'.'"

"What?"

"Never mind."

* * *

Wednesday I went down to Newark, had another exhausting, brain-bending day, and came home to a message from Jake asking when would be a good time for us to get together. He put a phone number in his e-mail, so rather than try to explain the situation with my mother via the written word, I called him.

"Jake, it's Kate."

"I'm so glad you called. I've had a lousy day. Say something to cheer me up."

"The Mets didn't lose last night?"

He laughed. "I'm a Yankees fan, but that was pretty good. How about dinner this weekend?"

So I told him about Mom.

"I know that things had never been easy between you when you were younger, and it sounds like it's gotten a lot worse," he said at last. "You're a good woman, Kate,"

"Maybe. Or I could just be a crazy woman. The thing is, I don't think leaving her alone at night is a good idea, at least not right away. So I was thinking about Sunday. Not dinner, but lunch. Maybe a picnic thing? Some green grass, find a lake somewhere? What do you think?"

"I think it sounds terrific. Call me again, though, on Saturday. If things get weird with your mom, we'll do it another time."

I didn't want to do it another time, but I appreciated the fact that he was being sensitive, so I said good night and tried to mentally prepare myself for driving down to Cape May the next morning and seeing my mother again.

For your information, there is no way to mentally prepare yourself for something like that. You just spend the night staring at the ceiling. And then you get up the next morning, drink too much coffee, and have to stop six times on the Garden State Parkway to pee.

But something happened that took away some of the doom of the morning. Just before I left, I got a phone call.

"Kate, it's Edward. Regan told me about the situation with your mother. I'm so sorry. This sounds like it's going to be a difficult stretch for you."

"Yes, it is, Edward."

"Listen, would you like me to drive down with you?"

I stared at the phone. "What?"

"It's a long drive, yes? Sometimes having someone in the car makes the time go faster."

"Edward, what an extraordinary offer. Thank you so much. But I'll be fine, really."

"Well, all right then. But please, if there's anything I can do, don't hesitate to ask."

"I won't. Thanks again." I hung up. I kept my smile all the way to Exit 82.

I had not seen my mother in eight years, although Laura had often shown me pictures. I was totally unprepared for Rose in the flesh. She was very thin, her thick gray hair pulled back tight against her scalp, and her face was pale and lined. She looked so much older than I'd expected that my jaw dropped open. I closed it slowly and walked into her room.

She was sitting beside the bed in a chair, her hands, clawlike, on the armrests, her eyes fixed on the television. Her jaw was still as strong as I remembered, even if the flesh around it was sagging.

"Hey, Mom."

She turned to look at me. Her eyes narrowed. "What the hell are you doing here?"

I forced a smile. "Good to see you, too, Mom. Didn't Laura call and tell you what's been happening? I'm here to take you home with me until we can figure out what comes next."

She snorted. "Going home with you? I don't think so."

I threw my purse on the bed. "Well, Mom, I'm sorry, but you don't have a choice."

Just then a very pleasant-looking woman breezed in. "Hello, Rose," she said. "I see your daughter is here. How lovely. We just have a few papers to sign, and off you can go."

My mother looked back at the television. "I'm not going home with her," she said, with some finality.

The woman turned to me and held out her hand. "I'm Gretchen Mars, the social worker here," she said as we shook hands. "Your mother has been quite a delight."

I grinned. "Yeah, that's Mom, all right. A delight."

Mom shot me a look. Gretchen shrugged. "Some of our residents adjust better than others," she conceded, "but considering the fact that your mother never wanted to be here in the first place, I think she did quite well."

"I didn't want to be here," Mom said, very loudly, "because there was no need. I just fell. People fall all the time. It was that quack in the hospital who sent me here, instead of sending me home where I belong, trying to get more money. Sure, I know Medicare pays for it, but that's no reason to put healthy people in places like this."

"Now, Rose," Gretchen said, "if you remember, the first few days you were here, you were very weak and could barely walk across the room."

"Why should I start walking marathons now? I get around my house just fine. You people and your obsession with exercise is insane. Old people sit; we don't sprint."

"You also had a few problems with remembering where you were," Gretchen said gently.

"That's what happens to a person when you put them in a strange place," Mom growled. "If you had let me go home, I'd have been fine."

"When I spoke to your daughter," Gretchen continued, foolishly thinking that she was speaking to a person you could actually argue with using logic, "she said you had been forgetting things for quite a while."

Mom shrugged. "Of course she'd say that. She hates me. Has for years. Just look at her; she's radiating evil as we speak."

Radiating evil?

"I meant your other daughter, Laura," Gretchen went on gamely. "Even Laura said you'd been having some problems."

Mom turned and fixed a cold eye on Gretchen. "Laura would never say anything against me."

Gretchen smiled brightly. "No one is against you, Rose. We all want what's best for you." She handed Mom a clipboard and pen. "Just sign at the bottom, and we can get you out of here."

Mom took the clipboard and stared at it. "I'm not signing anything without my lawyer looking at it first." She reached over to set it on the bed, then resumed her television watching.

Gretchen looked at me. "Somebody needs to sign the release," she explained. "It just says we're no longer responsible for her care."

I grabbed the clipboard and scribbled along the bottom.

Mom cackled. "There you go, putting your name to something that you haven't even read. I thought you were supposed to be so smart."

Gretchen grabbed the form gratefully. "It's a standard release, Rose. Saying that we are no longer responsible for your well-being, and that you will be going to a residence deemed safe and well monitored."

"I do not," my mother said loudly, "need to be monitored. I am quite capable of living by myself. I have for the past twenty-two years, ever since my youngest child moved out and left me alone."

"Mom, that was when Laura got married," I said.

She sniffed. "Whatever. I've been doing quite well without anyone's help for this long; I certainly don't need help now."

Gretchen grabbed Mom's hand and shook it. "It's been a pleasure, Rose. I'll send a wheelchair in to take you out to your daughter's car." To me, she rolled her eyes. "Bring your car up to the doors at the end of the hall. And, seriously, good luck."

I took a deep breath as Gretchen left. Then I reached over and grabbed the paper bag holding Mom's things. "I'll see you in the car," I told her.

I made it to my car and sat there for a few long moments, staring out the window. My mother had never been an easy woman, not even when she was young and happy with Dad. I remembered her being beautiful, and when she would get into one of her rages, where harsh words as well as pots, dishes, and furniture would be hurled around the house, my father would always hug me and whisper, "Lucky your mother is such a looker, or I'd have to trade her in for a quieter model." Then we would laugh together and wait for the storm to subside.

When he died, I know she was devastated, not only to lose her husband and number-one fan, but I'm sure she hated having to work, not to mention raising her children alone. I was fifteen then, and, like all teenagers, disliked her on principle. I spent a lot of years away from home during college and law school, and our times together were always short and not very sweet. We had done some mending of our relationship while I had been married to Adam, but by then her attention had moved to the kids. I felt like we never connected as two adults. The woman I had just left seemed like a total stranger.

I started the car and drove up to the double doors. Mom sat in her wheelchair, her purse clutched tightly to her chest, and I listened as the nurse read off a series of instructions; then she handed me a folder filled with notes. Mom sat heavily in the front seat and struggled with her seat belt. By the time I got around to the other side of the car, she was breathing heavily.

I looked at her. "You okay?"

She nodded. "Just catching my breath."

We drove in silence the twenty minutes from the rehabilitation center to Mom's development. I pulled into her parking spot and turned to her. "We need to decide what you want to bring up with you. You won't need lots of clothes, but we'll need other things, your checkbook, address book, things like that. Then we'll stop at the post office and have your mail forwarded. Do you know who was collecting your mail for you here?"

She was staring straight ahead. "Am I really going home with you?"

There was something in her voice that brought a rush of tears to my eyes. "Yes, Mom. I couldn't leave you down here by yourself. Laura and I talked about this. It's best. And we'll see about getting you into a place nearer to us. It's not going to work anymore, your living alone."

She unfastened her seat belt. "I'll need help with this car door," she said.

I got out, went around to her side, and opened the door. She grabbed my forearm and leaned against me as we went into the house.

She struggled for a few minutes with the key, then opened the front door. A blast of cold air hit me in the face.

"Mom, you left the air-conditioning on?"

"Of course," she said. "I was practically unconscious when they took me out of here, remember? I didn't think to tell them to shut it off."

Good point, Mom.

She made her way across the room, her hands going from tabletop to chair back, until she vanished into the bedroom. She reminded me of a spider, hunched over and moving slowly, but without the eight legs, of course.

I looked around. Her little house looked clean, but there were piles everywhere: stacks of magazines, newspapers, and opened mail. The air was very cold but stale. All her plants were dead, and some had been that way for a long time. The light was blinking on her phone, and there were dirty dishes in the sink. I looked in her refrigerator. It didn't smell too bad, but there were lots of plastic contain-ers. I opened one. It contained half an egg roll. I had forgot-ten that she had always been the leftover queen. I looked in a few of the cabinets. One box of crackers had a use-by date of October 2009.

I went into her bedroom. She was standing in front of her walk-in closet.

She turned to me. "My suitcase is up there. I need it on the bed."

Sure. No problem.

"Mom, while you're packing things, I'm going to clean out your refrigerator, okay?"

"Fine. My shopping bags are in the big drawer by the sink."

"Why would I need shopping bags?"

"To bring my food up to your house, of course."

"Mom, I'm not going to pack three eggs and leftover Chinese food and drive it all the way to Madison."

"You mean you'll just throw out perfectly good food?"

"I have food at my house, Mom."

"Well, maybe you have so much money that you can af-ford to waste it, but I don't."

I turned around and walked back to the kitchen.

I had three plastic garbage bags full by the time she came back out.

"What's all that?"

"Garbage."

"From my kitchen? That's not garbage, it's food."

"Mom, after two years, whether you want to or not, it's time to buy a new box of Cheerios."

She glared.

"Where are your garbage cans?"

"I don't know. I don't think I have any."

"Then how do you take out the garbage?"

"I can only carry a small bag at a time. I put them on the back porch and my neighbor takes them to the street for me."

I opened her back door, and, sure enough, there were half a dozen plastic shopping bags, tied neatly shut, each holding about four pieces of trash. I gathered them up and looked around. There, by the far corner of the house, were two large, faded garbage cans. I loaded both up and hauled them out to the curb. When I got back inside, Mom was at her dining room table, the overhead light on, going through stacks of paper.

"Are these your bills?" I asked.

"Why? Are you planning to throw them away, too?"

"No. Did you see your phone? It looks like you have messages."

She made her way over to the phone, and I went back into the bedroom. Her suitcase was packed full but wide-open on her bed. I took a look. She had packed about twenty pairs of underpants, one bra, a pajama bottom, and three wool sweaters.

I looked in her closet. She had obviously never thrown anything out. I recognized a black cocktail dress that she had bought for one of the Christmas parties Dad's work used to throw, back when she and my father would dress to the nines and go out for an evening, leaving Laura and me with a babysitter until two in the morning.

There were at least forty shoe boxes. I pulled one off the top of a pile and looked inside. A red-and-white spectator pump, probably from the fifties, size five, with the original tissue paper still crumpled in the toe.

What on earth was I going to do with all this stuff?

I found a few simple dresses, sandals, and slip-on sneakers, then went through her dresser. I pulled out pajama tops with matching bottoms, shorts, and neatly folded T-shirts, and a few more bras. Socks and a few light cardigans. I repacked her suitcase and took it out front.

She had a visitor. A handsome and healthy-looking gentleman was standing in her living room, bending down to listen as she whispered furiously in his ear. He caught my eye and made a small face, straightened up, and smiled.

"Why, Rose, is this your other daughter? Hello. I'm Fred, from across the street. Rose was just telling me about her plans."

My mother gave me a look that rivaled anything Medusa could have come up with.

"Nice to meet you, Fred. Yes, I'm Kate."

He nodded. "I was just telling Rose how much better she's looking. The week or so before her fall, her color was pretty bad." He put his arm around her shoulders and gave her a gentle squeeze. "Rose, I'm really happy you're going to be closer to your family now. We'll keep an eye on things; don't worry."

He kept that smile on his face and came over to me, picked up Mom's suitcase, and made for the door. "I'll help you put this in the car?"

"Sure," I said, and followed him outside.

"Your mother," he said as I opened the back of the Suburban, "is a real pistol."

"Yeah, I know."

"We tried to do more for her, but she's very independent."

"Or stubborn."

He chuckled. "Yes. So you're the evil daughter? I can't see the horns from here."

"No, they only come out at night. Thank you for looking after my mother."

"We've been neighbors a long time. She wasn't always like this. Ten years ago, when my wife was in the hospital for three months, she brought me a huge, hot dinner every Monday night. It would last me the whole week. Her heart has always been in the right place."

I took a deep breath. "I know."

"Will she be back, do you think?"

"Not to live. She can't be alone anymore. I'll bring her back to close the house as soon as we can talk her into it."

He patted me on the shoulder. "Good luck with that. Nice meeting you, Kate."

I went back into the house. My mother was seated at the dining room table, slowly rearranging her piles.

"Mom, we have to get to the post office before it closes. What else do you want to bring with you?"

She pointed to a battered recliner. I shook my head. "I bought you a new one. You can leave that here."

"But it's mine. It's comfortable."

"I'm sure the new one is, too. Besides, it's too heavy. I can't put it in the car without help."

"So why didn't you bring help?"

"Because, Mom, it's a three-hour drive down here. And it's a workday. Which means Bobby or Sam would have to take the day off to come down here with me. And I wasn't expecting to move furniture. I've got the clothes. There's your paperwork. What else?"

"My magazines? I always need something to read. Did you buy a new television, too? I can't miss *General Hospital.*"

I took out my cell phone and sent a text to Alisa to run out, buy a flat-screen, and make sure Sam had it ready to go when I came home.

Then I looked around at the magazines. "Which ones, Mom?"

"All of them."

"There are at least eight piles here. Haven't you read some of these already?"

"Yes, but I can't remember. Besides, I like to go back and cut out recipes."

"What do you mean, recipes? I didn't think you cooked." Her stove burners had been spotless, except for a thin layer of dust.

"I don't. Not anymore. But that doesn't mean I won't in the future."

"Mom, there isn't going to be a kitchen downstairs."

"Downstairs where?"

"You're going to be living in the basement of the condo."

"What condo?"

I closed my eyes. I had been sitting right across from Laura during the long, frustrating phone conversation she had had with Mom, where my sister went over, at least three times, all the details of where Mom would be living, for how long, and why.

"Mom, did you talk to Laura yesterday?"

She sniffed. "Of course I did. Laura is a good girl. She calls her mother every once in a while."

I clenched my jaw, then let it relax. "So, do you remember what you talked about? You know, my new condo, the space in the basement?"

"You want me to live in a basement? Are you crazy?"

I grabbed a stack of magazines and took them to the car. Then I took four more stacks. Then I grabbed several plastic shopping bags that Mom had scattered over the dining room table, each of them filled with three or four pieces of mail.

"Okay," I said at last. "We'll turn off the AC and lock up. Ready?"

"You can't turn off the AC," she said. "I can't breathe too good in the heat."

"You aren't going to be breathing here anymore, Mom. There's air-conditioning in the basement."

"Along with a lot of damp and mold, probably. But I don't want to come back to a hot house."

"You aren't coming back, Mom. Not for a while, anyway. Where's the thermostat?"

She pointed. I went over and turned it off. The house was suddenly silent. I did not realize how loud the hum of the AC had been. I looked at her.

"Ready?"

"No. But I know that doesn't make any difference, so let's go."

We stopped for gas. We stopped at the post office. We stopped at two rest stops. We exchanged perhaps twenty words in four hours. When we finally pulled up in front of the condo, she squinted into the dusk.

"Where the hell are we? This isn't your house."

The garage door opened, and there stood Bobby and Laura. Bobby ran to open Mom's door. Laura waved. I threw the car into park, shut off the engine, and leaned my head against the steering wheel.

"Kate?"

It was Alisa. She was standing outside the car door. I opened it and got out slowly.

"Sam and I will unpack the car. Why don't you just go on in?"

I nodded gratefully and went into my house. Eight was perched in her usual spot in the living room. I could see Seven slink downstairs, drawn by the sudden light and noise. I tried to remember—did my mother like cats? I went out onto the deck and sat down slowly. From there, I couldn't hear any voices, just a vague rumble of sound coming from downstairs. Boone came over, laid her head against my knee, and whined softly.

I scratched her ears.

My mother was home.

There was a pot roast in the oven. Laura had obviously been here for a while. It was after six, and I felt like the day had been three weeks long. I poured myself a glass of wine, and could hear laughter from downstairs. My mother's laughter. Laura and Bobby were working their magic. Then I heard Sam, and my mother exploded in laughter again. Good boy, Sam. Maybe this wouldn't be too dreadful after all.

Alisa came upstairs. I looked into my wineglass, not wanting to meet her eyes.

"I know what you're going to say," I said. "That she's a funny little old lady and what have I been so bent out of shape about for all these years?"

"Yes, she is a funny old lady. But I bet she's also a total bitch."

I looked up at her and broke into a laugh. "Alisa, you are by far the favorite of my children this week."

She smiled. "Laura wondered if we could bring down dinner. I guess she wants us all to eat together."

So I sliced the pot roast and arranged everything on a tray, while Alisa ran up and down a few times with plates, napkins, and wineglasses. I brought the tray of food down slowly.

The basement looked great. Alisa and Sam had fit their tiny dining table and two chairs into one corner. I noticed that the flat-screen television was not only on, but mounted to the wall on something that looked like it could swivel, making TV viewing possible from the love seat and the double bed tucked into the alcove. There were a bunch of daisies sitting on the refrigerator.

"Looks good, Mom. What do you think?" I said, setting the food on the table.

She shrugged. "I suppose."

"Now, Gram, you just said it looked like a suite at Disney World," Sam said.

"That was a great trip," Laura said. And it had been. Laura and I had taken Sam, then twelve, and her two sons, seven and five, along with Mom down to Orlando for a whole week. We had a blast. Even Sam, who kept complaining he was too old, had such a good time. That had been ten years ago, when my mother could walk the length of Epcot without having to stop once to catch her breath. Now I watched her as she put a small piece of meat on her plate and walked to the recliner. She put the plate down on the side table and lowered herself slowly, then sat back, her breath coming in short puffs. Her hand shook just slightly as she picked up the plate again.

"Is it as comfortable as your old one, Mom?" I asked.

She shrugged and chewed slowly.

Why was I so desperate to get any positive reaction from her? I knew better.

Bobby was talking with Sam about a project he was stuck on at work, and Laura and Alisa were discussing Regan's wedding. Mom ate, ignoring the talk around her, her eyes on the television. The pot roast was delicious. As I started clearing things up, I asked her if she wanted coffee or tea. She shook her head. The news was on.

"Well, Mom," Laura said, "I'm going upstairs, so I'll say good-bye now so I don't have to hobble down. Sleep good, okay?"

Mom waved her hand vaguely. The news was still on.

We all went upstairs and put things away in silence. Sam loaded the dishwasher. Alisa put leftovers in containers. Bobby took out the garbage. Laura and I sat side by side at the dining room table, just holding each other's hands.

"What are we going to do?" she asked me at last.

I shook my head. "I don't know. She can't stay here. Look at her. She hates it; she hates me; it's impossible. It shouldn't have to be. I mean, the room down there is perfect for her: plenty of space, I can cook for her, Sam and Alisa are here to keep an eye out, you're close. If she were any other mother in the world, we'd be set."

"I know. I'm so sorry, Kate, that she's still so mad at you. I'll never understand it. It was all so long ago." Bobby stood behind Laura, massaging her shoulders.

Alisa and Sam sat down with us.

"What did you two fight about in the first place?" Alisa asked.

"I told her I thought Adam had been cheating on me. She told me I was being paranoid, that I never appreciated him enough, and that I had always been looking for a reason to leave him. It wasn't true, I'd loved Adam and worked hard at our marriage, but she had really loved him, the son she never had." I glanced up at Bobby. "I think it was the fact that he was a doctor," I said. "She loved you, too, Bobby, I know that. But Adam represented something to her, I think. His own mother died when he was a kid, and he and Mom just really connected from the very beginning. She couldn't stand my being the least bit unhappy with him."

Laura shook her head sadly. "I'm sorry. I don't know what else to say. I will be over every day. The boys are home next week, and Devon can drive me over here. He's getting his license in October, and can use the practice."

"I can't deal with her. There is so much that has to be done—her house has to be emptied and sold, her things moved—but I cannot talk to her. Not about that. Not about anything, really. I mean, she can stay here as long as she needs to, but you'll have to deal with her, Laura. I can't do it."

I looked at Alisa. "The only commitment I have right now is on Wednesdays. Can you request not to work on Wednesdays? At least for the next few weeks? I don't want to leave her alone until I can get some idea what she's able to do and not do."

Alisa nodded. "Sure. I'm already off Wednesday this week, so there shouldn't be a problem."

"Okay. So, I guess I should be grateful I don't have a job, right? Although I do have a date this Sunday. Laura?"

"We'll pick her up and take her to our house, sure. But I thought you and Tom broke up?"

"It's with Jake," I said, trying to keep a straight face.

Laura smiled. "Well, well, well."

I just grinned.

Around eight thirty, I went back downstairs.

"Mom? Is there anything you need?"

She was sitting at the little table, her plastic shopping bags open, little piles of papers crowding the small tabletop.

"No. I'm fine."

"There's orange juice in the fridge, and a coffeemaker in the cabinet, along with coffee and sugar. What do you want for breakfast?"

"I usually have whole wheat toast and a little jelly."

"Good. I'll bring that down for you. What time are you usually up?"

"Well, I don't imagine I'll get much sleep. That bed looks all lumpy and not in very good shape."

"That bed is brand new and smooth as glass. What time?"

"It's pretty warm down here. I can't breathe in the heat."

"The thermostat is set at sixty-four down here, Mom. Just for you. I can almost see my breath. And I have the dehumidifier going as well. What time?"

"By nine."

"Okay, then. Good night."
She went back to her papers.
At the bottom of the stairs I stopped. I couldn't help it.
"Oh, and you're welcome."
She didn't even turn her head.

CHAPTER TEN

I made it through Saturday, because I knew I was seeing Jake on Sunday and did not want to be in jail for matricide when he came to pick me up. I had received a text from him late Saturday—just giving me a time and telling me to bring a bathing suit—but it was enough to spare my mother's life. Someday, if I ever spoke to her again, I'd tell her how much she owed him.

Regan appeared first thing Saturday morning with cheese Danish, Mom's favorite. She stayed downstairs for hours. They were talking about the wedding. I would occasionally pause by the top of the stairs and eavesdrop. Regan had brought her laptop, and they were working on designing the invitations. As much as I wanted to race down there and be part of the process, I knew that my presence would shut Mom down. So I waited it out until Regan came bouncing upstairs. She rolled her eyes at me and made a beeline for the deck. Once we were outside, the doors securely shut, she dropped into a chair and let out a string of expletives that would have done a dockworker proud. She finally let out a long breath. "Your mother is one tough son of a bitch."

I sighed. "Yes, I know. But I heard you laughing. I thought you were getting along."

"We were. We are. But she won't budge an inch on anything. I offered to buy her a cell phone, and she said no.
Period. When I told her that would save you from having
to put in another landline, she pretended not to hear me.
She also didn't hear my suggestions about going to the senior center here in town, joining water aerobics, or getting
a library card. Her selective hearing is phenomenal. But she
understood every single detail of the wedding. When I told
her I'd help her pick out a dress, she told me she couldn't
shop because she couldn't walk around. I said, 'Gram, we'll
just bring your walker.' She said, 'What walker?' I said, 'The
one right there in the corner.' She said, 'That's not mine;
I've never seen it before in my life.' What is wrong with that
woman?"

I tried not to laugh. "Regan, if I knew the answer to that
question, my life would be so much easier. So show me—
what did you decide for the invitations?"

Regan and Mom had done a pretty good job. I had
only four suggestions, all of which Regan vetoed. I asked
her, very casually, about Edward. Just curious. She said he
had driven up to Connecticut for the weekend to reconnect
with an old friend. Then she and I had tuna sandwiches on
the deck. She brought down lunch for Mom when we were
done, and stayed down there for another half hour before
heading out.

Sam and Alisa had spent the morning at the pool. Alisa,
I knew, swam laps, worked on her tan, and read paperback
romance novels. I had no idea what Sam did, as he always
came home dry and pasty-white. They picked up the dinner
shift with Mom, but were with her less than an hour. They
emerged looking beaten and battered.

My mother, Sam told me, did not like the cats. Or the dog. The room was too bright—could we find room-darkening drapes? She didn't like the sheets—were they really one hundred percent cotton? Because they felt very coarse. She needed a bigger table, because she didn't have enough space to spread out. Oh, and by the way? What kind of cable did I have that didn't carry the OWN network?

I had been down four or five times that day, just checking in, and every time I asked, she said everything was fine. Forty minutes with Sam, and there was a laundry list of crimes against the state. Really?"

I went downstairs again. "Mom, I've been down here a couple of times today. Why didn't you ask me about the cable? Or the sheets? Or a bigger table?"

She was changing the channel. She kept stabbing the remote with her index finger. "I didn't want to tell you because I didn't want you to think I was complaining too much."

"So you told Sam, and, what—thought he'd fix everything for you? This is my house, not his."

"Why in the world did you move into a tiny place like this? It's hardly big enough for three people. Let alone four."

"Well, when I bought it, it was more than big enough for one person, and I thought that's all who would be living here. I wasn't counting on Sam and Alisa. Or you."

"And what's with the cats?"

"I've always had cats."

"Your cable is pathetic, and this remote doesn't work."

"The cable I have is the only one available in this area. And that remote is exactly like the one you had for your TV. Stop jabbing it."

"The sunlight woke me up this morning. Can't you get different drapes?"

"Mom, did you close the drapes last night? Those drapes are fine."

"I need room-darkening."

"Did you close them?"

"If you don't have the money, I'll pay for them myself."

"*Mom!* Did you close the drapes before you went to bed?"

She finally looked from the television to me. "What has that got to do with anything?"

"Good night, Mom."

Then I went upstairs. Sam and Alisa were waiting for me in the kitchen.

"Well?" Alisa asked.

"I think I'm going to have to start drinking more."

Jake showed up at nine the next morning in a Mercedes convertible. He was dressed in white shorts and a bright Hawaiian-type shirt, with worn dock-sider shoes and no socks. His sunglasses probably cost more than my first car. He looked handsome and relaxed. He wouldn't tell me where we were going, but I would have followed him anywhere.

It's not easy having a conversation with someone in a convertible, going sixty miles an hour, but I managed to fill him in on Mom for the first twenty or so miles. Then I relaxed against the soft leather seat and tried to figure out where we were headed. We went north, into New York State, and after about an hour we went off the highway onto a quiet two-lane, then turned again onto a narrow drive that circled down and ended in front of a sprawling log cabin beside a silver-blue lake.

"Where are we?"

Jake grinned as he pulled a big wicker basket out of the trunk. "This place belongs to one of my vice presidents. He's going through a divorce right now, or he'd be up here himself with his kids. I've been here a couple of times, so when you mentioned a picnic and a lake, I thought of this place."

He opened the front door of the log cabin, which could have doubled as a movie set, and I could see the lake through a wall of glass. The place was gorgeous—high ceilings and comfortable leather furniture—but the star of the show was the clear blue water and white puffy clouds.

He gave me a quick tour, and of course I used the bathroom; then we walked out and across the grass to the dock, where a very sleek powerboat sat in the water, rocking gently.

He tossed the hamper on the deck, then held out a hand to help me climb in.

"Do you know how to drive one of these things?" I asked as I gingerly stepped on board.

"Yep. I've got one just like it down in my place in the Bahamas."

"You have a place in the Bahamas?"

"Sure. I'm one of the one percent, Kate. It's what we do."

"Really? You're really that rich?"

He nodded. "That was Jill's mission in life: to be rich. She never had the confidence to go out and do it on her own. That's why she was so involved in my career. In the end, she had earned almost as much of her own money, which is why, I think, she finally had the courage to leave me. She'd been unhappy for a long time. I think when she understood that she didn't need me to have the right house and the right car and the right vacation, she could finally let go." The boat was moving slowly away from the dock, the engine purring. Jake looked perfectly at home piloting the boat, one hand over the wheel, the other brushing his still-thick hair off his forehead.

"Are you happy?" I asked.

"I love my work, Kate. I didn't think I'd ever be that guy, the one who would rather be at the office than at home, but it's a challenge and a joy. Was I happy with Jill? Kind of. She was good for my career. That's why I married her in the first place, really. And because she was good at that, I was happy enough to be with her."

"That's the saddest thing I've ever heard," I said.

He looked surprised. "Is it? It doesn't feel sad to me. Maybe someday I'll look back with all kinds of regret, but not right now. I'm lonely, of course. That's why I ended up spending time with somebody like Sandra. But my life is good. I've got a bunch of money and can live anywhere and any way I'd like. I've got a foundation that does good things for hungry kids. I've got a job that keeps me sharp and moving forward. I enjoy food and wine and being on the water. And I get to impress my old girlfriend." He grinned. "Can't feel too sorry for me, can you?"

I had to laugh. "I guess not, Jake."

He turned the boat to the open water. I pulled off my T-shirt and sat in the sun in my bathing suit until I felt a tingle on my skin. I dug around in my tote bag until I found sunscreen, and started to slather it on. Jake, who'd been standing under a canvas canopy, saw what I was doing and cut the engine. He looked around. We were in the middle of the lake with no one in sight. He came to me and offered to do my back.

I turned, and his hands ran down the length of my spine. I felt a jolt all the way into my toes. His skin on mine had the same effect on me that it did thirty years ago. I kept facing away from him. If I looked at him now, I'd throw my arms around him, and that was the last thing in the world I wanted to do. Well, actually, it was the *only* thing I wanted to do. But the sane, logical part of my brain won out.

He handed me the bottle. I took it, bent forward, and made a very long production of putting it away.

When I stood up, the flash of lust had faded. He had started unpacking the big wicker basket he had brought on board. There was a cooler, and all sorts of things wrapped in yellow paper. Roast beef sandwiches on thick French bread. Sliced melon in a plastic container. Grapes and a wedge of pale, warm cheese. The cooler was full of bottles of hard cider. I was suddenly starving.

We sat in the sun, the boat moving gently up and down. We did not talk much at all. It was just like those Sunday afternoons when we were in college, when we would take a blanket to the park and lie out in the sun together, not talking, just feeling the hum of happiness bounce between us.

"Are you happy, Kate?" he asked at last.

"Yes. Very. Of course, my mother just moved in, and I feel that it's God's payback for my being so content for all those years. My kids are great. I have wonderful friends. I just found something to do with my brain. Regan's getting married. Jeff and Gabe are trying to have a baby. That's top-secret, by the way. Don't say anything to either of them, please. I'm lonely, too, but it's not as bad as I'd been imagining. I was seeing a man, just starting to get used to the idea of him. I really wanted to be happy with him. I thought if we worked at it, we could be a real couple. He just ended it. I'm more upset that he was the one to break it off than I am that it's actually over. But I'm really fine with it. I'm not dreading being alone again."

"You don't have to be, you know?"

"No?" I tried to keep my voice light, but my stomach suddenly knotted.

"Listen, you and I had a good thing going. Do you want to try to pick up where we left off?"

"No." The word was out of my mouth so fast, I shocked myself.

Jake looked pretty shocked, too. "I thought . . ." He looked out over the lake. "I guess it doesn't matter what I thought," he mumbled.

"Jake? Listen to me. Sitting here with you, I feel twenty-one again. But I'm not. I'm a very different person than I was back then. For one thing, I got my heart trampled by a man I loved more than anything else in the world, the man I trusted and thought I was going to spend the rest of my life with."

He was quiet for a really long time. I just sat back, sipping hard cider, watching his face. When he finally spoke, his voice was not quite steady.

"There hasn't been a day in the past thirty years I haven't thought about you, Kate. Even when I had convinced myself I was in love with Jill, and that she would do everything for me that you couldn't, that she could help me in my career the way you couldn't, I still would find myself thinking about you. I knew I'd lost you. I knew that I had betrayed you in the worst way possible, but I never stopped wondering about you. I am so sorry."

Okay—I was almost crying. I'll admit it. All the years that could have been flashed before my eyes like they never had before. But halfway through the vision of Jake and I spending our twenty-fifth anniversary on top of the Empire State Building, I stopped myself. If I had married Jake, I never would have had the three amazing kids I had right now. Maybe I would have three other amazing kids, but—seriously— the only possible combination for someone as terrific as Jeff or as independent as Regan or as brilliant as Sam was Adam and me.

"How would you feel," I finally asked him, "about starting all over again? Like we never knew each other before?"

He looked at me. Then he tilted his head and narrowed his eyes. "So, I couldn't suggest to you that we take the boat back and have sweaty 'Do we still have it?' sex on the dock?"

I kept my face pretty straight, considering that was exactly what I had been thinking. "No. And I'm not quite as easy as I was back then. You can't get me naked by waving a slice of pizza under my nose."

"Damn," he said. "There goes plan B."

"This particular phase of my life, the one where all my problems were supposed to have gone away and I was going to relax and be selfish about enjoying myself, is not exactly working out as planned. In fact, it's become more complicated than I could ever imagine. But once I've found a place for my mother to live, and Sam and Alisa find a place to live, and Regan is married, things should calm down. But until then, if you want to call me next week and ask me out to dinner, I will try to make time. What do you think?"

He leaned over and, very carefully, kissed me on the lips. "I think that's a great plan."

I stopped breathing. His eyes were so close and had that same little spark in them that used to make me crazy. Start over? Was I insane? Good old-fashioned horniness came rushing in so fast and so hard I practically had to jump out of the boat.

But I was strong. I was cool. I did not rip off any clothing. I did have to clear my throat. But just a little.

"It's a date."

He dropped me home right before six o'clock. I did not invite him in. My house was cool and quiet. Boone jumped off the couch to say hello as I walked in. Seven saw me, but chose to ignore. There was no background noise of the television downstairs, which I suddenly realized had been filling the house for the last few days.

I went downstairs.

Mom must have figured out about the drapes, because they were closed and everything was dark. The television had been left on after all, just muted. I turned it off and looked around.

Mom had unpacked every single thing we'd brought from her house. Someone must have helped her, because I couldn't imagine her emptying everything and putting it all away so quickly. There were magazines covering her dresser, the coffee table, and stacked on a pile by the love seat. The small round dining table had been replaced with a large folding table that jutted into the room, and it was covered with mail. The cabinet I had bought for the microwave had open shelves on top, and those shelves were now full of boxes of tea, five different cookies and crackers, and several cans of peaches.

I heard the sound of the garage door opener. My five minutes of peace and quiet were gone.

Mom came in from the garage, dressed in shorts and a T-shirt with a pink kitten face on it. Laura was right behind her. Bobby brought up the rear.

Mom ignored me and went straight into the bathroom. Laura slumped on her crutches. And glared at me.

"You'd better have had a really good time."

I nodded and kissed her cheek. "Yes. Thank you. Who bought all the food?"

Laura shrugged and sank into the love seat. "I think she sent Sam out early this morning. We brought in the table and I spent until lunchtime with her. Then Bobby picked us up, and we were at my house for the rest of the day. Our mother is a pain in the ass."

"I know."

Mom emerged, made her way to the recliner, and began groping for the remote.

"Have a good day?" I asked.

"Where were you since early this morning?" Her eyes were on the TV screen.

"I spent the day with Jake Windom. Remember him? My college boyfriend? I brought him home one Christmas."

"Isn't he the one who dumped you?"

"Why, yes, Mom. He is."

"Then what the hell are you doing with him again? You know what they say—insanity is doing the same thing over and over again and expecting a different result."

"You're probably right there, Mom, but we already know that I'm crazy. After all, I've been calling you up once a month for years, expecting you to talk to me instead of just hanging up."

"Exactly. He's going to do it all over again. Better get yourself a job quick, because you're going to need to bury your broken heart in something worthwhile."

I looked at Laura and went upstairs.

I took a shower and washed the coconut scent of sunblock off my skin. I slipped into a sleeveless linen dress, poured a huge glass of wine, and sat on the deck with the bottle and Boone until it was quite dark. Laura left at some point. I knew that Sam and Alisa were back from wherever, because the lights came on. But I sipped my wine alone, thinking about Cheryl and how she made the move from alcohol to pot.

I wasn't that bad.

Not yet, anyway.

The next morning, the phone company guy showed up to run a separate line for my mother downstairs. I then spent a great deal of time on the phone after that, disconnecting her phone in south Jersey, making sure the calls would be forwarded, and trying to convince her provider that she really didn't need cable anymore. Then I went downstairs and explained everything to Mom, giving her the new number, and telling her that if she wanted, she could call her friends and tell them about her move, and make sure they all knew how to get in touch with her now.

She scowled through my entire explanation.

"You disconnected my phone?"

"Yes, but anyone who tries to call you there will get redirected here. For the next thirty days."

"What happens on day thirty-one?"

"Well, hopefully, anyone who'd want to call you would have your new number by then."

"How would they get the new number?"

"You'd give it to them."

"How?"

"When they call you, Mom."

"But what if they don't call me?"

"Then you can call them."

"How will I know who to call? I don't know anybody's phone number."

"How did you call people before?"

"I had everything programmed into the speed dial on my phone."

"I thought you had your address book."

"I do. But that has addresses, not phone numbers."

"Then why didn't you tell me to bring your old phone with us when we were at your house?"

"Kate, I would have expected, at your age, that you'd be able to do a little thinking on your own."

"Grilled fish and wild rice for dinner?"

"Whatever."

I'd been spending mornings at the pool. If Alisa wasn't working, she'd come with me. We'd swim laps. She dove in the deep end and swam strongly, often going five or six lengths before coming out and lying in the sun. I tended to stay closer to the shallow end, and paddled back and forth across the shorter width, often treading water or stopping to chat with my fellow bathers. Then I, too, would stretch out in the sun.

When I told my mother that I'd be at the pool for a while, and asked whether she needed anything before I left, she fixed a cold, hard eye on me.

"What if I fall again?"

"Mom, you've been here for a few days, and I think you'll be okay for an hour or two."

"Then why the hell did you bring me all the way up here in the first place?"

"Would you feel better if I didn't leave you alone?"

"I'd feel better if you brought me back to my own house."

"That's not going to happen, Laura is trying to find you an assisted living place around here."

"I don't need any assistance, thank you very much."

"What if you fell again?"

"Why don't you go to the pool?"

"Good idea. I'll be back in an hour. If anything dire happens, call 911."

I went to the pool, paddled around, and watched the water aerobics class. There was a bunch of smiling ladies, all my mother's age, bobbing up and down. Would it be possible to get my mother into the pool with them? Probably not. But this was the same group of ladies who sat in the clubhouse every afternoon, sipping iced tea and playing something—cards? Mah-jongg? Whatever it was, it didn't look too stressful. And Marie often joined them. I might have an in.

I stopped at Marie's on my way home, declined her invitation for iced tea, cookies, and/or lunch, and explained the mother situation.

Marie took a deep breath. "It sounds like you and your mother are not on the best of terms."

"We're barely on the worst of terms. But she could be here a while, and I want her to do more than sit and watch television all day."

"Did you ask her if *she* wanted to do more than watch television all day?"

"No, Marie, but social isolation isn't good. I know that. There are studies. She needs to get back out in the world."

"Why don't I come over this afternoon? We can just chat."

"Perfect. Thank you so much."

When I brought down Mom's lunch, I told her about Marie, and that she'd be coming by to say hello.

"Why would she want to come over here?"

"Marie and I are neighbors. She's been over before. When I told her about you staying here, she thought she'd be nice and introduce herself."

"What's the point? You'll be shipping me out of here as soon as you find someplace to put me."

"The point is that you're going to be here for a while, and you might as well enjoy yourself. Marie and some of the other ladies here play cards together. You used to be a killer canasta player."

"I'm still a killer canasta player."

"Great to hear. And I'm not looking to 'ship you off,' Mom. You need to have a place to live."

"I already have a perfectly good place to live."

"You should be closer to Laura and me."

"So you keep saying. Your damn cat is trying to eat my sandwich. Don't you feed these animals?"

I scooped up Eight and went upstairs.

Marie came over later as promised. She came up after about an hour and asked if they could have some iced tea. I put some things on a tray and she took them down. There was laughter. Actual squeals of delight. Marie finally came back up with an empty tray and a big smile.

"Kate, your mother will be joining us poolside this evening for cards. I know you'll have to drive her over. About seven?"

"Marie, you're a wonder."

She took my hand and patted it gently. "Can I tell you how much I like Rose? I imagine she can be a complete terror, but she's also bright and lovely and great company. I think she'll do fine with the rest of us."

I was speechless, of course, so I just nodded.

At ten minutes to seven, I walked Mom out to the car and drove her the four blocks to the clubhouse. Luckily, there were no stairs, and she only had to stop twice. Marie and the other ladies had been there for a while, and they all had wineglasses in front of them and big smiles on their faces.

Marie took over. "Rose, welcome. They don't serve wine here, but they don't mind if we bring our own. I've got an extra glass. Let me introduce you." She turned to me. "Vivian here drove as well, so your mom has a ride home. Don't wait up."

I kissed my mother on her cheek. "Don't let them get you into trouble, Mom."

She actually smiled.

* * *

MaryJo's birthday was that Tuesday. I'd been calling my ex-roommate on her birthday for over thirty years. If I didn't call her, she'd immediately know that I had been in touch with Jake and was afraid to call her because she'd yell at me. If I did call her, she'd immediately ask if I'd been in touch with Jake, and she'd yell at me.

I thought about just changing my name and moving to Bolivia.

I was praying for the answering machine, but—"Happy birthday, MaryJo. Where are you going this year?" Every year for her birthday, MaryJo went away for a weekend to someplace amazing—usually a spa—where she would be steamed and massaged and wrapped in mud.

"I'm thinking New York. I've got reservations at a cute little boutique hotel around Gramercy Park and tickets to a Broadway show. Plus, I really need to go to the Museum of Natural History. Are you busy the weekend of the twenty-fifth?"

"Of course not! Oh, MaryJo! Finally, you're coming to see me? And in just two weeks! Did you run out of chichi New Age spas to visit?"

"There is always another chichi New Age spa to visit, but I thought I'd try a little culture and fun this year. I haven't seen you in six years, and you've been out here at least four times, so I figured it was my turn. Besides, I think we need to talk about Jake face-to-face."

Jake? Already with the Jake? Could I possibly bluff my way out of this? "What do we have to talk about?"

She sighed. Deep. Heartfelt. "Kate, how well do I know you?"

"Pretty well."

"Yes. Are you going to sit there and lie to me and tell me you have not had at least one serious conversation with that man?"

"No. We've had a conversation. Several, in fact."

"I know. I just hope you haven't done anything too stupid, like move in with him yet. But we'll talk about this when I get there. Can you make us preshow dinner reservations somewhere? For Saturday night?"

"Sure. How is everything else?"

"Fab. And you?"

"Regan's future father-in-law is here from England, and he's absolutely charming. And attractive. And he has a dry but terrific sense of humor."

"And?"

"And nothing. I'm just mentioning it, that's all."

"Hmmm."

"And my mother moved in."

"Oh, dear. Well, we'll talk about that, too."

"Oh, MaryJo, it will be so good to see you." And I meant it. I was so glad she was coming that I stopped thinking about her yelling at me.

Jake called. "Since we're starting from scratch, I think we should meet somewhere neutral for our date," he said.

"Oh? Did you read that somewhere?"

"Yes. Our dating site actually has guidelines, and it suggests a first meeting should be at a halfway point, preferably in broad daylight, for coffee. It also says that, depending on how things progress, we should pick someplace close enough to a good bar or restaurant, in case things go well and we want drinks and then dinner."

"Really? Guidelines?" I grinned happily. He was taking the idea of "first date" seriously. Pretty cute, Jake.

"Yes, and then, if dinner goes well, we should take separate cars to the nearest hotel, and whoever gets their clothes off last has to pay the bill."

I snorted. Also pretty cute. "Jake, I think you may have misread that part."

"No. I'm looking at it right now. Both parties should also bring their desired form of birth control."

"Well, I'll take your word for it. I'm feeling a little crazy with Mom here. How about next week? Monday? Hoboken? We can both take the train."

"True."

"And the place is loaded with coffee shops, bars, and restaurants."

"Sounds good. What about hotels?" His voice was a little teasing, a little hopeful.

"Jake, I thought your preoccupation with sex would have waned as you got older."

"Well, it hasn't, thank God."

I laughed. "Is this an appropriate conversation for two people who technically haven't even met yet?"

"Maybe not. Kate?"

"Yes?"

"I'm very glad we found each other again."

I felt a little squishy inside. "Me too."

Sam seemed a bit put off. "Mom, I was just getting used to Tom. Who is this guy again?"

"You were not used to Tom. You couldn't stand him. Jake is an old friend of mine. From college."

"Is he going to be showing up at the breakfast table, too?"

"Well, maybe, but not anytime soon. We're meeting in Hoboken next week."

"Good. So, you won't be sleeping with him."

"I won't be sleeping with him here, Sam."

He closed his eyes. "Mom. Please."

"Sorry."

CHAPTER ELEVEN

When I got back from my Newark adventure the next day, there was a message on the house phone—from the New Jersey Division of Youth and Family Services. According to the message, a complaint had been made against me, and would I please call the following phone number so that a social worker could come by and investigate?"

I had no idea what it was about, and when I called the number, the woman who answered was just taking the message. Would I be available tomorrow between ten and eleven? Was this the correct address? I was clueless, but said I'd be home. I went to bed wondering who thought I still had any children living with me, and what could they possibly be complaining about?

The next morning, at ten sixteen, the doorbell rang, and a rather pretty older woman introduced herself as Sonia Bing from DYFS. I invited her in, sat across from her at the dining room table, and took a deep breath.

"I have no idea why you're here," I told her. "I have no minor children living at home. My son is here with me, but he's over twenty-one."

Sonia went through her file. "The complaint is not concerning a child. The complaint comes from Mrs. Rose Freemont, who claims she is being kept here against her will in a single room in your basement, without so much as a stove to cook her own food."

I sat back and closed my mouth, which had, of course, dropped open. "My mother made the complaint?"

"Yes. Does she live with you?"

"Yes."

"Does she want to be here?"

"No, but—"

"Please. Answer the questions first. Then you can give your side of the story."

My side of the story? *My side?*

"Mrs. Freemont claims to be seventy-six years old and a widow. Is that correct?"

I gripped the seat of the dining room chair with both hands. "Yes."

"And, until recently, she was living in a senior community in Cape May County?"

"Yes."

"And she was taken, by you, from her home, and brought up here, even though she did not wish to move."

"Yes."

"How would you describe your relationship with your mother?"

Oh my God. I took a cleansing breath. "Strained."

"Oh? Can you give me an example?"

"Well, until I went down there two weeks ago, I hadn't spoken to her in over eight years."

Sonia sat back. "Really? Did you ever try to contact her on the phone?"

"Yes, as a matter of fact. I've called her the first Saturday of every month for, oh, about eight years."

"You called her?"

"Yes."

"What did you say?"

"'Hello, Mom.'"

"And then?"

"Then she'd hang up."

Sonia frowned. "You've called your mother once a month for eight years, and she hung up on you every time?"

"Mom is very big on routine."

She was still frowning, looking at her files again. "What about your sister, Laura?"

"Laura talks to Mom all the time. And visits her every couple of months. Laura broke her leg, which is why, when the hospital called, I had to be the one to go down and pick Mom up."

"What hospital?"

Apparently, Mom had been rather selective in her story-telling, so I gave Sonia the whole rundown. By the end, she was shaking her head.

"Well, obviously your mother needed to be placed somewhere safe, and I can understand that her presence here is only temporary, but I still need to see where she's staying. In a single room in a basement is not ideal."

I stood up. "No problem. Follow me. The Prisoner of Zenda awaits."

Sonia looked puzzled. Obviously not a fan of the classics.

Mom was sitting in her recliner, her feet up, watching television. The sunlight was streaming in through the sliding glass doors. The air was cool and smelled faintly of the roses that were sitting on the coffee table. Sam had brought them for her Saturday. She was drinking from a coffee mug, and I could see the steam rising faintly.

Sonia looked around, then at me, then rolled her eyes. "Mrs. Freemont?" she called.

Mom waved her hand. "I'm busy. Emeril's on."

Sonia crossed over and stood in front of the TV. "Mrs. Freemont, I'm from the state. The Division of Youth and Family Services. About your complaint."

Mom looked up, craned her neck to look back at me, then addressed Sonia. "Good. About time you showed up."

"Mrs. Freemont, you called us only two days ago."

"Well, it feels a lot longer when you're held against your will. I want to go home."

Sonia crouched down in front of her. "Mrs. Freemont, it doesn't appear that you were entirely honest in some of your statements. Is it true that the rehab center would not release you to go home alone?"

Mom sniffed. "They wanted me to stay there, charge me six hundred dollars a day to live in a tiny room and eat crappy food. I wasn't going to let them take any more of my money."

"But you had to live somewhere else, right? Is that what they said? Is your daughter trying to find you an assisted living place up here?"

"Well, she says she is. I don't know how hard she's trying. Why should she? She's got me trapped down here."

"In the dungeon," I said, trying to keep my voice steady.

"Exactly," Mom said.

Sonia shook her head. "Seriously, Mrs. Freemont, this may be one room, but it's bigger than my apartment. And brighter. With better carpet."

Mom wasn't going down without a fight. "I can't even cook for myself," she groused.

Sonia looked pointedly at the steaming cup and glanced around. "A microwave and a toaster oven?"

"And how am I supposed to roast a turkey in that little thing?"

Sonia looked at me. "I'll need the name and contact person at the hospital and the rehab center. I will need to confirm your story," she said to me. She shook Mom's hand. "Mrs. Freemont, I will finish up my investigation and send you a full report. But I think I can honestly say that, as of right now, I can find no proof of abuse, neglect, or intentional cruelty."

Mom glared, then turned back to the television.

I went back upstairs, found all the paperwork from the nursing home, and Sonia wrote everything down. Then she looked at me. "How is she doing?"

"I don't know. She shattered a mug in the microwave. We think she set the timer for thirty minutes instead of three. And she took a shower the other night, got out, got into bed, and left the water running. I had to go down and turn it off. I figure it was on at least two hours."

Sonia sighed. "Any luck finding her a place?"

"My sister is doing the looking. So far, it's tough. She'd be a Medicare bed, and those are hard to find."

Sonia took out her card and wrote down a few names. "Call these places. They're a bit off the beaten path, but I'd put my own mother in any of them. And I would certainly put your mother in one. As soon as is humanly possible."

I cracked a smile. "Thanks."

"I'll have to file my report, but I think you're safe."

"You mean you're not going to have to remove my mother from her current situation?"

"No."

"Damn."

Laura was not amused. "She called DYFS on you? You just had the phone installed Monday. It must have been her very first call. Is she crazy?"

"Laura, honestly, after all these years, how can you ask that question? The woman who came gave me the names of a few places. Can you check them out?" I rattled off the names. "Okay, I've gotta go. Oh, and by the way? Jake and I have a date next week."

"Again? Way to go, Kate."

"I know. I'm nervous. I'm trying hard not to have any expectations, but it's hard to forget about two years of perfect happiness, even if it was thirty years ago."

"Perfect happiness? Wow, that's pretty strong."

"Maybe. Later."

I'd spent lots of Friday nights alone. It had never bothered me. More recently, I wasn't spending any nights alone. Mom was around. So were Sam and Alisa. But Sam and Alisa were staying in on Friday night, and asked me why didn't I give somebody a call and get out of the house?

So I called Edward Pendergast. After all, he had been kind enough to offer to sit in a car with me for hours to get my mother. The least I could do was repay his kind thoughts. At least, that's what the logical side to my brain was saying. The other side just wanted his company, because he was charming and smart and had sparked a bit of something in me. He was back from the wilds of Greenwich, and would be happy to have dinner with me, as long as I didn't mind the restaurant in his hotel.

He was staying at the Westin in Morristown, a very classy hotel that just happened to have an amazing restaurant attached to it. I'd been to it a few times before. Not only was the food great, but going there meant getting dressed up just a little, and after one week of my mother, I really needed a distraction.

Edward looked so polished and suave that I was disappointed he didn't have a white silk scarf carelessly tossed around his neck. He drank gin, could raise just one eyebrow at a time, and for some reason, the waitstaff was falling over one another to cater to his every whim.

"So, you must be a great tipper," I finally said, "or have you decided to buy the hotel?"

He chuckled. I hadn't ever heard him actually laugh out loud. He was way too cool for that. "Maybe they know I'm a guest," he offered.

"No. I think it's the accent. When people hear a posh accent like yours, they automatically assume you're not only rich, but you probably know the queen. And anyone who knows the queen gets treated pretty well."

He shook his head. "I don't know Her Highness. And I don't think I'm all that rich. Most of my assets are not, as they say, fluid. And the way the economy in Europe is right now, I could be in the poorhouse next week."

"Does that bother you?"

He sipped gin. "I was married to Elaine for six years. It will take more than a major economic collapse to get me to break into a sweat."

"About that. How on earth did someone like you end up with Elaine?"

He shrugged. "I'd like to say I was under the influence of a complete mind-body takeover by a sadistic alien life force, but the truth is, she was beautiful. I hear she still is. I was a college senior, my parents kept telling me it was time to settle down, and she was right in front of me. And I must say, we were very happy in the beginning. And there's Philip, who is my joy. Of course, we were entirely unsuited for each other, but I didn't find that out until later. Let's face it, most twenty-two-year-old men tend to make a few mistakes at that age."

I thought of Jake and nodded. "I can vouch for that. Is there someone in your life right now? Over in England?"

"No. There was a lovely lady, but she passed away last year. Cancer."

"I'm so sorry, Edward."

"I should have married her. But once she found out how sick she was, she wouldn't let me. She said she wouldn't take a 'pity ring.' It wouldn't have been that, because I would have been very happy with her had she been my wife. How about you?"

"I've just reconnected with my former college sweetheart. It's been over thirty years. I can't tell if what I'm feeling is about being with him in the now, or remembering the then."

"That's a very tricky one. When do you think you'll decide?"

"Well, we've decided to start from scratch. We're going on our first official date next week."

"Ah, then it looks like I got a bit of a jump on him, then, doesn't it?"

I couldn't quite put my finger on what I felt right then, but it was kind of a tingle, kind of a rush of blood to the head. The same sort of thing that made me smile the very first time I saw him.

"Maybe you have," I said.

He smiled. "Do you feel like a walk? I found the most wonderful thing."

"Really? Here in Morristown? Lead the way."

We stopped in the parking lot so I could change my heels for canvas flats. Now, as we walked together, we were the same height. It was a cool night, and a full moon was starting to fill the sky.

"This is a fabulous neighborhood, by the way," he said.

I nodded in agreement. The houses here were older brick and Tudor-style homes set back from the road, all with wide lawns and swept sidewalks. In the bright moonlight, the street looked like something from a picture book.

"So, how did you find whatever we're going to see?" I asked.

"Just walking. But when I saw it, I immediately thought that, under a moonlit sky, it would be spectacular. I'm hoping I'm right, because I'd love to share it with you."

I smiled. "We're heading toward the Ford Mansion, you know. Where Washington stayed during the Revolution?"

"Yes. Quite the historic little town, this is. Plaques commemorating our defeat all over the place."

"I'm so glad you're being gracious about it."

The street was quiet except for the drone of crickets. A statue of Washington mounted on his horse stood in the middle of the road, and the moonlight was like a beacon on the black figure. I stopped and stared. Some trick of the shadows made the statue seem alive.

"Oh my. I've been by hundreds of times, even at night. It's amazing."

Edward bounced on the balls of his feet. "Isn't it? If you approach from this side, the artificial spotlight there isn't as obvious. But the real surprise is behind you."

I turned, and found myself looking at the Ford Mansion.

The mansion itself was a spare white colonial, two stories, shuttered, with three chimneys. I'd been through it with all my kids on various school trips, and had always admired its simplicity and grace. But tonight, it was bathed in moonlight, and the glass panes glinted, and the shadows from the trees danced across its wide, pale face. It looked enchanted.

"Edward, I never imagined it could look like this."

"I'm so glad you can appreciate it. I knew it would look like this, almost surreal. I'd love to paint it. Would I get in trouble, do you think, if I set up an easel on the front lawn?"

"You paint?"

He shrugged. "I dabble."

We stood there for a few minutes longer. A couple of cars drove by, and a police siren cut through the quiet as we turned to walk back to the hotel.

"Thank you," I said. "This was a real treat."

"The treat was mine. Even the smallest pleasures in life are so much more meaningful when you can share them with someone, don't you think?"

"Yes, I've always thought that."

"Ah, I knew we were kindred spirits." He glanced at me. "You do realize that there's something happening here, don't you?"

"Yes."

"What do you think we should do about it?"

I shook my head. "Oh, Edward. I have absolutely no idea."

I spent the entire weekend thinking about Jake and Edward. Edward knew about Jake. Should I tell Jake about Edward? Did I need to? Was it written in that dating guidebook somewhere that on a first official date, full disclosure was expected? By Monday morning, I decided that as appealing as Edward was, he was just visiting, and would be returning to England in a matter of months, and I should focus on the person who had a chance of maybe, just maybe, being in my life for the long haul.

Jake and I met at Arthur's.

"We're supposed to be having coffee first," he reminded me as we sat at the bar.

"I know. But I can't drink caffeine this late in the day. If I do, I'll be up all night, and I have trouble enough sleeping."

He had come over straight from work, and was in a beautifully cut suit that hid his thickened waist and made him look much younger. It was early, but there were a few women at the bar who turned to give him the once-over. He didn't appear to notice. He'd always been like that, completely unaware of his own good looks.

We ordered, a scotch for him and wine for me. "I have trouble sleeping most nights, too," he said. "I usually wake myself up snoring."

"I either have to pee, or a hot flash sets in and I have to stand in front of the open refrigerator."

He laughed. "Kate, how did we get old?"

I shook my head. "I don't know, Jake. I swear, I never saw it coming." I took a long sip of wine. "So, tell me about your company. What, exactly, do you do? I assume because you're on Wall Street you do banking or finance?"

"No. We're on Wall Street because the owner makes so much money, he can be wherever he wants. Nesco designs and manufactures marine navigational equipment."

"Do you mean marine as in boats, or marines as in G.I. Joe?"

"Boats, yachts, ocean liners, we cover it all. About twelve years ago, Steve Nessman patented a system so far ahead of the pack that his small private company exploded. He hired me to make sure he didn't drown in overexpansion. It was actually a fight, the first five years, to make sure we didn't grow too quickly. Steve went from offices and a plant in a warehouse in Teaneck to Wall Street and four manufacturing facilities across the country. I helped him get there. I know nothing about boats, except how to drive them. But I know how to manage a business. That, as they say, is why they pay me the big bucks."

"How big?"

"Last year I made twelve million, before bonuses."

"Dollars?"

He grinned. "Honestly, for a company with the assets that Nesco has, I'm incredibly underpaid. But Steve's a great guy to work for. He doesn't make much more than I do. All his employees are well paid with terrific benefits. The profits go right back into research and development. I have shares in the company, and complete access to any one of several properties in the world held by the corporation. So anytime I want to go to Paris or Bangkok or Rio, I've got a jet to take me there and a great place to crash. Besides, I'll be out of there in a few years, and Steve knows it, and I'll get a great package when I leave."

"It sounds like everything you always wanted."

He shrugged. "Almost."

"What do you mean? I remember very long recitations from you about how you were going to become a captain of industry, run an internationally known company, then retire early and spend the rest of your life signing dividend checks."

He laughed. "That's right, I did used to say that. But I guess I also assumed I'd have a wife and family to help me enjoy it. I didn't quite succeed with that part of it."

"True. So, why didn't you go with one of those matchmakers that specialize in the pretty rich?"

He laughed again. "I did. Right after Jill left. That's where I met all those women who were so intent on proving to me how great they were that they would never relax enough to have any fun. I just started the online thing a few years ago, and didn't really take it too seriously."

I had to ask. "And what was it about Sandra, exactly, that made you wave at her?"

He turned on the bar stool and looked into my eyes. "I'd just waved at you, and you didn't wave back. I didn't think it would matter to me. After all, you certainly didn't owe me anything. But still—somebody like Sandra is great for a bruised ego. She was young and beautiful, and I thought she'd fill in all the blank spaces in my life. It wasn't her fault her idea of a good time was nothing like mine. When I broke it off, she told me that she wasn't wife material, and if she'd known that was what I'd wanted, she never would have gone out with me in the first place." He shrugged. "And the thing is, I thought I was just looking for laughs. I didn't even realize that that was what I was looking for. A wife."

I was not expecting an answer like that. My throat was suddenly full and I had to think about breathing, because it took so much effort to keep looking into his eyes.

"And then we met. And I thought that maybe, just maybe, we could find some common ground again. So I told Sandra good-bye."

"Oh." Now the fullness was in my eyes, and I felt the tears starting to spill onto my cheeks. "Oh."

He handed me a cocktail napkin without a word, and I took it and held it against my eyes for what felt like an hour while I tried to rein in all the feelings that had suddenly come crashing down. When I took the napkin away, he was still sitting there, still looking at me, and apparently it had only been a minute or two, because he was still holding the same drink.

"I didn't mean to make you cry," he said, very quietly. There were tears in his eyes. "I never meant to make you cry."

"When you broke up with me, I cried for three days. Straight through. I even cried in my sleep. MaryJo almost called my mother. I felt the same way I did when Daddy died. It was such a loss." I sniffed. "And then I moved quickly into the betrayal and hatred phase, which was quite helpful for the healing process."

"Yes, I imagine it was," he said.

"We were so happy, Jake. How could you even look at someone else?" I blurted out the words. I didn't mean to. I had been feeling all along that he owed it to me to offer an explanation of what had happened so long ago. I didn't want to be the one to start that particular conversation. But after what he had just said, I needed to know.

He took a deep breath. "She kept telling me how great I was," he said softly. "She was smart, and had all these ideas about business and about management styles. We started out just talking about what she could do for me when I finally graduated. But after a few weeks, it stopped being about just my future career. It became about what we could do as a team. And it all sounded so real that it became the most important thing in my life. You were far away, Kate, and I missed you so badly, and Jill was right there, and everything she said seemed so possible."

He shook his head. "After a while, it was all I could see. This glorious future right there in front of me. And if I stuck with Jill, it would be so easy. I stopped thinking beyond that. I didn't want to think beyond that, I guess, because then I'd have to face what I was losing. And that would have been too hard to bear." He drained his drink and stared into the empty glass.

I had to clear my throat. Finally, a reason. Finally, I could stop racking my brain and playing out scenarios in my head. It had been so simple, really.

"Well. This is one hell of a way to start a first date."

He looked sheepish. "Yeah. Sorry about that. But you asked." He looked at me and smiled a little too brightly. "We could go backward a bit. I could tell you about how we're using satellites in improving the technology we're working on for submarines."

"And as fascinating as that sounds, no. I mean, it's okay." I finished my wine. "Why don't we walk? We can come back here for dinner if we don't stumble across someplace else."

So we walked around Hoboken, stopped at another bar, where we had another drink at an outside table. We talked. He told me he was leaving for Germany in a few days, and would be gone for a few weeks, but since our date seemed to be going so well, could we see each other when he got back?

Well, of course, Jake.

We watched people for a while before going back to Arthur's, because we both wanted steak, and then we went to the train station, and I got on the 9:23 back to Madison.

Alisa and Sam were still awake, and Alisa asked how the date went, but I waved her off and went into my bedroom. Boone jumped up on the bed, and I sat and scratched her ears for a very long time.

I kept running over Jake's words in my head. Boiled down to its barest bones, he had chosen his career over me. I knew it happened all the time. Adam had done it, although a doctor choosing his patients over his family sounds far less selfish than a businessman choosing power over love. It had really never been about me at all. It had been all about Jake. The little niggling that had been in the back of my head for thirty years, that maybe *I* had done something to drive him away, was finally put to rest. But knowing that didn't make sleep come any easier.

I called Regan in the morning. She and Phil had bought rings and booked the DJ. We talked wedding stuff for a while, and were trying to figure out how we were going to buy my mother a dress for the festivities if she couldn't walk through the mall.

"Mom, we really need to get Gram in a wheelchair."

"Honey, *you* get Gram in a wheelchair. I can't even get her to acknowledge her walker."

"But it would make her life so much easier. And she would be able to go outside and get some sun. I feel bad for her, holed up in the basement like that."

"Regan, in this humidity, being outside isn't possible for her. When it's cooler, maybe, but the thought of her wheeling down the sidewalks here is a little scary."

"We could get her one of those great big horns so she could warn people to get out of her way."

"Maybe I could ask the Widows' Mafia to work on her."

"The what?"

"Marie—you know, my neighbor across the street? She has a bunch of card-playing buddies that she calls the Widows' Mafia. They were all empty nesters who moved here with their husbands, and now they're alone. They call one another up every morning, just to make sure each of them made it through the night."

Regan made a noise. "And Gram is being drawn into the fold?"

"I hope so. She actually met with them last week and played cards. She even said she had a nice time. And even more amazing, she was invited back."

"Gram can be a real hoot when she wants to be."

"I know. I'm so happy wedding progress is being made."

"Me too. I can't wait for this to be over, though, so we can start planning for the baby."

"Jeff called you? Oh, thank God, now I can talk to you. I'm so excited. Isn't it just great?"

"Mom, believe me when I tell you I'm happier than you are about this whole thing, because now the pressure is off me."

"Regan, just a warning: The pressure will never be off."

"Perfect. So, we're seeing Edward tonight. Want to come over?"

"You're cooking?"

"Mom, don't sound so surprised. You know I like to cook."

I did know that. I was stalling for time. Did I want to see Edward again?

The short answer was yes. I really liked Edward. But I had just had a great evening with Jake. I had felt that old, familiar humming deep inside that I'd felt years before, when just being in the same room with him would make me happy.

"I'd love to. I'll have to see when Sam and Alisa get home. If they can stay with Mom, I'm all in."

What was I thinking?

I was thinking that Edward was so much like Jake—the same charm and smarts, the same easy laughter. Jake had an edge, and he was familiar and felt safe. Edward had softer corners, but was more of a mystery. And he had surprised me once, walking in the moonlight just to show me a two-hundred-and-fifty-year-old house. I was kind of looking forward to seeing what else he had in store. Even after the great evening before with Jake, I felt like I needed to blow off a little steam with Edward.

We hung up a few minutes later, and I spent the rest of the afternoon puttering around until Sam and Alisa came home. They were happy and excited, and had news of their own: Alisa would be going to France. She'd met with an ex-professor who had ties with the lab in France, and with one phone call he had arranged for her to fly over, all expenses paid, and work there until her classwork at Columbia started mid-October.

"I'm going to miss you," I said as I hugged her. And I would. Not only had she become excellent company, but what about my mother? Alisa had been home in the afternoons, allowing me time and freedom to do as I liked. Luckily, Laura would be off her crutches soon. She'd be able to pick up some of the slack. But the message was clear—I'd have to find a place for my mother, and soon.

Sam and Alisa said they'd cook hamburgers for Mom, so I drove over to Regan's for dinner. There was a strange car in front of their apartment, using up the one empty parking space, so I had to drive to practically the next county to find a spot for my car, then hike back to their place.

"When are you moving?" I groused as soon as I came through the door. "You two need your own driveway."

Phil clucked sympathetically. "Where did you end up parking?"

"Brooklyn. Hi, Edward." Why did just seeing this man make me smile?

He stood up and gave me a kiss on the cheek. "I'm sorry. Did I take your place in the car park? No worries. I'll drive you to your car when we leave."

Car park? God, I loved English word usage.

"No problem, but you need to talk these two into buying a nice house somewhere, setting down some roots."

Regan gave me her special look, the one that said, "Butt out." "Mom, you know we're saving. You know what kind of a down payment we're going to need. Unless you want us to move to Idaho, where we can buy a three-bedroom house for what a garage costs around here."

I took a glass of wine from Phil and shook my head. "No, I know. If you need any help, you could always ask."

Another special look. I drank wine.

Seeing Edward and Phil side by side was interesting. Edward was attractive, but Phil took after his mother in the looks department. Luckily, he took after Edward when it came to humor, patience, and charm. They were lovely together, close despite not being able to spend much time together.

"Edward," I said, "you should think about moving here. These two will be having babies soon, at least they'd better be thinking about it, and you'll be needed for grandpa duty."

He settled back on the couch next to me. We were finished with dinner, and Phil and Regan were in the kitchen, doing a quick cleanup. "I'd move in a heartbeat, Kate. Especially now that I've met you."

"Edward, you're making me blush," I said lightly. But inside, my blood really rushed around for a second.

He waved his hand. "And you're being coy. Sure, I could move, but that would involve selling all my business interests, and the way things are, I'd be selling them at a loss. I'm sure I'd still have enough to be very comfortable, but I do have a whole life I'm rather fond of over there." He looked at me, and when he smiled, the corners of his eyes crinkled.

"Besides, Elaine would be only three hours away by plane. That sort of proximity would make me very uncomfortable."

"We'd never tell her. Honest. She only gets out this way a couple of times each year. We'd all protect you, right, Phil?"

Phil had come in bearing a tray with coffee, cups, and a plate of cookies. "Right what?"

"If your father moved here, we'd keep him safe from Elaine."

Phil laughed as he poured coffee. "I've been trying to get him over here for years."

"I have a better idea," Edward said. "Why don't you move to England? You can all live in one of my apartment houses. Phil could help me run my business, Regan could certainly do exactly the same thing that's she's doing here, and since Elaine is terrified to fly over the ocean, we'd all be safe."

"And what would I do?" I asked.

"You, Kate, could dash about London, eating in expensive restaurants, going to the theater and the opera, whatever you want. I'd be happy to escort you, of course. And if by some chance you got bored, we could buy you a shop or something to keep you occupied."

Regan, coming in, laughed. "Forget it, Edward. Mom has just been told that her first grandchild is in the works. She's not leaving, even if she could live at the palace."

I looked at Edward. "Sorry," I said. "But it's by far the best offer I've had all week."

He made clucking sounds. "Then how are you and I going to live happily ever after? Long-distance relationships can work, but you here and me in London might be a special challenge."

I laughed. "Edward, I didn't know that you and I were working toward happily ever after."

He kissed me. Right there in front of Phil and Regan. It wasn't a long, deep, "Let's get naked" kind of a kiss, but I felt just a bit giddy.

"Maybe we should," he said, sitting back. "As I said before, I think we're getting off to a pretty good start, don't you?"

I stared at him. "You know what? I think we are." I was a little nervous, because I hadn't known him for very long. And let's face it, I had all sorts of Jake-thoughts crowding up my head. But Edward seemed full of . . . possibility.

Regan was stirring her coffee very intently, staring into its swirling depths as if the answer to all the questions in the universe were about to pop out. Phil was looking at his father with open-faced amusement.

"Dad," he said, "you are one smooth and subtle guy."

Edward waved a hand. "Kate here is being practical. I recognize the signs. She's seeing someone else already, trying to talk herself into thinking that she wants to be twenty again, and she doesn't want to be distracted by a rogue like me. Right, Kate?"

I thought hard for a minute. "Edward, being practical isn't all of it. I don't know you very well."

"True. But you like me and think that maybe, just maybe, I could offer you something unexpected. Right? I'm only here until the week after the wedding. Why don't we at least give it a fair shake?"

My first thought was—the man was a mind reader.

My second—Jake. Jake. Jake.

So why was I smiling? And why on earth was I thinking *Yes?*

* * *

Alisa gave her notice at the coffeehouse on Monday, packed on Tuesday, and Sam took her to the airport Wednesday morning. Since he wasn't going in to school, he agreed to stay home and watch Mom so I could go down to Newark. I told Dane the situation, that I didn't feel comfortable leaving my mother home alone for an entire day. I explained that until my sister's leg was out of the cast and she could drive over to stay with Mom, I wouldn't be back. He was understanding and sympathetic. I was upset about leaving Shadow People. So, of course, I called Cheryl.

"We need to go shopping," she said.

"I can't afford desperation buying. Besides, I don't need any more clothes."

"Then we'll go to Whole Foods."

"Oh, no. That's even worse."

"I'll pick you up in half an hour."

If you've never been to a Whole Foods grocery store, I'm sorry. Very sorry. They have food there that you have heard about, or maybe seen pictures of in a magazine, but never knew existed in the real world. The cheese department alone could bring tears to my eyes. Cheryl spent twenty minutes with the man behind the fish counter. Listening to them discuss shellfish was like watching a documentary on the Food Network. Then we spent ten minutes picking out cookies. By the time we were done with the produce department, we were so exhausted we couldn't bring ourselves to journey over to meats, so we checked out. I bought two hundred and forty-three dollars and eighteen cents' worth of food I didn't even know I needed.

And Cheryl wasn't even stoned.

"I never smoke when I drive," she explained when I asked. "Besides, Marco is coming over tonight. Late. After rehearsal."

"So, no more just one night a week? Good for you."

"I really like him, Kate, but he's getting on my last nerve. He really likes my breasts."

"Ah, Cheryl, that makes perfect sense. I mean, he is a man. What's the problem?"

"He spends an awful lot of time and attention on them. In bed, I mean. I think he thinks I like it. I used to, but seriously? At my age, only one erogenous zone works anymore, and time spent away from that is time wasted, as far as I'm concerned." She was stopped at a red light, so she could turn to me and give me a sly grin. "And how about you and Jake?"

"We had a great time. He's still one of the best people I know, honest and hardworking, and we're getting comfortable again, you know? Relaxed and happy with each other."

"When are you seeing him again?"

"When he gets back from Germany. We're going to take things slowly."

"Why on earth would you want to do that?"

"What am I supposed to do? Move in with him? We haven't been with each other in over thirty years. Some things have changed."

"You're so logical about things, Kate. You always were. It makes sense, I suppose, but wouldn't you like to throw caution to the wind and just enjoy spending time with the man?"

"I did that once, Cheryl. And he left me for another woman. We'd been living together, things had been great between us, and then he met someone else and, poof, we were done. And you know why? Because she was going to be better for his career."

"It happens all the time," she said.

"Yeah, well, it shouldn't."

"Should, shouldn't. What planet are you from again?"

"Besides," I said, then stopped.

"There's something else?"

"Yes. Phil's father is over from England."

"And?"

"And he's charming and funny. We had dinner together, and he walked me over to see the Ford Mansion, just because he wanted me to see it under a full moon. And it was absolutely beautiful. What kind of man does that? I was so impressed. There's a spark."

"Look at you, Kate Freemont, playing two men against each other."

"I am not," I said hotly, "playing them against each other. It's just that Edward thinks he deserves as much of a chance as Jake, and I can't argue with that."

"Are you sleeping with both of them?"

"God, no. I'm not sleeping with either of them."

"Well, that's very classy of you."

"Classy has nothing to do with it. I'm not comfortable double-dipping."

"So what are you going to do?"

"See Edward. See Jake. Try not to make an unholy mess of it. They're both very different men, but I like them both. A lot."

"Is this where I start singing 'Torn Between Two Lovers'?"

"If you do, I'll throw myself out of this car."

"Oh my God! Kate! Team Edward!"

"Cheryl, don't you dare. I mean it."

"And Team Ja—"

"Don't!"

She sighed. "You never let me have any fun."

She dropped me off, and I carried my bags into the kitchen, calling for Sam. He'd been downstairs with Mom.

"Are you going to be okay, baby?" I asked him as we unloaded the bags. "This thing with Alisa happened pretty quickly."

He shrugged. "I know. But it was such a great opportunity for her, I never thought to argue. Besides, it's only until October. I'll be fine." He had arranged some of the food I'd bought on the counter. "We can just heat this up, right?"

"Yes. That's why I bought it. I won't have to cook for the next couple of days."

"Can we all eat downstairs? Gram and I are watching *M*A*S*H* reruns."

Inside, I heaved a little sigh. "Sure, honey. Let's bring this down."

Mom and Sam sat side by side on the love seat, eating happily. Mom must have watched *M*A*S*H* for a long time, because she would say the lines along with the actors, making Sam laugh even harder. I sat back, ate my dinner, and watched them. My mother and I had never shared that kind of easy laughter. Even when I was a small child, she had never been completely relaxed around me, had never sat next to me on the couch, watching television, laughing, like she was doing with Sam. On one hand, I felt a twinge of jealousy. On the other hand, I was glad that Sam was so happy and comfortable with a woman who deserved an important place in his life, even as she remained a distant stranger to me.

CHAPTER TWELVE

MaryJo was arriving Friday, and had asked if I'd care to bunk with her in the city for the weekend. There was a flurry of activity as I made arrangements. Sam would be home most of the weekend. Laura could take Mom all day Sunday again. Regan was not on call at her clinic, and could fill in Friday evening until Sam came home from Columbia. I felt like I was running away from home, my little overnight bag packed, bus ticket in hand.

Her flight was delayed, so I sat in the tiny lobby of her hotel and thought a little bit about how my life was going. Still no job? Check. Still no permanent place for Mom? Check. Still hadn't joined the health club? Check. Hmmm . . . maybe I should focus on the things I *had* done. I'd found Jake. That was good. And I'd found Edward.

How did things manage to get so complicated so quickly?

I must have been thinking things over pretty intently, because I was suddenly jolted by a voice beside me.

"Oh, honey, you must be in one of those 'How's my life going?' modes. I'd recognize that look anywhere."

I stood up and hugged MaryJo for a long time. She had put on weight, and she was heavier than I'd ever seen her. Her hair was much shorter, but still age-defying blond, and her smile was the same despite the laugh lines and age spots.

"MaryJo, you're still a knockout."

"Oh, I know. I'm just knocking out a whole different class of men these days. But you—my God, have you even gained a pound?"

"No. Sorry. But look at these wrinkles. Do they make you feel better?"

"Maybe. But I've got those, too. Let me get us checked in so we can get some food and drink a little something. I need it."

The room was fine—two double beds and a view of the alley—but we wouldn't be spending much time there. We walked to a little bistro I'd found online and had steak frites and crêpes for dessert; then we sat in a small bar and listened to jazz and drank wine until they closed.

"This is way past my bedtime," MaryJo said.

"Mine too. But this is your birthday weekend. We haven't celebrated it together in a long time. We need to splurge."

In the morning, we had breakfast, then walked all the way uptown to the Museum of Natural History, had lunch, then meandered back to Midtown to wait for the play to start. Afterward, we bought a couple of bottles of wine. Mary-Jo wanted something stronger, of course, but I talked her out of her usual bourbon. We splurged on a cab back after the show. By midnight we were slightly drunk and giggling in our beds, having talked most of the day and night away.

I had told her all about Jake. Then I told her all about Edward. Then I sat there and looked at her. "Well?"

She gave me a very stern look and poured more wine into her glass. "Kate, you are a grown woman. What you choose to do with your own life is your own business. I know that when it comes to you and matters of the heart, logic doesn't stand a chance." She shook her head and sighed. "You are in a very interesting situation here, girlfriend. Where would you like me to start?"

"Jake?"

"Fine. Are the two of you happy?"

"Yes. Right now, right this minute, I am."

"But?"

"But what am I going to do about my mother? And Sam and Alisa? And I need a job. I mean, the kids will be okay. Sam is dependent on me right now, but not all that much, and I know that he'd be fine without my help. But my life is not where I want it to be, not if I want to think about a future with Jake."

"It seems to me that you thought out a very detailed future with Jake when you were both unemployed dumbasses who couldn't balance one checkbook between you." MaryJo glared. "And wasn't his mother sick at the time, cancer? And didn't you want your baby sister to come out and live with you? Not to mention you were going to go to law school without any idea how you were going to pay for it, all the while saving money to buy a mountaintop somewhere so the two of you could play Mr. and Mrs. Grizzly Adams." She shook her head. "There's never a time when your life is going to be where you want it to be. Has getting older taught you nothing? At least that younger, stupid version of yourself knew to grab for the good stuff before it's all gone."

"So you're saying I should really try to make a go of things with Jake?"

"Do not even try to put words in my mouth."

"So, what about Edward?"

"I don't know, Kate. What about Edward? He is the real clean slate. There's no history there, good or bad. There are no expectations, no memories. He's either the scarier choice, or the safer choice. All this with you and Jake is fine and wonderful and would make a great romance novel, but how does it play in the real world? Will you ever really trust him again?"

"I do trust him."

"And you've forgotten all about how he made you sick with pain and heartache?"

"No. I'll never forget that."

"Has Edward done anything you'll never forget?"

"You're no help to me here, MaryJo."

"That was never my job." She looked into her wineglass before taking another sip. "Enough about these silly boys. I am sorry about you and your mama. Old people get like that, hard and stuck in their ways. But you'll find a place for her to be safe, and that's the best you can do. We all think there will be happy resolutions at the end of our lives, but the truth is, she'll be the one dying without making peace. You've done all you could. Remember that."

"Thanks for that. You'll be out again for the wedding, right?"

"Of course. But do you still want me to stay with you? When we first talked about this, you didn't have your mother living with you, and I was going to camp out in the basement."

"Shit. You're right."

"I'll be happy to find a hotel."

"But I really wanted you to stay with me." I was thinking furiously. Where could MaryJo sleep? With Mom? With me?

"Wait. I have a blow-up bed. We could stash you in the den. Or you could bunk with me."

"Let's count on the den. By then, somebody else may be bunking with you."

"Good. Regan only let me invite six point two people. I hope you appreciate how valuable that invitation is."

"Yes. I believe I got a rather long e-mail from you about all that. You called your daughter a what?"

"I can't remember. I may have referenced a few heartless dictators. She is a girl who knows exactly what she wants."

"And whose fault is that?"

"Oh, shut up, MaryJo. I have to sleep now."

"Yes, me too."

"And nobody is going to be bunking with me anytime soon."

"Famous last words."

"Good night, MaryJo."

That Sunday evening, Marie came over to see Mom. She asked if they could have a couple of glasses of wine, took them downstairs, and soon the television was off and they were laughing. Mom had changed in one respect in the past few weeks—she had welcomed someone new into her life. She had never been one to make friends easily, and I thanked God for Marie.

On the way out, Marie found me on the deck and sat down. "Kate, I hope you don't think I'm interfering, but when Dane came by this weekend, he told me about your situation. I mean, now that Alisa is gone. I'd be more than happy to have Rose stay with me on Wednesdays, so you can continue to go down and help Dane until your sister can drive again."

I looked at her. "Really?"

She smiled gently. "I don't know what's going on between you two, and I don't care. Everyone at poker night thinks Rose is a real find. I so much enjoy her company. It would not be an imposition at all. And I know my son thinks very highly of you and the work you're doing with those people, so I'd be doing it as much for him."

"Did you ask her?"

Marie nodded. "Yes. She thinks it's fine. She also thinks that it's completely ridiculous that she has to be with you at all, but that's another conversation."

I smiled gratefully. "Oh, Marie, thank you."

"Good. It's settled. I'll call Dane tomorrow. And Wednesday morning, I'll come by and get Rose. I've already told her she'll need her walker, because I can't take half an hour to cross the street."

"Regan wants us to try to get her in a wheelchair. We need to find her a dress for the wedding, and that would involve a shopping expedition."

Marie frowned. "Please, Kate. I can only do one thing at a time. Don't start getting pushy."

I bit back a smile. "Sorry, Marie. You're right. One thing at a time."

"You need to call the post office," my mother said.

"Why? You seem to be getting your mail just fine."

"No, I'm not. I'm not getting any of my catalogs."

"Oh. Well, the post office only forwards first-class mail. That's why."

"So how will I get all my catalogs?"

"You won't."

"But how can I see what I need to buy without them?"

"Mom, if you need anything, tell me. I'll get it for you."

"That's not the point," she said impatiently. "I like to look through my catalogs. I get ideas. Sometimes I'll see something that I didn't know I needed."

"But you showed me your checkbook. You really don't have a lot of money for buying things you didn't know you needed."

"What about Christmas? I do all my Christmas shopping from catalogs."

"I'll come down with the laptop and you can shop on-line. It's the same thing."

"But I can't send a check online."

"You use your credit card."

"I'm not going to give a stranger my credit card number. Then anybody could use it."

"Mom, Laura told me about how many times someone has taken money from your account because they had your checking account number. Using your card online is safer than sending checks in the mail."

"No, it's not. And besides, I don't know how to use a computer."

"It's not that hard. All your friends here have computers. If you learned how to use one, you could go on Facebook, chat with them, do all sorts of things."

"And just when do you think I'll have time to spend playing around with all that stuff?"

"You sit down here all day and watch TV."

"Exactly. Because I don't have my catalogs to read."

Oh, Mom.

I had a really good time with Edward.

He picked me up right after Sam got home, and we went into Morristown. He'd made reservations at Roots, which was very trendy, and although it had been open for a couple of years and dinner cost a pretty penny, it was almost impossible to just walk in and get a table, even during the week, because the food was that good. We were early, so we had wine in a little bar where everyone was younger than we were, but we sat outside and watched people go by and had a great time. Dinner was delicious, and we spent the whole time talking about English tax law versus American tax law. Not the titillating conversation I was expecting, but once we got started, it was hard to stop. He was smart. Very smart. And he thought about things the same way I did, and looked at things from the same perspective. By the time we were done, I felt like my brain had run a marathon, and won.

As we walked by the bar again, we peeked in. There was a live band in the corner, playing an old Bee Gees cover, with a few couples on the dance floor.

"Let's go," he said, pulling me in.

"Where?"

"Here. Dancing. Do you like to dance?"

"Yes, but, Edward, look around. We're the oldest people in the room."

"Who cares?" He was grinning. "Come on; let's show them how it's done."

I had not spent much of the disco era strutting my stuff, because Jake had been a terrible dancer, and we never had the money to go to the nicer clubs. Most places we'd hung out in had a jukebox that catered to the Willie Nelson crowd. But I'd always kind of liked the music, and I had always loved to dance. Edward must have been the "Night Fever" king, because boy, he had some smooth moves. The band, once they realized we were practically a floor show, played one seventies hit after another. Pretty soon, there were so many people dancing that we kept getting pushed into a corner. I finally gave up and collapsed against the wall, sweaty and hot and out of breath.

"Edward, I am way too old for this."

"Nonsense. We were spectacular. Look at everyone out there, gyrating like fools. We've inspired an entire generation. Because of us, the glittery disco ball will be making a comeback."

"God, I hope not."

He was leaning against the wall right next to me, smiling. He'd worn a linen sports jacket over his polo shirt to dinner, and the lapel had turned up. I reached out to smooth it down, and he turned to me and leaned in, very close.

"I'm going to kiss you."

"Why do you think you have to give me a warning?"

"Because of Jake. I know you're still involved with him. I don't want to make things too complicated for you. I want to give you the chance to tell me not to."

"I think it's too late for that." I kissed him.

And then I kissed him again.

* * *

The next morning, Jake called me from Kennedy.

"Can you meet me in the city?"

"Oh, Jake, Sam already left for school, he won't be home till late. I can't leave Mom. Can you come out here?"

He made a noise. "No way. I've got meetings all day."

"How was Germany without me?" I teased.

"Lonely," he said. "How was the U.S. without me?"

Oops. Maybe I shouldn't have started this. "I had dinner with Regan and Phil. And Phil's dad, Edward. And I showed Edward a bit of Morristown." There, I didn't have to lie.

"Good. At least only one of us sat around, mooning. I'll call you when I can."

Wednesday morning I watched as my mother walked over to Marie's at what seemed to me to be breakneck speed. Hands firmly on the walker, she crossed the street, swung over onto the sidewalk, and finished the final twenty feet of Marie's walkway before going through the front door. Marie, who had stayed by her side, turned back and gave me the thumbs-up. Victory.

Jake had called again that morning, saying he could come into Newark and have lunch with me. When I told him the address, he started to laugh.

"Kate, life is a very funny thing. I'll see you around one."

When I got to Shadow People, I asked Dane if he knew Jake Windom. Dane broke into his beautiful grin.

"Jake? Of course. His company, Nesco, contributes about one-eighth of our yearly budget. The owner, Steve, is very interested in the homeless situation, and gives a lot of time and money to different organizations, including mine. Steve is on our board of directors, and he drops by every few months to sort out clothes. How do you know Jake?"

I gave Dane the abbreviated version of Jake and me. "He's coming by today to have lunch with me, and he knows you and this place already. Dane, do you believe in fate?"

He nodded. "Absolutely. I believe the path of each life is carefully laid out before us."

"But what about all that 'free will' stuff? I mean, don't you think we're in charge of our own lives?"

He looked shocked. "Of course we are, Kate. Our life may be planned for us, but we are wholly responsible for how that life is lived. Are you going to be angry or bitter when something bad happens, or are you going to be strong and make the best of a bad situation? When you accomplish something great, will you take all the blessings for yourself, or share them with those who helped you along the way? When a great gift is given, do you embrace and rejoice in that gift, or look for the strings you think are attached?" He spread his arms wide. "I see, every day, people who choose to live their lives with acceptance and gratitude. They are the happiest of God's creatures, even if they are the shadow people that most of society never sees. I also see the evil and hatred. That is also a choice. But never the right one." He smiled. "What is this about? Are you wondering if Jake is your fate?"

"Yes. I guess I am. It certainly seems that way. But how can you tell?"

"This could be one of those gifts, Kate. When a love is given to you, take it. Do not look too hard for a way out, because you can always find it. Rejoice in a good man."

"He is a good man." So was Edward. Why would his face come to me now?

"Yes." Dane patted my hand. "And you are a very good woman. If I could find the money, would you think about working here full-time?"

"Giving tax advice?"

He shook his head. "You are also an accountant, which we very much need. Right now I'm managing our funds, but I'm not very good at it, and it takes me a lot of time. If you could help with some of the office work, do the books, and keep the grant money coming, it would be a tremendous help. And since all my administrative people spend two days on the floor, you could still counsel and advise."

"I can't do anything until my mother is settled."

"Yes. But if I apply for funding now, it will take a few months, at least. I'm looking forward."

"I haven't done any accounting since college."

Dane grinned. "But you'll have plenty of time to brush up on your addition and subtraction skills. Will you think about it?"

I nodded. "Yes. I will."

Jake came by around eleven. When I saw him, my whole body kind of went squishy. He hugged me for a long time, and gave me a very good kiss. The man I had been talking to about what he was going to say to the IRS about his five-years-late payment watched with some interest. Then Jake wandered off to talk to Dane until lunchtime.

Dane, Jake, and I ate tacos in the sun. Jake and Dane, being practically old friends, talked sports. I sat and leaned slightly against Jake, grateful for his company. I was so glad to see him. But I had to tell him about Edward.

I walked him to his car and gave him a long kiss.

"I need to talk to you," I said.

"Sounds serious."

I nodded. "I think it is."

He opened the back door. "Get in. We can take a drive."

The inside of the Town Car was cool and dark, with one of those glass partitions between the front and back seats. Jake told the driver to head toward Weequahic Park, and closed the glass.

"What's up?"

"Phil's father is here. From England."

Jake nodded. "You told me about him."

"And I've been spending some time with him." I had been looking at Jake, making myself look right into his eyes, even though it was harder than I thought.

He nodded again, a little slower this time. "Okay. You told me that, too."

"And I kissed him."

Jake took a deep breath. He was still nodding. He was still looking at me. "I see."

"I'm a little confused right now, Jake. I'm not exactly sure what's going on with me."

"Kate, listen to me, okay?"

"I'm listening."

"I never stopped loving you. More than that, I never stopped being in love with you. It took me about ten minutes with you for everything to come rushing back. But I know that it's been a long time, and that we're different people now. I never expected you to feel the same way." He made a face. "Hoped, maybe, but didn't really expect. You don't owe me anything."

I swallowed hard. "It's not that I don't trust you, Jake, because I do. At least, I think I do. But whatever is going on has nothing to do with that." I swallowed hard again, and tried to figure out where the tears were coming from. "I don't want to hurt you."

"I know," he said gently. He reached over and pulled a few tissues out of nowhere to give to me.

"Why is it that you're always handing me tissues?"

"I don't know, because I really never mean to make you cry."

"I know." I sat and sniffed for a few minutes. "Listen, why don't you come over this weekend."

"I'd love to. I'd like to see your mother again, actually."

"How odd. And you could meet Sam, although he may be going somewhere for the weekend, now that I think about it. It's Labor Day. Wow, the summer is over already. I feel like I should be buying school supplies."

"We could do that Saturday. Pencils and crayons?"

I smiled. The crisis was over, just like that. We were back into a happy, familiar rhythm. "Pink backpacks. I'm sorry you never had kids."

"Sometimes I am, too. We could go back up to the lake."

"Could we? I loved that house. And the boat. That would be perfect."

"He's selling it. Rather than split it in the divorce, they're splitting the profit."

"What a shame. Does that mean you won't be able to go up there anymore?"

"That means if you like it, I could buy it."

"Just like that? You'd buy a million-dollar house?"

"I'd wait until the White Plains house is sold."

"Are you trying to bribe me?"

He laughed. "Hey, if that's what it takes."

"Must be nice being that rich."

"It's great. Is that a plan, then?"

"Yes." I leaned over and kissed him gently. "I need time, Jake. Please give me time."

"As much as you need."

"I'll call you."

When I got home I walked over to Marie's to pick up Mom. Marie let me in, and I was surprised to find something of a crowd. I recognized a few of the card-playing crew, but also some younger, unfamiliar faces. They were standing around Marie's dining room table, and all looked up and waved as I came in.

"We're organizing the Saturday potluck," Marie explained. "We get a very good turnout if the weather's nice. Were you planning on stopping by?"

I'd seen the flyer at the pool. I shook my head. "No, thanks, Marie. I've made plans."

She nodded. "That's fine. But Rose wants to go. In fact, she says she's very good at planning this sort of thing. And she wants to make deviled eggs."

My mother had been an outstanding cook, and I remembered her deviled eggs. They were delicious, the yolks fluffy and smooth, with a hint of sweetness.

Mom looked up. "I'll need at least four dozen eggs. Can you get them for me?"

"Sure, Mom. Ready to go?"

She shook her head. "No, not yet. I'll be home a little later."

"By yourself?"

A redhead in cutoffs looked up. "Don't worry. One of us will walk with her."

Well, all righty then. Apparently, my mother was acquiring minions.

I went home, took a shower, poured myself some wine, and started looking around for something for dinner. Sam came down and said hi, pulled a Coke from the fridge, and sat expectantly at the breakfast bar.

"Can I help you?" I asked him.

"Do you know you've got half a dozen marijuana plants growing on the deck?"

"Sam, of course I know. I just keep forgetting they're there. They blend in pretty well with the cherry tomato plants. Are they getting too big, do you think? "

"Mom, why are you growing pot? Does Gram have glaucoma or something?"

"No, Gram does not have glaucoma. It's because Cheryl had the seeds, and it seemed like a good idea at the time. You going to be around this weekend?"

"Tim has friends who are doing a thing on Long Island on Saturday, so I was going to stay at his place Friday night and go with him, and then I figured I'd go to Aunt Laura's Sunday." My sister always had a huge cookout the Sunday of Labor Day weekend. "Is that okay? Will that work with Gram?" he asked.

"Your grandmother is making her own plans these days, and she's already booked for Saturday. I was going to ask Jake to Laura's. Are you okay with that?"

"If I weren't, would it matter? Besides, Alisa told me this guy might turn out to be the one who sticks."

"She's a smart girl. She may be right. I miss her."

"Me too. Skype is fine, but it's not quite the same as curling up on the couch and going over the day, you know?"

"Yes. I do know."

Somebody called hello from downstairs, so I hurried down. Mom was in her recliner. The redhead was there, looking concerned.

"Hi, Kate. She's out of breath, she says. Doesn't she have oxygen?"

I shook my head. "She's been very resistant to that idea."

The redhead frowned. "I'm Lauren Mitchell. I'm a nurse. She really should have oxygen."

I raised my voice. "Hear that, Mom? Lauren says you need oxygen."

My mother waved a hand. "I'll catch my breath in a minute. I always do. Why should I pay for oxygen to sit here month after month if I might never use it?"

"Rose, you could use it every day. Even just moving around down here would be so much easier for you," Lauren said.

My mother had found the remote and turned on the TV. Loudly.

Lauren sighed. "I work with lots of older people. They hate admitting they need the help."

"Yeah."

"It was good meeting you, Kate. Your mom is a real character."

"Good meeting you, too. Thanks for walking her home."

I let Lauren out and went over to Mom.

"Burgers on the grill okay for dinner?"

She nodded. The news was on.

"What else do you need for your eggs?"

She hit the mute button. "Sweet gherkins. Lots of mayo and Dijon mustard. I'll make a little list tomorrow. And I'm also going to help Marie with her meatballs, so it looks like I'll be sleeping over there Friday night."

"Sleeping over?"

"Yes. It would just be easier than getting up early and going over. You know I'm a little slower in the mornings. And if you want, you can ask one of your boyfriends to stay over."

I maintained a straight face. "Thanks, Mom, but nobody's staying over."

She glared at me. "Are you ever going to reintroduce me to Jake?"

"I'm bringing him to Laura's. He'll meet the whole family."

"What about that other man, Edward? After all, he's going to be part of the family pretty soon, no matter what happens between you two."

"I'm not seeing Edward this weekend. He's going up to Canada to see some friends. It's just Jake."

"Jake was pretty good-looking when he was young."

"He still is, Mom."

"Well, that's good. 'Cause you're a beautiful woman, Kate. I know that you didn't think you were pretty enough for him. And back then, maybe you weren't. But you've gotten better-looking with age. Some women do. Your face suits you now. It's the face you've always deserved."

I was shocked. "Thanks, Mom," I managed.

"Too bad you're so flat chested. You get that from your father's side of the family. His mother looked like a diving board. If you'd been lucky, you'd have taken after me more. If you had a body like mine at your age, you'd have more than just two men knocking on your door."

"Right. I'll bring down the burgers in a bit."

"Well-done. I don't eat pink meat."

"I know, Mom."

Jake came over early Saturday morning, and we drove back up to New York and enjoyed another day on the lake. We spent a long time walking through the log cabin. It was beautiful.

"It's not quite a cabin in Colorado," Jake said, "but it's already built, and it would be an easier commute. I'd keep the town house, of course, but this is perfect for the weekends."

"Yes." In my head, I was redecorating. The great room needed brightening up, the master bath was a gut job, and all the antler chandeliers had to go. He was behind me, and he came close, wrapped his arms around me, and brought his head over my shoulder. We stood there for a few minutes. I could feel the pounding of his heart against my back, and the heat of him came through my clothes. His breath was warm against my neck, and he kissed my ear. Thirty years ago, I would have turned to him and drawn him down onto the leather couch, peeling his clothes off slowly before easing myself onto him.

But my head wasn't ready for that yet, as much as my body might have been. I wasn't going to make love to Jake, not with Edward crowding in so close in my head. Besides, this was someone else's house, and leather was cold, uncomfortable, and would have made funny noises against bare skin.

"If you buy this house, we need to get rid of all the leather furniture," I said.

"Why?"

"I hope I can tell you someday."

* * *

The house was empty when we got home. The potluck was still going strong. I felt a little guilty sending Jake home, knowing he'd be driving back the next morning, but he was sweet and good-natured about the whole thing.

I'd given Mom the remote control for the garage so she could get in and out by herself. I also figured it would be an early warning system, letting me know when she got back. I did not hear the garage open until late, almost eleven. I had been reading in bed, but got up when I heard it and went downstairs.

"Hey, Mom, this is pretty late for you. You must have had a good time."

She looked tired, and her breath was short. She was in the recliner. She nodded and held up a finger. "Wait."

I sat, and when she caught her breath, she actually smiled. "It's nice to be around people again. When I first moved down to Cape May, I knew everybody. But all my friends died off or went to nursing homes. The new people didn't want to be bothered with a crabby old lady, so most of them left me alone. But the folks here are pretty nice."

"Mom, I think you've probably got more friends here than I do. I know Marie, and a few people from walking the dog and hanging out at the pool, but I would never be asked to help plan a potluck."

"You'd never want to. You were never that kind of woman. You've got sunburn on your cheeks."

"I know."

"Got sunburn on your other cheeks?"

"No, Mom. Outdoor sex is not on the agenda at my age."

"He's coming to Laura's?"

"Yes."

"Good. I'll see him then."

"Okay. Good night, Mom."

Jake was there so early the next morning that he brought down my mother's tray. I sat at the breakfast bar and waited, my eyes closed, hoping for the best. When he came back up, he was grinning.

"What?"

"She wants me to drive her to the cookout. She says she's never been in a Mercedes before. And she wants the top down."

"Do you mind?"

"No. I was going to take my car anyway. I have to head straight back to the city this afternoon. There's a lot going on next week."

The front door crashed open and Boone got all excited. Sam was home. He came into the kitchen with his usual bounce, grinning.

"Great car," he said to Jake, holding out his hand. "I'm Sam."

Jake shook his hand. "Thanks. Jake Windom."

Sam nodded and turned to me. "What time?"

"We'll leave here around noon. I still have potato salad and brownies to make."

"Cool. Need help?"

"Oh, how sweet." I looked at Jake.

"I could use an hour or two at my computer," he said. "If it's okay."

"Jake, you were always a major distraction in the kitch-
en. Sam here can at least boil potatoes and knows how to cut
things."

Jake gave me a quick kiss and went off into the den. Sam
brought his duffel bag upstairs, and when he came back
down, we boiled potatoes, chopped celery and hard-boiled
eggs, and baked two batches of brownies from scratch. He
talked nonstop. He'd had a great time in Long Island, and
mentioned someone named Vin six times before I realized Vin was Vincenza, a young woman who had apparently
made a big impression on my son.

"Who is she again?"

"Tim's sister's roommate. She's down on Wall Street.
Usually I find those businesspeople pretty boring, but she
was pretty cool. Big online gamer, you know?"

"No. I haven't a clue. Your grandmother wants to go
over with Jake, so it will just be you and me. Got your swim-
suit?"

"Yep. Jake seems nice."

"You didn't even talk to him."

"Yeah, but what a great car."

"And that makes him nice?"

Sam shrugged. "I'll put this stuff in the car."

Jake followed me to Laura's. My sister lived in an old
farmhouse with an in-ground pool and a yard big enough
for the boys to play regulation soccer, which they did pretty
much every day. Luckily, the weather was perfect: hot, but
no humidity, and a breeze. That meant Mom could sit out
on the screened porch and not have to huddle in the air-
conditioned house.

Jake helped her around to the back of the house. I looked for any visible signs of harassment, but he was all smiles. So was she.

"What did you talk about?" I asked.

"Alfred Hitchcock."

"What?"

"She's a fan. So am I."

"That's it?"

He shrugged. "What were you expecting?"

Anything but Alfred Hitchcock.

Laura had been told she could walk on her ankle again, and had been to physical therapy a few times, so she was getting around pretty well. She gave Jake a big hug and introduced him to everyone. Jeff and Gabe were already there; so was Bobby's sister and her husband and three boys. Devon had his arm draped around a pretty little girl named Brianne who looked twelve years old. Wade was in the pool with his cousins. Sam changed into his suit and joined them. I went into the house to help Laura, leaving Jake talking wine versus beer with Bobby and Gabe.

Jeff followed me into the kitchen. "Jake spend the night?" he asked.

"No."

"Why not?" He looked indignant.

"Really, Jeff? Sam went crazy because I was having sex, and you're acting bent out of shape because I'm not." I cleared my throat. "It's getting complicated."

"How is it getting complicated? I thought this guy was the one, with a capital O."

"I've been spending some time with somebody else."

Laura looked up. "What? Wait a minute. A few weeks ago you told me you and Jake were starting all over. Where did another man come from?"

"England. Phil's dad."

"Awkward," Jeff muttered.

"No, it's not. Each of them knows about the other, and let's face it, I'm not sixteen. I'm not going 'steady.' I'm a grown woman who's examining all her options."

"You make it sound perfectly civilized," Jeff said.

"It is. We're all grown-ups here." I looked around. "It's fine."

Laura was pouring homemade marinade over chicken. "Kate, I hope it all works out for you; I really do."

"Me too," said Jeff. "But I'm rooting for Jake. Nothing against Edward—Regan says he's a perfectly nice man—but if we're looking to add value to the family, Jake is a better bet. He doesn't have any kids of his own, does he? He really needs a family to leave all that money to."

"Jeff, don't be crude," I scolded.

Regan came in and gave me a kiss. "Jeff is always crude. Who was he talking about this time?"

"Jake," I said. "He's out back."

Regan looked out the window. "The tall guy? And Gram's here? How did that go over?"

"They bonded over Alfred Hitchcock," I told her. "Who knew?"

"Mom, didn't you go out with Edward a few times?"

"Yes, I did. But we didn't sign any vows of undying loyalty, so I'm still seeing Jake as well."

"You go, Mom. You're really taking this whole dating thing to heart, aren't you?" Regan said.

"Don't be fresh. Listen, did you order a cake?"

"From Swiss Chalet in Morristown."

"And what about music for the church?"

Regan gave me a look. "Mom. It's covered. We have only one possible disaster looming."

"What?"

Phil answered. "My mother is coming into town two weeks before the wedding. She's staying at the Westin. The Governor Morris."

"That's where Edward is staying," I said.

Laura finished chewing a bit of melon from Regan's salad. "That's bad?"

Regan rolled her eyes as Phil nodded. "Very," he said. "You don't know my mother very well, but she can be a total raving bitch. And she hasn't spoken to my father in twenty years."

Jeff sighed happily. "I so love a little drama at weddings."

Regan stuck her tongue out at him. "Well, if this gets too dramatic, Phil and I will just cancel."

"No, you will not," I said sternly.

Laura shook her head. "Why did your parents divorce, Phil?"

He shrugged. "Because my mother is a total raving bitch?"

"No, really," Laura chided.

"No," I said. "Really."

"Mom," Regan said. "You bait her."

"*Moi?* Never."

"Wait till she finds out that you and Edward are, were, well, whatever," Regan said, looking a little worried.

"Oh my. I hadn't thought of that. Well, we just won't mention it, will we?" I said, glaring around the room. "Like, ever."

Jake came in the back door. "Bobby sent me in to break up the kitchen party and move everyone outside."

Laura laughed. "Good idea."

"Jake," I said, "this is my daughter, Regan, and her husband-to-be, Phil."

Jake shook hands. "Good to meet you both. Kate has been filling me in on the wedding details."

"I'm sure she has," Regan said. "And I'm sure she's been very open and honest about her feelings about the situation."

"What are you talking about? Your mother has always been reserved in her opinions. Unless you mean how she mentioned about having to slash her list of guests, and how you're only having a buffet instead of a six-course sit-down meal, and the whole 'She's not even having a real band' rant?"

Regan laughed. "That's Mom."

Jake grinned. "She's actually slowed down. In her prime, she was completely terrifying."

Regan nodded. "She still can be. But these days, she tries to use her powers for good."

"Enough," I said loudly. "We can dissect my personality outside. Leaving Bobby out there with my mother is cruel and unusual."

Jake reached out and patted my cheek. "Only to you, Kate."

Laura handed everyone a dish to carry out, and we trailed out of the kitchen. Jeff, coming up behind me, whispered in my ear.

"Meryl is pregnant."

"Meryl? The wonderful woman in Maine who's going to be carrying my grandchild?" I set a bowl of pickles on a table and hugged him. "I'm so happy. Okay, we need to keep our fingers crossed and think good thoughts."

"She says she feels good. It's only a few weeks, but it's a great start."

"Let me know when I can start planning the shower. I'm thinking we could get a room at Rod's Ranch House. Would your friends come out from the city? We'll do a Saturday luncheon."

"Do you have a guest list for this, too?"

I looked skyward. "Maybe."

He kissed me on the cheek. "Knock yourself out, Mom. And I'm happy that you're happy."

We ate under a striped tent that had been staked in the middle of the yard. Jake had been hovering over the grill with Bobby, but after the table had been loaded down, he sat between me and my mother, his plate piled high, an icy bottle of water at hand.

"No beer?" I asked.

He shook his head. "Nope. Driving. I never drink and drive anymore. God spared me too many times during my misspent youth; I'm not pushing my luck now."

"Luckily," I said, "most of our favorite haunts back then were in walking distance."

Regan looked over and shook her head. "Mom, one or two glasses of wine, well, that's okay, but anything more than that and you're a little embarrassing. I can't imagine you going out drinking."

Jake threw back his head and laughed. "You should have seen her trying tequila for the first time." He grinned at me.

"At the Varsity," we said together, and I laughed with him. Laura leaned in. "Do tell."

"Well, the Varsity was a fairly nice club," I began.

"For a sports-themed bar on a college campus," Jake said.

"Yes. And on Tuesdays they had contests," I went on.

"For ladies only," Jake put in.

"Yes. And one month we were a little short on rent, and I thought I could get us an easy fifty bucks."

Jake shook his head. "She'd never had tequila before."

Laura made a noise. Devon was leaning in, listening closely. She hit her son on the arm and glared at him.

"Remember," she said sternly, "your aunt was of legal drinking age at the time. And I'm sure this kind of thing is not allowed anymore. She could have gotten really ill."

"Oh, I did," I said. I looked at Devon. "I was so sick, Jake had to practically carry me home. I spent the night on the floor in our bathroom."

"I did, too," Jake said. "I was afraid to leave her."

"Nothing in my life felt so good as that cool toilet bowl against my cheek."

Wade yowled with laughter. "Oh, that's gross."

Jake nodded. "Yes. The whole night was kind of gross. But she learned a valuable lesson. So did I. I never let her drink like that again." He looked at me. "I was so worried about you. I still feel sick when I remember how badly I was frightened."

I remembered, too. I could hear his voice, as though it were yesterday, asking me if I was okay, telling me he was going to call an ambulance. I'd kept shaking my head no, and he'd held me, lying with me on the cold tile floor.

"I didn't drink for a month," I said. "I couldn't even look at a beer."

"But," Jake said with a grin, "you got over it."

I made a face. "And how about the time you decided to drink yourself sober, and tried to finish off the keg at eight in the morning?"

Jake groaned and we all laughed. Phil raised his hand. "I've done that," he said. "Usually, it doesn't end well."

"This time it didn't, either." He pointed a finger at me. "You never tried to stop me."

I waved my hand at him. "Could I ever? But I did call some people to come over and help you out."

Devon yelped, "At eight in the morning?"

Jake and I spoke together—"That's what friends are for." And we all laughed.

My mother, sitting primly on Jake's other side, sniffed. "It's a miracle the two of you managed to graduate at all."

Jake leaned over her. "Your daughter had the best study habits I'd ever seen. True, when she let loose, it could get crazy, but she would sit at her desk and shut out the world to get her work done. She was something to see. Her concentration was so intense, sometimes she'd forget to eat."

"That would not happen now," I muttered, and we all laughed again.

A few hours later, Jake had left, Mom and Bobby's sister had gone inside to watch some TV and cool off, and there was a soccer game going on, involving everyone under the age of forty. Bobby was acting as ref, a few neighborhood kids had come by to fill in the ranks, and they all seemed to be having a great time. Regan had declined the invitation to play, and was sitting with Laura and me on the screened porch, watching her husband-to-be race down the field, trying to get the ball from a very determined Brianne.

"The girlfriend," I observed, "is a bit competitive."

Laura nodded. "I think that's why Devon was attracted to her in the first place."

Regan sighed. "First love is so sweet."

"At that age," Laura said, "I was such a baby. I never would have had the nerve to jump into a game like Brianne. I would have been happy to be the cheerleader."

"That's because you always wanted to be a cheerleader," I reminded her.

"True. I wasn't cool enough."

"But you did have a boyfriend," I said. "Your freshman year. I remember a very tall kid with long hair who didn't say anything."

Laura smiled. "Freddy. Yes, my very first high-school crush. I was so in love. Until you brought Jake home for Christmas. After that, Freddy never had a chance."

Regan sat up. "Oh?"

Laura shook her head at the memory. "Can I tell you? Jake Windom in his prime took your breath away. I mean, he's still a good-looking guy for his age, but then? He was something else."

Regan looked at me. "Well, I have to admit, I can really see what the attraction is. He's a lot more fun to be around than Tom was. And I can tell you mean something to him,

Mom. The way he looks at you?" She was quiet. "Daddy never looked at you that way."

I reached over and grabbed her hand. "Honey, your father and I were very happy for a long time. We had you kids and a life together that worked. At some point, things started to fray. But for a long time, it was all good."

"I know, Mom." Regan squeezed my hand. "But he still never looked at you the way Jake does."

We sat for a few minutes.

"So, what about Edward, Mom? I mean, I've got kind of a stake in this."

"I know, sweetie. And I wish I could give you a nice, simple explanation of what's going on. But I can't. I really like Edward. I really like Jake. At some point, something will change."

"Yes, Mom, but in the meantime . . ." She shook her head. "It would be so cool if you and Edward ended up together. But Jake would get hurt."

"I know. I'm very aware of that, Regan."

We sat for a few more minutes.

"Mom seems pretty happy, too," Laura said.

"Yes. She has somehow fallen in with a group of women who find her good company. She's got more on her social calendar right now than I do," I said.

"What's going to happen?" Regan asked.

"Happen when?"

"When you find her another place to live?"

Laura and I looked at each other. I'd been so relieved at my mother's good mood that I hadn't thought of that.

"I don't know," I said. "How's that coming?"

Laura made a face. "I have somebody calling me next week about the possibility of a bed. It would be available October first. In Hackettstown."

"That's pretty far," Regan said. "And if Gram is happy . . ."

I shot her a look. "She can't live with me permanently. I hope to be starting a full-time job in the next few months. And it's still the Cold War between us. Granted, we've actually had some spontaneous conversations, but it's still pretty much a don't-speak-until-spoken-to situation."

"Maybe," Regan said, "you could find her a condo in your development."

"Honey," I explained, "she cannot live by herself. She forgets things. Important things. You know that. And her health is only going to get worse. She should be on oxygen. She needs to be using her walker at all times. Doing every-day things is going to get harder and harder for her. And I don't live in an assisted living community. Somebody would have to be paid to come in and stay with her."

We were quiet again, watching the soccer game.

"How can they play in this heat?" Laura said at last.

"They're young," I said.

"But still. Look at Jeff. He's not enjoying this," Laura said.

"He never smiles when he's sweating," Regan said. "Ever see him run? He looks like he's about to kill someone."

"Nobody ever looks happy running," I said. "Ever notice that? If all those endorphins are pumping, you'd think all runners would be smiling all the time."

"Sam looks happy, though," Regan said. "I bet you miss Alisa."

"Yes, I do," I said. "And not because she kept Sam on the same plane as the rest of us. I really got to like her. Sometimes she'd say or do something so sweet, I'd elevate her to favorite-child status."

Regan made a noise. "Mom, I thought that since I was getting married, I was your favorite."

"Sadly, Jeff chose this time to get some woman in Maine pregnant with my first grandchild. The two of you are in a dead heat most days."

"And I guess Jake will be your guest at the wedding?" Regan asked.

"If I say yes, you can't take away from the number of people I can invite."

"Mom. We have a finite number of seats. Jake coming means somebody else can't."

"No, Regan," Laura cut in. "Sorry, but I'm siding with your mother on this one. A guest of the mother of the bride who is also her date is in a completely different category, and cannot be lumped with other guests."

"You just made that up," Regan said.

"No. Look it up. It's a rule."

Regan waved a hand. "Whatever. He'll look great in the pictures. That's the important thing."

"My, my," I clucked. "Aren't we getting a bit coldhearted?"

"Mom, planning this wedding has been the most exhausting, frustrating, and calculated thing I've ever had to do. Worse than getting into veterinary school, and you know how hard that was. If it weren't for you, I think we would have eloped."

"Weren't for me?"

She grinned. "I really wanted that favorite-kid status."

I laughed. A few minutes later, Bobby's sister came out. "Kate? Your mom says she's ready to go."

Regan stood up. "I'll bring Sam home, Mom. He's on Phil's team, and they need all the help they can get."

I said my good-byes and helped Mom into the car. She was very tired, I could tell, and she put her head back on the car seat and napped all the way home. Her breathing was still labored as we walked into the garage, and she had to immediately sit down before she could stand up again to get ready for bed, but she seemed calmer, less angry about the world. She did not look gray and pinched like she had a month before.

"This was a good day, wasn't it, Mom?"

She nodded. I waited for her to reach for the remote, but she just sat there.

"He apologized," she said.

"Who, Mom?"

"Jake. He said he was sorry about hurting you. He wanted me to know."

That took me back a bit. "That was nice of him, but why would he apologize to you? I'm the one who got stomped on."

She glared. "Because you were my firstborn, and the one dearest to my soul. When your heart broke, mine did, too. I felt so bad for you, and I knew there was nothing I could do to make it better. I felt angry and helpless, and I wanted to kill that boy."

I stared. "Why didn't you ever tell me that?"

She rolled her eyes. "Were we even talking to each other then? And then you got all geared up for law school, and there was that whole fight. I wanted you to come home for a while but, no, you went off again, and then by the time things were good between us, you were with Adam, and I didn't want to drag up anything about Jake. I knew you still

299

loved him." She sniffed and straightened her shoulders. "Then you became a mother. I thought you would have figured it out for yourself. I still don't know why people keep saying you're so smart." She leaned back in the recliner and closed her eyes. She looked very peaceful. "He's smart, Jake is. He knew. I still don't trust him, but at least he's smart. And now he knows if he's going to screw you over again, he'd better wait until after I'm dead."

I leaned over and kissed her cheek. "Thanks, Mom."

And then I went upstairs and got into bed. But I did not sleep. Not for a long, long time.

Chapter Thirteen

Seeing two men at the same time wasn't as logistically hard as I thought it was going to be. As soon as Edward heard that Elaine was going to be in the same hotel, even though it was weeks away, he found a short-term rental in a fabulous complex and moved. He was in Jersey City, a bit farther from me, but closer to his old friends and business connections in the city. I saw him once a week, during the week, and on Sunday afternoons.

Jake came to Newark every Wednesday to have lunch with me, and spent all day Saturday.

After a few weeks of this, I was no closer to deciding which of them I wanted more. Actually, I wanted them both, and seriously thought about how long I could possibly keep doing this. I knew how selfish I was being, but I just couldn't stop. Being with Jake was like curling up with my favorite blanket, soft, warm, and safe. He knew me so well, I didn't have to finish half of my sentences most of the time. Being with Edward was like climbing into the front car of a roller coaster. I never knew what was coming next, but there was a good chance it would leave me smiling.

* * *

Cheryl came by and helped me dig up my marijuana, which, in spite of its limited growing space, had managed to cause so much shade that my tomatoes were small and under-ripe.

She arrived wearing hot-pink capris, a sleeveless flowered tunic, and jeweled sandals. Her official pot-harvesting outfit. She did not get a speck of dirt on her. The woman was a real pro.

"Okay. We need to hang these upside down in a cool, dark place to dry out. I suggest the garage."

I brushed some dirt off my jeans. I was, as you can guess, filthy. "That would involve sneaking them past my mother, or taking them in through the outside door, in which case the entire neighborhood will see them."

"Them" were six plants, over three feet tall and almost as wide, with trailing root systems still caked with dirt.

She made a face. "How about tonight? We'll just leave them here for now."

"The problem is that Mom and all her friends come in and out of the basement through the garage. They might get noticed."

Cheryl frowned, a sign that she was thinking. "We could disguise them."

"As what? Christmas garland?"

"Maybe. Do you have any tinsel?"

"Can't we just put them in a plastic bag and stick them in a closet?"

She shook her head. "No. Upside down and in open air is best."

"Cheryl, since when did you become such an expert?"

"Kate, the Internet is a wonderful place. You should spend a little time there."

"Listen, why don't you just take them and hang them up with all your own plants. I still don't know why I grew these in the first place. If I ever feel the need to get stoned, I'll just call you, okay?"

"Okay. By the way, who are you dating these days?"

"Please, Cheryl, don't. Both of them. Can we not talk about this?"

"Of course. Are you sure you don't want me to leave a little behind? I bet you could use some serious relaxation."

"Thanks, but no thanks. My brain doesn't need any more messing with."

So we packed the plants into a garbage bag and Cheryl took them. I spent a few more minutes on the deck filling in the holes in my planters with mums. I was feeling smug and accomplished when I was done.

My mother, in the weeks since she had moved in, had carved out a very nice little routine for herself. She had a standing card-playing night. Marie had become her good friend and had talked her into a wheelchair. Regan and I got her to Macy's and bought her a lovely dress for the wedding. Mom on wheels was a sight to behold. When the weather was right—not too hot, no dampness in the air—she would be wheeled around by one of her growing number of lady friends, as well as an older widower who was living in the development with his divorced middle-aged son.

But she had also tried to warm up two cupcakes in her toaster oven, causing the frosting to catch fire and burning up the inside. Sam had been home at the time, and had simply smothered the burning unit with one of Mom's pillows. When I refused to buy her another toaster oven, she pouted for three days.

She opened her sliding glass doors to let in some fresh air, which was fine, but then she opened the screen door as well and left it open all night. The drapes had been closed, so I didn't notice it until I went down the next morning. By then, both cats had slipped out, and it took Sam, Regan, Jake, and me all day to find them. Eight had made it as far as the walking trails. Seven climbed up a tree and had to be coaxed down with tuna fish.

Twice, my mother had to be told who Wade was. Then she insisted that Laura only had one son.

I kept pushing the worry to the back burner. I was making myself crazy with Jake and Edward. And then Alisa sent me an e-mail.

I'd gotten e-mails from her before. We kind of chatted back and forth every few days. First, she would tell me a single fact about her day that I did not remotely understand. Then she'd describe something amazing that she'd eaten. Finally, she'd tell me how much she missed Sam, and how I should watch him and make sure he was okay. She was exhausted and thrilled and happy to be in France, but could not wait to come home.

But this particular e-mail was something else.

"Hi, Kate—I know this may sound stupid, but I think there's something going on with Sam. We still talk every night on Skype, but it's different. I can't explain it, but there's something wrong. Could you talk to him?"

I stared at the screen and was twenty-one again. Jake had been at Penn State six weeks. We called each other every night. One Saturday I hung up the phone, turned to MaryJo, and said to her, "Something's going on with Jake." She had laughed, and said I was imagining things, that Jake loved me like crazy and I needed to get a grip. I shook my head. My stomach had turned to knots and there was a tightening in my heart. I couldn't explain it. There was something wrong. Three weeks later, Jake said good-bye.

I left the den and went upstairs.

Sam was in the second of the two bedrooms, the one he had set up as an office. I could hear him talking. He was on the computer with someone. He was laughing.

I stood outside the door. No, he was not talking to Alisa. Whoever she was, she sounded very different from Alisa; her voice was clear and little-girl-like. She was giggling. I did not want to know what they were talking about. I did not care.

"Hey, Sam."

He looked up from the computer and his face froze. "Mom?"

"Are you talking to Alisa? Can I say hi?"

"Ah, no. This is Vin." He looked at the screen. "I've gotta go, Vin. I'll talk to you later." He closed the laptop and pushed the chair away from his desk.

"Vin?" I asked. "The girl you met over Labor Day?"

"She's not a girl, Mom; she's twenty-four."

"Right. And have you been spending time with her?"

He didn't look at me. "Yeah, a few dinners, stuff like that."

"Have you slept with her yet?"

He rolled his eyes. "Mom."

I sat on the edge of his desk and kicked back his chair with my foot. It rolled backward. He looked up at me in surprise.

"Alisa—" I began.

"Is not here," he said loudly. He met my eyes briefly, then looked at his hands, clenched in his lap. "She's not here," he said again. "Vin is just so different, you know? She's not all planning this and managing that. She's fun, but at the same time, she cares about what I do. She has really good ideas, from the business side of things, about what I can do with my life."

I took a deep breath. "Sam, I really want to understand this. Not just for your sake, and Alisa's, but for my own. How can a man be in love with a person—really, truly in love—and even look at another woman?"

He shrugged. "She came after me, Mom. It's flattering. Women don't chase me, you know. They never have. All of a sudden this really hot woman thinks I'm the greatest thing she's ever come across. It's hard to resist."

"But, Sam, Alisa thinks you're the greatest thing, too."

His eyes filled with tears. "Mom, I know. And I love her—Alisa. I miss her like crazy. I want her here. I don't want us to be apart. I know it can't be helped, and I'm trying to be the stand-up guy here. But . . ." He stood up and threw back his head, chest heaving as he took in a long, stuttering breath.

His eyes were closed. And when he opened them, he looked right at me. "Alisa is the known entity, Mom. I love her. And I know that she loves me, and I know that we are good together. I do know that. But Vin is like this little flicker in the corner of my eye. She's bright and new and she won't go away. And the more time I spend with her, the more I keep thinking that something really exciting is just about to happen."

"Then stop spending time with her."

"You say that like it's easy. I'm lonely, Mom."

I stood up and went over to him. "Sam. Listen to me. Do you think Jake and I are a good couple?"

He frowned, thinking. "Yeah, I guess you are."

"And you know our history, right? We loved each other, Sam, the way that you and Alisa love each other. We were just right together. And then someone bright and shiny came into Jake's life. Do you want to wake up one day thirty years from now and realize that you've been living your life with the wrong person?"

He looked at me a long time. "Are you saying that Dad was the wrong person?"

I sighed. "Life happens the way it's supposed to, Sam. Somebody I really respect recently told me that our lives are already planned out for us, and all we can really do is live that life as the best person we can be. Your father and I were meant to be together, Sam. He was not the man I had wanted to marry, but I knew he loved me and would give me a good life, so I took a leap of faith and married him. I grew to love him, and I have no regrets. So maybe you and Vin are supposed to be together. Maybe Alisa was just for practice." I grabbed both of his hands in mine and held on tight. "But I want you to think about what you're giving up. Think hard. All those plans that the two of you have made. You will never be able to get those back, Sam, if you give up on Alisa. Even if you and Vin live a long and happy life, and she dies, and you find Alisa again and realize what you still mean to each other, you will have lost all the things that you once wanted more than anything else in the world."

He was looking at me, and I could see the wheels in his brain spinning around. *Gotcha*, I thought. But I was so wrong.

"Mom, if that's how you feel about Jake, then what are you doing with Edward?"

Oh my God.

What was I doing with Edward?

I stepped back. "I love you, honey. And once again, you're the smartest person in the room. But this isn't about me. Well, maybe it is, but let's make it about just you, okay? Please don't make any stupid mistakes, because if you do, I'll kick your ass out on the street before I'll send Alisa away."

I turned and went back downstairs, took Boone for her evening stroll around the cul-de-sac, and said good night to my mother. Then I crawled into my bed and cried for a very long time, for all the lost things in my life that even now, with Jake back, I would never get back again. And when I thought about all the things going forward that I might not have, I cried even harder.

CHAPTER FOURTEEN

I had no idea what to say to Edward. I just knew I had to talk to him. I drove over to his new place the next evening, walked in the door, and instead of kissing him hello blurted, "I need some advice."

He stepped back to look at me, raised one eyebrow, and said, "Indeed."

"Yes, Mr. Spock. Indeed. About Jake."'

"Oh?"

"He does that one-eyebrow thing, too, you know."

He smiled. "No. I didn't know. Do you think we should sit down?"

We sat on the couch. I stared at my hands, which were clenched tightly.

"Here's the thing," I began.

"Yes?"

"My first marriage was good, but it was never what it could have been, because I never got over Jake. I'm afraid of that happening again. I spent so many years wondering what our lives together might have been, I can't stand the thought of never knowing if we would have been good together or not."

"You already know that, don't you? The two of you were perfect together. Until he left you."

"But I keep thinking I need to give Jake another chance. He's what I wanted thirty years ago, and it all feels the same way now."

"And why do you think that's a good thing?" he asked.

"What do you mean?"

"People change, Kate, and what was good once may not be good again. Have you looked at the two of you together, today? Or have you only been looking back?"

A hot flash suddenly hit. I pulled back and forth at the front of my shirt, trying to create a breeze.

"I have been looking back."

"What about now?"

I looked at him, his eyes steady and kind, his lips curled in a slight smile. "I can't find a now, Edward. That's the thing. I realized that everything I thought was real is like an echo. I can hear it, even feel it, but I don't think I can hold it in my hand. Do you think that's enough?"

He shook his head. "Kate, am I really the person to ask? Don't you think my opinion of what you should do with Jake might be clouded by the fact that I want you for myself?"

"But you're an honest man, Edward. And the fact that you do care about me makes me hope you'd want what's best for me."

"I would be best for you," he said simply. He reached over, picked a magazine up off the coffee table, and fanned me. The air felt so cool and good, I sighed from happiness. Who else in my life had ever done that for me?

I looked at him. "How could you and I work anything out? You have your life in London, and I'm tied to so many things here, I could never leave. Not permanently."

"Nothing is permanent, Kate, except how people feel about each other. Everything else can be rearranged. I could move here."

"But what about all your businesses? You said you'd have to take a loss."

"Kate, listen to me." He took my hands in his and leaned in close. "You are a remarkable woman. I've never felt such a connection with anyone as quickly, and as strongly, as I've felt with you. That sort of thing doesn't happen often, and it's not worth losing because of business." He took a deep breath. "I've learned that taking too much time to make up your mind might mean losing what could have made you the happiest. I won't make that mistake again."

He kissed me very softly, and when he did I wanted to slip right into his arms and hold him. He had just offered me the very thing that Jake had denied me years ago, to put me first in his life. Was it possible that what could make me happy was right here, right now?

I pulled back. I had to ignore all those bells and whistles and look at everything through a clearer lens.

"Thank you, Edward. I need to think. God, do I need to think. I know I'm not being fair to either of you. I promise, I'll figure this out soon." I took a deep breath. "Now, can you promise me something?"

"Anything."

"In any conversations you might have with Elaine in the next few weeks, don't ever mention that we spent any time together."

His face became solemn. "Kate, I swear. Never."

"Good. Then maybe we both have a chance of surviving this wedding after all."

* * *

Laura called to tell me that someone wanted to rent out Mom's house. We had told the manager of the development that Mom would be moving out at some point. We'd been paying her monthly fees as well as her electric bill to keep the lights on. But someone had stopped by the manager's office and asked if there was anything that could be rented, and he had thought to call Laura.

"It would be a good thing, Kate. She would have additional income every month. These people were willing to pay eight hundred dollars a month on a long-term lease."

That seemed to me like a lot of money for a two-bedroom house, but the development had some great amenities—swimming pool, tennis courts—and it was only an hour away from Atlantic City.

"When would we have to clear out the house?" I asked.

"By November first. We'd probably have to do it before then, and get the place painted. Is it manageable, do you think?"

"Sure. The unmanageable part is telling Mom. What about that place in Hackettstown?"

Laura sighed. "The room is Mom's if she wants it. However, the home has to wait until the person who is in it now either goes to a different facility or dies."

"Oh, Laura, is that what this is going to be about now? A deathwatch?"

"Kate, we're talking about old people. Someday, we'll be on the other side of this, flipping a coin between extended care or pulling a plug. I'm going to tell the boys to set me out on an ice floe, rather than put them through this."

"But if she goes into this home as a Medicare patient, doesn't she have to sell the house?"

"I was thinking we could help her out. Between what she makes from the rent, plus her Social Security, then Dad's pension and her pension, she could just about make it every month. Bobby and I could kick in an extra couple of hundred dollars."

I sighed. "So could I. I can't believe she's still getting Dad's pension."

"He was in a union, remember? She started collecting when she turned sixty-five, and it will go on until she's gone. Thank God for that. It's the only thing that's kept her afloat all these years."

"Well, it will be easier for Mom to move if she doesn't have to sell the house and give all her money away. When can you come over?"

She sighed. "This afternoon."

When Laura arrived and we went downstairs, Mom had company. Marie was there with another woman whom I recognized from the Widows' Mafia. I had brought down a pitcher of iced tea and some cookies that I had made, and the three of them were happily munching away. The sliding glass doors were closed, of course, and the air-conditioner was humming loudly. It was so cool down there, I wanted a sweater.

Mom's eyes narrowed. "The two of you? Together? This can't be good."

Marie made clucking noises. "Rose, now behave. You need to talk to them anyway. Don't be such a bitch," she said, smiling sweetly.

Mom actually cackled with laughter.

Laura cleared her throat. "As a matter of fact, Mom, we do need to talk to you. Perhaps your friends could come back later?"

"No, they can't. Because I have to talk to you two, and Marie and Gail are part of it. I need money from you girls so I can move in with Gail here."

Laura and I looked at each other. I wanted to sit, but the little bentwood chair was stacked high with magazines.

"Move in with Gail where, Mom?" I asked.

"On the other side of the clubhouse. Section seven," Mom said.

Gail, who looked a bit older than Mom, with bright blue eyes and silver hair wrapped around her head like a crown, smiled gently. "I was one of the first people to move in here, almost twenty years ago," she said. "My husband and I sold our house in Livingston after the kids moved out. Peter died six years ago. I'm doing pretty well for myself, but things are starting to get tight. My place is paid for, but the taxes are killing me. I don't want to move at my age. On top of all that, I fell last year and can't get around the way I used to. I'd like to hire a girl to come in and take care of things, and make sure I don't accidentally burn the place down. I know that Rose is here with you on a temporary basis, so I thought if she moved in, she could help share some expenses."

Laura and I looked at each other again. Could it be that the light at the end of the tunnel was actually sunshine? And not an oncoming train?

"How much more money would you need, Mom?" Laura asked.

"Another twelve hundred a month."

Marie leaned forward. "I know that sounds like a lot. But these ladies can't just hire anyone, you know. I know of an agency that will send someone over every morning, seven days a week. The ladies will have two or three regular girls to help them out, drive them where they need to go, and do light cooking and cleaning. And at night, well, they can watch over each other."

I took a deep breath. "Mom, you know that in a few years, it won't be enough to have somebody during the day. You're going to have to be someplace where trained people can take care of you."

My mother scowled. "Kate, do I look stupid to you? Do you really think I don't know my own body? I'm the one who's talked to the doctors, not you. I know what to expect. But for the next few years, I can still live my life the way I want to. There are nice people here. I like being around them. I know you want to send me off someplace you think is safe, but for right now, I'd rather be happy. Can you two manage the money or not? It would only be until I get the house sold, and then I'll pay you back."

"Mom, I just got a call from Frank at your development. Somebody wants to rent your house. Eight hundred dollars a month," Laura said.

Mom smiled. "Do it."

"We'll have to go down and empty out the house," Laura continued.

"So? We'll go down and empty out the house. We'll have a yard sale."

"Mom," I said, "you've spent most of the summer telling me you want to go back to your house, and now you're going to leave it? Just like that?"

Laura shot daggers in my direction. I know—what was I thinking? But I had to know.

My mother shook her head sadly. "I'll be keeping my house, Kate. I won't be selling it. And I'll be living in a place I can call my own again, not in my daughter's house. If you can't see the difference, then maybe you should try getting another degree."

"Okay, then," Laura said quickly. "That sounds like a plan. Nice meeting you, Gail. I guess I'll be seeing you soon."

Laura and I both turned around and went upstairs, not looking at each other. We both went directly outside to the deck and shut the sliding doors tightly behind us. Then Laura threw back her head and gave a loud whoop that shook the leaves off the trees.

"How did that happen?" she yelled. "Oh my God! Saved!"

I sank into a chair and laughed weakly. "Laura, one of us has amazing karma for something like this to happen. Un-freaking-believable."

"I know. Is it too early to drink? I feel like cracking open a bottle of champagne."

"This is so good. So, at least for the next few years, we're off the hook, Mom-wise. Call Frank, before those renters change their minds. "

"Yes. And I'll call Hackettstown and let somebody else have that bed. Oh, Kate, I feel like such a burden has been lifted."

I got up and hugged her. "Me too."

Marie opened the sliding door and came onto the deck, grinning. "Are you girls celebrating out here?"

"Marie, you are such a lifesaver," I said.

She kissed my cheek. "I happen to like your mother, dear. And I think she and Gail will get along fine. They're both lonely. Gail knows about your mom's problems, so she's not going into this blind. I wouldn't do that to her. But Gail's mind is still pretty sharp, even if her body is failing. She'll make sure Rose doesn't do too much damage." She hugged Laura. "You are two good daughters. I'm glad you won't have to do anything against your mother's wishes. Not right now, anyway. When Rose is happy, everybody's happy."

Laura rolled her eyes. "You are so right. Thank you. Okay—I've got to get home and make phone calls. And buy Devon new shoes for this wedding." She gave me a quick hug and went.

Marie looked around the deck. "Those mums are looking very nice, Kate, but what did you do with all those pot plants?"

"What? I gave them to my friend Cheryl. She's, ah, drying them out for me."

"Oh, that's too bad. I was hoping to score a bag. I found out a long time ago that if I took a few hits before bed, I'd sleep like a baby. Beats anything you can get out of a prescription bottle."

"Well, Marie, I'll see what I can do for you."

"Why, thank you, dear. I'll let myself out."

I looked around. There was just a hint of fall in the air, that crisp kind of feeling that reminds you to look for sweaters and warm socks. The leaves were just starting to turn. The air smelled like apples. A little over six months ago, I thought I had myself a nice little life planned out. True, things were not going quite the way I had planned for them to, but that was okay. Right here, right now, everything was looking pretty good.

Elaine Pendergast did not like the place Regan and Phil had picked out for their wedding. She did not like the menu; she did not like the centerpieces for the tables. She did not like the fact that Regan's maid of honor and lone bridesmaid had gotten to pick out their own dresses, and that the ushers would be in suits, not tuxedos. Only one limo? How would she get to the church? No band? What was this, a sweet-sixteen party, with a Rastafarian DJ named SallyJ?

She sighed heavily. "Honestly, Kate, I can't believe that you just sat back and let them create this mess. Didn't you care enough to give a little advice?"

I was sitting between Regan and Phil when she said this. Both of them, under the discreet white linen tablecloth of the restaurant where we were having dinner, reached over and placed a restraining hand on my knee. The fact was, I had exactly those same reactions, but I did not like thinking about Elaine and I being on the same page about anything.

"Mom, we didn't ask for any advice. Both Regan and I knew the kind of wedding we wanted. Kate actually had some very strong opinions, and was actively pushing for a more traditional reception, but she was outvoted," Phil explained calmly.

Elaine raised a thin, bleached eyebrow and shrugged elaborately. "Yes, well. I guess we should all be grateful we won't be barefoot on a windy beach somewhere with the dogs as ring bearers."

Regan and Phil had two scruffy rescue mutts, one white and one black. The thought of them wearing little bow ties and carrying ring boxes in their mouths made me smile for the first time that evening.

I glanced at my watch. I had asked Jake to join us. I wanted to show up with a date, since Elaine was going solo, and asking Edward was out of the question. Even though it was a Friday night, he'd been held up at the office and he had said he'd be late. I looked at the menu again, sipped some more wine, and took deep, cleansing breaths.

I had not seen Elaine since she flew out for Phil's birthday last February. It appeared she'd had some work done. Some more work done. When I had first met her, three years ago, she admitted to having just recovered from her second boob job. She had actually had a reduction, telling me she felt that 32DD was no longer appropriate at her age. I'd only seen her a handful of times since then. Her alimony payments could have paid for more frequent trips east to visit her only son, but, thankfully, her social schedule kept her in Denver.

This time, I noticed that her jawline was much tighter, and the lines around her mouth had disappeared. For the first time, I was jealous. I had spent lots of time the past few years staring in the mirror, pulling at the skin by my ear and watching the parentheses around my mouth disappear, and thinking that could be a good look for me.

"I must say, Elaine," I said brightly, "you look great. At least ten years younger."

She beamed. "Thanks for noticing, Kate. I had my neck done for the wedding."

"Oh, good for you. Me, I just had my hair done."

She raised an eyebrow again, and then she sat up a little straighter and turned on her porcelain—and I mean that literally—smile.

"Hello, everyone, sorry I'm late," Jake said, sitting down across from me.

He was in another one of those killer suits, with a gray silk tie, and Elaine practically purred when they were introduced. At last, something she approved of.

"So, you're the long-lost boyfriend? How terribly romantic for the two of you," she said, looking at Jake like he was an oyster she couldn't wait to crack open and swallow whole.

Jake smiled easily. "Yes, it's pretty amazing how we managed to find each other again after all these years. And the great thing is, we've fallen right back into our old ways."

I felt something right then, a wrenching in my heart. Our old ways? Was that how he really felt? Our old ways had ended with him leaving me. I had been hoping we had started over fresh, but Jake had obviously never seen it that way.

I looked at Jake. "Although sometimes going back to the old ways is not such a good idea."

Elaine sighed dramatically. "I don't know; it sounds good to me. Maybe I should try looking up all of my old college beaus."

Phil looked puzzled. "Mom, I thought you met Dad your freshman year. When could you have had other college beaux?"

Elaine shrugged her shoulders. "Darling, just because your father and I were a couple doesn't mean that other men weren't interested. I could have had my pick." She leaned over and practically put her whole mouth in Jake's ear. "I was voted the most beautiful pledge in my sorority my first year out, you know."

"No," Jake said. "I didn't know. But I'm not surprised."

She beamed.

After Jake arrived and she was significantly distracted, things went along pretty smoothly until Phil's father was mentioned again. By Jake. So I'm pretty sure he ended up on Elaine's list after all.

"So, Elaine, did you know that until recently, Edward was staying in this same hotel?" he said.

Elaine set down her wineglass so hard, it splashed a little bit on the table. I'm sure she could have used even more force, but she was drinking red, and probably didn't want to risk getting anything on her winter-white suit. "Really."

Regan looked a bit panicked. "Yes, Elaine, but he moved out a few weeks ago. He's in a condo now. In Jersey City. Which is, like, more than half an hour away."

Elaine made a very small, inelegant noise that suggested possible strangulation. "I had no idea. What has he been doing here all this time?"

Now it was my turn to panic. I did not want Elaine to know how Edward was spending his time. I also didn't want Jake to know.

Phil dived in. "He's been catching up with old friends, and talking with businesspeople. He was in Toronto for a while, and remember Carl Latowski? His college roommate? He spent a few weekends with him."

Regan looked like she was desperate for a new topic, but I think Phil was enjoying it. "And it's been great showing him around. So much has changed since he was here last."

"When did he move to England?" I asked. I knew the answer, of course, but I couldn't resist. Regan gave me a warning look. Hey, we were already talking about him, right?

Phil thought for a second, then turned to his mother. "He was born there, but his family came over here when he was in his early teens. He went back—when was the last time you took him to court for more alimony, Mom, 1995?"

"Somewhere around there," she said shortly.

Phil grinned. "He returned to England right after that."

"Really?" I said, feigning complete and total surprise. "You drove him right out of the country, Elaine?"

Under the table, Regan kicked me. Hard.

Elaine did not appear amused. But it didn't take her long to load her next round.

"So tell me, Kate, have you found a job yet?"

I smiled. "Yes. I'll be working for a nonprofit. The funding has just been approved, and I'll start November first."

"Well, dear, I hope you won't be taking too big a cut in salary. Those nonprofits are notoriously tight."

"True," I countered. "Luckily, I've got enough stashed away that I don't really need a big salary."

She sniffed.

Two points for me.

Believe it or not, none of us wanted dessert, so the party broke up soon afterward. Elaine played kiss-kiss and headed for the elevators up to her room. As soon as she was out of sight, Regan burst out laughing.

"Mom," she sputtered, "you have got to stop. Please, it's going to be a long two weeks. Don't make it worse."

Phil put his arm around her. "Regan, it's not all Kate's fault. My mother has a habit of bringing out the worst in people."

Jake looked at Phil. "Did she really drive him out of the country?"

Phil shrugged. "He says he was planning on going back anyway. She says he left the country so she couldn't get any more money from him."

Regan looked stern. "Mom, you have to promise. Remember, if you don't behave . . ." She looked at me knowingly.

I kissed her. "I promise. Good night."

As I watched them leave, Jake reached for my hand and held it tightly. "How about an after-dinner something? The bar is right here."

I nodded. "Good idea."

We ordered Amaretto, something we both loved. A thousand years ago, when Jake and I lived together, we'd save all our pocket change until we could afford a bottle; then we'd hide it from our friends, saving it for special occasions.

"You do know that I'm incredibly jealous of your family," Jake said.

"Jake, in two weeks, Elaine will be part of my family."

"Still. You are so lucky to have them. And I consider myself very lucky to be an outsider looking in."

We were sitting across from each other in a corner of the bar. He looked happy and handsome, and I was about to ruin his evening.

"Jake, I don't think I want to do this anymore," I said.

He frowned. "Do what?"

"Be with you." My mouth felt dry as dust, and I could hear my blood pounding in my ears.

"What?"

"Believe me, this is about the hardest thing I've ever had to do, but I don't want to see you anymore. It's not that I've stopped loving you. I'll never stop. But we had our moment, Jake. We had everything together. And it wasn't enough for you. We'll never be able to get that back, no matter how hard we try. And even if, by some chance, we came close, it would still not be enough for you."

He shook his head. "You're wrong, Kate. I know the mistake I made. I would never do that again."

I nodded. "I know. But that's not the point. It wouldn't be enough. And I'd know it."

His face changed, and went blank and pale.

"I'm sorry, Jake."

"Kate, I'll be retired in a few years. I told you. We'd be able to do anything you wanted."

"What I want is to be the most important thing in your life. All the time. I know that maybe sounds selfish, but I'm getting a little cranky in my old age. If I'm willing to give that much to someone—and I am more than willing, to the right person—then that's what I expect in return."

He slumped back in his chair. "Is this about what's-his-name? Edward?"

I shook my head. "Edward is a lovely man, and it may be that he's the one I've been waiting for, but he has nothing to do with this. This is all about me, Jake. And you should understand that. Because last time, it was all about you."

I got up, leaned down to kiss him good-bye, and walked quickly out of the bar. I didn't even cry. When I got home, I took Boone for her walk, and crawled into bed.

And I still didn't cry.

I didn't sleep, but I didn't cry.

The phone rang early, and I grabbed it on the third ring, which was pretty good, considering I'd been fast asleep.

"Mom? I'm bringing Gabe out to meet Gram."

"How brave you are, my son. Did you have to call me at seven eighteen to tell me that?"

"Yes. We're leaving now, stopping for bagels, and we'll all have breakfast in about an hour. Will she be up?"

"No, but then we all can have a nice chat. I broke it off with Jake."

"Oh, Mom. I'm so sorry."

"Me too. See you in a bit."

Jeff and Gabe brought bagels, lox, three kinds of cream cheese, fresh-squeezed orange juice, a small bag of Gabe's favorite coffee, and strawberries. My mother was not awake when they arrived, so the three of us sat outside and feasted on the best breakfast in the history of breakfast.

"So, Jake?" Jeff asked. He'd waited until we were almost finished eating.

I shrugged. "Jake left me years ago because what we had together wasn't enough for him. He wanted success and power more than he wanted to be with me. I could have forgiven him all that, honestly, but I would have still known it. We could never have gone back to the before."

Gabe sighed. "You're very brave, Kate. Most people would be willing to settle."

I shrugged. "I don't feel brave. I feel empty. But at least I've stopped wondering. That's huge." I looked at both of them. "Okay, boys, time to take the plunge. Are you ready for this?"

Jeff frowned. "Mom, what's the big deal? Gram knows I'm gay, right?"

"Yes, honey. But there's a difference between knowing in the abstract and actually meeting the boyfriend. Let's head down."

Mom did not like lox, thought the strawberries were overripe, and what was wrong with Maxwell House? She also kept looking at Gabe as though she didn't know why he was there, although Jeff introduced him as his partner, sat at his feet, and at one point kissed him on the lips. They stayed until almost noon, insisted on leaving the bagels behind, and headed home.

Alisa came home.

Sam picked her up from the airport late that night. I wanted to stay up and welcome her, but thought about what I would have wanted, at that age, to do with Jake if I hadn't seen him in months, so I didn't.

I would have thought that between the jet lag and her welcome home, she'd have slept in. But she came down fairly early the next morning and threw her arms around me, hugging me for a long time. When she finally stepped back, she was crying.

"Alisa, honey, what's wrong?" My heart was in my throat. Instead of throwing her down, caveman style, had Sam broken up with her last night instead?

"I'm just so glad to be back. And everything with Sam—he told me about that girl, and what you said to him. Thank you, thank you. You saved us. You really did."

"Oh, Alisa, I'm so glad everything's fine. Men are so stupid. Even the seemingly smart ones like Sam are capable of supreme idiocy." I stuck a coffee mug in the Keurig. "And if I hadn't had to talk to Sam about what an idiot he was being, I would not have seen my own situation for what it really was. I told Jake good-bye."

"Kate, really? Oh, I'm so sorry for you. I thought he made you happy."

"He did. But it was false happiness. Like eating a candy from your childhood. You remember it as being the best thing ever, but when you taste it again, it's all sugar and fluff that just melts away." I shrugged. "Now. Tell me about all that wonderful food."

She went up a bit later to shower; then Sam came down, looking very happy. "Mom, life is good," he said, head in the refrigerator. "Very good."

"Yes, Sam, it sure is. So, I guess that means everything with Alisa?"

"Everything with Alisa is better than good. I don't know what got into me, Mom. But right after we talked, I told Vin I was making a mistake. She got a little pissy, I guess, but you were so right about everything." He closed the fridge, a container of yogurt in one hand, orange juice in the other. "Thanks."

"Hey. No problem. Do you have a suit?"

"For what?"

"The wedding? This weekend?"

"I have a suit. Besides, I'm not in the wedding party, just showing people to their seats. It's no big deal."

"Of course it is. What are you doing today?"

"Alisa needs to talk to some people at Columbia. She starts next week. I'm going with her, even though I don't have a class."

"On your way home, go to the mall. Alisa already has a dress, I think. She can help you. That suit you've got is old, and you can't wear khaki if you're an usher. Get something navy blue. And new shoes."

He put the juice back in the fridge and drank the whole glass in one gulp. "If Alisa and I get married, I don't want any of this big wedding crap, okay?"

"Big wedding? You call this a big wedding? You really need to get out more. And what do you mean, if?"

He shrugged. "We don't think that we need to be married to live our lives together."

"No, honey, you don't. But being married means something; don't let anyone tell you different. And besides, it would make me happy, and isn't that what you really want out of life?"

He grinned. "Sure, Mom. Okay, I'll get a new suit."

I beamed. Smart boy.

Cheryl called. "I have no idea what to get your daughter for this shower."

"I know. They have an excessive amount of sheets and towels, because Regan refuses to use the same towel more than once without washing it. Phil had been living in his place for a few years before Regan moved in, and since he knew nothing about cooking, he bought every single pot, pan, and appliance on the market. And they both hate the cutesy kind of stuff. But they're seriously looking at houses, and I imagine they'll have something by the beginning of next year, so they can use all their new, shiny stuff in the new place."

"Is it a surprise?"

I made a noise. "Are you kidding? Regan planned the whole thing out with Kim, down to the favors. But they did throw her an impromptu shower at her clinic, and that was a surprise. She got a gift card from Home Depot, and silver serving spoons."

"The bachelor party?"

"Thursday night, in the city. They're going to see the Blue Man Group, then dinner at a 'gentlemen's club.'"

"How civilized."

"Yes. If you'd like, you can come over to the house. I'm having a mother-of-the-bride party."

"And what's that?"

"I'm not sure, but MaryJo will be there, so I imagine alcohol will be involved."

"Anything else?"

"What do you mean?"

"Should I bring something?"

"Great idea."

The next morning I picked up MaryJo at Newark Airport. We stopped at the Short Hills Mall and had crab cakes at Legal Seafood, then walked around, window-shopped, and talked before coming home. When I told her that Jake was out of the picture, romance-wise, her jaw dropped open.

"Kate, I am so proud of you. I can't even imagine how hard that must have been. Poor Jake. I bet he never saw it coming."

I shook my head. "No, I really surprised him. I kind of surprised myself. And I'm sad, but it is such a burden lifted off my shoulders. I'm never going to have to think about him again."

She gave me a quick hug and kiss. "I bet that's not at all what you figured this would feel like, no?"

"No. And it feels great."

Once again, Alisa had saved the day by agreeing to stay with Mom, and when we finally got to the house, I found them downstairs playing gin rummy.

Mom and MaryJo had met several times in the past, and MaryJo being MaryJo, she sat down with them and asked to be dealt in. I went upstairs, made about a hundred phone calls, and was trying to figure out dinner when both Alisa and MaryJo came upstairs, chatting like BFFs.

"We want Chinese takeout for dinner," MaryJo announced. "And after that, Alisa and I are wheeling your mom to play cards. Want to come? You can bring the dog."

"Why, thanks, I'd love to."

"I'll go get the food," Alisa offered. "And MaryJo wants me to pick up a bottle of bourbon."

"No need," I said, reaching into the cabinet and pulling out an unopened bottle of Wild Turkey. "I know my roomie. I'm prepared."

Having a roommate like MaryJo in college was a blessing for many reasons, not the least of which was my introduction to drinking hard liquor. She had always been a brown-booze kind of girl, and getting drunk with her those first few months was what had turned me into a wine drinker. I had spent many a night hugging the porcelain god. It took me a while—in fact, until after I'd graduated—but it finally sank in that I just couldn't handle the stuff. But MaryJo had mastered the art of drinking a shot—her wrist stiff, a smile on her lips, and down it would go in one neat, quick motion.

We spent most of the night doing more talking, and MaryJo, Sam, and Alisa put a big dent in the bottle. The next morning, Sam looked a bit washed out, and Alisa didn't make it downstairs until after ten. I wasn't going to Newark, and spent the day trying not to obsess about the bridal shower.

Regan's shower took place in the American Legion Hall in Whippany, where thirty women and Phil sat around for several hours, eating catered deli food and drinking too much. Regan got lots of towels and sheets, three coffeemakers, a KitchenAid mixer that caused my heart to twist with envy, and several hundred dollars' worth of gift cards.

I introduced MaryJo to Cheryl. MaryJo gave her a big hug. "I feel like we should be playing catch-up," she said, "instead of being introduced." We sat with Alisa, Mom, and Elaine. Elaine was horrified at the shabby carpet and leather folding chairs, as well as the poor quality of the gin. Mom pretended to be going deaf in her left ear, so that every time Elaine said anything, she'd have to repeat it to Mom, very loudly. All the people at the surrounding tables soon knew exactly what kind of mother-in-law Regan was getting. Mom remained deadpan throughout her entire performance. The rest of us were in hysterics. Elaine never caught on.

Thursday night Cheryl came over. Alisa joined us. She had been invited to go out with Regan and her friends, but decided to stay close to home. We broke out the rest of the Wild Turkey. When that bottle was gone, Cheryl found the Sambuca. MaryJo insisted we drink it with a coffee bean, and also suggested we set it on fire. Something about intensifying the flavor. At that point, I was so far gone that I tried to drink my shot before the flames had died down, almost burning out all my nose hairs. Thankfully, God was looking after me, so I did not set fire to my face, which would have made for unfortunate wedding photos. Although it was getting cool on the deck, we went out and smoked a bit of Cheryl's latest crop. Then things got really fuzzy.

I called Edward before I crawled into bed. He had been invited to the bachelor party, but I had heard Sam come in a few minutes earlier and thought Edward might be home.

"Did I wake you?" I asked.

He chuckled. "No. Just came through the door. You sound like you've had a rather interesting night."

"It's MaryJo's fault. You'll meet her tomorrow. She's an evil person who forced brown liquor down my throat, and now I'm going to die."

He made a few clucking noises. "Drink lots of water; you'll be fine."

"When are you coming?"

"I'll be there by five. Do you need me to bring anything?"

"No. I've done all I can do. It's in God's hands now."

"Kate, it's only a rehearsal dinner."

"Edward, any mother of the bride knows you can never put the words 'only' and 'rehearsal dinner' in the same sentence."

He laughed again. "Good night."

"Good night."

CHAPTER FIFTEEN

The people who cleaned my house agreed to make an extra trip out before the dinner so everything would look perfect. I did not expect them quite so early. MaryJo, completely unfazed by the prior evening's activities, had let them in. When I finally dragged my old, sorry butt out into the kitchen, she and Alisa were halfway through their second cup of coffee and were both looking disgustingly chipper.

"I get Alisa," I growled. "She's young. But, my God, MaryJo, do you have a deal with the devil?"

"Oh, honey, I was a schoolteacher, remember? Drinking heavily comes along with the job. If I didn't do something to let off a little steam, I'd have been a tragic statistic long ago. Your mom's had breakfast, and we took Boone for a walk. I actually met one of your cats this morning. Not very friendly, are they?"

"They're cats. They don't do friendly. And if you insist on being so cheerful," I said, "you may have to sleep somewhere else tonight." I made myself a cup of coffee and stirred in lots of sugar.

MaryJo beamed. "Don't be silly. You know you love me."

"I do. With all my heart. Even when you make me drink brown liquor, which you know I can't take. Can you do something about all this sunlight?"

"Sorry, baby. No. Do you have anything to do today? Hair, manicure, something like that?"

"Manicure at one, but I'm going to cancel."

Alisa reached over and picked up my hand, looking critically at my nails. "Why?"

"Because," I said, taking another gulp of coffee, "my nails hurt too much."

MaryJo chuckled. "You'll feel much better by then. I have to tell you, Kate, you have wonderful friends. I had such a fun time last night. And Alisa here is a dream. You are so lucky to be surrounded by such great women."

"If they're so great, why did they let me get totally drunk the night before my only daughter's rehearsal dinner?"

Alisa shook her head sadly. "After you found the tequila bottle, I don't think anyone or anything could have stopped you."

"Oh, God. Tequila. Why?" I put my head down on the counter and waited for the rush of caffeine to hit me and make me feel better. "That noise? Is that the wind?"

"They're vacuuming upstairs. Maybe," MaryJo suggested gently, "you could drink a second cup. And eat some bacon and eggs. Hot, greasy food has always made me feel better on mornings like these."

She bustled around the kitchen as I stared off into space, listening to the pounding in my head and wishing I had thought to put floor-to-ceiling, room-darkening drapes on all those damned windows.

"Here," MaryJo said with a flourish, and set a diner-perfect breakfast in front of me: two eggs over easy, crispy bacon, perfectly buttered toast. I ate everything on the plate in silence, while MaryJo and Alisa went off into the living room. I heard Sam's voice at some point. I put the plate in the sink and went into the living room to join them.

"Hey, Mom," he said, way too loudly. "Looks like you had a crazier night than the boys did."

I gritted my teeth and tried to remain civil to my youngest child. "And did the boys have a fun time?"

"Great," he gushed. "Edward is way cool and paid for the whole dinner, even though Phil's best man—what's his name?—was going to."

"His name," I told him as I sank into the chair, "is Mike. They were roommates at Pitt."

"Yeah, whatever. It was a good time."

I managed a smile. "That's nice, Sam. Can you just keep your voice down a little?"

"And you got high with Alisa? All summer long, I was watching the stuff grow, and never pinched a leaf for myself. You could have offered me a taste."

"Sam," MaryJo said, "it's against all the rules of parenthood for a mother to offer her child a joint. Believe me when I tell you that. Last night, your mother was celebrating, and I must say, we all did a few things that, in the bright light of day, were possibly not the best choices. But sometimes it's acceptable to revert to earlier behavior, especially after Wild Turkey shots. You will never, ever speak of this to your mother again, understood?"

Sam nodded, and he and Alisa went off to do whatever young, bright-eyed people in love do.

MaryJo cleared her throat. "It's eleven thirty. What do we have to do?"

"I have to go back to bed."

"I think not."

There was a knock on the door. Boone looked vaguely interested, and Cheryl let herself in. She looked at me critically, then shook her head.

"Now I know why, in all the years I've known you, you never drank anything but wine or the occasional vodka martini," she said. "But I must say, you're pretty entertaining when you're shit-faced."

"If you're not part of the solution, Cheryl," I told her, "I may have to kill you."

"I am here to help," Cheryl said. "I know you need it, and as awesome as MaryJo is, she can't do it all on her own. How many people are here tonight?"

I closed my eyes and tried to do a count in my head. "Six hundred and thirty-two," I said at last.

Cheryl and MaryJo shared a chuckle. How cozy.

"And why," MaryJo asked, "did you insist on having it here instead of at a restaurant?"

"Because I didn't know I'd have the hangover from hell, and thought it would be nice to have the most important people in my daughter's wedding here at my home. Under normal circumstances, I could be charming and totally in control. Now, I don't think I can even remember who the caterer is."

"Well, luckily, I know who it is," Cheryl said. She looked at MaryJo. "I think she has a mani/pedi this afternoon with Regan and a few of the other girls."

MaryJo nodded. "I'll get her there."

"Have you talked to Rose?" Cheryl asked.

"Not since breakfast," MaryJo said.

Cheryl nodded and went downstairs. The cleaning people were leaving. They smiled at me and left their little card. MaryJo closed the door behind them and settled back on the couch. "We'll take care of everything, Kate. You'll feel so much better this afternoon."'

Cheryl came back upstairs. "Your mother," she told me, "wants to come upstairs for the festivities. She insists that if she takes her time and rests every couple of steps, she can make it up."

I sighed. "Dinner is scheduled for seven. She'd better start by five, five thirty."

"Oh, stop," MaryJo said. "If you must, go back and lie down for just a half hour. Then take a long, hot shower. You need to get your act together, honey."

So I took a nap, and she was right, of course. After a shower, I did feel better, and I drove myself to the nail salon. Regan had booked all the chairs for her wedding party. Even Elaine was there, looking very frosty.

"How are she and Edward getting along?" I asked Regan.

She grinned. "Mom, it's the best show in town. She's trying everything to make him angry, and he refuses to even blink."

"Just so you know, I broke it off with Jake."

She stared at me. "After all that?"

I shrugged. "I know, right? But it's all about looking forward, honey. Getting caught in the past will only drag you down. There's nothing wrong with moving in another direction."

She kissed me, then tilted her head. "So, where does this leave Edward?"

I grinned. "In a very good place," I said, and she laughed.

I had my pedicure sitting between Kim, Regan's best friend and maid of honor, and Foster, her lone bridesmaid. Foster had been Regan's roommate all through veterinary school, and was very quiet and very intense. She and her partner, Willa, had come down from Syracuse for the wedding. Kim and Foster kept up a running conversation about the Kardashians. I sat back and listened, nodding occasionally. Mostly, I watched Regan.

I remembered the day before my wedding to Adam. He and I had gotten into a fight. We'd moved into our apartment three months earlier, and I had started clerking for a municipal judge. Adam was, at that time, in his second year of residency.

We had planned a fairly large wedding, almost two hundred people. That is, I had planned it. Adam had very little to do with anything, and barely knew what the menu was. But he had said he'd take care of the limousines, and then had forgotten all about making the call. I was already stressed out, and had started crying when, in the middle of our own rehearsal dinner, we realized there was no way for anyone to get to the church the next morning. He got angry because I was crying. I started yelling at him. He started yelling back. His father had to step between us and literally carried me into the next room, where I screamed and sobbed for what seemed like hours.

Adam made phone calls. By the time my eyes had dried and my mascara was back on, everything had been arranged. The dinner continued. We got married the next day. But

I never quite forgave Adam for forgetting the one, single thing I had asked him to do for our wedding.

Regan, on the other hand, seemed happy, relaxed, and completely in control. She wasn't going to have a meltdown about anything. She had been enjoying every minute of the past few days. Maybe there was something to this whole small-wedding thing after all. But I'd never admit it. Not to her, anyway.

I had my nails done a deep iridescent brown. I hardly ever had my nails manicured, and would normally never have considered anything but pale pink or mauve. But I had brought in a sliver of fabric from my dress, and they matched the color. This was Regan's idea. Everyone raved about the color of my dress, and how the polish would be so complementary, and since the reaction caused Elaine to wince, I went with it.

When I got home, the flowers had been delivered, and Cheryl and MaryJo had hung streamers and balloons in pale blue and silver. They'd rearranged some furniture, and covered tables with stiff white paper tablecloths. The sliders to the deck were open, and I could see flowers and candles out there as well. Everything looked beautiful.

"Thank you. I forgive you both for getting me drunk last night," I told them.

Cheryl shook her head. "You're welcome. But wherever you got last night was all your own doing. I'll see you tomorrow at the church."

Cheryl left, and MaryJo went off to shower and change. She was not going to the church rehearsal, but was staying behind to let the caterer in and help Mom with her momentous ascent. I could hear Sam and Alisa upstairs. They were coming with me to the church. Phil was having his best man stand with him at the altar, but had no groomsmen, just Sam and some others walking folks down the aisle.

Regan had gotten her undergraduate degree at the College of Saint Elizabeth, and was getting married in their chapel. It was a beautiful building, and the priest there was young and easygoing.

On the groom's side of the aisle, Elaine was sitting stiffly in the front row. Edward came in. I hadn't seen him since I had asked him what to do about Jake. He looked great, gave me a hug and a cool kiss, then went off to do battle. He sat right next to her. He seemed to be enjoying himself. Elaine fidgeted. She tapped her foot, drummed her fingers, and generally could not sit still. And she kept looking over her shoulder, shooting me daggers. Every time she did, I smiled and waved. Alisa and I had fun watching her.

It took less than an hour, and we all headed back to the house. I rushed ahead and found the food looking perfect, smelling delicious, and my mother and MaryJo sitting happily together. Mom looked very nice in a bright red pantsuit. She was in her wheelchair, next to the fireplace.

I smiled and filled a wineglass with seltzer. Everyone arrived in a rush, and the house was crowded and noisy. I had slipped Boone a little doggie Prozac, and she had curled into a corner and was not barking at anyone. Laura and Bobby arrived. Cheese, crackers, and wine flowed. Things were humming along very nicely.

Jeff drew me aside. "I tried to get to you in the church," he said, "but you refused to take the hint. We're having a girl."

I choked up. "A baby girl? Oh, Jeff, I'm so happy."

Gabe slipped around on my other side. "We'll tell everyone after the wedding," he said. "Don't want to steal the bride's thunder."

"Absolutely. But names—we have to think about names."

"Done," Gabe said. "My mom is Leighton. So she'll be Kathleen Leighton Everett-Braun. We'll call her Kayleigh."

"Perfect, Gabe. I'm so excited for you both. And for me. When do we start redecorating the guest room?"

"We may be moving to the 'burbs," Jeff said. "You know, fresh air, green grass, all that good-parent stuff."

"As long as you don't move to France. I promise I won't say a word. Thanks, you guys, for telling me."

We ate and drank. Well, other people drank. I sipped seltzer until the desserts were laid out, watching everyone happily eating away. I noticed Edward sitting with Mom for a while, and she was positively beaming. After he moved off, I went over and sat beside her.

"How are you doing, Mom? Can I get you anything?"

She shook her head. "No, I'm fine, Kate. I must say, that Edward is quite a nice young man."

I had to smile at "young." "Yes, he certainly is." I reached over and grabbed her hand, giving it a squeeze. "Adam would have been so proud of her, don't you think?"

She looked over at Regan, who was laughing and starting to pour champagne into glasses. "Yes. The two of you managed to make some wonderful children."

I felt sudden, unexpected tears. "Yes. We were good at that."

Mom pulled her hand away and waved it at me. "You'd better get yourself a glass," she said.

I stood up, grabbed a glass, and found Edward, and stood next to him as everyone quieted down.

Phil had his glass raised. "Regan and I want to thank everyone here for being a part of this," he said, his arm around Regan's shoulder. "I wish that Regan's dad could have been with us all tonight. I know what that would have meant to her. But I know that he's looking down on us, and I hope he's happy with how everything has turned out."

Regan smiled up at him. "I want to thank you all, too. I miss Daddy, but I'm so grateful to have so many new and wonderful people in my life. So, here's to your helping us become a brand-new family."

We all raised our glasses and drank.

Later, MaryJo found me on the deck. "The food was unbelievable."

"Did you try that potato-pimento-cheese thing? I've never met a potato I didn't love, but that was exceptional."

"I know. And that Viennese coffee thing they did? Heavenly."

"Everything has turned out just right, " I said.

"Yes, Kate, it certainly has."

Edward came up behind us. "Ladies, how are you enjoying this amazing evening?"

"Very much," I said.

"I could not help noticing," Edward said, "that your good friend Jake is not here."

MaryJo waved bye-bye to me and slid back into the house.

I smiled at Edward. "I told Jake that I didn't want to be with him anymore."

"Ah. Really? I must say I'm a bit surprised. I thought he was the one you were going to settle on."

"Me too. But then I decided *not* to settle. And it wasn't really as awful as I thought it would be. I've discovered in the past few months that a slight change of plan is not such a bad thing."

"How wise."

"Yeah, that's me, all right. Wise. When are you heading back to London?"

"Next Tuesday."

"Could you maybe stay a little longer?"

He smiled, and took me in his arms. "I can stay just as long as it takes."

He kissed me.

In that moment, I heard the laughter of my children, felt the autumn breeze on my skin, and saw a serene white mansion, bathed in moonlight.

In that moment, the possibilities were endless.

Author's Note

Once again, in spite of the fact that this book was written while I sat alone in my office, there are many people I need to thank for helping me bring this book to you all.

My agent, Lynn Seligman, comes first and foremost. She was always a believer.

Then there's Carly Hoffmann and the folks at Montlake, who reached out to me, tapped me on the shoulder, and said, "So, you wanna?" YES! Thank you all so much. I can't begin to describe what it's like for a little ol' indie like me to publish with the big boys.

Big thanks to Tiffany Yates Martin, for—seriously—making this book what it is today.

Karen Y. gets a shout-out for her online dating stories, a few of which are related here—and believe me, they're the ones you think I MUST have made up.

Please—feel free to contact me at dee@deeernst.com. I love hearing from my readers. And you can wander on over to my website, www.DeeErnst.com, check things out, and sign up for my newsletter. I promise you, I'll only send you real news, like when my next book is coming out.

I've gotten a lot of e-mails from women who've said they're happy that I was finally able to make my dream of writing come true. I'm not the only one out there moving to "The Second Act" and making it work. It's never too late to do what you love.

ABOUT THE AUTHOR

Dee Ernst attended Marshall University, where she majored in journalism. Several years, career changes, and a few daughters later, she heard a guest on a radio show make the suggestion that if you want to be happy, you should go back to what you were doing when you were ten and try to make it a career. Since Dee was writing stories when she was ten, she decided to give writing another go. After three novels and many rejection letters, she self-published *Better Off Without Him*. In the spring of 2013, she signed with Montlake Publishing. Though Dee finds a lot in common with all her heroines, she is happily married and living in New Jersey.